The Son of the Bear Hunter

Unabridged Translation of the
Original Karl May Manuscript Published under the Title

Der Sohn des Bärenjägers

A Travel Narrative
by
Karl May

Translated by
Herbert Windolf

Original German text by Karl May [1842 – 1912]
First published 1887
in 'Der Gute Kamerad', in serial format

English translation by Herbert Windolf

ISBN: 978-0-9794855-2-7

This book is printed on acid free paper.

Nemsi Books - rev. 11/11/2007

Acknowledgements

Der Sohn des Bärenjägers' – The Son of the Bear Hunter' – was first published in serial form in the youth magazine 'Der Gute Kamerad' – The Good Comrade – between January and September 1887.

The translation is based on a download from the Karl-May-Gesellschaft web site with Hans Grunert's permission, which I gratefully acknowledge.

The pictures, illustrating this translation, date from the original German publication and were kindly made available by Hans Grunert of the Karl-May-Gesellschaft.

A number of editorial comments of historical nature and grammar were kindly suggested and inserted by Michael Michalak.

For the Foreword, Marlies Bugmann provided the information on Prince von Wied's American exploits and the historical connection to Karl May and, in turn, to one of The Son of the Bear Hunter's protagonists, the Indian Wohkadeh.

As to the editing, I am greatly indebted to Zene Krogh, who patiently tracked down and corrected my Teutonic terminology, grammar and punctuation.

Herb Windolf, Prescott, Arizona

Karl May – translated by Herbert Windolf

Foreword

Karl May's extensive work also includes a particular genre of about eight narratives he called *'Jugenderzählungen'*, 'Stories for Youngsters': These were and are not only read by youngsters, but are also appreciated by adults. Most of them are of the Western kind. In addition to the following story, The Son of the Bear Hunter, which May penned in 1887, other titles are:

The Ghost of Llano Estacado
The Treasure of Silver Lake
The Oil Prince
and
Black Mustang

These and a number of others are listed in the register at the end of this book.

In the years 1832 to 1834, the German Prince von Wied, accompanied by the Swiss painter, Carl Bodmer, ventured into the American West, and visited the Mandan with their chief, Mato Tope (Four Bears) among other tribes. This party may have once more exposed the Mandan to smallpox, just as the earlier Lewis and Clark expedition may have. However, as Michael Michalak pointed out, the Mandan were already exposed to smallpox in the 16th century and by similar epidemics every few decades on. To quote Michalak verbatim: "In June of 1837, the St. Peter arrived at Fort Clark, sixty miles north of present day Bismarck, North Dakota. Knowing there were men aboard the boat with smallpox, F. A. Chardon and others of the American Fur Company tried to keep the Mandan away from the boat, but to no avail. The two Mandan villages that had provided aid to Lewis and Clark the winter of 1804-1805 were devastated. Thirty-one Mandans out of a population of sixteen hundred survived the epidemic...these figures vary."

In the following story, the young Indian Wohkadeh, a Mandan, explains to Fat Jemmy, his fellow adventurer, the near extinction of his people through smallpox, and that Mah-to-toh-pah (Four Bears), his mother's brother, was then chief of the Mandan.

Fifty years after von Wied's travels, Karl May, who spent much time at the Dresden library and who, supposedly, was an avid reader of the Prince's Western exploits, appears to have taken Wohkadeh's account from this background.

In his narratives, Karl May tried to convey values such as honesty, courage, love of fellow human beings, and more, to his young readers. Years later, as adults, many a German has visited the West of the United States and the locales Karl May described in his stories.

iii

Karl May – translated by Herbert Windolf

Karl May wrote at a time of rising German patriotism and, yes, at a time of *German innocence,* as well. He died prior to the terrible experience of WWI. Although his many stories have been translated into more than forty languages, he wrote first and foremost for German readers. It follows, therefore, that many of his frontiersmen are German or of German parentage.

Writing more than a hundred years ago, the author may not have always been politically correct by today's standards or in matters of ethnicity in the opinion of the translator (as demonstrated by the character, Bob). However, he was, after all, a man of his times. And yet, his caring for the American Indian, whom he saw correctly with both his strength and his failings, was ahead of the period in which he was writing in, that is, from approximately 1875 to 1910.

We, ourselves, have come a long way since – in some ways improved, in others still sadly lacking. Let us hope that some of May's 'old-fashioned' values will have a positive affect on the people of today.

Herb Windolf, Prescott, Arizona

Contents:

Karl May – translated by Herbert Windolf

The Son of the Bear Hunter

Karl May – translated by Herbert Windolf

1. Wohkadeh

Not far to the west where the corners of the North American states of Dakota, Nebraska and Wyoming meet, rode two men whose appearance, at any other place than this western one, would have caused a justified stir.

They were of very different build. Being taller than six feet, the figure of one of them was almost frighteningly lean, while the other was considerably shorter but so corpulent that his body almost resembled a ball.

Nevertheless, the faces of the two hunters were at the same level, for the little one rode a very tall, rawboned nag, while the lanky character sat on a low slung, seemingly weak mule. This is why the leather thongs, serving the corpulent one as stirrups, did not even reach the lower belly of his companion's mount. The tall one had no need for any stirrups, since his large feet hung down so far, that it took just a small sideways movement to touch the ground with one or the other foot, without him even sliding in his saddle.

To be sure, one could not talk about a saddle for either one, because the little one's consisted simply of the rear-parts of a killed wolf with its hide left on, and the skinny one was using an old Saltillo blanket which was so tattered, that he actually sat on the bare back of his mule.

Their condition hinted that they had had a long and hard ride behind them. This assumption was irrefutably confirmed by the appearance of their outfits.

The tall one wore leather pants, which must have been cut for a much bigger man. They were much too wide for him. Under the changing conditions of heat and cold, of dryness and rain, they had shrunk extremely, however, only in length. Thus it was that the lower seams of its legs barely extended past its owner's knees. In addition, the pants displayed an extraordinary greasy shine, the cause being that, at every opportunity, its owner used them as a towel. Anything he did not care to keep on his fingers, he wiped off on his trousers.

His bare feet were stuck in absolutely indescribable leather shoes. They gave the impression that Methuselah had already worn them, and that, since then, every one of their subsequent owners had repaired them by patching them with several pieces of leather. Whether they had ever seen any shoe polish was impossible to determine, could not even be guessed, since they glittered in all the colors of the rainbow.

The lean body of the horseman was covered by a leather shirt, which had neither buttons nor hooks, thus leaving his tanned chest uncovered. Its sleeves extended only slightly beyond the elbows, from where his sinewy, scrawny forearms protruded. Around his long neck, the man had wrapped a cotton cloth. Whether it had once been white or black, green or yellow, red or blue, even its owner no longer knew.

The main attraction of his outfit, however, was the hat, perched on his high, pointy head. Once upon a time, it had been gray and had had the shape, referred to by non-respectful people, as a stovepipe. Ages ago, it may have graced the head of an English Lord, yet had afterwards begun it's incessant descent, finally ending up on the head of a prairie hunter. This man, not possessing the taste of an Old-English Lord, had thought its brim to be unnecessary and had simply cut it off. Only in the front, a piece of the brim had been retained, partly to shade the eyes and partly for easy removal of the head cover. Furthermore, he must have held the opinion, that a frontiersman's head needed airing, which had caused him to take a variety of stabs into the top and sides of the hat with his Bowie knife, enabling the westerly, easterly, northerly and southerly winds to say "hello" inside.

For a belt, the tall one wore a rather thick rope, which he had wrapped several times around his waist. Stuck in it were two revolvers and a Bowie knife. In addition, hanging from it, were a bullet bag, a tobacco bag, a sewn-up cat skin to carry flour, the prairie punk, and a number of different items whose purpose had to be a riddle for the uninitiated. On his chest rested, suspended on a thong, a tobacco pipe – but what a one it was! It was the hunter's own artwork. The stem was made of an elder twig from which the pith had been removed to hollow it out. Long ago, he had chewed its stem off to just before its head, and it now consisted only of the latter. A passionate smoker, the tall hunter had the habit of chewing the little elder piece for some time once he had run out of tobacco.

To protect his honor, though, it needs to be said, that his outfit did not only consist of the shoes, the pants, the hunting shirt and the hat. Oh, no. He also wore a garment not everyone could acquire, that is, a rubber coat, the real American kind which, right after the first rain, shrank to half of its original length and width. For this simple reason, he was no longer able to put it on, and therefore, had it slung colorfully around his shoulders like a hussar's jacket. Furthermore, he carried a lariat, hanging from his left shoulder to his right hip. In front of him, across his legs, he held a rifle with which the experienced hunter never missed his target.

It was impossible to tell the age of the man. Numerous creases and folds covered his lean face, and yet, it had an almost youthful look. Some roguishness seemed to peer from every crease, large and small. Despite all these many wrinkles and the inhospitable territory he found himself in, his face was shaved totally smooth. There are many, many frontiersmen, who particularly pride themselves on this. His large, wide open, sky-blue eyes displayed the sharp look one can observe on seamen and the inhabitants of wide-open plains. And yet, one could have called his look childlike.

The mule, mentioned already, was only seemingly weak. It carried the heavy, bony rider with ease and, at times, even delighted in causing a scene. But every time it was squeezed forcefully by the thighs of its master, it quickly quit any resistance. These animals are favored for their steady pace, but are also known for their tendency for obstinate insubordination.

What was striking about the other rider was that he wore a fur despite the heat with which the sun shone on the two. Of course, when this fur was slung back by a move of the tubby one, it revealed that it suffered quite critically from a high degree of 'hairlessness'. Only here and there, a small, thin tuft was still attached, just as, in an infinite desert, an oasis is to be found only at times. Even the collar and lapels had thinned so much, that there were larger than dollar-size bare spots. From below this fur protruded, to the right and left, giant fold-over boots. A much too large broad-brimmed Panama hat graced the man's head, forcing him to push the piece far back on his neck in order to see. The sleeves of the fur were so long, that one could not see his hands. Thus, one could see only his face, however, this face was worth a closer look. It, too, was shaved smooth; not a trace of beard could be seen. The red cheeks were so plump, that the little nose made an almost unsuccessful attempt to show itself to effect. Just as much happened to the small, dark eyes, deeply hidden between the brows and cheeks. They gave an impression of the man's good-natured, cunning nature. In general, his face seemed to say: "Look at me! I'm a small, splendid fellow, easy to get along with; but be kind and understanding or you'll have come to the wrong address. Understood!"

A gust of wind rose pulling the little one's fur apart. Now, one could see that underneath he wore pants and a shirt made of cotton. Around his substantial waist a leather belt was buckled in which, in addition to the items carried by the tall one, there was also an Indian tomahawk. His lasso hung from the pommel of his saddle, together with a short-barreled Kentucky rifle, from which one could glean, that it had served in many a fight as both an attacking and defensive weapon.

Who were these two men? Well, the little one's name was Jakob Pfefferkorn, and the tall one carried the name of David Kroners. Had one mentioned these two names to any frontiersman, a squatter or trapper, they would have said, shaking their heads, that they had never heard a word of these two hunters. And yet, it would have been an untruth, for they were very famous scouts, and for many years, and over many a campfire, their adventures had been told. There was not a place between New York and Frisco and from the lakes in the north to the Gulf of Mexico, where these two famous prairie runners had not been praised. Of course, only they personally knew the names Jakob Pfefferkorn and David Kroners. On the prairie, in the forest, and particularly among the redskins, no one asks for a birth certificate. There, everyone soon receives a name expressive of his characteristics, which will very soon spread far and wide.

Kroners was a full-blooded Yankee and wasn't called any other name but Long Davy. Pfefferkorn had come from Germany and was called either by his given name, Jakob, or Fat Jemmy, the latter being the Anglo-Saxon term for 'little Jacob'.

3

By these names, Davy and Jemmy, they were known everywhere, and one would have rarely met a person in the Far West unable to recount one or another heroic deed of theirs. They were known as being inseparable. At least, there was no one who could remember ever having seen either of them alone. If the fat one stopped by the campfire of strangers, people would involuntarily look out for the tall one and, if Davy entered a store to buy powder and tobacco, he was immediately asked what he also wanted to take along for Jemmy.

The two animals of these frontiersmen were just as inseparable. The big nag, despite great thirst, would not have drunk at any creek or river, if the small mule had not bent its head to the water at the same time. And the latter would have kept standing with head raised in the most beautiful, juiciest grass, if the former had not softly snorted at it, as if wanting to whisper: "Hey, you. They've dismounted and are roasting a buffalo loin; now let's eat too, because there'll surely be nothing more before late evening!"

To leave each other in any kind of trouble would never have occurred to the two animals. Already their masters had many times saved each other's life. Without any hesitation, one would enter into the greatest danger for the other. Just like that, the animals had often come to each other's help when it was called for, to bite its comrade free or, with their strong, sharp hooves, to defend it against an enemy. The four characters, humans, as well as animals, simply belonged to each other, not knowing it any other way.

Thus, they trotted happily along in a northerly direction. There had been water and succulent grazing for horse and mule in the morning, and for the two hunters, water and the leg of a red deer. The nag carried the remainder of the meat, so that no starvation was to be feared.

By now, the sun had reached its zenith and sunk slowly lower. Although it was very hot, a fresh breath of wind blew across the prairie. The myriad of flowers spread throughout the carpet of buffalo grass did not yet show the brown, burnt color of fall. Its fresh green pleased the eye. Spread across the wide, wide plain were giant, rocky, mountainous cones, lit by the now slanted rays of the sun. Brilliantly illuminated, their westerly faces shone in glowing colors, while to the east they wrapped themselves more and more in deeper, darker shadows.

"How much further are we riding today?" asked the fat one when, for hours, they hadn't exchanged a single word.

"As far as every day," the tall one answered.

"Well!" the little one laughed. "Then on to our next camp site."

"Aye!"

Davy had the peculiar habit of always saying 'aye' instead of 'yes'.

Some time passed. Jemmy took great care not to receive another such reply to one more question. From time to time, he watched his comrade through his cunning little eyes and waited for his moment of revenge. Finally, the silence became too pressing for the tall one. Pointing with his right hand toward the direction they were headed, he asked:

"Do you know this area?"

"Very much so!"

"Well. Then what is it?"

"America!"

Annoyed, the tall one pulled up his legs, gave his mule a blow, and then declared:

"Bad fellow!"

"Who?"

"You!"

"Ah! Me? How so?"

"Vindictive!"

"Not at all. I just continue in the way I've been talked to. If you give me a stupid answer, I don't see at all why I ought to be brainy when you ask me."

"Brainy? Oh my! You and brainy? You consist so much of flesh, that there's no room for brains."

"Oho! Did you forget what I had to go through over there in the Old Country?"

"One class in the Gymnasium[1]? Yes, I recall that. I will never be able to forget, since you remind me daily at least thirty times."

"And that's necessary. Actually, I ought to mention it forty to fifty times, I being a man you can't have enough respect for. And then, I didn't pass only one class!"

"No, three."

"Well then!"

"But for any more, your brain wasn't good enough."

"Be quiet! The money ran out; I would have had more than enough brains. And, by the way, I knew very well what you meant earlier. I'll not forget this area here. Remember, we got to know each other over there behind this rise."

"Aye! It was a bad day. I had spent all my powder and was pursued by the Sioux. Finally, I could not go on, and they beat me down. You came that evening."

"Yes. The stupid fellows had started a fire one could have spotted from way up in Canada. I noticed it and crept up to it to see five Sioux who had tied up a White. Luckily, I hadn't spent all my powder like you. I shot two of them. The other three fled, since they didn't know that they were only dealing with a single attacker. And you were free."

"Free I was, but also very angry at you!"

---

[1] German upper level educational system encompassing 9 grades from 5th to 13th, its final two to three classes being equivalent to Junior College level.

"Yes, that I hadn't killed the two Indians, but had only wounded them. However, an Indian is also human, and I would never think to kill a person, if it's not absolutely necessary. I happen to be German, not a cannibal!"

"But am I one?"

"Hm!" the little one snorted. "Nowadays you are, of course, different. Before, like many others, you were of the opinion that one couldn't exterminate the redskins fast enough. I literally had to convert you to my belief."

"Yes, you Germans are peculiar fellows. Mild, and soft as butter, but at other times, when it's necessary, you bear a man's part like no other. You'd like to touch the entire world with kid gloves, and yet you strike right away with the butt of the rifle once you think you need to defend yourselves. That's how you all are."

"And I'm pleased that it is like that and no different. But look, there seems to be a trail crossing the grass."

He reined in his horse and pointed to a rock outcrop at whose base passed a long, dark line.

Davy, too, stopped his mule, shaded his eyes with his hand and examined the respective area, then said:

"You could force me to devour a hundredweight of roasted bullets if those aren't tracks."

"I think so, too. Shall we have a closer look, Davy?"

"Shall we? Who's talking about 'shall' when one must? On this old prairie one must not be careless when coming across tracks. One ought to always know who's ahead and who's behind. Otherwise, it can easily happen that one will awake dead in the morning, having bedded down alive in the grass in the evening. Let's go!"

They rode close to the outcropping and halted there to inspect the tracks with expert eyes.

"What do you say about them?" Davy asked.

"They're tracks, of course!" the fat one laughed.

"Yes, no way it's a tower rope. I see that, too. But what kind of tracks are they?"

"That of a horse."

"Hm! Every child can see that. Or do you mean I'm of the opinion a whale has swum past here?"

"No. Because only you could have been that whale, and as for you, I know that you didn't leave my side. By the way, I find these tracks very suspicious."

"Why?"

"Before I answer, I first want to inspect them more closely, since it won't be any fun to make a fool of myself with you, old chap."

He jumped off his mount and knelt in the grass. His old nag, as if possessing human intelligence, stuck its nose into the trampled grass and snorted softly. The

6

mule, too, stepped close, waved its tail and its long ears, seemingly observing the tracks.

"Well?" asked Davy, who found the examination going on too long for his taste. "Is it that important?"

"Yes. An Indian rode past here."

"You think so? That would be unusual, since we are not on the hunting or grazing grounds of a tribe. Why do you think it was an Indian?"

"I see from the hoof tracks, that the horse was schooled the Indian way."

"Yet, it could have been ridden by a White."

"I told myself that too, but – but –"

Pensively, he shook his head and followed the tracks a short distance further. Then he called back:

"Follow me! The horse wasn't shod. It also was very tired and yet, was forced to gallop. The rider had to be in a hurry."

Now, Davy also dismounted. What he had heard was important enough for a careful examination. He followed the fat one, the two animals coming after them, as if they thought this to be self-evident. Reaching Jemmy, the two walked farther alongside of the tracks.

"Jemmy, the horse was truly tired," he offered, "and it often stumbled. Whoever pushed his animal in such a way must have a valid reason to do so. Either the man was being pursued, or he had reason to reach his destination as quickly as possible."

"The latter is the case, not the former."

"How so?"

"How old are those track?"

"About two hours."

"I'd say so, too. Yet, there's no sign of pursuers, and whoever is ahead by two hours, needn't ride his horse to death. There are also so many dispersed outcroppings here that it would have been easy for him to lead his pursuers astray by riding in a circle unnoticed. Don't you agree?"

"Yes. For us two, for example, a lead of several minutes would be sufficient to send pursuers home with a bloody nose. I agree with you. The man wanted to reach his destination quickly. But where might that be?"

"In any case, not far from here."

Astounded, the tall one looked into the face of the fat one.

"You seem to be all-knowing today!" he responded.

"To find this out doesn't require omniscience, but only a bit of reflection."

"Well, I, too, am reflecting, but in vain."

"That's no surprise with you."

"How so?"

"You are too tall. Before your considerations about the tracks get from down here to your brains, thousands of years might easily pass. I tell you that the destination of this rider isn't far from here, or he would have spared his horse."

"So! I hear the reason, but I'm not comprehending it."

"Well, I figure, that if the man had to do a day's ride still, his horse would have been too tired for such a distance. Therefore, he would absolutely have had to rest a few hours to then catch up for this loss of time. But, because he knew the place he was to reach to be close, he believed he could still cover this distance today despite the tiredness of his horse."

"Listen, dear old Jemmy, what you say doesn't sound so bad. I agree with you once more."

"This praise is entirely unnecessary. Whoever has stumbled across the prairie for almost thirty years, can occasionally hit upon a smart idea. Of course, we now aren't that much smarter than we were before. Where is the place this

Indian is heading for? That, we would naturally want to know. In any case, the man must be a messenger. He found his task very urgent, so it must have been of great importance. In all probability, an Indian is a messenger between Indians. Therefore, I figure there are redskins nearby."

Long Davy whistled softly between his teeth and looked around thoughtfully.

"Annoying, utterly annoying!" he growled. "Then, this fellow comes from Indians and goes to Indians. That puts us between them without us knowing where they are hiding. That's how we can easily come across one band and carry our scalps to the country fair."

"That we must be concerned for. But there's an easy means to obtain certainty."

"You mean to follow these tracks?"

"Yes."

"Right! That way we know they are ahead of us, with them knowing nothing of us, and we have an advantage. Then, it's my opinion to follow the Indian, since his tracks aren't diverging very much from our own direction. But I'm still curious as to which tribe he might belong."

"I, too. It's impossible to guess. Up in northern Montana, there are the Blackfoot, the Pigan and Blood Indians. They don't come down here. At the bend of the Missouri, there is the Riccavee tribe's camp, who have little, if anything, to do here. The Sioux? Hm! Did you by chance hear, that they recently took up the war tomahawk?"

"No."

"Then, let's not ponder too much, but let's be careful. Behind us is the North Platte, as you may recall from our last expedition. We are now in the area we know very well. If we aren't foolhardy, nothing will happen to us. Come on!"

They mounted up again and followed the tracks, keeping a sharp eye on them, and looking just as sharply to each side in order to spot anything dangerous.

About an hour passed and the sun sank lower and lower. The wind rose increasingly, and the day's heat was rapidly abating. Soon they noticed that the Indian had fallen back to a trot. At an uneven spot his horse seemed to have stumbled and have fallen onto its knees. Jemmy dismounted at once to examine the place.

"Yes, it is an Indian. He jumped off. His moccasin was decorated with porcupine quills. There lies a broken tip[2] of one. And here – ah, the fellow must be very young."

"Why?" asked the tall one, who had remained sitting on his steed.

---

[2] It should be noted that the hollow shafts of the porcupine quills were used much like beads. The tips were usually discarded.

9

"The spot is sandy, with his foot leaving an exact imprint. I assume it wasn't a squaw, then ..."

"Nonsense! No woman comes here by herself."

"Then, it's a boy, at most eighteen years old."

"Well, well! That sounds dangerous. Certain tribes use these young chaps as scouts. Let's be cautious!"

They continued their ride. While so far they had passed through true flowery prairie, now, here and there, a bush appeared, eventually increasing in numbers. There seemed to be trees in the distance.

They arrived at a spot where the rider had briefly dismounted to allow his horse a brief rest. He had then continued on foot, leading the animal by its reins.

From time to time, the bushes ahead obscured the view to such an extent that twice as much caution was now called for. Davy rode ahead with Jemmy following. Suddenly, the latter said:

"Hey, lanky one, it's a black horse."

"Really! How do you know?"

"Here on this bush, there's a hair from its tail."

"Then we know a bit more already. But don't speak so loudly! At any moment we could come across some men here, and we'll see them only after they've killed us."

"I'm not afraid of that. I can rely on my horse, which snorts as soon as it smells an enemy. We can continue confidently."

Long Davy followed this request, but immediately stopped again.

"By the devil!" he exclaimed. "Something happened here!"

The fat one drove his horse on and, after only a few paces through the bushes, arrived at an open area. Ahead of them rose one of those cone-shaped rock outcroppings, of which there were many on this prairie. The tracks led up to it, passed close by it, and then diverged at a sharp angle to the right. This, the two saw clearly, but also something else. Namely, that from the outcrop's opposite side, other tracks led to the single one to join it.

"What do you think of that?" Davy asked.

"That some people camped behind the outcrop, then followed the Indian when they saw him."

"Maybe they returned there!"

"Or some stayed back. Stay behind these bushes here! I'll stick my nose around the corner."

"But don't stick it right into a loaded rifle barrel ready to be fired!"

"No. Your nose would be better suited for that."

He dismounted and handed the reins of his nag to the tall one. Then he ran speedily towards the outcrop.

"Smart fox!" Davy grumbled contentedly. "Creeping up here would take too much time. It's hard to believe that the fat one can run like this!"

Arriving at the outcrop, the little fellow crept slowly and carefully forward and disappeared behind a protruding edge. He soon reappeared to give the tall one a signal by describing an arc with his arm. Davy understood very well that he was not to ride directly towards the rock and, therefore, rode in an arc through the bushes. When he hit upon the new tracks he followed them, arriving at the outcrop where Jemmy stood.

"What do you say about that?" asked the little one, pointing to the place in front of them.

There had been a campsite. A few iron kettles still lay on the ground, several hoes and shovels, a coffee grinder, a mortar, and several smaller and larger parcels – but there was no trace of a campfire.

"Well," Davy answered, shaking his head, "those who settled in so neatly here, seem to be very careless people or still very green in the West. There are tracks of at least fifteen horses without a single one having been staked down or hobbled. It seems they had several pack horses. Those are also gone. Where to? This is a big mess! One ought to give these people a good thrashing!"

"Yes, that they deserve. So little experience and they head for the Far West! Then, not everyone can have gone to the Gymnasium ..."

"Like you!" the tall one injected quickly.

"Yes, like me. But everyone should possess a little common sense and deliberation. The unsuspecting Indian came around the corner here and, as soon as he saw them, preferred to ride off quickly instead of turning back. Then, the whole gang went after him."

"Might they have seen him as an enemy?"

"Of course, or they would not have pursued him. That may become disastrous for us. To the redskins, it's all the same whether their revenge is exacted on the perpetrators or any other."

"Then let's follow in a hurry to prevent a calamity."

"Yes. We won't have to ride a great distance, because the Indian will not have made it very far with his tired horse."

They remounted and, in a gallop, followed the trail, from which several hoof prints spread to the left and right, likely those of bolting pack horses. Despite their previous assumption, they had to ride a considerable distance through some varied terrain. Jemmy, being ahead, suddenly reined in his horse. He had heard loud voices and quickly led his horse sideways into some shrubbery where Davy followed. Both listened. They heard several voices talking.

"That's them," the little one opined. "The voices aren't coming any closer; so they mustn't be returning yet. Shall we spy on them, Davy?"

"Of course. We'll hobble the horses for the moment."

"No, that could give us away. If we want to remain unseen, we must tie them up, so that they can't move further than we permit."

'Hobble' is a trapper term meaning 'to tie the front legs of a horse together', so that it can make only small steps. That is done only if one feels safe. Otherwise, the animals are tied to trees, bushes, or to short stakes pounded into the ground. Hunters customarily carry such pointed stakes in the wood-poor prairie.

Thus, the two inseparable chaps tied their steeds to some bushes and crept in the direction from where the voices were coming.

They soon arrived at a small river, or rather a creek, which did not carry much water at the time. Its high banks, however, indicated that it carried substantial amounts of water in the spring. Here, at a bend, nine wild-looking men stood or rested in the grass. In their midst lay a young Indian, with both hands and feet tied so that he could not move a limb. On the other side of the creek, below the high bank, which it had been unable to climb, lay the horse of the redskin, loudly snorting and huffing. The Whites' horses stood with their masters.

They did not give a good impression. Seeing them, a true frontiersman would tell himself immediately that here was a sample of that unruly rabble of which only Judge Lynch could maintain the upper hand in the Far West.

Crouching behind a bush, Jemmy and Davy, observed the scene. The men talked among themselves, seemingly conferring about the fate of their captive.

"What do you think of them?" the fat one asked softly.

"Just like you, that is, not much."

"Rotten faces. I pity the poor Indian boy. What tribe do you think he belongs to?"

"I'm not sure about that yet. He wears no paint and no other distinguishing mark of any tribe. But one sure thing is that he's not on the warpath. Shall we take him into our protection?"

"Of course, since I don't think that he gave them any reason for their enmity. Come on. Let's have a few words with them."

"And if they don't listen to us?"

"Then we have the choice of enforcing our will either by force or with cunning. I'm not afraid of these characters. However, a bullet hits home even when fired by a cowardly scoundrel. Let's not let them know that we have horses, and it will be better to approach from the other side of the creek so that they are unaware of us having observed their camp already."

Taking their rifles, they crept towards the creek but kept enough distance from the men, so that they could not yet be seen. Then, they climbed down the bank, jumped the narrow water, and climbed up the opposite side. After creeping in a short arc, they reached the creek right at the place where the men rested on the opposite side. Arriving there, Jemmy and Davy acted as if they were totally surprised about their presence.

"Hello!" Fat Jemmy called. "What's this? And I thought we were all alone on this blessed prairie, but now we find a full meeting going on here. I hope we are permitted to partake."

The men who had rested in the grass got up, and all of them faced the two arrivals. For the moment, they did not seem to be pleased about their sudden appearance, but once they took in the figures and dress of the two, they broke out in loud laughter.

"Thunder and lightning!" one of them replied. He carried a whole arsenal of weaponry on his body. "What's happening here? Are you holding a carnival and masquerade in the midst of high summer?"

"Aye," the tall one nodded. "We are just short a few more fools, which is why we have come for you."

"Then, you've come to the wrong address."

"I don't believe so."

With these words, Davy took a single step across the water with his eternally long legs and, in a second, stood before the speaker. The fat one took two steps to join him and said:

"So. Here we are. Greetings, gentlemen. Do you have something good to drink?"

"There's water!" was the speaker's response, pointing to the creek.

"*Fie*! I don't care to water my insides? My grandpa's grandchild wouldn't think of it! If you don't carry anything better with you, you ought to head quietly home for this good prairie isn't a fitting place for you."

"You seem to think of the prairie as a restaurant!"

"Of course! The roasts amble about in front of one's nose. One only needs to get them to the fire."

"And you seem to be very much taken by it!"

"Sure!" Jemmy laughed, patting his belly comfortably.

"And what you have too much of, your comrade is missing."

"Because he is on half rations. I can't permit his beauty to be spoiled, for I took him along as a scarecrow, so that no bear or Indian comes too close to me. But, with your permission, mister, may I ask what actually led you to this pretty water?"

"No one led us. We found the way ourselves."

"His buddies laughed at this reply, which they thought to be a very witty snub. But Fat Jemmy answered quite seriously:

"So? Really? I didn't think you capable of it, since your physiognomy doesn't let anyone guess that you are capable of finding any path without help."

"And yours makes me guess that you wouldn't see the trail, even if your nose was right on it. Since when did you actually leave school?"

"I haven't even entered it yet since I haven't reached the right size yet. But I hope to profit from you enough to learn to say at least the multiplication tables of the West tolerably well. Would you care to be my school master?"

"Haven't got the time. I've actually more important things to do than to drive stupidity out of others."

"So! And what are these important things?"

He looked around and acted as if he had only now seen the Indian, and then continued:

"Behold! A captive, and at that a red one!"

He backed up as if scared by the sight of a redskin. The men laughed, and the one who had spoken so far, seemingly their leader, said:

"Don't faint right away, sir. Whoever hasn't seen such a fellow, can easily be left with a dangerous shock. One can get used to the sight only slowly. I assume that you haven't come across an Indian yet?"

"I've seen a few tame ones, but this one seems to be a wild one."

"Yes. Just don't get too close to him."

"Is it that bad? But he's tied up!"

He intended to approach the captive, but the leader blocked him and said:

"Stay away from him! He's none of your business. I must finally ask who you are and what you want here from us."

"You can learn that at once. My comrade's named Kroners, and my name is Pfefferkorn. We ..."

"Pfefferkorn?" he was interrupted. "Isn't that a German name?"

"With your permission. Yes."

"Then the devil may get you. I can't stand people of your kind of rabble."

"That must be a failure of your nose not being used to finer things. And speaking of rabble, you must be measuring me by your very own yardstick."

This he had now spoken in a very different voice from his previous easy banter. The other raised his eyebrows angrily and asked almost threateningly:

"What do you mean by that?"

"The truth. Nothing but."

"What do you think we are? Spit it out!"

He reached for the knife in his belt. Jemmy made a disdainful move with his hand and replied:

"Keep your knife where it is, mister. You can't impress us with it. You've been rude to me and can't expect that I will splash some *Eau de Cologne* on you. I don't want to give such deep sorrow to the Farina Company in Cologne by the Rhine. I can't help it, if you don't like my outfit. Here in the Far West, I wouldn't think of putting on a tailcoat for your sake, its tails to the front and twelve-rowed kid gloves to the legs. If you judge us by our get-up, then it's your own fault if you end up in a wrong sleeve. Here, the coat doesn't count, but the man who can demand courtesy first of all, does. I answered your question and now expect some information from you when I inquire as to who you are."

"My name's Walker. That's enough. The other eight names you couldn't remember anyway."

"Remember them, I could quite easily. But if you think that I needn't know them, you are quite correct. Yours is entirely sufficient, for the one who has a look at you knows exactly what kind of mind he's dealing with."

"Mister! Are you trying to insult me?" Walker shouted. "You want us to go for our weapons?"

"I wouldn't advise it. We've got twenty-four revolver shots, and you would get at least half of them, before you would be able to aim your weapons at us. You think us to be greenhorns, which we are not. If you want it to come to a test, we don't mind."

Lightning-fast, he drew his two revolvers, with Long Davy already holding his. When Walker wanted to reach for his rifle on the ground, Jemmy warned him:

"Let your shooting iron lie there! If you touch it, you'll get my bullet. That's the law of the prairie. Whoever fires first is right and the victor."

Upon the appearance of these two, seemingly so miserable-looking men, the others had been so incautious as to keep their rifles lying in the grass. Now they didn't dare reach for them.

"By the devil! You act exactly as if you want to swallow us!"

"Wouldn't think of it; you don't look tasty enough. We don't want to know anything else but what this Indian has done to you."

"Is that any of your business?"

"Yes. If you lay hands on him for no reason, then every other White is endangered without being guilty. That is, he's exposed to the revenge of his people. So! Why did you take him captive?"

"Because we wanted to. He's a red scoundrel, and that's reason enough. You'll get no further answer. You aren't our judge, and we are not boys who must give the first one showing up information."

"That's answer enough for us. We now know that the man gave you no reason for enmity. Quite redundantly I'll ask him myself."

"Ask him?" Walker laughed sneeringly, his companions joining him in the laughter. "He doesn't understand a word of English and hasn't answered us with a single syllable."

"An Indian doesn't answer his foes, even when tied up, and you may have treated him in such a way that he wouldn't speak a word even if you would take off his fetters."

"He got a thrashing. That's right."

"A thrashing? Jemmy called out. "Are you crazy? To beat an Indian! Don't you know, that this is an insult which can only be washed off with blood?"

16

"He may go for our blood, but I'm curious how he's going to do that."

"He'll show you as soon as he's free."

"He'll never again be free."

"Do you intend to kill him?"

"What we want to do with him is no concern of yours. Understood! The redskins must be squashed wherever they are found. Now, you have our response. If, before you get lost, you want to talk to the fellow, I don't mind. He won't understand you, and neither of you look like you are professors of Indian languages. I'm very eager to listen to this conversation."

Jemmy shrugged his shoulders disdainfully and turned to the Indian.

He had lain there with half-closed eyes, and with no look or expression, had given away whether he had understood a word of the conversation. He was still young, just as the fat one had said, maybe only eighteen years old. His dark, simply kept hair was long; no hairstyle gave indication to which tribe he belonged. His face was not painted and neither ocher nor cinnabar colored the crown of his head. He wore a hunting shirt of soft leather and leggings of deer leather, both tasseled at their seams. Not a single human hair could be seen among these tassels, a sign that this young man had not killed an enemy yet. The neat moccasins were decorated with porcupine quills, just like Jemmy had guessed. There wasn't a single weapon in the red cloth he wore as a belt. But on the opposite bank of the creek, where his horse had risen now and was greedily drinking the creek's water, lay a long hunting knife, and on the saddle hung a rattlesnake-covered quiver and bow made from the horns of mountain sheep. They might have fetched the price of two or three mustangs.

This simple weaponry was a sure sign that the Indian had not entered this area with hostile intention. At the moment, his face was without any expression. The Indian is too proud to display any feelings in front of strangers, particularly enemies. His features were still youthfully soft. Although his cheek bones protruded a bit, this in no way took anything away from his pleasant physiognomy. When Jemmy approached him, he opened his eyes for the first time fully. They were black like shining coal, and their friendly look greeted the hunter.

"My young red brother understands the language of the palefaces?" asked the hunter.

"Yes," the young man replied. "How do you know, my older white brother?"

"From the look of your eyes, I saw that you had understood us."

"I have heard that you are a friend of red men. I am your brother."

"Will my young brother tell me whether he has a name?"

This question, asked of an older Indian, is to him a serious insult, because the one who does not yet have a name, has not yet proven his courage by some deed and is, therefore, not counted as a warrior. But considering the youth of this captive, Jemmy could permit himself the question. The youth answered:

"Does my good brother think me to be cowardly?"

"No, but you are still too young to be a warrior."

"The palefaces have taught red men to die young. My brother may open my hunting shirt to learn whether I possess a name."

Jemmy bent down to open his hunting shirt. He pulled out three, red-colored feathers of the war eagle.

"Is it possible?" he exclaimed. "You can't be a chief yet!"

"No," the young man smiled. "I am allowed to carry the feathers of the *Mah-sish* since my name is Wohkadeh."

These two words were of the Mandan language, the first meaning war eagle and the latter being the hide of a white buffalo. Since white buffalo are very rare, the killing of such a one counts more with some tribes than the killing of several enemies, even permitting the carrying of the feathers of the war eagle. The young Indian had killed such a buffalo and thus received the name of Wohkadeh.

By and large, this was nothing unusual, but Davy and Jemmy were surprised by the name, derived from the Mandan language. This is why the little one asked:

"To which tribe does my red brother belong?"

"I am a *Numangkake* and Dakota at the same time."

The Mandan call themselves *Numangkake* with Dakota being the collective name of all Sioux tribes.

"Then you were taken in by the Dakota?"

"It is as my white brother says. My mother's brother was the great chief Mah-to-toh-pah. He carried this name, because he slew four bears at once. The white men brought us smallpox. My entire tribe perished except for a very few who, wishing to follow their departed to the Eternal Hunting Grounds, provoked the Sioux, and were killed by them. My father, the brave Wah-kih (Shield), was only injured and was later forced to become a son of the Sioux. Thus, I am a Dakota, but my heart belongs to my ancestors whom the Great Spirit has called to himself."

"The Sioux are presently beyond the mountains. How did you cross them to get here?"

"I do not come down from the mountains my white brother has in mind, but from the high mountains in the west to bring an important message to a small white brother."

"This white brother lives nearby?"

"Yes. How does my older white brother know this?"

"I followed your tracks and saw that you had driven your horse like someone being close to his destination."

"You thought correctly. I would have been at my destination by now, but these palefaces pursued me. My horse was too tired and could not make the jump across this water, so it fell. Wohkadeh came to lie underneath it and lost consciousness. When he came to, he was tied up."

In a grating tone, he added in the Sioux language:

"They are cowards. Nine men tie up a youth whose soul had parted! Had I been able to fight them, their scalps would be mine now."

"They even beat you!"

"Don't speak about it, for every word of it smells of blood. If my white brother will remove my fetters, then Wohkadeh will deal with them as a man."

He said this with such confidence, that Fat Jemmy asked smilingly:

"Didn't you hear that we cannot command them?"

"Oh, my white brother is not afraid of a hundred men of their kind. Every single one of them is *Wakon kaneh* (an old woman)."

"You think so? How can you know that I'm not afraid of them?"

"Wohkadeh has open eyes. He has heard talk of the two famous white warriors, called Davy-honskeh and Jemmy-petahtsheh, and recognized them from their figures and words."

The little hunter wanted to reply, but was interrupted by Walker:

"Hold it, man! That wasn't our arrangement. I permitted you to talk with the fellow, but it must be in English. I can't allow some pidgin, since then I will expect you to hatch some plans against us. It's sufficient for us to have learned that he knows English. We don't need you any longer, and you can go back from where you came. And if that doesn't happen quickly, I'll get you running!"

Jemmy's look went to Davy who gave him a signal with an eyebrow no one else noticed. However, for the fat one this lightning-fast twitch from above the eye was clear enough. The tall one had drawn his attention to the bushes to the side of them. Jemmy took a quick sharp look over there and noticed that, close to the ground the mouths of two double barreled rifles pointed out a little from between the twigs. Two men must be lying there at the ready. Who were they? Friends or foes? The carelessness Davy displayed, calmed him. He answered Walker:

"The legs you are referring to, I'd like to see! I don't have reason like you for running off quickly."

"Like us? Who ought we to run away from?"

"The one whom these horses still belonged to yesterday. Understood!"

With these words he pointed to the two brown geldings standing close next to each other, as if they knew that they belonged to each other.

"What?" shouted Walker. "Who do you think we are? We are honest prospectors on the way to Idaho where new gold fields have been discovered."

"And since you were short the necessary horses for this trip, you became, on the side, just as honest horse thieves. You can't deceive us!"

"Man. Say another word and I will gun you down! We have bought all these horses and paid for them.

19

"Where then, my honest mister Walker?"

"Down in Omaha."

"So! There you also picked up a supply of hoof black? How come the two browns are as fresh as if they'd just come from a coral? Why do they have freshly blackened hooves, while all your other nags are jaded and run about in neglected slippers? I tell you that the browns had another master yesterday and, that the theft of horses here in the Far West is punished by the beautiful death of hanging."

"Liar! Slanderer!" Walker screamed, bending down for his rifle.

"No, he's right!" a voice sounded from between the bushes. "You are miserable horse thieves and must get your reward. Shall we gun them down, Martin?"

"Don't shoot!" Long Davy shouted. "Use the butts! They aren't worth a bullet."

He reversed and raised his rifle and hit Walker with such a blow, that he fell to the ground unconscious. Two figures jumped from the bushes, a sturdy boy and an older man, and threw themselves onto the alleged prospectors.

Jemmy had bent down and, with two quick cuts, had released Wohkadeh's fetters. He sprung up, jumped at one of the enemies, grabbed him by the neck, pulled him down and catapulted him across the water where his scalping knife lay. No one would have attributed such bodily strength to him. To leap after his victim, grab the knife with his right hand, kneel on the enemy and take his hair with the left, was the work of only a moment.

"Help, help, for God's sake, help!" the man screamed under pain of death.

Wohkadeh had raised the knife for a killing stab. His flashing eyes looked at the face of his foe, distorted by terror, and his hand fell together with the knife.

"Are you afraid?" he asked.

"Yes. Oh, have mercy, mercy!"

"Tell me you are a dog!"

"I'm pleased to say it. Yes, I'm a dog!"

"Then, stay alive to live with your shame; an Indian dies courageously and without lament. Wohkadeh cannot carry the scalp of a dog. You did beat me, and for that your scalp is mine. But, a rabid dog cannot insult a red man. Take off. Wohkadeh is nauseated by you."

He gave him a kick with his foot. A moment later the man had disappeared.

This had all happened much, much faster than one can tell. Walker lay on the ground next to another. The others had quickly turned tail. Their horses had run after them. The two brown ones still stood there and rubbed their heads on the shoulders of the two helpers who had so unexpectedly shown up.

The boy might have passed for about sixteen years, but his body was well developed for his age. Fair skin, blond hair and blue gray eyes hinted of Germanic descent. He was bareheaded and dressed in blue linen. From his belt protruded a knife, the handle of which was of rare Indian work. The double-barreled rifle he held in his hand seemed almost too heavy for him. His cheeks were quite red from the fight, and yet he stood so calmly just as though nothing had happened. Anyone who now observed him would tend to assume that such events, like the one that had just happened, were nothing unusual for him.

His companion was a peculiar sight. He was a small, slender man whose face was framed by a dense, black beard. He wore Indian moccasins and leather pants, together with a dark blue coat fitted with high shoulder pads and shiny brass buttons. This latter piece of clothing must have dated from the first quarter of the century. At that time, a cloth had been fabricated which seemed to have been made to last for eternity.

Of course, the tailcoat was extremely worn and faded, and its seams had been often freshened up with ink. However, there wasn't yet a single small hole to be seen. One finds such old pieces of clothing quite often in the far West.

There, one isn't embarrassed to wear old-fashioned dress, for people think that the man counts more than his dress.

The little man wore a giant black Amazon hat, adorned with a large, yellow-colored ostrich feather. This beauty must have once belonged to some lady in the East, and then been driven off its course to the Far West by some capricious fate. Since its extremely broad brim protected one very well against sun and rain, its current owner had had no scruples about assigning it to its present location.

The little man was armed with rifle and knife. But a belt was missing, a sure sign that the little one wasn't presently on a hunting expedition.

Walking back and forth across the small battlefield, he inspected several items abandoned by their owners in their hurry to flee. One could see that he limped with his left leg. Wohkadeh was the first to notice this. He stepped towards him, placed his hand on his arm, and asked:

"Is my white brother perhaps the hunter the palefaces call Hobble-Frank?"

The little man nodded a bit surprised and confirmed it in English. That's when the Indian pointed to the young White and inquired further:

"And this one is Martin Baumann, the son of the famous Mato-poka?"

Mato-poka is a word composed of the Sioux and Ute languages and means 'Bear Hunter'.

"Yes," the other replied.

"Then you are the ones I am looking for."

"You want to see us? Might you want to buy something? Because we have a store and trade everything a hunter needs."

"No. I have a message for you."

"From whom?"

The Indian thought about it for a moment, glanced around, and then answered:

"Here is not the place for talk. Your wigwam is not far from here near this creek?"

"Yes, we can be there in an hour."

"Then let us go there. When we sit by your fire, I will tell you what my message is. Let us go!"

He leaped across the creek and retrieved his horse, which by now should have been able to carry him for this short distance. He mounted and rode off without looking back to see if the others were following.

"He's a quick one," the little man offered.

"Is he going to give a speech that's even thinner and longer than myself?" Long Davy laughed. "A redskin like him knows very well what he's doing, and I advise you to follow him right away."

"And you? What are you going to do?"

"We'll come along. If your palace is that close, it would be a most discourteous of you, if you wouldn't invite us for a sip and two bites. And since you have a trading post, you may be able to earn a few dollars."

"So! Have you got some dollars on you then?" the little one asked in a voice that betrayed his doubt of the two hunters being millionaires.

"That will be your business only when we want to buy something. Understood!"

"Hm, of course! But if we leave now, what's to happen to the fellows who stole the two horses from us? Shall we not give their leader, at least this Walker, a memento to remember us by?"

"No. Let them run. They are cowardly thieves who run from a Bowie knife. It brings you no honor to busy yourself any longer with them. You've got your horses back. That's good enough!"

"Had you only reached out a bit more when you clubbed him. The fellow only lost consciousness."

"I did that on purpose. It's not a pleasant feeling to kill a human being one can disable this way."

"Well. You may be right. Come along then and pick up your horses!"

"Ah? You know where our horses are?"

"Of course. We would be poor frontiersmen, if we hadn't reconnoitered before we made our presence known to you. When we discovered that two horses had been stolen from us, we followed the thieves' tracks. Unfortunately, we discovered the theft too late, so we only caught up with them here. The horses graze in the open and we only look after them in the evening. Let's go!"

He mounted one of the recovered animals. His young companion jumped on the other. Both directed their horses exactly to the spot where Jemmy and Davy had hidden theirs in the shrubbery. Those two also mounted up. With the four now following the tracks of the Indian, they soon saw him up ahead. He did not quite let them catch up however, but kept his distance knowing exactly the direction he had to take to get to his destination.

Hobble-Frank kept to the side of Fat Jemmy, to whom he seemed to have taken a liking.

"Don't you want to tell me, mishter, what you are actually looking for in this area?" he asked.

"We actually want to get a bit farther up into Montana where there's better hunting than here. There, one still finds reasonable forest and prairie men who hunt for hunting's sake. But hereabouts, one literally butchers the animals. The Sunday rifle rages among the poor buffalo which are being killed by the thousands and only because their hides are better suited to make drive belts than common neat's leather. It's a sin and a shame, isn't it?"

"You are correct there, mishter. It was much different in earlier times. Then, it was man againsht man. That is to say, the hunter faced the game honeshtly,

23

fighting for the meat he needed under danger of losing his life. Nowadays, the hunt is almost a cowardly murder from ambush, and the old shtyle hunters are gradually dying out. People like you are rare these days. I don't trust you to have much money, but your names sound fine."

"Do you know our names?"

"Shure."

"Where from?"

"Wohkadeh mentioned them when I was lying in the bushes with Martin, shpying on you. You don't actually have the right figure for a frontiershman. Your waist is better suited for a German baker or municipal guard officer, but ..."

"What?" the fat one interrupted quickly. "You are talking of Germany. Do you know it?"

"Shure, and how! I'm German with skin and bones!"

"And I with body and soul!"

"Is it true?" Frank asked, holding back his horse. "Yeah, it's true. I should have known right away that you couldn't be a Yankee with your body circumference. Give me your hand, man! You are mosht welcome!"

They clapped hands so that both of them hurt. Then the fat one suggested:

"Urge your horse on again. We needn't stop here because of that. How long have you been in the States?"

"About twenty years."

"Then you might have forgotten your German by now?"

Both had spoken English so far. Hearing this last question, Frank raised his small stature as high as possible in the saddle and answered in an insulted voice:

"I? Forgotten my language? There, for the mosht part you are all wrong. I am a German and remain a German, the more so since we now have an emperor. Might you know by chance where my cradle once shtood?"

"No. I wasn't around then."

"If so! You musht have notished right away from my pronunshiation, that I am from the province where the puresht German is shpoken."

"So! And which is that?"

"Always, only Saxony! You undershtand? I have shpoken with other Germans, but I never undershtood those as well as when they happened to have been born in Saxony. Saxony is the heart of Germany. Dresden has class; the Elbe river has class; Leipzig has class, the Saxon Swiss Mountains have class, and the Sun Shtone, too. The mosht beautiful and puresht German is heard on the shtretch between Pirna and Meissen. Just about between those two towns, I have seen the firsht light of this world. And afterwards or later, I shtarted my career in the very same locale. You know, I was a foreshtry assishtant in Moritzburg, which is a famous royal hunting castle with a mosht famous painting gallery and large carp ponds. You can see that I was a real employed official with a twenty taler monthly salary. My besht friend was the local school mashter with whom I played Sixty-six every evening and afterwards talked with him about the arts and sciences. There, I acquired a very special general education and, for the firsht time, learned where America is located. We were very good in German, which is why I know, in fact, that in Saxony the mosht beautiful syntax is shpoken. Do you doubt it? You make such a miserable face!"

"I don't want to fight about it, although I once attended the Gymnasium."

"What? Is it true? You shtudied in the Gymnasium?"

"Yes, I also declined *mensa*."

The little one threw him a cunning sideways look and said:

"Declined *mensa*? You musht have misspoken there?"

"No."

"Well, then your Gymnasium ishn't worth much either. It is not *decline*, but *declaim*, and neither is it *mensa*, but *pensa*. You declaimed your pensa, maybe the *Singer's Curse of Hufeland* or the *Freischuetz* by Mrs. Maria Leineweber. But lets not become enemies because of that. Everyone learns as much as he can and no more, and when I see a German, then I'm happy, even when he's not such a shmart fellow or a Saxon. How is it then? Shall we be good friends?"

"Of course!" the fat one laughed. "I've always heard that the Saxons are the most good-natured fellows."

"That we are, yes! Of that, there's no doubt. That's native intelligence."

"But why did you leave your beautiful state?"

"Precisely because of the arts and sciences."

"How's that?"

"That happened very suddenly and like this: We were talking of politics and world hishtory in a reshtaurant one evening. There were three of us at the table, the boots, the night watchman, and myself. The schoolmashter sat at another table with the distinguished ones. But since I've always been a very affable person, I took a seat with the other two, who were quite happy about this kind of loyal lowering of myself. Talking about world hishtory, we came across old Papa Wrangel, and the fact that he had picked up the habit of using the verb '*merschtentels*' (for the most part; in High German spelled '*meistenteils*') at every opportunity. At this, the two fellows began to quarrel with me about the proper orthographic shpelling and pronunciation of this word. Each had a different opinion. I said it had to be pronounced '*merschtentels*', but the boots claimed '*mehrschtentels*', and the night watchman even said '*meerschtentels*'. During this quarrel, I got more and more into a fit. Finally, I got so hot that I would have loved mosht to jump in with all fours, but, as a learned official and citizen, I kept my shtrength for what little was left of my self-control and turned to my friend, the schoolmashter. Of course, I was right, but he might have been in a bad mood, or had a touch of learned insolence. In short, he didn't agree with me and said that all three of us were wrong. He claimed there had to be two '*ei*' in the word '*merschtentels*'. But since I knew for sure that there was only a single

25

word with two '*ei* ', that is '*Reisbrei*', (rice mash), I became disagreeable. While I don't want to schpoil anyone's dialect, I exspect mine also to be reshpected, the more so since it's the right one. However, the night watchman didn't appreshiate that. He said, I also didn't pronounce it correctly. At that, I did what every honorable gentleman would have done: I threw my insulted self-reshpect at his head together with my beer shtein! Of course, there now erupted several different scenes without shtage wings, and at the end I was indicted for dishturbing the peace and for inshury to an intended body. I was to be punished and demoted. I'd have taken the punishment and demotion, but saw that I was also going to lose my employment, which was too much for me. I couldn't overcome that. So, when I had put the punishment and discharge behind me, I took off. And since everything I do I do properly, I went immediately to America. Therefore, only old Wrangel must take the blame for you having met me here today."

"I'm grateful to him for I like you," the fat one assured him, nodding kindly to the little man.

"So? Is that true? Well, right away I, too, felt a kind of secret affection for you, which has good reason. Firsht, you aren't a bad chap; second, I'm also not so bad. Thus, third, we can become good friends. We have already shtood by each other, so the tie is actually already made and will embrace us lovingly. You will kindly notice that I'm always moving in shoice terms, from which you can conclude, that I will prove worthy of your feelings of friendship. The Saxon is always noble, and if an Indian wanted to shcalp me today, I would politely tell him: 'Please, make a kind effort! Here'sh my scalp lock!'"

At that Jemmy replied, laughing:

"If he would then be just as polite, he'd have to leave you your scalp lock. But, to speak now about another matter. Is your companion truly the son of the well known Bear Hunter?"

"Yes. Baumann is my assoshiate and his son, Martin, calls me uncle, although I am the only child of my parents and was never married. We firsht met down in St. Louis when gold fever drew diggers to the Black Hills. We had both saved a little sum and decided to open up a shtore up here. In any case, this was more advantageous than to dig for gold. It worked out quite well. I took over the shtore, and Baumann went hunting to supply us with provision. Later, however, it turned out, that no gold was to be found hereabouts. The diggers left, and now we live here all by ourselves with the supplies we didn't sell, since we wouldn't have received payment. Only little by little were we able to get rid of them to hunters who happened to come by. We conducted the lasht business two weeks ago. That's when a small group showed up, who wanted to hire my assoshiate to accompany them to the Yellowshtone. Supposedly, there were semiprecious shtones to be found en masse, and these people were shtone polishers. Baumann let himself be talked into it for a considerable fee, sold them a subshtantial quantity of munitions and other useful things, and then left with them. Now, I'm

26

all alone in the log house with his son and a Negro we took along from St. Louis."

During this dry report, he had barely used his home dialect, which Fat Jemmy noticed, he being used to observing everything. He looked sidewise at the little one inquiringly and asked:

"Does Baumann then know the Yellowstone River?"

"He previously went up it a goodly dishtance."

"But that is highly dangerous."

"Not any more."

"You don't think so? No, since the wonders of this area have been discovered, the Congress of the United States has sent several expeditions up there to survey the area. It has been declared a national park, which doesn't mean anything to the Indians, however. Between here and there, the Snake Indians continue to hunt."

"They have buried the war tomahawk."

"Well, I heard that they have recently taken it up again. Your friend is most likely in danger. Then, there's the messenger coming today. I don't expect anything good."

"Then I musht hurry and catch up to him."

He drove his horse on in order to reach Wohkadeh. As soon as the latter noticed this, he pressed his horse's flanks, speeding up. If Hobble-Frank did not want to enter into a race, he had to give up, for now, the idea of talking with the Indian.

In the meantime, the Son of the Bear Hunter had stayed with Long Davy, who was obviously also interested in learning something about the circumstances of the boy's father. Although he received information, it was not as extensive as he had wished. The boy was very reserved and monosyllabic.

Finally, the creek made a turn around a rise after which the men saw a log house. Its location made it a small fort, which provided good protection against an Indian attack.

The rise dropped off so steeply on three sides that it was impossible to easily climb it. A double fence protected the fourth side. Below were a cornfield and a small area for growing tobacco. Nearby, two horses were grazing. Martin pointed to the two and said:

"The men stole our horses from there when we weren't home. Where is Bob, our Negro?"

He put two fingers to his mouth to sound a shrill whistle. That's when a black head peered from between the tall corn plants. Between his broad lips, two rows of white teeth, a jaguar would have been proud of, could be seen. Then, the Herculean figure of the Negro stepped out. He carried a heavy, thick pole in his hand and said with a laugh:

"Bob hide and watch. If scoundrels come to steal two more horses, then he smash their heads with pole."

He swung the pole with such ease as if it were a light willow switch.

The Indian did not pay him any attention. He rode past him, up the rise, to the double fence. There, he jumped off his horse and then over the fence to disappear up top.

"What coarse fellow red man is!" the Negro said angrily. "Ride past *Massa* Bob without saying 'Good Day!', jump over fence, and not wait until *Massa* Martin permit to enter. *Massa* Bob him make polite!"

The good black man gave himself the title '*Massa* Bob', that is master Bob. He was a free Negro and felt very insulted not to have been greeted by the Indian.

"You are not going to insult him," Martin warned. "He's our friend."

"That is different thing. When red man is friend of massa, then be also friend of *Massa* Bob. *Massa* got horses back? Killed scoundrels?"

"No. They escaped. Open the fence!"

In a long stride, Bob went ahead and pushed the two heavy wings of the gate open as if they were made of paper. The others then rode into the space enclosed by the fence.

In its midst stood the square log house, though actually not a log house since it was not built from fitted logs. The material for its construction consisted of stones, loam and branches. The shingles for the roof must have come from far away.

Its door stood open. When the men entered, they found the Indian sitting in the midst of the room. He did not seem at all concerned for the whereabouts of his horse. It had entered the enclosure together with the others.

Now, Martin and Hobble-Frank greeted their two guests with a hearty handshake, as they looked around the room. The store was in the back, however, its inventory had been very much depleted. A few crate lids hammered onto posts served as tables. The chairs were nailed together from the same material. Beds were located in a corner, and were so precious, that one could have envied the residents of the log house for them. They consisted of a number of piled-up coats of the terrible gray bear, the most dangerous carnivore in America. If such a grown grizzly rises on its hind legs, it is easily two feet taller than a man of good size. To have killed such a bear was seen by Indians as a most heroic deed, and even the better-armed White avoids this animal, rather than enter, without need, into a fight with it.

Various weapons, together with war and hunting trophies, hung on the walls, and next to the fireplace large pieces of smoked meat hung from wooden pegs.

The afternoon had mostly passed, and since the dusky light entered through small wall openings, which were only furnished with shutters, not windowpanes, it was rather dark in the hut.

"*Massa* Bob will light fire," the Negro said.

He dragged in a load of dry brushwood and, by means of a punk, lit a fire in the fireplace. Tinder for his prairie lighter, the punk, consisted of dry, easy smoldering material from the innards of rotting trees.

The flames glaringly lighted the giant figure of the Negro during this task. He wore a wide outfit of the simplest calico and did not wear a hat. This had a reason. Good Bob was a bit vain. He didn't want to appear pure African. Unfortunately, a thick forest of short, curly locks covered his head, and since this 'wool' gave away his origin most convincingly, he had made every effort to make others believe that he possessed no 'wool' but rather smooth hair. For this reason, he had rubbed his head heavily with deer fat and had braided the short, unruly hair into innumerable little plaits, which now pointed in all directions from his head like the quills of a hedgehog. With the illumination of the fire, this made for a truly grotesque sight.

Up to this point, only a few words had been exchanged. Now Hobble-Frank addressed the Indian in English:

"My red brother is now in our house. He is welcome and may deliver his message."

The Red threw an inquiring look around and replied:

"How can Wohkadeh speak when he has not yet tasted the smoke of peace?"

That's when Martin, the Son of the Bear Hunter, took an Indian calumet from the wall and stuffed it with tobacco. When the others had then sat down near the redskin, he lit the tobacco, took six draws, blew the smoke upwards, downwards, and into the four main directions of the heavens, and then said:

"Wohkadeh is our friend, and we are his brothers. He may smoke with us the pipe of peace and after that, tell us his message."

He handed the pipe to the Indian, who accepted it, rose, took the same six draws, and then answered:

"Wohkadeh has never seen the palefaces and the Black. He was sent to them and they rescued him from captivity. Their enemies are also his, and his friends may also be theirs. Howgh!"

The Indians' 'howgh' means to them something like 'yes' or 'certainly'. It is used as an expression of affirmation or agreement, particularly when pausing or at the conclusion of a speech.

He passed the pipe on. While it continued its round, he sat down again and waited until Bob, as the last one, had confirmed brotherhood by the smoke of tobacco. During this greeting, Wohkadeh acted like an old, experienced chief, and Martin, still half a boy, also showed seriousness, demonstrating his conviction that he was the actual host of this house in the absence of his father.

When Bob had put the pipe away, Wohkadeh began:

"Do my brothers know the great paleface called *Nou-pay-klama* (The Hand which Shatters – Shatterhand) by the Sioux?"

"You mean Old Shatterhand?" Long Davy replied. "I have not met him yet, but just about everyone has heard of him. What's the matter with him?"

"He loves the red men although he is a paleface. He is the most famous tracker. His bullet never fails and with his unarmed fist, fells the strongest foe. That is why he is called Old Shatterhand. He spares the life and blood of his enemies and solely wounds to incapacitate. Only when his own life is in danger will he kill his adversary. Several winters ago, he was hunting up at the Yellowstone, the first paleface ever to enter this area. He was attacked by the Sioux-Ogallalla and fought them – he alone against many. He stood on a huge rock. They could not reach him with their bullets, but he did not shoot at them since he believes that all humans are brothers. Two days and two nights they besieged him. Then, he stepped out and offered to fight with three of them, they armed with the tomahawk, he without a weapon. He killed all three with just his fist, although Oihtka-petay (Brave Buffalo), the never vanquished chief, and Shi-tsha-pah-tah (Evil Fire), the tribe's strongest man, were among them. That is when a tremendous lament arose in the mountains and plaintive sounds were heard in the wigwams of the Ogallalla. They have not abated even today but rise always anew on the day of the death of the three warriors. Now a '*shakoh*', a period of seven years, has passed, and the bravest warriors of the tribe have left for the Yellowstone to sing their death songs at the graves of the three slain braves. A white man, they came across during this venture, is lost. He will be tied to the stake near the graves of the ones killed by Old Shatterhand to die in the greatest agony, so that his soul accompanies the three dead into the Eternal Hunting Grounds.

He paused. Martin jumped off his seat and called:

"Bob, quickly, saddle the horses! Frank, hurry and pack munitions and provisions. In the meantime, I shall oil the rifles and sharpen the knives!"

"Why?" the little Saxon asked in surprise.

"Didn't you understand Wohkadeh? My father has been captured by the Sioux-Ogallalla and is to be miserably butchered at the stake. We must save him. We'll set out in an hour at the latest!"

"By the devil!" Frank shouted, quickly jumping up. "The Reds will pay for that!"

The Negro, too, rose and picked up the pole he had earlier brought in. He said:

"*Massa* Bob come along! *Massa* Bob slay all red dogs of Ogallalla!"

That's when the Indian raised his hand to say:

"Are my white brothers flies who buzz around angrily when provoked? Or are they men who know that quiet consultation must precede action? Wohkadeh has not finished yet."

"Then first say whether my father is in danger or not?" Martin urged.

"You will hear it."

"I demand that you say so, immediately, at once!" the youth erupted.

That's when Fat Jemmy warned:

"Calm down, my young friend! Make haste slowly. Have Wohkadeh talk first, then we can deliberate after which we shall act."

"Act? You too?"

"That's self-evident. We did smoke the calumet and are, therefore, friends and brothers. Long Davy and Fat Jemmy have never let anyone down yet who's in need of their help. Whether the two of us ride up to Montana to hunt buffalo, or whether we take a detour to Yellowstone before, to dance a waltz with the Ogallalla Sioux is all the same to us. But everything must take place in the necessary order. Otherwise, it's no real fun for old hunters like us. Therefore, sit down again and stay calm as is called for. Our red friend is right: We are men. Understood!"

"This is correct!" the little Saxon chimed in. "Excitement isn't helpful to a problem. We musht deliberate properly."

Once the three had taken their places again, the young Indian continued:

"Wohkadeh was raised by the Sioux-Ponca, who are friends with the palefaces. He was later forced to become an Ogallalla. However, he waited only for an opportunity to leave them. He was with them when they attacked the Bear Hunter and his companions by night in their sleep. The Ogallalla need to be cautious on this ride. The Shoshone living in these mountains, are their enemies. Wohkadeh was sent out as a scout to spy on the wigwams of the Shoshone, which he did not do. Instead, he rode east in great haste to the hut of the Bear Hunter to inform his son and his friend that he had been captured."

"That is very brave. I shall never forget that!" Martin called out. "But does my father know about it?"

"Wohkadeh did tell him and had him describe the direction. He spoke so secretly with the Bear Hunter that no Sioux noticed it."

"But they will figure it out if you don't return to them!"

"No, because they will believe that Wohkadeh was killed by Shoshone."

"Did my father give you particular instructions?"

"No. Wohkadeh is to tell you only that he was captured together with his companions. Now, my young white brother will know himself what to do."

"Of course, I know! I will take off immediately to free him."

Again he wanted to jump up, but Jemmy took his arm and held him back.

"Stop, my boy! Do you want to ride through the air and arrive tonight with the Indians only to also be captured by them and then roasted? Wait a little while, young man! Fat Jemmy will be glad to help you but isn't inclined to run with his head through your wall. We haven't learned anything yet. Wohkadeh will tell us the place where your father was attacked."

The Indian answered:

"The water the palefaces call the Powder River comes together from four branches. The attack happened on the western one."

"Good! That would then be beyond Camp MacKinney and south of Murphy's Ranch. This area isn't unknown to me. But how can the famous Bear Hunter be so incautious to let himself be attacked?"

"The Hunter slept, and the man who was posted as a guard was not a man of the West."

"This alone explains it. What direction did the Ogallalla take then?"

"Toward the mountains the Whites call the Bighorn."

"To the Bighorn Mountains then. Go on?"

"They moved past the head of the bad spirit ... "

"Ah, Devil's Head!"

"... and headed for the water which springs from there and runs into the river of the Bighorn. There, we heard of hostile Shoshone, so Wohkadeh was sent off to spy on them. And so, he does not know where the Ogallalla rode from there."

"That's not really necessary. We have eyes and shall find their tracks. When did the attack happen?"

"Four days have passed."

"Oh my! When's the execution to take place?"

"The night of the full moon that the three warriors were killed on."

Jemmy did some calculating in his mind and then said:

"If that's the case, we have enough time to get to the Reds. There's still twelve days to full moon. But how strong are the Ogallalla?"

"When I left them, they counted five times ten and six."

"Then, they are fifty six warriors. How many captives did they take?"

"Six, with the Bear Hunter."

"Then we know enough for the time being and can consider what we intend to do. However, we need not talk long about it. Martin Baumann, what are your intentions?"

The young man rose from his seat, lifted his right hand as though to take an oath, and replied:

"I herewith promise to rescue my father or to avenge his death, even if I have to pursue the Sioux and fight them all by myself. I may die, but will not break my oath."

"You won't be traveling alone," little Hobble-Frank said. "Of course, I will ride with you and, in no case, abandon you."

"And *Massa* Bob also go along," the Negro declared, "to free old *Massa* Baumann and beat Sioux-Ogallalla to death. All must go to hell!"

Saying this he made such a fierce face and gnashed his teeth so loudly, that it was dreadful to behold.

"And I will come along, too!" said Jemmy, the fat one. "It will be my pleasure to snatch the captives from the Reds. And you, Davy?"

"Don't be stupid," the tall one answered, even-tempered. "Do you think I will stay here to repair my shoes or grind coffee while you go on such a marvelous lark? I thought you knew your old chum better than that!"

"Well, you old raccoon. Finally, there's something serious. Shooting animals becomes boring with time. But, Wohkadeh, what will our red brother be doing?"

The Indian replied:

"Wohkadeh is a Mandan, at most a foster child of the Ponca-Sioux but never an Ogallalla. If his white brothers give him a rifle with powder and lead, he will accompany them and die with them or defeat the enemies."

"Good chap!" the little Saxon said. "You'll get a rifle and everything else, even a fresh horse, since we have four, one being a shpare. Yours is tired and can run along with us until it has recovered. But when are we going to leave?"

"At once, of course!" Martin answered.

33

"Indeed, we ought not to lose any time," the fat one agreed, "but to be too hasty isn't advisable either. We will pass through areas, which are poor in water and game and, therefore, we must provision ourselves. That we will take along lots of munitions is self-evident. Actually, such an expedition must be prepared with the best of care, so that nothing's missed and forgotten. As we stand here, we are six men against fifty-six Ogallalla. That is a lot. Also, we don't know if the nine horse thieves we recited the multiplication table to today, are planning something evil for us. We must make sure that they have left the area or will leave it. And what about this house? Do you intend to leave it unprotected?"

"Yes," Martin replied.

"Then, it's very possible that you'll find it burned down, or at least cleaned out upon your return."

"We can prepare against the latter."

The young man took a hoe and, in a square, hacked the hard-packed floor open. A loam-covered, secret trap door appeared, below which was a very large space. Everything that was not to be taken along could be hidden inside. Even if the building was burned down, it could be expected that the hard-packed loam floor would protect the hidden items from destruction.

The men now got to work to deposit the contents of the room into the cavity, as far as they weren't required for their expedition. The bear skins, too, went down there. One of them was of a particular great size and beauty. When Jemmy looked at it admiringly, Martin took it from his hands and dropped it into the hole.

"Leave it!" he said. "I can't look at this fur without thinking of the most terrible hours of my life."

"That sounds very much, as if you had already a long life and a whole series of terrible events behind you, my boy."

"Oh ho! I'm not bragging!"

Martin gave the fat one an almost angry look. He asked:

"Do you think that the Son of the Bear Hunter hasn't had enough opportunities for adventure?"

"Obviously, I don't want to dispute this."

"Then, I will tell you that I did fight already, as a four-year-old boy, with the fellow who lived in the hide you just now admired."

"A four-year-old child against such a powerful grizzly? I know that the children of the West are cut from a different stock than the boys who put their little feet against their fathers' bed warmers. I've seen many a boy who, in New York, was an ace in spelling, but also knew how to use his rifle like an older man. But – hm! What happened then with that bear?"

"It was down in the mountains of Colorado. I still had my mother and a most sweet little sister of three, a year younger than myself. Father had left to hunt for meat; mother was outside in front of our hut cutting firewood. It was winter and very cold in the mountains. I was all-alone with little Luddy in the room. She sat between the door and the table playing with her doll, which I had carved from a piece of wood. I stood on the table to cut with the big carving knife, an M and an L into the strong support beam, which extended to the gabled roof. These were the first letters of my given name and of my dear Luddy. As boys do, I wanted to immortalize both of us. Absorbed in this hard work, I barely paid attention to a shout from my mother outside. Since it wasn't repeated, I continued unconcerned with my carving, sweating from exertion. Then I heard the door latch being forcefully opened. Being of the opinion, that mother had entered so noisily, because she was carrying wood in her arms, I didn't even turn around, but only said: 'Ma, this is for Luddy and myself. Then, it will also be your turn and Pa's."

"Instead of her reply, I heard a deep, deep growl. I turned. You must understand now, gentlemen, that it wasn't day yet. But outside, snow was glistening, and on the big fireplace burned a large log whose flame illuminated the room. What I saw by its shine was absolutely terrible. Right in front of poor Luddy, who couldn't utter a sound from terror, stood a giant gray bear. Its fur was shaggy with ice and its breath was steaming. In a begging gesture, my speechless, little sister held the little wooden doll up to the animal as if wanting to say, 'Here, take my doll, but don't do anything to me, you bad, dear bear!' But the grizzly knew no mercy. He tossed Luddy down with a single blow of his paw, and then crushed the little, sweet, blonde head with a single bite. You must know gentlemen that a bear's first bite goes for the head of its victim, the brain being its greatest delicacy. Today, still, I hear the gnashing and cracking. Heavens, I cannot forget it, never, never ... !'"

He stopped in his recollection. No one broke the silence that had ensued. Then he continued:

"I, too, could not move from horror. I wanted to call for help, but could not make any sound. I saw my sister's members disappear into the jaws of the monster, until nothing was left but the wooden doll that had fallen to the floor. Convulsively, I held the long knife in my hand. I had wanted to jump off the table and fight the bear for Luddy's life, but I was paralyzed by terror. Then, the monster approached me and raised itself by its forelegs on the table. God be thanked! At that moment, the use of my limbs returned. The bear's terrible, penetrating breath reached my face. That's when I took the knife between my teeth, grabbed the beam with both arms, and swung myself up onto it. He wanted to follow and, in the process, toppled the table. That was what saved me.

Now, of course, I shouted for help, but in vain. Mother did not come, although she ought to have heard my voice since the door stood open letting in a cold draft of air. The grizzly stretched to its greatest height to snatch me from the beam. You've seen its hide and, therefore, must believe me when I tell you that he could have reached me with his front paws. But, I held the knife in my right hand, held fast with the left, and stabbed at the paw he raised towards me.

How am I to describe the fight, my upset and my fear! How long I defended myself, I don't know. In such a condition, a quarter of an hour becomes an eternity. But my strength waned. Both front paws of the bear had been punctured and cut multiple times. Then, I heard, despite its growling and howling, the bark of our dog, which father had taken along. Outside our hut a voice rose like I've never heard before – the voice of a dog. He rushed in and immediately leaped upon the giant carnivore. Every one of you has probably witnessed several dogs fighting a bear. But a single dog against such a grizzly, without his master being present with rifle and knife that you ought to see and also hear. You are aware that dogs that have become wild are a real plague in the States. They decimate herds of sheep. It is estimated, that in Ohio alone, up to sixty thousand sheep are killed by these rapacious dogs who have escaped from their owners. And in the entire United States, half a million die from such attacks annually. These dogs are distinguished by their extreme daring and will even attack bears. We had tamed and domesticated one of those. He was an ugly cur, but immensely strong and faithfully devoted to us. When he threw himself onto the bear, he did not howl. No, he literally roared like a carnivore! He grabbed onto its throat to tear it apart, but instead the bear tore him to pieces with its mighty paws. Only a minute later the dog was dead – torn apart, and the ferocious grizzly then turned back to me.

"But how about your father?" Davy asked, who had, like the others, listened with close attention. "Where there's the dog, the master can't be far away."

"That is true. Just when the grizzly, his back turned to the door, reared up again below the beam to reach for me, my father appeared, his face pale like living death.

"Father, help!" I screamed while stabbing at the bear.

He did not reply. His throat was constricted. He raised his loaded rifle – now he's going to shoot! But, no, he lowered it again. He was so upset, that the rifle wavered in his hands. He threw the gun away, yanked the Bowie knife from his belt and leaped upon the animal from behind. Grabbing its fur with his left hand, he stepped forward on one side and stabbed the long blade up to its handle between the known two ribs. But immediately he jumped back so as not to be seized by the bear in its death throws. The mighty beast stood immovable. It groaned, its throat rattling indescribably. It reached into the air with its front paws, and then collapsed dead. As it later showed, the blade had entered directly into his heart."

"God be thanked!" Jemmy exclaimed, exhaling loudly and deeply. "That was help in the greatest need. But what happened to your mother, young sir?"

"Her – oh, I never saw her again."

He turned away as if ashamed, and with a swift move of his hand, wiped a couple of tears from his eyes.

"You never saw her again? How so?"

"When father had lowered me from the beam, both of us trembled all over. He asked for little Luddy. Loudly sobbing, I told him what had happened. I never again saw a human face as that of my father's when he heard this. He was ashen-faced and like stone. He let go a scream, a single one, but what a one it was! May God help me that I never again must listen to such a cry! Then, he fell silent. He sat on the bench and covered his face in both hands. He did not respond to my endearing words. When I asked him about mother, he shook his head. But when I wanted to go outside to look for her, he grabbed my arm so hard that I screamed from pain!"

"Stay!" he demanded. "That's not for you!"

He sat down once more and remained there for a long, long time until the fire had burned down. Then he locked me up and began work behind the hut. I tried to remove the moss stuffed between the individual logs at one spot and was successful. When I then peered through, I saw that he was digging a deep hole. Before entering the hut, the bear had attacked my mother and torn her apart. I didn't even see how father prepared her for her final rest, because he surprised me in my spying and made sure that I could no longer see through the wall."

"Terrible, terrible!" said Jemmy, while he wiped his fur's sleeve across his eyes.

"Yes, that was truly horrible! Father was ill for a long time, and our closest neighbor sent a man over to care of him and me. But then, when he had recovered, we left this area and became Bear Hunters. When father hears that a bear has been seen somewhere, he will not rest until he has given it a bullet or the blade. And I – well, I can tell you, that I, too, have done my share to avenge my poor little Luddy. At first, my heart was beating tremendously when I aimed my rifle at a bear. But I have a talisman which protects me, so that I'm just as calm against a grizzly as if I were shooting a raccoon."

"A charm?" Davy asked. "Pah! That doesn't exist, young man. Don't believe in such nonsense. That is sinning against the first commandment!"

"No, the talisman I mean is of a different kind than you think. Look at it! There it hangs below the bible."

He pointed to the wall where upon a small board lay an old, big bible. Below it, on a peg, hung a small piece of wood, about one and a half fingers in length and about a finger thick. One could see clearly that the upper part represented a head.

"Hm!", grumbled Davy who, like all Yankees, held firmly to his belief. "I don't want to believe that this thing is the representation of an idol."

"No. I am no heathen, but a good Christian. What you see is the wooden doll I had carved for my little sister to play with. I preserved this little keepsake to remember the terrible events and always hang it around my neck when I'm accompanying father on a bear hunt. If a danger seems to me too great, I take hold of the doll, and the bear's lost. You can rely on that!"

At that Jemmy, deeply touched, put his hand on the youngster's shoulder and said:

"Martin, you are a brave boy. Consider me your friend, and you'll not be disappointed. As fat as I am, as fat can be your trust in me. I shall prove it to you!"

2. Tokvi-tey

Five days later, in the afternoon, the six horsemen had put the area of the Powder River behind them, and were now headed for the Bighorn Mountains.

The tracts extending from Missouri to the Rocky Mountains are today still some of the wildest parts of the United States. The area is almost entirely solitary, treeless prairie, where the hunter must ride for several days until he finds a bush or a source of water. The country rises gradually towards the west, at first forming soft rises, then hillocks becoming higher, more abrupt and fissured the farther one moves west. But the lack of wood and water remains the same. This is why the area is called *Mah-kosietsha* by Indians, and by the Whites, Badlands. Both terms mean the same, that is, poor country.

Even important rivers, spreading widely like the Platte, carry only little water in summer. Farther to the north, where the headwaters of the Cheyenne, Powder, Tongue and Bighorn Rivers are located, the land becomes more hospitable. The grass is richer, and the bushes form extensive brush forests. Eventually, the frontiersman's foot walks even in the shade of hundred or more-year-old giant trees.

Here, the hunting grounds of the Shoshone and Snake Indians, the Sioux, Cheyenne, and the Arapaho are located. Each of these tribes divides again into subgroups. Since every one of these groups pursues its own particular interests, it is no wonder that there is a continuous change of war and peace between them. And should the red man be, at times, inclined to keep the peace for awhile, master paleface comes along and pokes him, first with needles and then with knives, until the Indian takes up the war tomahawk again and starts warfare once more.

Under these circumstances, it is self-evident that, where the grazing grounds of many different tribes and groups meet, the safety of an individual is questionable, even highly threatened. The Shoshone and Snake Indians have always been embittered enemies of the Sioux, which is why the tracts extending from Dakota south of the Yellowstone to the Bighorn Mountains, have drunk the blood of the red, and also that of the white man, quite frequently.

Fat Jemmy and Long Davy knew this very well, which is why they took great care, as far as possible, to avoid meeting Indians no matter the tribe.

Wohkadeh rode in the lead, since he had already traveled this same distance on his way to meet the group. He was now armed with a rifle and on his belt carried several bags filled with the incidentals no prairie man can do without. Jemmy and Davy hadn't modified their appearance at all. Of course, the former rode his tall nag, and the latter hung his eternally long legs from the sides of his little, obstinate mule, who every five minutes made the all too well known, fruitless attempt to toss off its rider. Davy needed only to put his left or right shoe to the ground to gain a firm hold. On his mount, he resembled one of the inhabitants of the Australian isles, who equipped their dangerous boats with outriggers and, for this reason, could never be tipped over. Davy's outriggers were his two legs.

Frank, too, wore the same kind of outfit he had been seen in by his two new friends the first time: moccasins, leggings, blue tailcoat and Amazon hat with a long yellow feather. The little Saxon sat very well on his horse and, despite his odd outfit, gave the impression of an able frontiersman.

It was a pleasure to see Martin Baumann sitting in the saddle. He rode at least as well as Wohkadeh, was at one with his horse, and maintained the forward-bent position. This eased the load for the animal and enabled the rider to endure the exertion of a month-long ride without becoming fatigued. He wore the leather outfit of a trapper, and his equipment and weaponry left nothing to be desired. His entire soul was with the task at hand. Whoever looked into his fresh face and bright eyes became immediately aware that he was quite at home on the prairie. He definitely gave the impression that, although still half a boy, he would, nevertheless, stand like a man when required. Had not the deep concern for his captive father thrown a shadow on him, he might have been called the most cheerful member of the little party.

It was funny to watch black Bob. Riding had never been his passion, thus he sat in an absolutely indescribable position on his horse. He had his difficulties with the animal, as it had also with him, since he was unable to maintain a firm seat for even ten minutes. Every step of the animal shifted him back by a fraction of an inch, despite his moving forward to the neck of the horse. Thus, he slid and slid, until he was in danger of falling off the back end. Then he again pushed himself as far forward as possible and the slide began anew. Over time, he such came quite involuntarily into ridiculous positions not even a circus clown could have contrived. Instead of a saddle, he had attached only a blanket, since he knew from former experience, that he was unable to keep himself in a saddle. With a somewhat faster tempo, he had always ended up behind the saddle. He held his legs far from the horse. When asked to keep his legs firmly against the horse's body he always replied:

"Why should Bob squeeze poor horse with legs? Horse has not done him any harm! Bob's legs are no pair of pincers!"

The horsemen had reached the edge of a shallow, almost circular depression, whose diameter was approximately six miles. Surrounded on three sides by barely noticeable rises in terrain, it was bordered on the west by a substantial elevation, apparently covered by bushes and trees. There might have been a lake here in former times. The ground consisted of deep, infertile sand, and, except for a few hardy tufts of grass, showed only the grayish gleaming, useless mugwort vegetation characteristic of the sterile areas of the far West.

Without much consideration, Wohkadeh drove his horse into the sand, making a beeline for the distant rise.

"What kind of area is this?" Fat Jemmy asked. "It's unknown to me."

"The warriors of the Shoshone call this place Pa-are-pap," the Indian replied.

"The Sea of Blood. Oh my! Then let's not wish to meet Shoshone here."

"Why?" inquired Martin Baumann.

"Because we would be in trouble. Here, at this place, Whites butchered a hunting party of Shoshone to the last man entirely without cause. Although about five years have passed since, the tribal members of the murdered would mercilessly kill every White, unfortunate enough to fall into their hands. The blood of the fallen calls for revenge."

"Do you think there are Shoshone nearby, sir?"

"I hope not. I've heard that they are presently far to the north by the Musselshell River in Montana. If this is true, we are safe from them. Wohkadeh will tell us if they have moved south by now."

The Indian heard these words and commented:

"When Wohkadeh passed through here seven days ago, there was not a single Shoshone warrior nearby. Only the Arapaho had made camp by the spring of the river the palefaces call Tongue River."

"Then, we are safe from them. The area here is so flat and open that we can see every horseman, even people on foot, for more than a mile. Therefore, we will be able to take the necessary measures in good time. Forward then!"

They rode straight west for about half an hour when Wohkadeh halted his horse.

"Uff!" he exclaimed.

Indians use this word mostly as an expression of surprise.

"What's the matter?" Jemmy asked.

"Shi-shi!"

This word of the Mandan language actually means feet, but signifies tracks.

"Tracks?" the Fat One asked. "Of people or an animal?"

"Wohkadeh does not know. My brother may look at them himself."

"By gosh! An Indian not knowing if the tracks are that of a human or a beast! I've never come across that! These must be very strange tracks. Let's have a look at them. But dismount properly and don't ride over them, men, or they won't be recognizable any longer."

"They will still be recognizable," the Indian suggested. "They are so large and long, coming from the south and moving far to the north."

The men dismounted to investigate the strange tracks. Every three-year-old Indian boy is capable of distinguishing the footprints of a person from those of an animal. That Wohkadeh was unable to make this differentiation was totally incomprehensible. But even Jemmy, when he looked at the impressions, shook his head. He looked to the left from where the tracks came, and then to the right

41

where they led. Again he shook his head, and then said to the long David Kroners:

"Well, old Davy, did you ever in your life see anything like that?"

The other shook his head doubtfully, looked also left and right, contemplated the impressions in the sand, shook his head once more, and then answered:

"No, never!"

"And you, Mister Frank?"

The Saxon also studied the tracks, likewise shook his head and announced:

"Only the devil may know these tracks!"

Martin and the Negro voiced the same opinion, stating that this matter was very puzzling to them as well. Long Davy first scratched himself behind the right ear, then the left. He usually did this two times which was always a sign that he was embarrassed. Then, he made the wise comment:

"But some kind of creature passed by here. If that's not true, I'll be forced to drink the entire Mississippi including its tributaries within two hours!"

"Look, what a smart ass you are, oldster!" Jemmy laughed. "If you hadn't said so, we truly wouldn't have known that these were tracks. So, a creature walked along here in any case. But what kind? How many legs did it have?"

"Four," everyone answered, except the Indian.

"Yes. That, one can see clearly. Then it was an animal. But can anyone tell me now what kind of four-legged creature we are dealing with?"

"It's not an elk," Frank opined.

"God help us, no! An elk doesn't ever leave such giant impressions."

"A bear, maybe?"

"Of course, a bear leaves such large and clear imprints in sand that even a blind man could read them with his fingers. But, these tracks have not been made by a bear. The impressions aren't long and fainter towards the back, like those of a sole-walker. They are almost circular, more than the span of a hand in diameter and stomped in straight, like with a seal. They are raised only slightly in the back and, at their base, are totally flat. Thus, the animal cannot have toes or claws, but must have hooves."

"A horse then," Frank suggested.

"Hm!" Jemmy growled. "A horse ...?"

"But it cannot have been a horse either. One ought to be able to see at least a small indication of a horseshoe, or, should the animal have been unshod, the wall and the frog. The tracks are at most two hours old, too brief a time for these indentations to have disappeared. And the main point: Could there ever be a horse with such exceptionally large hooves. Were we in Asia or Africa and not on this old, cozy prairie, I would assert that the granddaddy of an elephant had stomped by here."

"Yes, it looks just like that!" Long Davy laughed.

"What? It looks like that?" Jemmy asked.

"Sure! You just said so!"

"Then, have them return your apprentice moneys! Have you ever seen an elephant?"

"Two even."

"Where?"

"In Philadelphia, at Barnum's, and now here, Fat One!"

"If you want to make a joke, buy a better one for ten bucks. Understood! These tracks do resemble those made by an elephant! The prints are large enough, I admit, but an elephant would have a totally different step width. You didn't think of that, Davy. It was also no camel, or I would maintain that you had stomped by here two hours ago. And now I admit that I'm at the end of my wisdom."

The men walked a distance ahead and back again in order to inspect the wondrous tracks closely, but none was able to offer a halfway believable explanation.

"What does my red brother say about it?" asked Jemmy.

"*Maho ahono!*" the Indian answered, while making a gesture with his hand indicating reverence.

"The Ghost of the Prairie, you mean?"

"Yes, because it was neither a human nor an animal."

"Oh my! Your ghosts seem to have terribly large feet. Or might the ghost of the prairie suffer at times from rheumatism of the foot and put on felt slippers?"

"My white brother ought not to mock. The Ghost of the Prairie can appear in all kinds of representations. We must look at his tracks with reverence and ride on quietly."

"No, that we shall not. I must positively know what this means. I've never seen such tracks and shall follow them until I know who made them."

"My brother will perish. The Ghost does not tolerate searching for him."

"Madness! Later, when Fat Jemmy tells of these tracks and cannot say who made them, he will be laughed at, even declared a liar. It is literally a question of honor for a good frontiersman to explain this puzzle."

"We do not have time for such detours."

"I don't demand that from you. There are still four hours until dark. Then, we must set up camp. Does my red brother perhaps know of a place where we can camp?"

"Yes. If we ride straight ahead, we come to a place where the distant mountain has an opening. After an hour, a side canyon opens into this valley on the left. We shall rest in there, since it holds bushes and trees, which will make our fire invisible from the big valley. There is also a spring with water for us and our animals."

"That's easy to find. Ride on then! I shall follow these tracks, then meet you at the campsite."

"May my white brother be warned!"

"No way!" Long Davy called out. "A warning is totally out of place here, Jemmy is absolutely right. It would be shameful to have discovered these incomprehensible tracks without investigating who is responsible for them. It is said that, before Earth was created, there were animals against which a buffalo would appear like an earthworm beside a Mississippi steamer. Maybe, a beast from these times has been left over and now runs around in the sand here, counting by its grains how many hundreds of years old it is. I believe such an animal is called *mammo*."

"Mammoth!" the Fat One corrected.

"Could be, too! Again, shame on us, if we come across such a prehistoric beast's tracks and not at least one of us tried to get to see such an animal. I'll ride along, Jemmy!"

"That won't work."

"Why not?"

"Because both of us, not to be presumptuous, have the most experience, and are, so to speak, the leaders. Therefore, we can't leave together. One must stay behind and someone else better ride with me."

"Master Jemmy is right." Martin responded. "I shall go with him."

"No, my young friend," replied Jemmy. "You would be the very last one I'd invite to accompany me."

"Why? I burn from desire to discover this unknown animal!"

"I do believe that. At your age one is always ready for such adventures. But the ride may be dangerous, and we've taken on a silent obligation to watch over you and unite you unharmed with your father. It's, therefore, not consistent with my conscience to take you along into unknown danger. No, if I'm not to ride by myself, someone else must accompany me."

"Then I will come along!" lame Frank said.

"Yes, I have nothing against that. Mister Frank once fought already '*merschtentels*' in Moritzburg with the boots and the night watchman and is unlikely to be afraid of a mammoth."

"I? Be afraid? Wouldn't think of it."

"Then, that's it. The others will ride on, and the two of us will veer to the right. Your horse won't mind the detour much, and for my nag, trotting is his greatest passion. Earlier, before he assumed his present horse form, he must have been a runner or mailman."

Martin had some objections, but not for long. Long Davy warned them to be cautious. Wohkadeh once more described the campsite and admonished Jemmy's intentions, which would provoke the prairie ghost's wrath. Then, the others continued the interrupted ride, while the Fat One followed the tracks northward with the Saxon.

Since the two had a detour ahead of them, they gave their animals the spurs, and so a short time later, the others could no longer see their companions.

Later on, the tracks diverged from their previous direction and turned west toward the distant mountains, so that Jemmy and Frank now rode parallel to their companions, but most likely more than an hour's ride apart.

They had remained silent until now. Jemmy's rawboned nag had thrown its legs so easily forward that Frank's horse had had trouble keeping up in the deep sand. Now the Fat One changed the strenuous trot to an easier gait enabling Frank to keep readily at his side.

While with the other expedition members, these two had chosen to speak English. Now that the two Germans were by themselves, they preferred to use their mother tongue.

"Am I right," Frank began, "that thing earlier with the mammoth was only a joke?"

"Of course."

"I thought so right away, because such mammoths don't exisht anymore."

"Have you heard of these prehistoric animals before?"

"I? Shure and how! And if you don't believe me, then I feel mighty sorry for you. You know, the Moritzburger schoolmashter from way back, who was actually my shpiritual mother, he was on top of things, particularly in plant-zoology. He knew every tree, from the shpruce down to sorrel, and also every animal, from the sea shnake to the littlest sponge. At the time, I profited downright abundantly from him."

"I'm truly pleased," the Fat One laughed. "Maybe I can also profit from you."

"That is '*merschtentels*' (for the most part) self-evident. For example, espeshially what concerns the mammoth, I can give you the best authentic information."

"Might you have seen one?"

"No, because at the time, before the creation of the world, I haven't been with the current police; but the schoolmashter did find the mammoth in old books. How large do you think the monshter was?"

"Substantially larger than an elephant."

"Elephant? That's by far not enough! If the mammoth shtumbles over a rock and looked down at it, then this rock was 'merschtentels' an Egyptian pyramid. Now think how tall this animal was! And if a fly might have alighted on the tip of its tail, it took fourteen days for it to become aware of it in his brain up front. Now think of the length of such a creature! Our today's mind is much too weak for the menagerie of that time. Today, when we want to see something grand, we musht peer through the back-bullock-clover-grass-teleshcope. Then, it's at leasht close to somewhere around the deluge."

Jemmy looked very surprised.

"What?" he asked. "What's the name of this telescope?"

"Why don't you pay attention? Once I'm in the middle of instruction every dishturbance is impertinent to me. It's the back-bullock-clover-grass-teleshcope. Can you remember that? If you really were a Gymnasiast, then you musht have had also lessons about the acoushtics of teleshcopes. The darker the focus, the larger are the shtars one can see, since in the sciences merschtentels the reverse relationship musht be calculated. Do you undershtand that?"

"Yes," nodded the Fat One, who made every effort to keep a serious face. "But now I begin to understand what kind of telescope you meant."

"Well, what kind then?"

"None. You mistook the designation. You didn't mean a telescope, but a microscope."

"Microshcope! Yes, yes, right! Because the correct word was abshent for me at the moment, I subshtituted it meanwhile, as I've always been quick-witted."

"And you meant the hydro-oxygen-gas-microscope!"

"Of course! That's self-undershtood. But why should I talk Danish, if I'm fully a mashter of the German language? If I say back-bullock-clover-grass-microshcope, then even an uneducated person will undershtand me. The schoolmashter always said: 'One must lower oneself to the child's mind. Only then is one to harvest palms on sandy ground.' You see, I'm throwing plenty of metaphor examples around. That's because I've always been a diligent autodidact. If back then the quarrel about father Wrangel's favorite word hadn't erupted, I'd have made it nolens coblenz to the Tharandt Foreshtry Academy, and wouldn't need to bang around in the Wild West and have the Sioux shoot me lame."

"Ah, you weren't born lame?"

Frank looked at the Fat One almost angrily.

"Born lame? How could that be possible with a pershonality of my ambutation! A lame person can never ever become a foreshtry official! Naw, I've had my healthy legs as long as I can think of myself. But when I came with Baumann to the Black Mountains to shtart the trading posht among the gold diggers, Indians came also at times to make their purchases. Merschtentels they were Sioux. These are the worsht anthropological savages there are, particularly since upon the leasht gesture one can make, they right away shtab and shoot. It's the best not to deal with them at all. Good day and good travels, fare well and good-bye! I've always been true to this saying, being a friend of principles; but once I had a weak hour in my character, and for that I'm shtill limping today."

"How did that happen?"

"Quite unexpectedly, like everything one doesn't know in advance. It's shtill so real before my mental sight as if it were that reshpective day. The shtars were shining and the bullfrogs roared loudly in the nearby shwamp, since, unfortunately, it wasn't by day, but in the night. Baumann was away to pick up new supplies at Fort Fetterman. Martin was ashleep, and the Negro Bob was off to collect debts and hadn't shown up yet. Only his horse had returned without him to its beloved home. Negsht morning he came limping in with shprained limbs and without a penny's worth of money. He had been thrown out by all our debtors and subshequently even thrown off his horse. That's called life's folly to enjoy firsht hand. You see that I can even talk in verse! Right?"

"Yes. You are a little genius."

"I've told this often to myself, but never to others, since no one believes it. So, the shtars shone from the heavens, when someone knocked at the door. Here, in the West one must be very cautious. That's why I didn't open right away, but asked from the inside who it was wanting to come in from the outside. To make it short, it was five Sioux Indians who wanted to trade furs for powder."

"You didn't let them in?"

"Why not?"

"Sioux, in the middle of the night?"

"Oh, please! Had we had a clock, it would have been half pasht eleven. That wasn't too late yet. I, as a frontiershman, know very well that one cannot always be showing up at the proper visitation hour, and that time can, in some circumshtances, be immenshely precious. The Reds said they shtill had to travel through the night and, therefore, my good Saxon heart appealed to me – I let them in."

"What incautiousness!"

"Why? I've never been afraid, and before I opened the door, I demanded them to leave all weapons outside. To their honor, I musht admit, they honeshtly followed that demand. Of course, I had a revolver in my hand when I served them, which, as savages, they couldn't take badly. I shure did a brilliant business with them, bad powder against good beaver pelts. When Reds and Whites trade with each other, the Reds are always the cheated. While I'm sorry for it, I alone can't change it. Negsht to the door hung three rifles. When the Indians left, the last one remained shtanding in the door. He turned and asked me, if I might add perhaps a sip of firewater to the deal. Now, although it's forbidden to give the Indians brandy, I had, as I said, made a good profit and was, therefore, willing to do them a favor. I turned and went to the corner where the brandy bottle stood. The moment I returned with it, I saw the fellow disappear with one of the rifles he had torn from its peg. Of course, I quickly put the bottle down, took the negsht rifle and jumped out the door. Obviously, I leaped sideways, since I'd have offered a clear target in the light of the doorway. But since I had come so quickly from the light into the dark, I was unable to see clearly right away. I heard quick shteps, then it flashed from across the fence. A shot rang out, and I felt as if something had hit my foot. Now I saw the Reds in the process of swinging over the fence. I aimed and fired, but at the same time felt such a shtabbing pain in the foot that I collapsed. The bullet missed, and the rifle was lost. Only with difficulty did I make it back to the hut. The Indian's shot had penetrated my foot. Was it because of the darkness or because the Sioux had a strange rifle? Today I still cannot comprehend how he could make this peashooter shot. Only months later was I able to use the foot again, but that made me the Hobble-Frank. But I took good note of the Red and shall never forget his face. Woe to him, should he somewhere and some time cross my path! We Saxons are known as the mosht good-natured Germans, but our national merits can never commit us in the course of the night, when the shtars shine from the heavens, to be robbed and shot lame. I believe the Sioux was a member of the Ogallalla and when – What's the matter?"

"What's the matter? he replied. "I wonder myself. Do I actually have eyes?"

He looked in total surprise from his horse to the sand. Frank, too, now saw what his companion meant.

"Ish it possible!" he exclaimed, "the tracks are suddenly very different!"

"Of course! At first they were pure elephant tracks and now they are clearly horse tracks. The animal was shod, and with new irons, making imprints as sharp as they are. The grabs as well as the studs are not the least worn."

"But these tracks are wrong!"

"That is precisely what I can't comprehend! Until now the tracks moved away from us and now they approach us!"

"But are they really the same tracks?"

"Of course! There behind us, rock is surfacing, but the area is barely twenty feet wide. On the rock, the tracks are invisible. Beyond it, they come as elephant tracks from the east, and over here, they come as distinct horse prints from the west. Look around! Are there any other tracks?"

"No."

"Therefore, despite their difference, these imprints must have been made by the same animal. It's redundant, but I'll get off my horse to convince myself that there's no error."

Both dismounted. Their accurate investigation of the ground gave the same result. The elephant tracks had changed on the narrow, rocky place into horse tracks. If that wasn't very strange, then the circumstance that both tracks came from opposite directions to meet at the rocky ground, was absolutely perplexing. Both men looked at each other helplessly and shook their heads.

"If that isn't magic someone is playing tricks on us," Jemmy said.

"Playing tricks? How?"

"Yes, that's what I can't understand!"

"But there's no magic!"

"No. I'm not superstitious."

"This looksh to me like the magician Philadelphia, who's supposed to have thrown a ball of yarn up into the air and then climbed up on it!"

"Since the elephant came from the east and the horse from the west and both tracks terminate here, then both animals must have climbed the twine at this location and have disappeared up there in the air! Explain that who will; I'm unable to do it!"

"I'd like to know now what the Moritzburg teacher would say if he were here!"

"He wouldn't look any smarter then you and I!"

"Hm! With permission, you don't look particularly ingenious either, Jemmy."

"And, right now, one can also not see what a talented 'autopetrefact' you are. I'd actually like to see the pershon who could solve this riddle."

"But it must be solvable, because the famous Archidiakonus said: Give me a firm point in the air and I'll lift every door from its hinges!"

"Archimedes, you mean!"

"Yes, but he was Diakonus on the side, for when the enemy soldiers came on Saturday evening, he was just learning next morning's prayer and called to them: 'Don't dishturb me and be quiet!' That's when they killed him. That's why the point in the air was losht again."

"Maybe you'll find it again. I, however, don't feel qualified to do it, since I can't even resolve this contradiction here."

"But we must do something!"

"Of course! We aren't returning. If there's an explanation at all, it lies ahead of us, not behind. Let's mount up again and ride ahead!"

They rode on following the horse tracks. These were clearly recognizable and, after about half an hour, led from the sandy terrain to better ground. There, they found grass and sporadic brush. The big rise was close now. Dense forest crept up its slopes. Beginning down below with individual trees, then, the higher one looked, the denser they became. Here, too, the tracks were clearly visible. After a while, however, they came upon an area covered by small pebbles. There the tracks suddenly and completely stopped.

"That's the solution!" mumbled Frank.

"Incomprehensible!" declared Jemmy. "The horse must have come from the air and disappeared up there again. Or was it truly the ghost of the prairie? If so, then I wish he'd show himself for once. I'd very much like to learn what a ghost looks like."

"This wish can be fulfilled. Turn around, gentlemen!"

These words came in German from a bush by which they had stopped. With a shout of surprise both turned. The speaker now left the bushes behind where he had taken cover.

He was not very tall and not very broad in stature. A dark blond, full beard framed his sunburned face. He wore tasseled leggings and a hunting shirt similarly tasseled at its seams. Long boots reaching above his knees completed his outfit and a broad-brimmed felt hat, all around whose string were attached the ear tips of the gray bear. In his broad belt, braided from individual strands, stuck two revolvers and a Bowie knife. It seemed to be filled with cartridges around its entire circumference. From it also hung several leather bags, two screw-on horseshoes, and four, almost circular plaited contraptions made of straw and rushes equipped with straps and buckles. From his left shoulder to the right hip he carried a braided lasso, and around his neck, on a strong silken twine, a peace pipe decorated with hummingbird skins. Engraved in the peace pipe were Indian characters. In his right hand, he held a short-barrelled rifle, its lock and bolt of a very peculiar design, and in his left – a burning cigar, from which he, just then, took a good draw, blowing the smoke away with obvious pleasure.

The true prairie hunter doesn't give anything for shine and cleanliness. The more decrepit he looks, the more he is supposed to have experienced. Anyone taking care of his exterior is looked upon with a great disdain. His greatest abomination is a brightly polished rifle. According to his firm conviction, a frontiersman does not have the time to occupy himself with such tittle-tattle.

Now, on this young stranger, everything looked so clean as if he had only yesterday left St. Louis for the West. His rifle looked as if it had come from the hand of the gunsmith only an hour ago. His boots were immaculately polished, and the spurs had nary a trace of rust. No wear was noticeable on his outfit and, truly, his hands were even washed.

The two stared at him and, in their surprise, forgot to answer him.

"Well," he continued with a smile, "I suppose you wish to see the Ghost of the Flats? If you believe to have followed his tracks, you see him standing before you."

"By the devil! That, *merschtentels*, shtops my mind!" Frank exclaimed.

"Ah, a Saxon! Right?"

"Even a born one! And in any case, you are a pure, uncorrupted German?"

"Yes. It's my honor. And the other gentleman?"

"Oh, he's from the same beautiful area. This pleasant scare left him shpeechless. But it won't take long for him to talk again."

He was right, for now Jemmy jumped from the saddle and offered the stranger his hand.

"Is it possible!" he called. "Here at Devil's Head to meet a German! One shouldn't believe it!"

"And my surprise is twice as great, since I'm meeting two. And, am I not mistaken, your name is Jakob Pefferkorn?"

"What? You know my name!"

"It's easy to see that you are Fat Jemmy. And if I couldn't guess it from that, I need only to look at your nag. If one meets a fat hunter with such a nag, it must be Jemmy. And, it so happened, I learned, that this well-known frontiersman's name is actually Jakob Pfefferkorn. But where you are, Long Davy with his mule cannot be far. Or might I be mistaken?"

"No, he's really close by, not too far from here to the south, where the valley enters the mountains."

"Ah! Do you intend to camp there tonight?"

"Sure. And my companion's name here is Frank."

Frank had also dismounted and shook hands with the stranger, who looked him over closely, nodded and asked:

"Might you be the Hobble-Frank?"

"By Jemineh! You know also my name?"

"I see you are limping, your name being Frank. That makes it an easy question. You live with Baumann, the Bear Hunter?"

"Who told you that?"

"He himself. I met him casually several years ago. Where is he now? At home? I believe that's about a three-days' ride from here?"

"Exshactly. But he's not home. He has fallen into the hands of the Ogallalla, and we are on the way to see what we can do for him."

"That's a scare. Where did it happen?"

"Not far from here, at Devil's Head. They dragged him up to the Yellowshtone, together with five companions and plan to kill them at the grave of Brave Buffalo."

The stranger listened.

"For revenge, I assume?" he asked.

"Of course. Might you have heard of Old Shatterhand?"

"Yes, I think I remember."

With these words a peculiar smile played over his face.

"Well, he killed Brave Buffalo, Bad Fire, and a third Sioux. Now the Ogallalla are under way to visit the graves of the three and, in the process, Baumann has fallen into their hands."

"How did you learn that?"

Frank told him of Wohkadeh and everything that had happened since the young Indian had appeared. The stranger listened with serious attention. Only sometimes, when the lame one fell too much into his home dialect, a quick smile flashed across his face. When the report was finished he said:

"Then, the misfortune of the Bear Hunter is actually Old Shatterhand's fault. It is on his conscience."

"No. It's none of his doing; Baumann was careless."

Well, let's not argue about it. It is brave of you not to shy from the dangers and depravations you will certainly encounter in your attempt to free the captives. I wish you success from the depth of my heart. My particular interest is in the young Martin Baumann. Maybe I will get to see him."

"That's easily possible," Jemmy remarked. "You only need to come with us, or rather ride with us. Where's your horse?"

"How do you know that I'm no woodsman, but have a horse?"

"Well, aren't you wearing spurs!"

"Ah, that tells you. My horse is nearby. I left it for a while so as to watch you riding past here."

"Did you then notice our approach?"

"Of course! Half an hour ago I saw you stop out there to discuss the difference of the tracks."

"What? What do you know about them?"

"Nothing more than that they are my own tracks."

"What? Yours?"

"Yes."

"By the devil! Then it's you who tricked us?"

"Did I really fool you? Well then, this is a great satisfaction for me to have tricked a frontiersman like Fat Jemmy. However, this wasn't meant for you, but for very different people."

The Fat One didn't seem to know anymore what to think of the speaker. Shaking his head, he looked him over from head to foot, then asked:

"But who are you actually?"

The other laughed bemused and replied:

"Well, you noticed right away, that I am a newcomer to the Far West."

"Yes. One notices right away the greenfinch. You can easily go for sparrows with your Sunday's rifle, and your outfit can't be more than a few days old. You must've been with some party here and likely belong to a group of tourist hunters. Where did you get off the train?"

"In St. Louis."

"What? That far east? Impossible! How long have you been here in the West?"

"This time for eight months."

"Oh, please, don't take it wrong! You aren't serious, or are you trying to fool me?"

"I wouldn't think of telling you an untruth."

"Pshaw! And you claim to have deceived us also."

"Yes, the tracks are mine."

53

"No policeman believes that! I bet you are a teacher or professor and are riding around here with several colleagues to collect plants, rocks and butterflies. Let me give you some good advice. Get out of here quickly! This area is no good for you. Life doesn't hang hourly here by a hair, but for every minute. You don't know what danger you are in."

"Oh, but I know this very well. Not too far from here more than forty Shoshone are camped."

"Heavens! Is that true?"

"Yes; I know for sure."

"And you say this so calmly!"

"How else am I to say it? You feel the few Shoshone are to be feared?"

"Man, you aren't aware of what dangerous territory you are in!"

Oh, yes! Out there lies the Sea of Blood, and the Shoshone would be delighted to catch us, or even one of us."

"Now I really don't know what to think of you!"

"Don't you think I can trick these Reds just like I did you. I've already met many a good frontiersman, who was mistaken about me, only because he used a common yardstick to measure me. Please, come along!"

He turned and walked slowly into the bushes. The two followed, leading their horses by the reins. Quickly they arrived at a truly magnificent hemlock, at least a hundred feet tall, rare for such a tree. Next to it stood a horse, a splendid black stallion with red nostrils and a particular hair swirl in his long mane, which to Indians is a sure sign of excellent breeding. The saddle and leatherwork were of Indian type. A rubber coat was buckled behind the saddle. From one of the saddle bags the case of a telescope protruded. On the ground lay a double-barreled Bear Killer of the heaviest caliper. When Jemmy saw this rifle, he took a few steps, picked it up and said:

"This rifle is – it is – ah, I've never seen one, but recognize it immediately. The Silver Rifle of the Apache chief Winnetou and this Bear Killer are the most famous rifles of the West. The Bear Killer belongs ..."

He halted and stared totally disconcerted at its owner, then continued:

"Now, ah, now it dawns on me! Those who have met Old Shatterhand for the first time always thought him to be a greenhorn. He owns this gun, and the rifle in your hand isn't a Sunday rifle, but one of only eleven Henry rifles that have ever existed. Frank, Frank, do you know who this man is?"

"No. I've neither seen his birth certificate nor his inoculation pass."

"My dear fellow, leave the jokes aside! You stand before Old Shatterhand!"

"Old Shat ..."

Hobble stepped back a few paces.

"Goshamighty!" he uttered. "Old Shatterhand! I've always imagined him to be completely different!"

"Me, too!"

"But how then, gentlemen?" the hunter asked smilingly.

"Long and broad jusht like the colossus of Varus!" the learned Saxon replied.

"Yes, of giant stature," agreed his rotund companion."

"In that case, you can see that my reputation is larger than I deserve. Something told around the first campfire will be embellished around the second fire, threefold, and around the third campfire, six fold. And so it happens that one is deemed a veritable miracle when, in fact, one is only human, just like everybody else."

"No. What I've heard about you, that is ..."

"Pah!" Shatterhand interrupted him short and commanding. "Leave it be! Better have a look at my horse. It's a *N'gul-itkli*, found only with the Apache. It is barefooted. If I want to confuse possible pursuers, I'll tie these reed shoes onto its hooves. They are commonly used in China. They will leave behind tracks, especially in sandy soil, that could be mistaken for those of an elephant. Here on my belt hang two pairs of horseshoes, which simply slip onto the hoof and screw on tight. One pair is fashioned in the customary shape, but the other pair is made back to front. Naturally, a track will turn out back to front as well, and those who come across it will believe that I rode in the opposite direction."

"By the devil!" Frank said. "Now it's finally becoming bright daylight with my intelligence. Then these are vexation-irons! What would my Moritzburg teacher say to that?"

"I don't have the honor to know this gentleman but have the pleasure to have hoodwinked you. On rocky ground no trace is left. That's why I got off my horse there to exchange the reed shoes for the irons. Of course, I had no idea that I had fellow-countrymen behind me. I saw you only later. I took this precaution because, from certain signs, I had to conclude the presence of hostile Indians. And this assumption was confirmed when I arrived at this fir."

"Are there vestiges of Indians?"

"No. The tree is the point where I intend to meet Winnetou today, and ..."

"Winnetou!" Jemmy interrupted. "Is the Chief of the Apache nearby?"

"Yes. He arrived here before me."

"Where, where is he? I must absolutely see him!"

"He left me a sign that he has been here already and will be back today. Where he is at this time, I don't know. He will spy on the Shoshone, of course."

"Does he know of their presence?"

"He's the one who made me aware of them. He carved a sign into the bark of the tree, it being just as comprehensible to me as any other writing. I know that he was here and will return, and that forty Shoshone are nearby. All else I must wait for."

"But what if the Shoshone find you here?"

"Pah! I don't know for whom the danger is greater, whether for me, if they find me here, or for them, when I discover them. With Winnetou at my side, I need not be afraid of this little bunch of Shoshone."

This sounded so simple, so self understood, that Hobble-Frank exclaimed admiringly:

"Not fearing forty enemies? I'm no hare's foot either, but my character's temperament for daring hashn't made it that far yet. *Veni, vidi, tutti*, said old Blücher, and then he won the battle at Belle-Mesalliance, but he washn't just two againsht forty. I simply don't comprehend this!"

"The explanation is very simple, my dear sir: much caution, much cunning and a bit of decisiveness when needed. If one is in possession of weapons upon which one can rely, then, as matters stand, one is even superior to the many. Here, at this place, we are not safe at all. If you are smart, you'll soon ride on to meet your companions."

"And you will remain here?"

"Until Winnetou arrives, yes. Then I will come to your campsite. We have another destination, but if he agrees, I'm willing to ride with you to the Yellowstone."

"Really, truly?" asked Jemmy, with great delight. "In this case I'd swear that we'll liberate the captives!"

"Don't be so confident! I am the indirect reason for Baumann being in danger, which is why I feel obligated to assist in his liberation. Therefore ..."

He stopped in mid-sentence, as Frank had emitted a subdued exclamation of concern. With his hand he pointed between the bushes out onto the sandy plain where a group of Indians on horseback could be seen.

"Quickly! Onto the horses and off!" Old Shatterhand called. "You haven't been noticed yet. I'll follow."

"The fellows will find our tracks!" Jemmy said, while he quickly mounted up.

"Off, off!! That's the only thing that will save you."

"But they will discover you!"

"Don't worry about me! Go, go!"

The two now were in their saddles and rode off. Shatterhand looked carefully around. Just like him, the two had not left any tracks on the pebbly ground. Down below the rubble covered the slope widely, narrowing the steeper it became, until it was lost under the dense cover of firs. He hung the Henry Rifle on the saddle, slung the Bear Killer over his shoulder and, in the language of the Apache, only said one word to his horse:

"*Peniyil* – come!"

As swiftly as possible, he began to climb the incline taking large steps. The animal followed him like a dog. It might be thought impossible for a horse to climb like this, and yet both reached the trees at the top after a short, but very strenuous effort. Laying his hands onto the horse's neck he said:

"*Ishkuhch* – sleep!"

Immediately, it lay down and remained completely motionless. It had had Indian schooling.

The Shoshone had noticed the tracks. Had they been those of Old Shatterhand's, the Indians would have assumed that they led from here east, due to the reversed hoof impressions. But Frank's and Jemmy's tracks were too clear; they couldn't be mistaken. The Shoshone followed them and came quickly closer.

By the time the Indians arrived at the hemlock, barely two minutes had elapsed since the two Germans' departure.

"*Ive, ive, mi, mi* – here, here, ahead, ahead!" one of the Indians called.

He had found what he was looking for. The Reds immediately disappeared. Up at his hiding place, Old Shatterhand heard them follow the two fugitives at a gallop.

"Now it depends on developing the requisite smartness and speed," he thought. "Jemmy is likely the man for it."

That's when his horse sounded a soft snort, a sure sign, that it wanted to direct its master's attention towards something. The animal looked at him with large, smart eyes turning its head sideways up the slope. The hunter took the Henry Rifle, knelt down ready to shoot, while keeping a sharp look upwards. The trees stood here so densely that it was impossible to see far. Soon, however, he put the rifle down again. Looking below the lower branches, he had spotted a pair of porcupine-decorated moccasins, and knew that their wearer was his best friend. Soon there was a rustling in the branches, and there he stood.

He was dressed like Old Shatterhand, only he was wearing moccasins instead of high boots. He also wore no head cover. His long, dense, black hair was arranged in a high, helmet-like bun, woven through with a rattlesnake skin. No eagle feather adorned his hairdo. This man had no need for such a symbol to be recognized as a chief and honored as such. Whoever looked at him was immediately convinced that here stood an important man. He carried a medicine bag around his neck, the peace pipe, and a threefold chain of bear claws, trophies he had fought for under threat of his life. His hand held a double-barreled rifle whose wooden parts were studded with silver nails. This was the famous Silver Rifle, its bullets never missing a target. His serious, handsome face could almost be called Roman; his cheekbones barely stood out, and his skin color was a soft light brown with a touch of bronze.

This was Winnetou, the Apache Chief, the most splendid of Indians. His name lived in every log house and at every campfire. He was just, smart, faithful and brave to the point of being audacious without falseness, a friend and protector of all those in need, whether they be of red or white color. He was known across the entire length and width of the United States and beyond her borders.

Old Shatterhand had risen. He intended to speak, but was asked for silence by a hand move of Winnetou's. A second signal of the Apache urged him to listen.

From afar, monotonous sounds could be heard, coming quickly closer. They were minor tones in a four eight measure, the two first eighths in the minor third, the quarter then in the prime, something like *cc a - cc a*. Then sounded the high fifth *e*, a shrill shout of joy.

The two listeners now heard loud horse steps, and the words that were sung could also be understood. They were actually only one word: "*totsi-wuw, totsi-wuw!*" and meant simply 'scalp'.

Old Shatterhand now knew that the two Germans had not escaped but had been captured.

Down below the Shoshone rode past with the two hunters, in Indian style, one behind the other. However, two of the Redskins kept the captives between them. They had been relieved of their weapons tied to their horses with lassos but seemed not to be hurt. Maybe, no fight had ensued. Convinced that resistance was useless they had likely surrendered once the Indians caught up to them.

None of the Shoshone guessed that spies were nearby. The captives, however, thought of Old Shatterhand who they had left here. They looked around, to the right, the left and uphill. Shatterhand had to give them a signal that he was well aware of them. Doing this, he, of course, risked the chance that such a signal might also be seen by one of the Shoshone. He stepped forward a bit and waved his hat. When he saw that Jemmy had seen him, he quickly retreated again.

The Reds disappeared. Briefly, one could hear the monotonous "*totsi-wuw, totsi-wuw*", then it became quiet.

Now, without uttering a word, Winnetou turned and left the place where he had stood next to Old Shatterhand. The latter waited quietly. After maybe ten minutes the Apache returned, leading his horse by the reins. It was truly amazing how this animal was able to wind itself safely through the dense forest on such sloping ground. It was the same kind and color as Old Shatterhand's horse, however, the latter probably deserved preference. The noble-minded chief had made his friend the gift of the better horse.

Now, they stood side by side, two men who needn't be afraid of an entire Indian tribe. A close look at the face of the Apache told Old Shatterhand that there was no need to give him a detailed account of the events that had transpired. The two knew each other so well that they could readily read each other's thoughts. The White asked:

"Has the Chief of the Apache discovered the place where the warriors of the Shoshone have made camp?"

"Winnetou followed their tracks," was his reply. "They rode upwards in the dry river bed where once the waters from the mountain flowed into the Sea of Blood. Then, their tracks led to the left across the height to a *Nastla-atahehle* (circular valley) where they have set up their tents."

"Are they set up for a long term?"

"No, these are war tents – only three – and all are occupied. Winnetou has counted their tracks and written on the tree how many there are. Their leader lives in the tent decorated with eagle feathers. It is Tokvi-tey, Black Stag, the bravest chief of the Shoshone. Winnetou saw his face from a distance and recognized him by the three scars on his cheeks."

"And what has my red brother decided?"

"Winnetou does not intend to show himself to the Shoshone. He does not fear them, but since they are on the warpath, a fight would be unavoidable. He does not wish to kill any of them, since they have not done anything to him. But now they have captured the two palefaces. My white brother wants to free them. Therefore, Winnetou will have to fight them after all."

He was so sure of the thoughts and intentions of Shatterhand's that he could speak like this. The latter found it so normal that he did not comment on it but simply inquired:

"Has my brother guessed who the palefaces are?"

"Winnetou has seen the figure of the fat one and, therefore, knows that this is Jemmy-petahtsheh, Fat Jemmy. The other limped when he got off his horse.

His animal was so fresh and his outfit was still so clean that the man cannot have been in the saddle for long. He must not live too far from here, which means he is likely Inda-hish-shohl-dentshu, the palefaces call Hobble-Frank. He is the companion of the Bear Hunter."

The Apache have no special word for 'limping'. The chief's four words meant: 'the man who is bad on foot'. He had guessed quite right and, as was so often the case, gave proof of his shrewdness.

"My red brother has guessed the names of the two hunters," said Old Shatterhand. "He has seen Hobble-Frank limping and must have been nearby when I spoke with the two."

"Yes. Winnetou watched the Shoshone and saw that a group of them rode off in the direction of the Sea of Blood. Since he knew that his white brother would come there, he rode across the heights and the forest straight for the tree of meeting. Eventually, the horse prevented him from advancing quickly to warn his brother, which is why he left it behind and hurried on on foot. From up here, he then saw his brother standing down there with the two palefaces. He also saw the Shoshone, who found the tracks of the Whites. Those two hurried off, but were captured by the Reds. Of course, Old Shatterhand will free them, and Winnetou will stand by his side. He assumes also, that the two Whites are not alone here at the Sea of Blood and the Devil's Head. They likely came across Old Shatterhand's tracks and split from their companions in order to follow his trail. My white brother will know where these companions are, and we shall now go to them to get their help in liberating the captives."

This was another proof of his unusual acumen. Old Shatterhand told him briefly what he had learned from Jemmy and Frank. The Apache listened attentively, then said:

"Ugh! Then the dogs of Sioux will learn that Old Shatterhand and Winnetou are not going to tolerate the Bear Hunter's death at the stake. Today we will free the Fat One and the limping one and then ride with their companions up to the Yellowstone. There we will show the Sioux of the Ogallalla tribe that Old Shatterhand, who once slew their three bravest warriors with his bare fist, is once again in the mountains of *Toli-tli-tsu*."

This four syllable word means 'Yellow River', thus nearly the same as Yellowstone River.

To Old Shatterhand it was a relief to know that Winnetou was prepared to come to the aid of Baumann of his own free will. He said:

"My red brother has guessed my wish. We have not come here to spill the blood of red men, but will also not permit innocents to suffer death for my long ago actions. Winnetou may follow me to the ones who left to save them!"

They led their horses up the final steep incline, mounted and quickly rode in the same direction Jemmy and Frank had taken earlier in their unsuccessful flight.

60

It was getting dark, which is why they led their horses at a quick pace. Soon, they reached the spot where the Shoshone had caught up with the fleeing men. They stopped there to check the tracks.

"There was no fight," Winnetou observed.

"No. The two palefaces have not been wounded. Had they felt it necessary to defend themselves, they would not have fallen unhurt into the Shoshone's hands. They were smart enough to realize that a fight would have only been to their disadvantage and thus surrendered of their own free will."

Winnetou made a peculiar, sharply-defining gesture with his hand and said:

"Smart enough, my brother says? I might ask him whether he and Winnetou would have surrendered if they had been the ones being pursued by the Shoshone?"

"Surrendered? Us? Surely not!"

"Howgh!"

"We would have fought to the death, and many of the Shoshone would have died before they could have taken us."

"We might also not have had to fight. Winnetou would like to see the Shoshone, who could catch up with him and Old Shatterhand on our two stallions. And isn't Old Shatterhand a master in finding the tracks of others and in hiding his own? The Shoshone would have been like men the Great Spirit struck with blindness. None of their eyes would have noticed our tracks. Courage is the honor of a man, but with acumen, he beats more foes than with the tomahawk."

They rode on straight south, along the foot of the mountain. To the left of them lay the sink of the former lake.

"Does my brother already have a plan for the liberation of the two Whites?" Old Shatterhand asked.

"Winnetou needs no plan. He will return to the Shoshone and take the captives from them. This is what he thinks. These Snake Indians are not worth Winnetou thinking about a plan. Old Shatterhand has proof that they have no brains in their heads."

Shatterhand knew right away the meaning of his words.

"Yes," he said. "None of them thought that most hunters do not travel alone. Had they thought of this, they would have sent out some scouts. We are, therefore, dealing with people whose smarts we need not be afraid of. Had Tokvi-tey, the chief himself, been with this group, we would now surely have some scouts riding ahead of us."

"They would not find anything, for Winnetou and Old Shatterhand would draw the attention of these men onto themselves and lead them astray."

They had now reached the place where the canyon cut almost straight west into the mountain. There, they found the tracks of the Whites' party, however, it was already too dark for them to clearly see the impressions. They turned right to follow them.

The canyon was rather wide and easily passable. Despite the darkness the two horsemen made good progress. The hoof beats of their unshod horses made so little noise that they could only be heard nearby.

Then, a side canyon opened up branching off to the left. The two stopped. The canyon was narrow. Could it be the one where the four Whites intended to camp?

While they stood there silently, Winnetou's horse softly pawed the ground and produced the signifying snort, a sign that the animal had scented something foreign, maybe even hostile.

"We are on the right track," Old Shatterhand announced. "Let's veer to the left here. The horse is telling us that someone is in there."

They rode for about ten minutes when the canyon made a turn. Shortly after passing it, they saw a fire burning about a hundred paces ahead. The canyon had broadened here and formed a tree-covered bay in the middle of which a spring gurgled from the ground, but whose little water soon disappeared again in the sandy soil.

The trees receded at the spring, leaving a small area for a fire. The two newcomers saw three people sitting by it, whose faces they were unable to identify due to the distance.

"What does my brother think?" Winnetou asked. "Are they the right ones?"

"They're only three, and we are looking for four. Before we make ourselves known, let's see who we have here."

He dismounted, Winnetou following him.

"It's enough if I walk a bit closer to them," Old Shatterhand said.

"Fine! Winnetou shall wait."

He took the horses by the reins and led them as far as possible to the side where the rock face made further retreat impossible. Old Shatterhand carefully scurried forward to the trees, where he advanced from trunk to trunk. Then he lay down behind the last one and could now easily observe the three men. Even their words were understandable.

They were Long Davy with Wohkadeh and Martin Baumann. Bob, the Negro, was not to be seen. Good Bob was extremely enthusiastic about the adventurous ride. He felt like a knight of the prairie and had very much decided to act like one. That's why, when he had eaten, he had risen from the fire and declared that he was going to take care and post guard for the safety of the young *massa* as well as the other two *massas*. Davy had tried in vain to explain to him that it was unnecessary here.

Now, instead of guarding the entry to the canyon from which danger could arise, he was patrolling the opposite direction. There, he had not found anything suspicious, which is why he returned to the fire precisely at the moment when

Old Shatterhand took up his post behind the tree. However, the Negro did not sit down, but walked on.

"Bob," Davy said. "Stay here! What's the use of wandering about! Certainly there are no Indians nearby."

"How *Massa* can know that?" Bob replied. "Indian can be everywhere, right, left, this side, that side, up, down, behind, up front ..."

"And in your head!" Long Davy laughed.

"*Massa* may laugh. Bob know his duty. *Massa* Bob is great, famous frontiersman, make no mistake. When Indian come, *Massa* Bob right away beat dead."

He had torn off a dead spruce sapling and carried its four inch thick trunk in his mighty fists. He felt more secure holding this weapon than a rifle.

Now he walked off in the opposite direction.

Old Shatterhand was now convinced he could face the looked-for party. He could have made his presence known, but since Bob now headed right for the point where Winnetou stood, a small intermezzo was certainly to be expected. This is why the hunter remained quietly behind the tree.

He had not miscalculated. The Negro approached the respective spot. There's an old tale that says that Indian horses do not easily become friends with Negroes. The reason lies in the transpiration. The two stallions smelled Bob from afar and became restless. Winnetou had noticed the dark skin color of the approaching man, and since he had heard from Shatterhand that a Negro was among the other party, he was now convinced he was facing friends. This is why he took no hostile action and quietly let the Black approach.

One of the horses snorted. Bob heard it. He stood still and listened. A repeated snort convinced him that someone or something was nearby.

"Who be there?" he asked.

No answer.

"Bob asking, who be there! When not answer, *Massa* Bob beat dead who there!"

Again no answer.

"Well, then must die who there!"

He lifted the club and stepped closer. Winnetou's stallion, its eyes flashing, raised its mane. It reared up, threatening Bob with its hooves. The Negro was now very close and saw this giant figure in front of him. He saw the sparkling eyes and heard the threatening snorts. One of the hooves passed by his head, and then on the way down, the horse tossed him aside.

He was a brave chap, but to engage with such an opponent was just too dangerous for him. He dropped the club, ran off and screamed with all his strength:

"Woe to me! Help, help, help! He *Massa* Bob want to kill! He want *Massa* Bob swallow! Help, help, help!"

63

The three by the fire jumped up.

"What's the matter?" Davy asked.

"A giant, big beast, a ghost, want throttle *Massa* Bob!"

"Nonsense! Where?"

"There, by rock, over there."

"Don't be ridiculous, Blacky! There are no ghosts."

"*Massa* Bob have seen it!"

"It likely was an oddly shaped rock."

"No, not was rock!"

"Or a tree!"

"Not tree either. It be alive!"

"You must be mistaken."

"*Massa* Bob not mistaken. Ghost was big, so, like so!" At that he raised both hands as far as possible above his head. "It have eyes like fire, open mouth like dragon and blow at *Massa* Bob, that he fall down. *Massa* Bob saw big beard of giant."

Despite the darkness he had seen the long hairs of the stallion's mane, thinking them to be a giant's beard.

"You are out of your mind!" Davy insisted.

"Oh, but *Massa* Bob be of clear mind, very clear mind! He know what he seen. *Massa* Davy only go there and see, too!"

"Well then, let's go and have a look at what kind of thing the Negro has taken to be a giant or ghost!"

He was about to leave when, from behind him, a voice said:

"In God's name, stay here master Davy! It truly isn't a ghost."

He quickly turned and raised his rifle to his cheek. Simultaneously, Wohkadeh also held his rifle at the ready, with Martin Baumann following suit. All three barrels were aimed at Old Shatterhand who had risen from behind the tree and had stepped forward.

"Good evening!" he greeted. "Put your shooting gear away, gentlemen! I come as a friend and bring greetings from Fat Jemmy and Hobble-Frank."

At that, Long Davy lowered his rifle. The others, following his example.

"To say hello from them?" he asked. "Then you've met them?"

"Of course."

"Where?"

"Down there by the edge of the Lake of Blood where they had followed the elephant tracks."

"That's true. Did they discover who the elephant was?"

"Yes. It was my horse."

"Thunder and lightning! Does it have such giant, flat feet, sir?"

"No. It even has rather dainty little feet. Of course, it isn't my fault, that you mistook the shoes here for its feet."

He pointed at the four reed shoes hanging from his belt. The Long One understood immediately what he was talking about:

"Ah, how smart! This strange master buckles such shoes to his horse to make people crazy when they see the tracks! Gosh, that's a very good idea. It is so excellent, that I could have come up with it!"

"Yes, of all the hunters, riding and walking between the two oceans, Long Davy always has the best ideas!"

"Don't mock me, sir! I'm as smart as you are. Understood!"

Saying this, he examined the clean appearance of Old Shatterhand with a disparaging look.

"I don't doubt that," was the reply he got. "And, since you are so smart, you can probably also tell us who the ghost is your good Bob has encountered?"

"I'll eat a hundredweight of rifle bullets, and that without butter and parsley, if it wasn't your horse!"

"I think you guessed it."

"To guess this, one didn't have to go to the Gymnasium like Fat Jemmy. But tell me now where Frank and Jemmy are actually hiding. Why do you come alone?"

"Because they've been detained from coming themselves. They've been invited to supper by a bunch of Shoshone."

The Long One made a frightened move.

"Heavens! Are you saying they have been captured?"

"Unfortunately, that's what happened."

"Really? Are you sure? Is it true?"

"Yes. They were attacked and taken away."

"By the Shoshone? Captured? Taken away? That we shall forbid! Wohkadeh, Martin, Bob, quickly on your horses! We must follow the Shoshone right away. They must relinquish the two, or we will mash them like Russian salad!"

He hurried to the horses grazing by the spring.

"Stop, sir!" Old Shatterhand told him. "You won't be able to do this that quickly. Do you know where the Shoshone are to be found?"

"No, but I hope you can tell us!"

"And how many there are?"

"How many? Do you think, I'd dream of counting them, when to free my Fat Jemmy is what's called for? If it's a hundred or only two, it's all the same to me. I must get him out!"

"Then, at least wait a bit before you strike! I think we must first talk a little. I'm not alone. Here comes my friend, who wishes to bid you a good evening as well."

Winnetou had noticed that Old Shatterhand was speaking with the men, which is why he now approached with the horses. Although Long Davy was surprised to see a redskin in the company of a White, he didn't consider the chief as particularly noteworthy, so he said:

"A redskin who also looks like he's been peeled fresh from an egg, just like you! You can't be a real frontiersman?"

"No. Actually not! You guessed that right away."

"Thought so! And this Indian is probably also a resident one who had himself given a handful of land from the Great White Father in Washington?"

"Now you are mistaken, sir!"

"Unlikely!"

"Certainly so. My companion isn't the man to have himself presented land by the President of the United States. He's rather ..."

He was interrupted by Wohkadeh, who let go of a joyous shout. The young Indian had stepped over to Winnetou and had noticed the rifle in his hand.

"Uff, uff!" he exclaimed. "*Maza-skamon-wakon* – the Silver Rifle!"

The Long One knew enough Sioux to understand what Wohkadeh meant.

"The Silver Rifle?" he asked. "Where? Ah, here, here! Mind showing it to me, my red sir?"

Winnetou let it be taken from his hands.

"It is *Maza-skamon-wakon*," Wohkadeh shouted. "This red warrior is, therefore, Winnetou, the great Chief of the Apache!"

"What? How? Impossible!" the Long One said. "But this is how his rifle has been described to me."

He looked at Winnetou and Old Shatterhand inquiringly. At the moment, his face did not really give an expression of great wisdom.

"It is the Silver Rifle," Old Shatterhand answered. "My companion is Winnetou."

"Listen, mister, don't make any foolish jokes with me!"

"Pah! If you absolutely insist, then think of it as a joke. I've no desire to paint the Apache's family tree onto your back."

"You'd not get away easily with that, sir! But if this red gentleman is truly Winnetou, then who are you? In that case you'd have to be ..."

He stopped in mid sentence. The thought that had just occurred to him made him forget to close his mouth. He stared at Old Shatterhand, clapped his hands, leaped in the air and continued:

"Well, then I've truly goofed, more than a full-grown elephant! Here I insulted the most famous frontiersman on whom the sun has ever shone! If this Indian is Winnetou, then you are none other than Old Shatterhand, since these two go together just like Fat Jemmy and me. Am I right, sir?"

"Yes, you aren't mistaken."

"Then, to my joy, I'd love to grab all the stars from the heavens and hang them there in the trees and by their illumination celebrate the evening I got to know you! Welcome, gentlemen, welcome to our campfire! Forgive my stupidity!"

He offered both his hands and pressed theirs very hard. Bob, said nothing at all. He was very much ashamed to have thought a horse a ghost. Wohkadeh had stepped back to the trees. He leaned against one and rested his eyes admiringly on the two arrivals – among Indians, youth is accustomed to being modest. Wohkadeh would have thought it the biggest mistake had he remained standing like an equal with the others. Martin Baumann also closely observed the two men whose many heroic deeds he was familiar with. He was facing two examples he was most eager to emulate, although he could not hope to ever equal them in his lifetime.

Winnetou had taken Davy's handshake. To the others, he nodded in greeting in his serious way. Old Shatterhand, on the other hand, being of a more cheerful nature and uncommonly jovial, shook hands with all including the Negro. This touched Wohkadeh so much that he put his right hand to his heart and softly affirmed:

"Wohkadeh will be happy to give his life for Old Shatterhand! Howgh!"

The welcome finished, Shatterhand and Winnetou joined them by the fire. The former began with further explanations; the latter added not a word but took his pipe and stuffed it. This was the sign for Davy that he wanted to 'smoke friendship' with them. Of course, he was delighted about it from the bottom of his heart. His assumption was proven right. Old Shatterhand declared at the close of his report, that Winnetou and he were prepared to free Jemmy and Frank as soon as possible, and then to ride with them up to the Yellowstone River.

Now, Winnetou lit the pipe and rose. After he had blown the smoke into the prescribed directions, he declared that he was to be the *nta-je* (older brother) to his new acquaintances, and passed the pipe on to Shatterhand. From him it went to Davy. After he had taken the ceremonial puffs, he was greatly embarrassed. The two famous men had smoked from it. Was he now permitted to pass it on to the boys and the Negro?

Winnetou guessed the thoughts of the Long One. He inclined his head towards the other three and said:

"The Son of the Bear Hunter has already killed grizzlies, and Wohkadeh is the victor over the white buffalo. Both are great heroes. They will also smoke the peace pipe with us, just like the black man, who even dared to clobber a ghost."

This was a jest, which they might have laughed about, but the smoking of the peace pipe is an act calling for avoidance of such hilarity. However, Bob felt like trying to reinstate his honor, which is why, when he received the pipe, he took several mighty draws, raised a hand, spread all five fingers far apart, as if he wanted to give a fivefold oath, and called:

"Bob be *Massa* Bob, a hero and gentleman! He be friend and protector of *Massa* Winnetou and *Massa* Old Shatterhand. He clobber dead all their enemies. He do everything for them; he – he – he even beat dead himself!"

This was friendship sworn to in a superlative way! While stating it, he rolled his eyes and gnashed his teeth to show that his assurance was spoken in sacred seriousness. The recipients accepted it with due respect.

Now, what needed to be said had been said. To develop a plan was not possible as yet, since the situation of the captives was still unknown. They had to find the camp of the Shoshone first. Once having located it, they could decide on further action, but not before.

Of course, Long Davy was extraordinarily angry to learn that his Jemmy was in the hands of the Reds, and Martin was very much concerned for Hobble-Frank. Both were prepared to risk their lives to free the two. Wohkadeh did not say much more than:

"Wohkadeh knew that the two palefaces would encounter misfortune. He warned them, but they would not listen to his voice."

"And with that you were right," Davy affirmed. "But had they not followed the 'elephant' tracks, they would not have come across the Chief of the Apache and Old Shatterhand. Although they were captured in the process, we shall get them out. We have two helpers in these new friends, and we cannot ask for better ones. So, let's go for the Shoshone! They will get to know Long Davy!"

They broke camp. As fast as possible, the six rode back the same way they had come, down both canyons. At the mouth of the main canyon, they turned left and headed north. They had not progressed far, when Winnetou halted his horse. The others, of course, followed suit at once.

"Winnetou will ride ahead," he said. "My brothers must not follow me any faster than at a good trot, avoiding every noise. They will do everything Old Shatterhand asks of them."

He dismounted and occupied himself briefly with his horse's hooves. Then, he remounted and galloped off. The noise his horse now made was barely audible. It sounded so quiet, so dull, as if a person was hitting the ground with his fist. The others followed as quickly as he had demanded.

"What did he do?" Davy asked.

"Did you not notice that he has the same irons and reed shoes hanging from his belt as I do?" Old Shatterhand asked him. "He put these shoes on his stallion so that he cannot be heard but can hear better himself."

"Why that?"

The Shoshone, who took your companions captive, didn't hit on the idea that the two captives might have comrades nearby. Tokvi-tey, the Chief of the Shoshone, is smarter and more deliberate than his warriors. He will know that two hunters will not dare enter a dangerous area like this by themselves. Thus, it can be expected that he will subsequently send out scouts."

"Pah! That would be a totally useless venture. How do the fellows intend to find us in the dark? They don't know where we are, and cannot see our tracks."

"Your name is known as that of a good frontiersman, which is why I'm surprised about your talk, master Davy. These are the Shoshone's hunting and grazing grounds and, therefore, they are familiar with the area. Or don't you think so?"

"Of course!"

"Well then, continue with your conclusions! Will cautious hunters camp here in the open, in the sands of the former lake?"

"Obviously not."

"Where then?"

"Here. In the mountains."

"That is in one of the valleys or a canyon. Now, you could ride along this entire distance and, except for the old waterway the Shoshone followed, you wouldn't find any other valley opening up than the one you camped in. There, and only there, are you to be found."

"By the devil! You are right, sir. One notices right away that one's riding with Old Shatterhand!"

"Thank you for your compliment, which isn't one, however, for what I have told you, anyone would tell himself who had lived in the West for only a few months. To continue, comrades don't usually separate for any length of time in locations like this one. From that it follows that you can't be far from Jemmy and Frank. Therefore, your camp could not be too far away in the canyon. And there being a side canyon, which every reasonable frontiersman would prefer to camping in the main canyon, the Shoshone know very well where they must look for you. That which you earlier thought impossible is, therefore, an enterprise without difficulties. Thus, the chief of the Shoshone will know, and Winnetou will, too. That's why he rode ahead to prevent us being spotted by any scouts."

Davy mumbled something and then said:

"Very well, sir! But now the undertaking of the Apache appears to me to be a totally hopeless one."

"Why so?"

"How can he, in this darkness, notice scouts approaching him without being seen by them or at least heard?"

"You can't ask this when talking about Winnetou. First of all, he has a superior horse, which has had excellent training of which you, seemingly, have no idea. Earlier, at the entrance to the side canyon, it told us, for instance, that you were in there. Now, it will warn us again since we are riding into the wind. It will make its master aware of the approach of any other creature from a substantial distance away. Then, you don't know the Apache. He has the senses and sharpness of a wild animal. What sight, hearing or smell won't tell him, he will notice, due to this indefinable sixth sense possessed only by people who have lived in the wilderness from their youth. It is a kind of perception, an instinct, upon which anyone possessing it, can rely, just like his own eyes."

"Hm, I've a bit of that, too!"

"I, too, but I can't compare myself with Winnetou in this respect. Furthermore, you must take into account that his horse wears the reed shoes, while the Shoshone, should there truly be some around, will make no effort to avoid loud hoof beats."

"Oho! They too will be cautious!"

"No, for they will think that such caution is unnecessary here and would even be detrimental."

"Why detrimental?"

"Because they would forfeit the necessary speed. They would feel certain, that you would wait for your comrades at the campsite. Assured of not coming across anyone here, they wouldn't hold their horses back at all."

"Hm. When you explain it this way, one must absolutely agree with you. Frankly, I'd like to tell you that I've gone through quite a bit and have outsmarted many an enemy, which is why I've always thought myself to be a right smart old fellow. But now I must concede to you. Winnetou said earlier that we ought to submit to your will. He, so to speak, proclaimed you our leader. I quietly fretted a little bit about this, but now I admit that he was right. You are mightily superior to us, and I'll gladly submit to your command in the future."

"That's not how it was meant. On the prairie, all have the same rights. I'm not presuming any privilege. Everyone of us serves the other with his gifts and experiences, and no one can begin something without the other's agreement. Thus, it must be, and thus, we'll handle it this way, too."

"Well! We'll find out. But what shall we do should we come across scouts, sir?"

"What do you think?"

"Let them go?"

"You think so?"

"Yes. They can't do us any damage. We'll have acted before they return."

"We can't be sure of that. If we let them pass, they will find the abandoned camp site and the extinguished camp fire."

"What harm's that?"

"Very much so. From it, they'll know that we've left to come to the captives' aid."

"You really think they'll assume that? Can they not think, just as well, that we've continued our ride?"

"Not at all. People expecting companions don't continue on a ride. That's obvious."

"Then you would render the scouts harmless?"

"Absolutely."

"Kill them?"

"No. You know that human blood is an immensely precious fluid. Winnetou and Old Shatterhand are fully aware of this and have never spilled a single drop if it wasn't absolutely necessary. I am a friend of the Indians and know who's right. The Indians are, not those who again and again force them to defend their good rights to the knife. The red man fights the desperate battle. He must succumb. But every Indian's skull that is later plowed from the soil will shout the same silent scream to the heavens. This is told in the forth chapter of Genesis. I spare the Indian even when he's facing me as an enemy, because I know that he was forced to it by others. This is why today it wouldn't occur to me to commit murder."

"But how would you render the Shoshone harmless without killing them? Should they encounter us, there'll be a fight in any case. They will defend themselves with rifle, tomahawk and knife ...!"

"Pah! I don't wish to meet enemies. But for the sake of your question, I'd wish them to send out scouts. Then, you'd have the opportunity to see how one seizes such people."

"But if there are too many?"

"We need not be concerned about that. Many would only be a hindrance to them. More than two wouldn't be sent out and – hold it, I think Winnetou is coming!"

Without them having heard him, the next moment Winnetou stood before them.

"Scouts!" he said briefly.

"How many?" Shatterhand asked.

"Two."

"Good! Winnetou, Davy and I shall remain here. The others will ride quickly out onto the sand. They'll take our horses along and wait until we call them."

He jumped off with Davy following. Winnetou had already handed the reins of his horse to Wohkadeh. In a few seconds, the other three had disappeared.

"What do we do now?"

"You haven't anything to do, but watch," Old Shatterhand told him. "Lean against this tree here so you can't be seen. Listen, they are coming."

He and the Apache had handed their rifles to their companions right away.

"*Shi darteh, ni owjeh* – I take this one, you that one!" the Apache said, making a move with his hand to the right and left. Then, he had disappeared.

Long Davy leaned close to the mentioned tree. Barely two paces from him, Shatterhand lay down flat on the earth. The two Shoshone approached at a rather fast speed talking to each other. Their dialect showed that they were truly Shoshone. That was sufficient. They approached, then passed.

Long Davy saw Old Shatterhand rise from the ground and take a forceful run.

"*Saritsch*! – dog!" one of the scouts shouted, but no further word was heard.

Davy jumped out. He saw two men on a horse or, rather, four men sitting on two horses, the two attackers behind the attacked. The horses shied, kicking front and back and bucking sideways, but for naught. The two famous men had their victims with their horses in a firm grip. Following a brief fight between man and animal, the attackers were victorious, and the horses stood still. Right from the first moment, the Shoshone had been unable to defend themselves.

Shatterhand jumped off carrying one of the scouts, who was unconscious, in his arms.

"*Sarki* – finished?" he inquired to the right.

"*Sarki* – finished!" Winnetou replied.

"Hello, men, come on back."

Following this loud call, Wohkadeh, Martin and Bob rode up.

"We've got them. They will be tied to their horses with their lariats and shall accompany us. That way we have two hostages who will be of use to us."

The Shoshone, who had been throttled, soon came to. Their weapons had been taken from them, and their hands had been bound. They were now tied to the horses. Hands bound behind their backs, their legs were tied together with the lasso below the belly of the horse. Old Shatterhand told them that they would be killed upon the least attempt to resist. The ride then continued.

Although the scouts had been captured, Winnetou again rode ahead. This was a rule of caution the Apache found absolutely necessary.

After a while, the watercourse they had to follow leftward into the mountains had been reached. The horsemen continued alongside it. No word was spoken, since it was possible that one of the scouts understood English.

73

After about half an hour, they again met up with Winnetou who, riding far ahead, had waited there.

"My brothers may dismount," he said. "The Shoshone crossed the forest here to the height. We must follow them."

This was not easy with the captives having to sit on the horses. Below the trees, it was totally dark. With one hand, the men had to grope forward and, with the other, pull the horses after them. Winnetou and Old Shatterhand had taken on the most difficult task. They walked ahead leading the horses with the captives. Now, the value of their two stallions demonstrated itself. They followed their masters like dogs and, despite the troublesome path, did not snort in the least, while the other horses could be heard far off.

When this great exertion was over, the Apache stopped.

"My brothers have arrived at their destination," he said. "They may tie up their horses and help tie the captives to separate trees."

The men followed this request. Once the two Shoshone had been secured, they were gagged, so that they were able to breathe through their noses but could not speak or shout. The Apache then asked his companions to follow him.

He led them only a few paces from where the height, which they had ascended from the east, sank rather steeply to the west. Down there was the steep valley of which Winnetou had spoken, where a large and bright fire shone. Of course, it was impossible to have a good look at what was going on down there. One saw the fire's flames, but no more. All else lay in deep darkness.

"So, down there sits my Fat One." Davy said. "What might he be doing?"

"Only what a captive of the Indians can do – nothing," answered young Baumann.

"Oho! There you don't know Jemmy, my boy! He'll surely have dreamed up a way to take a little walk tonight without the permission of the Reds!"

"It's unlikely he'll be able to do it without our help," Old Shatterhand said. "By the way, he heard from me that we will be coming and can thus assume that I'll be bringing you along."

"Well, then let's not lose any time and get down there quickly, sir!"

"We must do this silently and carefully, one behind the other. But someone must remain back here with the horses and the captives, one we can rely on. That is Wohkadeh!"

"Uff!" the young Indian exclaimed, very much delighted about the great trust Shatterhand expressed.

But since he had met him today for the first time, it was actually a risk to leave the young Indian all by himself with the captives and horses, loaded with all the owners' belongings. However, the sincerity with which Wohkadeh had told Old Shatterhand that his life was his, had won the hunter's heart. Then, too, Shatterhand was confident that the red youngster possessed the cold-bloodedness required for this responsible posting.

"My red brother will sit with the captives, knife in hand," he told him, "and if one of the Shoshone should attempt to escape or make a single noise, he will stab the knife into his heart!"

"Wohkadeh will do it!"

"He will stay here until we come back and, under no circumstances, will he leave this place!"

"Wohkadeh would sit here and starve to death if his brothers would not return!"

He said that with a voice, which imparted how serious his promise was. He pulled out his Bowie knife and sat down between the captives. Old Shatterhand explained to them what they could expect if they did not remain totally quiet. The five men then commenced their difficult descent.

As mentioned, the decline was rather steep. The trees stood close to each other. Between them was so much brush that these daring men, with the caution required, made very slow progress. No noise could be made. The cracking of a twig would give their approach away.

Winnetou went ahead. His eyes were the sharpest at night. Behind him was Martin Baumann. Then came Long Davy, followed by the Negro. Old Shatterhand brought up the rear.

It took them more than a quarter of an hour to cover a distance which, in daylight, would have required at most five minutes. Then they reached the bottom of the valley, which was covered by grass. There was not a single tree to be seen, and only here and there rose a lone bush.

The fire burned brightly, not at all maintained the usual Indian way. It was a sign the Shoshone felt very safe.

While Whites put the logs on top of each other to produce a high-flaring fire, visible from afar with much smoke-spreading flame, Indians usually place the logs in a circle, their ends meeting at the center. At this center burns a small flame, fed by pushing the logs inward once their ends are burned off. This makes a fire sufficient for all the redskins' purposes. It forms a small, protected flame and causes so little smoke that it will not be noticeable more than a short distance away. In addition, they know what kind of wood to collect to produce very little smoke when burning. The scent of smoke is extraordinarily dangerous in the West. The Indian's sharp nose can perceive it from a very great distance.

The fire here was fed in the Whites' way, and the scent of roasted meat had spread across the entire valley. Winnetou tested the air inhaling and whispered:

"*Mokasshi-si-tsheh* – Buffalo loins."

His sense of smell was so sensitive that he could even determine the body part of the animal from which the meat had been cut.

Three large tents stood there forming the corners of a pointed triangle, one of which, faced the five listeners. This tent, next to them, was decorated with eagle feathers indicating the one in which the chief lived. In the center of the triangle, the fire burned.

The Reds' horses grazed freely. The warriors sat by the fire and cut their portions from the roasts, grilling them on a branch over the flames. Unlike Indian custom, they were very noisy. Having captured two prisoners had put them in an excellent mood. Despite the security they felt, they had posted several guards who were slowly patrolling back and forth. However, judging by their demeanor, they appeared to feel unjustly treated for not being permitted to sit with the others by the fire.

"This is a devilish situation!" Davy grumbled. "How will we get our two comrades out? What do you think, gentlemen?"

"First we would like to hear your own opinion, master Davy," Old Shatterhand answered.

"Mine? Gosh! I don't have one."

"Then have the kindness to think a little!"

"That won't help either. I thought the issue to be rather different. These red yokels have no sense. There they all sit by the fire in the midst of the tents, so that it isn't at all possible to get into one of them! They could have been more cooperative!"

"You seem to love convenience, sir! Do you wish the Indians to build a racetrack from the tents in order to send your Fat Jemmy here in a carriage? Well, then you ought not have come to the West!"

"Very true! And one also ought not let himself be caught. If we only knew in which tent the two have been put!"

"Of course, in the chief's tent."

"Then I have a suggestion."

"Well?"

"We sneak up on them as close as possible and, as soon as they notice us, we attack them. We'll make such a terrible ruckus that they'll think we are a hundred men. They'll run off in terror. We get the prisoners from the tent and also run away as fast as possible."

"That's your suggestion?"

"Yes."

"You want to add something more?"

"No. Do you like it?"

"Not at all."

"Oho! Do you figure you can think of something better?"

"Whether it's something better, I can't say, but certainly not something more imprudent."

"Sir! Is that to be an insult! I am Long Davy, you know!"

"I've known that for some time already. There won't be any talk of an insult. You can see from here that the Indians have their weapons handy. They won't be so stupid as to overestimate our numbers like you wish. If we attack, they will be startled for a moment, but only for a moment. Then, we will be facing a tenfold superiority."

"I thought you weren't afraid?"

"Precisely. I need not be afraid, because I'm not risking an attack whose result would be our certain demise. Even if we were victorious, a great deal of blood would be spilled. That can be avoided. What do you gain from freeing the captives if you yourself would be shot dead? Isn't it better to find a way which takes us to our goal without spilling any blood?"

"Yes, sir, if you find such a way, I'd praise you very much."

"Maybe it has been found already."

77

"Quickly, explain it then. I'll do my best."

"It may be that we'll not have to trouble you at all. I want to hear what the Apache has to say to my plan."

For a brief time he spoke with the chief in an Apache dialect the others did not understand. Then he turned back to Long Davy:

"Yes, I'll do the trick with Winnetou alone. You stay quiet once we have left. Even if we don't return within two hours, do not leave your place and dare not do anything. Only if you hear a cricket chirp loudly three times are you to enter into the action."

"In what way?"

"By coming as quickly and as quietly as possible to the tent next to us. Winnetou and I will creep up on it together. Should we need you there, I'll sound the mentioned signal."

"Can you imitate a cricket's chirp?"

"Of course! It is a great advantage if hunters can imitate the voices of certain animals. Only it must be of animals whose voices would normally be heard at the same time that one is apt to use this imitation. As is well known, the cricket chirps during the night, so the Shoshone will not find it unusual when they hear my chirping."

"But how to you reproduce it?"

"Simple! With a blade of grass. One folds the hands together in such a way that the thumbs are side by side, and puts a tightly stretched blade of grass between them. Between the two lower members of the thumbs is a small gap in which the grass blade can vibrate. This makes it a kind of tongue instrument. If one then blows a brief '*frr-frr-frr*' onto the blade by placing the lips firmly onto the thumbs, a chirp springs up which resembles that of a cricket. However, it takes a lot of practice."

That's when Winnetou said:

"My white brother may explain these things later. We do not have the time now. Let us begin."

"Good! Shall we take our token along?"

"Yes! The Shoshone will then learn that we paid them a visit."

Many frontiersmen, as well as outstanding Indians, make use of a token, a sign, by which one recognizes the owner's identity. Some Indians cut their sign into the ear, the cheek, the forehead, or the hand of the one they have killed. Whoever then finds the body later and knows the sign, recognizes who has defeated and scalped the dead.

Winnetou and Old Shatterhand cut several short twigs from an adjacent bush and stuck them into their belts. With them they could make the signs known to every Red as being theirs.

They handed their rifles to their companions so as not to be hindered in their moves. Then, they left by lying flat on the ground and inching forward towards the respective tent at a distance of about eighty paces.

This approach was certainly not easy. Without major danger, and if there is no concern about leaving noticeable tracks, one can creep ahead on hands and knees. That, however, produces a very obvious trail, particularly in grass. But when forced to avoid this, then locomotion is only by means of fingertips and toes. Doing so requires arms and legs stretched out for the body to stay very close to the ground it is not to touch. Then, the body's entire load rests on the finger and toe tips. To endure this for even a short time requires exceptional strength, dexterity, and long years of practice. Like swimmers who speak of a swimming cramp, frontiersmen talk of creeping-up-cramp, which is no less dangerous than the former. It can lead to discovery with death sure to follow.

While the frontiersman creeps up on the enemy in this manner, he must consider the terrain very closely and may not place a hand or foot tip on the ground before he has inspected the respective spot carefully. If, for instance, a hand or foot hits a small, unnoticed dry twig, which then cracks, this slight cracking may lead to the worst consequences. There are experienced hunters who can hear from a crack whether man or animal has caused it. By necessity, the frontiersman's senses become so sharpened with time that, even lying on the ground, he can hear the noise made by a running beetle. Whether a dry leaf has dropped on its own or was stripped off carelessly by a hidden enemy, he will hear it, for sure.

A good spy will also put the toe tips of his shoes precisely onto the spot he has previously touched with his fingertips. This produces less visible tracks, which can be more easily and quickly effaced than if there were more numerous and larger impressions.

It is often necessary to 'efface' the tracks, a term used by the frontiersman. It is upon retreat that the most strenuous and difficult part of the venture occurs. No one is to learn quickly that the visit took place. That's why every impression one has caused must be effaced while moving feet-backwards. This is done with the right hand, while one maintains equilibrium, supporting oneself on both toe tips and the fingertips of the left hand. Whoever has tried to hold this difficult position for only a minute, will soon comprehend the terrible exertion to the hunter to maintain it for a long time.

So it was here.

The two – Old Shatterhand in the lead with Winnetou following – slowly moved forward in the way described. When touching the ground, the White had to test it inch by inch, and the Indian had to endeavor to stay exactly in the impressions the former had produced. This is why their advance was extremely slow.

The grass was rather high, almost a foot tall. On one side this was advantageous since it hid the body; on the other side, it had the disadvantage that tracks were more visible in the tall grass.

The further they advanced, the clearer they were able to discern the camp's details. Between it and them, a guard patrolled back and forth. How was it possible then to reach the tent unnoticed?

It seemed that the two experienced men had no problem with this.

"Is Winnetou to take the guard?" the chief of the Apache whispered.

"No," replied Shatterhand. "I know I can rely on my blow."

Quietly, like two snakes, they wended their way through the grass, closer and closer to the guard who was totally unaware that two such foes were that close to him. The two spies could see the man rather clearly against the light of the fire. He seemed to be still young and carried no other weapons than a knife in his belt and a rifle, which he held comfortably across his shoulder. He was dressed in buffalo skin. It was impossible to recognize his features, since they were covered alternately by red and black stripes, the colors of war.

He never looked towards the approaching spies, but preferentially directed his attention towards the camp. Maybe the aroma of the meat roasting over the fire interested him more than was advisable for a guard.

But even had he glanced at the place where the two crept up, he would have been unable to spot them, since their dark bodies were impossible to differentiate from the dark grasses. That is to say, they slyly moved only in the shadows made by the tent on the fire's opposite side.

And yet they were as close as eight paces from him!

He had trampled the grass walking back and forth. The attack on him had to take place where he walked if its traces were not to be noticed.

Just then, he turned at one end of his walk and now returned slowly, walking from the right to the left, as seen from the position of the two spies. The guard walked past them and was now, just like them, in the shadows.

"Quickly!" Winnetou whispered.

Old Shatterhand rose. Two giant leaps brought him behind the Indian who heard the noise and turned quickly. But then Old Shatterhand delivered a blow to his temple with his fist, and the guard collapsed.

With two similar leaps, Winnetou stood next to him.

"Is he dead?" he asked.

"No, just unconscious."

"My brother may tie him up. Winnetou will take his place."

Lifting the Shoshone's rifle from the ground and shouldering it, he walked off in the same posture the Shoshone had held previously. From afar, he would look like the guard. Thus, he now patrolled back and forth. This was rather daring, but necessary. In the meantime, Old Shatterhand advanced to the chief's tent. The hunter tried to lift the canvas a bit to look inside. Since the tightly stretched hide prevented this he had to loosen the string holding it to a pole.

This had to be done with extreme caution. It could be noticed from the inside, in which case everything would be lost. Cowering close to the ground, he brought his eyes as close as possible to the ground. Quietly, quietly he pushed the edge of the hide upwards. Now he was able to look inside.

What he saw surprised him. The captives were not in there. Only the chief sat on a buffalo skin and smoked harsh-smelling *Kinnikinnick*, composed of tobacco and willow bark or the leaves of wild hemp. All the while, he looked out of the half open tent, silently observing the lively scene playing around the camp fire. His back was turned towards Old Shatterhand.

The hunter knew very well what had to be done here, but did not want to act without the Apache's agreement. He, therefore, lowered the canvas again, turned away from the tent, pulled out his blade of grass and took it between his thumbs.

A soft, singular chirp sounded.

"*Tho-ing-kai* – the cricket is singing!" sounded a Shoshone's voice from the camp.

Had he only known what kind of cricket it was! The chirp was the signal for Winnetou to come. The Apache maintained his slow, dignified moves until he stepped into the shadow of the tent and could no longer be see by the Shoshone. There, he put the rifle into the grass, lowered himself, and crept as fast as possible to the tent. Arriving there he whispered:

"Why is my brother calling me?"

"Because I need your consent," Shatterhand answered just as softly. "The captives are not in the tent."

"That is not good. Now we must retreat and, from the other side, creep up on the other tents. This will take too long, even till morning."

"Maybe this isn't necessary at all, for Tokvi-tey, Black Stag, is sitting inside."

"Uff! The chief himself! Is he by himself?"

"Yes."

"Then we need not get the captives!"

"That's what I thought, too. If we capture the chief, we can force the Shoshone to set Fat Jemmy and Hobble-Frank free."

"My brother is right. But can the Shoshone who are around the fire look into the tent?"

"Yes! But the fire's light does not reach the point of the tent where we will be."

"But they will notice right away, that their chief no longer sits there."

"Then they'll think that he retreated into the shadows. My brother may be ready to help me if my first grab is unsuccessful."

This was said so softly, that not a breath could be heard inside the tent.

81

Now Winnetou quietly and slowly pulled up the canvas far enough that Old Shatterhand could creep inside as close as possible to the ground. This the daring hunter did noiselessly so that Black Stag couldn't possibly notice the encroaching danger.

Then, Shatterhand moved inside the tent. The Apache followed part way to assist immediately should it become necessary. Shatterhand stretched out his right hand and was just able to reach the Shoshone. A quick, forceful grab for the man's throat and Black Stag dropped his pipe, waved his arm once, twice through the air, then sank as he lost his breath.

Old Shatterhand pulled him from the circle of light back into the shadows of the tent, lowered him to the ground and, dragging him from behind, pulled him out of the tent.

"Success!" Winnetou whispered. "My brother carries the power of a bear in his hand. But how do we get him away? We must carry him, yet simultaneously efface our tracks."

"That will be immensely difficult."

"And what do we do with the guard we tied up?"

"We take him along, too. The more Shoshone we have in our hands, the more readily the Reds will free their two captives."

"Then my brother may carry the chief, and Winnetou will take the other. Doing this we will not be able to efface our tracks, which is why we must return once more."

"Unfortunately! Precious time will pass and we ..."

He stopped. Something happened which quickly ended all their considerations. A loud, shrill scream was heard.

"*Tiguw-ih, tiguw-ih*!" the voice sounded. "Enemies, enemies!"

"The guard woke up. Go, quickly!" Old Shatterhand said. "We'll take him along!"

Already Winnetou was leaping in quick strides towards the spot where the Shoshone lay. He snatched him up and ran off.

Now Old Shatterhand demonstrated the kind of frontiersman he was. Although danger lurked close by, he still stayed for a moment behind the tent. He pulled out the little twigs he had previously cut, lifted the tent hides once more and stuck them in such a way into the ground that they crossed like Spanish Horsemen. Only then did he pick up the chief and hurried off with him.

The Shoshone had been sitting close to the fire. Their eyes, which had accommodated to its brightness, could not change quickly to the darkness as Shatterhand had guessed. They had leaped up and, although they stared into the night, could not see much. Besides, they had been unable to differentiate from which side the cry for help had sounded. This is how it happened that Winnetou and Old Shatterhand were successful in completing their retreat.

The Apache even had to stop once on his way back. He had been unable to shut his captive's mouth entirely with his hand. Although the man had been unable to shout for help once more, he had, nevertheless, produced such a loud groan, that the Apache had to stop for a moment to throttle him.

"Thunder and lightning, who are you bringing here? Long Davy asked as the two dropped their captives to the ground.

"Hostages," answered Shatterhand. "Quickly, put a gag into their mouths, and tie up the chief."

"The chief? Are you kidding, sir?"

"No, it's him."

"Heavens! What a prank! People will talk of it for a long time! To fetch Black Stag from the midst of his warriors! Only Old Shatterhand and Winnetou could accomplish that!"

"No useless speeches now! We must be off! Up the hill to our horses."

"My brother need not hurry," the Apache said. "From here, we see better what the Shoshone will do than from up there."

"Yes, Winnetou is right," Old Shatterhand admitted. "The Shoshone will not think of coming here. They don't know with whom and how many they are dealing. They will need to limit themselves in order to secure their camp. Only upon daybreak will they be able to try something."

"Winnetou will give them a warning which will pluck their courage and discourage them from leaving their camp."

The Apache took his revolver and held its muzzle very close to the earth. Shatterhand understood at once.

"Hold it!" he said. "They must not see the flash of the shot or they will learn where we are. I think there will be an echo, which will deceive them. Give me your jackets and coats, gentlemen!"

Long Davy took his famous rubber coat off his shoulder, the others followed Shatterhand's demand. The clothing was held up after which Winnetou fired twice. The shots rang out. They reverberated from the valley walls, and since the flash could not be seen, the Shoshone were unaware as to where they had been fired. They replied with a penetrating howl.

When they had heard the shout, '*tiguw-ih, tiguw-ih*', the Shoshone had leaped from the fire in an effort to spot the enemy. Only slowly did their eyes become adapted to the darkness, and by that time, Old Shatterhand and Winnetou had already reached safety. Thus, the Reds could not see anyone.

Obviously, they were not being attacked. If there had truly been enemies, they would not have hesitated to attack the camp. The alarm call must, therefore, have been in error. But who had sounded it? One of the guards, of course. He had to be found and asked. To call him was the chief's duty. But how was it possible that he had remained so quietly in his tent?

Several warriors stepped to the tent's entrance. They looked in and found it empty.

"Black Stag has already gone to check on the guard," one of them said.

"My brother is mistaken," another replied. "The chief could not have left his tent without being seen by us."

"But he is not here!"

"And he also cannot be gone!"

"Then, *Wakon-tonka*, the bad spirit, has made him disappear!"

That's when an old warrior pushed the others aside and said:

"The bad spirit can kill and bring misfortune, but he cannot make a warrior disappear. If the chief did not step from the tent, yet has disappeared, he can have left it only in such a way, that ..."

He stopped. Before, only part of the canvas forming the entrance flap had been opened; now it had been completely removed, allowing the firelight to illuminate the entire inside.

The old one stepped in and bent down.

"Uff!" he exclaimed. "The chief has been taken away!"

No one answered. What the old one had said was too unbelievable, however, they were not allowed to contradict such an old and experienced warrior.

"My brothers do not believe me?" he said. "They may have a look. Here the tent's canvas has been opened, and here twigs are stuck in the ground. I know these tokens. It is the sign of *Nou-pay-klama*, who the palefaces call Old Shatterhand. He has been here and has taken Black Stag."

That's when the two shots of the Apache reverberated. That loosed the tongues of the Shoshone, erupting in the aforementioned howl.

"Quickly, extinguish the fire!" the old one commanded. "We must not offer the enemies clean targets."

He was obeyed. The flaming branches were quickly pulled apart and the fire stomped out. With the chief having disappeared, the Shoshone freely submitted to the oldest warrior. Now it was dark in camp. Everyone had reached for his weapon and, upon the old one's command, the warriors formed a circle around the tents to make ready for the enemy from whatever side he might come.

Four guards had been posted to protect the camp on all four sides. Once the shots had been heard, three of them had quickly returned to their posts. The fourth, however, was missing. As it happened, this one was the most esteemed, Moh-aw, the chief's son. This Shoshone word means something like 'mosquito' and signified that the young Indian had proved already that he was brave, and could sting.

One of the most daring men offered to look for him and received permission to do so. He lay down in the grass and crept into the night in the direction where the missing guard had been. After awhile, he returned with Mosquito's rifle. It was a sure sign that the chief's son had encountered misfortune.

The old one held a brief council with the most outstanding warriors. It was decided to guard the tent in which the captives were kept and stake down the horses in close proximity to the camp. Then, they would await the dawn when, who they were dealing with, would be revealed more clearly.

In the meantime, the frontiersmen had made sure that the two captives, both of whom had now regained consciousness, could not make a sound, and then remained silent themselves keeping an eye out. Nothing was to be heard except the grass-dampened stomping of the horses.

"My brothers may hear that the Shoshone are gathering their horses. They will tie them up close to the tents and not try anything until daybreak," Winnetou explained. "We can go now."

"Yes. Let's retreat," Old Shatterhand agreed. "However we will not wait until morning. Black Stag is to learn, as soon as possible, what we demand of him."

He walked to the captives, who had been separated and laid down away from the group, so that they could not hear what was said. He still wasn't aware that their catch was even more precious than he had so far assumed. He lifted Black Stag from the ground, put him on his shoulder and began the ascent. The others followed, Winnetou carrying Mosquito.

For anyone else, it would have been almost impossible to carry such a load in deepest darkness up the forested mountainside. For these two, it did not seem difficult at all.

Arriving at the top, they found everything in order. Wohkadeh had done his job.

Long Davy unwound his lasso and said:

"Hand me the fellows! We'll tie them up with the others."

"No!" Old Shatterhand responded. "We are leaving this place."

"Why? Do you think we aren't safe here?"

"Yes, that's my opinion."

"Oh, I'm sure the Shoshone will be happy not to bother us. They'll be relieved that nothing happened to them."

"I know that just as well as you, master Davy. But we must speak with the chief, and maybe also with the others. It's, therefore, necessary to remove their gags, and if we do this here, they can easily give a signal by calling to their people which, from here, could be clearly heard down there."

"My brother is right," the Apache said. "Winnetou was here today to observe the Shoshone. He knows a location where he and his brothers, together with the captives, can camp."

"We need a fire," remarked Old Shatterhand. "Is that possible there?"

"Yes. Tie the captives to the horses!"

This was done, after which the little group moved off into the night and through the dense forest with Winnetou in the lead.

Advancing only step by step, progress was extremely slow. In daylight the distance covered would have taken only five minutes, while it now took them half an hour. Then, the Apache stopped.

Of course, the captives were unaware into whose hands they had fallen and were also unclear about each other's identities. Due to the darkness the two scouts had not even been able to see that two more prisoners had been captured, while the latter did not know anything about the former. The chief had no inkling that he had been taken together with his son, and his son did not know, that his father had been captured as well.

For this reason, they were kept apart once the new campsite had been reached. Old Shatterhand pursued his policy of not letting Black Stag know how strong his enemy was. This is why he intended to deal with the chief first and alone. The others had to withdraw. Then, he gathered dry twigs from the ground to light a fire.

Old Shatterhand and the Chief of the Shoshone found themselves in an open space only a few paces wide. In daylight, the Apache had seen how well suited it was as a hidden campsite, and his sense of place was so acute, that he succeeded in finding it even in the dark.

It was surrounded by trees, below which ferns and thorn brush formed a rather dense enclosure. This prevented the fire's light from being seen from a distance. With the aid of his punk, Old Shatterhand lit the dry material easily and then, with his tomahawk, chopped off the lower dry branches from the surrounding trees to maintain the fire. It served only to illuminate the immediate area and, therefore, did not need to be big.

Lying on the ground, the Shoshone observed the activities of the white hunter with a scowl. When Old Shatterhand was finished with his preparations, he pulled the captive over to the fire, raised him to a seated position and took off the gag. No facial expression or a breath of air revealed the Indian's relief. For an Indian warrior it would be considered shameful to show his thoughts and feelings. Old Shatterhand sat down facing him from the opposite side of the fire. At first, he only observed his enemy. Black Stag was built very sturdily and wore a buffalo outfit of Indian cut without any adornment. Only the seams were decorated with scalp hair, and on his belt, he carried something like twenty scalps. They were not whole, which would have taken up too much space, but only dollar-size, well-prepared crowns of the head. Still stuck in his belt was his knife, which had not been taken from him.

His face was not painted, so that the three red scars on his cheeks could be seen clearly. He sat quietly, his features unmoving, and stared into the fire not indulging the White with a single look.

"Tokvi-tey does not wear the colors of war," Old Shatterhand began. "Then why does he act with such hostility against peaceful people?"

He received no answer and no look, which is why he continued:

"It seems the Chief of the Shoshone has fallen silent from fear, since he cannot reply to my question with even a single word?"

The hunter knew quite well how to deal with an Indian. The result showed immediately. The captive threw him a flashing look of anger and answered:

"Tokvi-tey does not know fear. He does not fear the enemy nor death!"

"And yet he acts precisely as if he were afraid. A courageous warrior paints the colors of war onto his face before he attacks. That is honest and courageous for then, the opponent knows that he must defend himself. The warriors of the Shoshone, however, did not wear color. They wore the faces of peace and yet attacked the Whites. Only a coward acts like this, am I not right? Does Black Stag find a word for his defense?"

The Indian lowered his look and said:

"Black Stag was not with them when they chased the palefaces."

"That's no excuse. Were he an honest and courageous man, he would have set the palefaces free the moment they were brought to him. We also did not hear that the warriors of the Shoshone had taken up the tomahawk of war but instead were grazing their herds as if in deepest peace at the Tongue and Bighorn waters. They visited the homes of the Whites, and yet Black Stag assaulted men who had never insulted him. Does he have anything to say when a brave man thinks that only a coward could act in this way?"

The Red gave the White only half a look, but this look proved that he was really angry. Nevertheless, his voice was controlled when he answered:

"Are you perhaps such a brave one?"

"Yes," Shatterhand replied even-tempered, as if this self-praise was self-evident.

"Then you must have a name!"

"Don't you see that I'm carrying weapons? Therefore, I must also have a name."

"The palefaces may bear arms and have names even when they are cowards. The greatest cowards among them carry the longest names. You know mine. Therefore, you will know that I am no coward."

"Then set the two captured Whites free and later fight them open and honestly!"

"They dared to come to the Lake of Blood. Therefore, they shall die."

"Then you will die, too!"

"Black Stag has told you already that he does not fear death. He even wishes for it!"

"Why?"

"He was captured, and taken by a White from his own wigwam. He has lost his honor. He can live no longer. He must die without being able to strike up the song of war. He will not sit proudly upright in his grave on his battle horse, draped with the scalps of his enemies, but will lie in the sand being hacked apart by the beaks of stinking carrion vultures."

He said this slowly and monotonously without a single move of his features, and yet, from each of his words spoke a pain bordering on hopelessness.

And, according to his belief, he was totally correct. It was an enormous shame for him to have been snatched from his tent, surrounded by his warriors, and made a prisoner.

Old Shatterhand felt sorry for the man, but did not show any sign of his compassion. It would have been an insult and would have caused the chief's thoughts of death to grow ever deeper. This is why he continued:

"Tokvi-tey deserves his fate, but he can stay alive even though he is my prisoner. I am prepared to return him to freedom, if he commands his people to free the two palefaces in return for him."

It sounded like proud scorn when the Red replied:

"Tokvi-tey can no longer live. He wishes to die. You might as well tie him to the stake. Although he may not speak of the deeds which did spread his fame, he will, nevertheless, not twitch his eye brows despite all tortures you can apply."

"I shall not tie you to the stake. I am a Christian. Even when I must kill an animal, I kill it in such a way, that it will not suffer any pain. But you would die uselessly. Despite your death, I would free the captives from the hands of your people."

"Try it! You were able to sneak up and stun me with a cunning grip and drag me away in the dark of night. But now the warriors of the Shoshone are warned. It will be impossible for you to free the palefaces. They dared to appear at the Lake of Blood and shall suffer this by slow death. You may have overcome Black Stag to die, but Moh-aw, his only son, the pride of his soul, lives and will avenge him. Already now, Moh-aw has painted his face with the colors of war, for he had been assigned the blow of death against the captured palefaces. He will paint his body with their warm blood and then be protected against the enmity of all palefaces."

There was a rustling in the bushes. Martin Baumann appeared, bent down to Old Shatterhand's ear and whispered to him:

"Sir, I am here to tell you that the captured guard is the son of the chief. Winnetou drew it out of him."

This information was very convenient for the hunter. He answered just as quietly:

"Have Winnetou send him here right away."

"By what means? The Red is tied up and cannot walk."

"Long Davy may carry him and then remain sitting here with him."

Martin left. Old Shatterhand turned back to the Indian and said:

"I do not fear Mosquito. Since when does he carry a name and where does one hear of his deeds? I need only wish it, and I'll take him prisoner like I did you."

This time the Stag could not quite keep his composure. The hunter had spoken disdainfully of his son. His brows narrowed, his eyes flashed, and he said angrily:

"Who are you that you dare speak in such a way of Moh-aw? Try to fight him. From his look already you will scurry away and hide in the earth!"

"Pshaw! I do not fight children!"

"Moh-aw is no child, no boy! He has battled the Sioux-Ogallalla and overcome several. He has the eyes of an eagle and the hearing of the night birds. No enemy can surprise him, and he will take bloody revenge on the fathers and sons of the palefaces for his father, Black Stag!"

That's when long Davy arrived carrying the young Indian on his shoulders. With his eternally long legs he strode over the densest shrubbery, put the Indian down and said:

"Here, I bring the boy. Am I to 'blue' his back that he remembers not to play games with men?"

"There's no talking of beating, master Davy. Seat him upright and take the place next to him. You can also remove the gag. It is no longer required, for here we talk."

"Aye, sir! But I'd like to know what the boy can contribute here."

The Tall One obeyed. When Mosquito sat upright, the two Shoshone looked fearfully into each other's eyes. The chief said nothing and made no move, but despite his dark skin color one could see that the blood had drained from his face. His son was not able to keep control of himself.

"Uff!" he called. "Tokvi-tey has also been captured! That will cause a wailing in the wigwams of the Shoshone. The Great Spirit has covered his face from his children."

"Be silent!" his father thundered at him. "No squaw of the Shoshone will shed a tear when Tokvi-tey and Moh-aw will be devoured by the fog of death. They had their eyes and ears closed and were without brain like the toad, which is swallowed by the snake without offering resistance. Disgrace be on the father and disgrace on the son! No mouth will speak of them, and no one will talk about them. But with their blood also the blood of the palefaces will flow. Already, two Whites are in the hands of our warriors, and already, the scouts of the Shoshone are under way to open the pathways to new victories. Disgrace for disgrace and blood for blood!"

That's when Old Shatterhand turned to Davy and softly issued the command:

"Fetch all the others. Only Winnetou is not to let himself be seen!"

The Tall One rose and left.

"Well," asked Old Shatterhand, "does Black Stag perhaps see that I'm not scurrying into the earth before the look of his son? I do not wish to insult you. The Chief of the Shoshone is famous for being a brave warrior and wise in the council of elders. Moh-aw, his son, will enter into his footsteps and be also as brave and wise. I give both their freedom against the freedom of the two captured white hunters."

Something like joy flashed across the son's face. He loved life. However, his father threw him an angry look and answered:

"Black Stag and Mosquito fell without battle into the hands of a miserable paleface. They do not deserve to live any longer. They want to die. Only by their death can they atone for the disgrace into which they have fallen. So, it is also that the palefaces shall die who have been caught already, and the ones, who will yet become the prisoners of the Shoshone ..."

"He stopped. His frightened look was on the two scouts who were now brought by Davy, Bob and Martin Baumann.

"Why does Black Stag not continue?" Old Shatterhand asked. "Does he feel the fist of terror reaching for his heart?"

The chief lowered his head and, for a long time, gazed silently down. Behind him branches moved without him noticing it. Old Shatterhand saw the head of the Apache appear and threw him a questioning look. A silent nod was his answer. The two understood each other without a word being spoken.

"Now Tokvi-tey may see that his hope for new victories is in vain," the hunter continued. "Yet, I repeat my offer. I shall set you free at once, if you promise that you'll also free the two white hunters."

"No, we shall die!" the chief shouted.

"Then die for nothing for, despite your deaths, we shall free your captives."

"Yes, maybe you will, because it seems that Manitou has forsaken us. Had he not struck us with blindness and deafness, then palefaces with no name, would not have succeeded in seizing the Chief of the Shoshone."

91

"No name? Do you wish to learn our names?"

Disdainfully he shook his head.

"I do not wish to hear them. They are not worth anything. This, precisely, is the disgrace! Had Tokvi-tey been conquered by *Nou-pay-klama*, the palefaces call Old Shatterhand, or by a hunter with a similarly famous name, he could take comfort from this. To be outwitted by such a warrior is no disgrace. But you are like dogs without masters. You ride in the company of a black Nigger. I do not want mercy from your hands!"

"And we don't want either your blood nor you yourself," Old Shatterhand replied. "We did not set out to kill the brave sons of the Shoshone, but to punish the dogs of Ogallalla. If you don't want to free our friends, then we will not be as cowardly as you are. We will permit you to return to your tents."

He rose, stepped up to the chief, and undid his fetters. He knew he was playing a daring game, but he was knowledgeable about the West and its inhabitants and was convinced that he would not lose this game.

The chief had totally lost his composure. What this White did was absolutely incomprehensible, entirely nonsensical! He set his enemies free without obtaining his friends' freedom in return. By that time Old Shatterhand had stepped up to Mosquito and also freed him as well.

Black Stag stared at him totally disconcerted. His hand reached for his belt and felt the knife there. A wild joy glowed in his eyes.

"Free we are to be!" he called. "Free! We are to see how the old squaws point with their fingers at us and tell how we were attacked and torn down by nameless dogs! Are we to lie on the earth in the Eternal Hunting Grounds and eat mice, while our red brothers delight on the loins of undying bears and buffalo? Our names are sullied. No blood of an enemy, only our own blood can wash off our shame. Tokvi-tey will die and send his son's soul ahead of his own!"

He tore the knife from his belt, jumped towards his son to stab the blade into his heart, and then kill himself. Mosquito did not move. He was prepared to receive his father's stab.

"Tokvi-tey!" Someone shouted from behind the chief.

This voice could not be resisted. His arm raised high with the knife, he turned. Before him stood the Chief of the Apache. The Shoshone lowered his arm.

"Winnetou!" he exclaimed.

"Does the Chief of the Shoshone think Winnetou to be a coyote?" the Apache asked.

The coyote is the wild prairie dog, also the little wolf of the West. The animal is so cowardly and often befallen with hideous mange, so that it is a great shame to be compared with a coyote.

"Who dares say this!" asked the Stag.

"Tokvi-tey has said so himself."

"No!"

"Has he not called those who defeated him, nameless dogs?"

At that, the Shoshone dropped his knife carelessly. Something dawned on him.

"Is Winnetou the victor?"

"No, but his white brother is, who stands here beside him."

He pointed at Old Shatterhand.

"Uff! Uff! Uff!" Black Stag exclaimed. "Winnetou has only one brother. He, who he calls his white brother is no other than *Nou-pay-klama*, the most famous among palefaces, who call him Old Shatterhand. Have Tokvi-tey's eyes the pleasure to see this hunter here?"

His looks moved questioningly between Shatterhand and Winnetou, who answered:

"My red brother's eyes were tired, and just as tired was his mind to reflect. Whoever takes Black Stag's breath with a single grip of his hand cannot be a nameless dog. Could my red brother not have told this to himself? Is my red brother a sick earth owl, one can easily take from its nest. He is a famous warrior, and whoever takes him from his wigwam despite the warriors guarding him, must be a hero carrying a great name."

The Shoshone stroked his fist over his head and answered:

"Tokvi-tey has a brain but had no thoughts in it."

"Yes, there stands Old Shatterhand, his conqueror. Need my red brother therefore enter death?"

"No," it sounded with a heavy, redeeming sigh. "He may stay alive."

"Yes, because by wanting to enter the Eternal Hunting Grounds by his own free will, he proved, that he possesses a strong heart. And it was Old Shatterhand who struck Moh-aw down with a blow of his shattering hand. Is that a disgrace for the young, brave warrior?"

"No, he, too, may stay alive."

"And it was Old Shatterhand and Winnetou who took the scouts of the Shoshone captive, not as enemies, but to exchange them for the captured palefaces. Is my red brother therefore condemning the scouts?"

"No. For then he would have to condemn also himself and his own son."

"And does my red brother not know, that Old Shatterhand and Winnetou are the friends of all brave red warriors? That they never kill their red enemies, but only disable them, and that they take the lives of their enemies only if they are forced by them to do so?"

"Yes, this, too, Tokvi-tey knows."

"Then, he may choose what he wishes to be, our brother or our enemy! If he is our brother, then his enemies will also be ours. But should he chose the other, then we shall set him, his son and his scouts free. However, then much blood will flow for the freedom of the two white captives, and the children of the Shoshone will have reason to cover their heads and begin their lament in every wigwam and by every camp fire. He may chose. Winnetou has spoken!"

Deep silence ensued. The impression made by the personality and the speech of the Apache was great. Tokvi-tey bent down, picked up the knife he had dropped, stabbed the blade to its haft into the earth and answered:

"Just like the sharpness of this knife has disappeared, so the enmity between the sons of the Shoshone and the brave warriors standing here has disappeared!"

He then pulled the knife out again, held the blade up threateningly, and continued:

"And, just like this knife is the friendship between the Shoshone and their brothers, it will strike all foes who are against this union. Howgh!"

"Howgh, howgh!" sounded all around.

"My brother has made a smart choice," Old Shatterhand said. "Here he sees Davy-Honskeh, the famous hunter. Does he know the names of the palefaces lying in his tent?"

"No."

"They are Jemmy-petahtsheh and the limping Frank, who is the companion of Mato-poka, the Bear Hunter."

"Mato-poka!" the Shoshone exclaimed in surprise. "Why did the limping one not say this? Is not Mato-poka the brother of the Shoshone? Has he not saved the life of Tokvi-tey when the Sioux-Ogallalla followed his tracks?"

"He has saved your life? Well, here you see Martin, his son, and Bob, his faithful black servant. They took off to save him with us accompanying them, for Mato-poka has fallen into the hands of the Ogallalla and is to be killed together with his five companions.

Tokvi-tey was still holding his knife. He threw it to the ground, stomped on it with his foot and called:

"The dogs of Ogallalla want to torture the Bear Hunter? Great Manitou will destroy them. Are their numbers many?"

"They are only fifty and six."

"And were they even a thousand, they ought to perish. Here, like this knife, they will be stomped into the earth by the warriors of the Shoshone. Their souls shall flee from their bodies, and their bones bleach in the rays of the sun! Where are they? Where can one find their tracks?"

"They have gone up into the mountains of the Yellowstone River to the grave of Brave Bull."

"Did not my brother Old Shatterhand slay Brave Bull and two of his companions with his bare fist? Then, also those who have dared to lay hands on the Bear Hunter, shall perish. My brothers may follow me down to the camp of my warriors. There, we will smoke the pipe of peace, and there, the men will sit by the council fire to consider which way the dogs can be reached most quickly!"

Of course, everyone was ready for it. The two scouts were also relieved of their shackles, after which the horses were brought in.

"Sir, you are a devil of a guy!" Long Davy whispered to Old Shatterhand. "Whatever you start has class, is extraordinarily daring, and yet succeeds exquisitely, as if it had been a trifle. I lift my chapeau to you!"

He pulled off his brimless top hat and waved it emphatically as though he wanted to drain a carp pond with it.

They took off. Pulling the horses behind them, the hunters groped their way back to the drop-off. Obviously, their fire had been extinguished. Arriving at the valley's rim, Tokvi-tey held both hands to his mouth and shouted into the silent valley:

"*Khun, khun, kin-wah-ka* – the fire, the fire, start the council fire!"

The shout echoed back many times. It had been heard down there and understood, for loud voices arose.

"*Hang-pa* – who's coming?" a question sounded from the valley.

"Moh-aw, Moh-aw!" the chief's son replied.

A loud, joyous '*ha-ha-hih*' resounded, and minutes later the flames of the quickly restarted fire could be seen. It was a sure sign that the Shoshone had recognized the young Indian's voice. Otherwise, they would have been on guard so as not to facilitate the attack of a possibly approaching enemy, wanting to deceive them by his call to illuminate the camp. Nevertheless, they were cautious enough to send some men towards the approaching group, who were to ascertain that, truly, there was nothing to be concerned about.

When the chief and his company entered the camp, his people were joyful about his and his son's return. They were also eager to learn how the mysterious disappearance of the two had happened, yet none let on to this. Of course, they were utterly astonished when they saw the strange palefaces arriving with him. However, being used to hide their feelings, they did not display any sign of surprise. Only the old warrior, who had taken over command, approached the chief and said:

"Tokvi-tey is a great magician. He disappears from his tent like a spoken word."

"Did my brothers truly believe that Black Stag disappeared without trace, like the smoke rising into the air?" the chief asked. "Did they not have eyes to see what happened?"

"The warriors of the Shoshone have eyes. They found the token of the famous white hunter that Shatterhand had spoken with their chief."

This was a very considerate paraphrase of the fact that Black Stag had been abducted by Old Shatterhand. The old one used such words in respect for their leader.

"My brothers guessed right," the chief affirmed. "Here stands *Nou-pay-klama*, the white hunter, who strikes down his enemies with his fist. And on his side stands Winnetou, the great Chief of the Apache."

"Uff, uff!" arose from the circle.

The Shoshone looked admiringly and respectfully at the two famous men, and by stepping back deferentially, the circle that had formed around the arrivals widened.

"These warriors have come to smoke the pipe of peace with us," the chief continued. "They want to free their two companions lying over there in the tent. They held the lives of Black Stag and his son in their hands and yet did not take them. This is why the warriors of the Shoshone may untie the fetters of the captives. Instead, my brothers may get the scalps of many Sioux-Ogallalla who, like mice, scurried from their holes to be throttled by the hawk. Upon daybreak, we shall follow their tracks. But now the warriors may gather around the council fire to ask the Great Spirit whether he will let the campaign be successful!"

Not a word arose, although the message they had just heard was fit to rouse great interest. Some of them quietly went to the respective tent to execute the chief's command and soon led the two captives to the fire.

Their walk insecure, they arrived in a stagger. The fetters had cut so deeply, that they had prevented proper circulation of the blood. It usually takes some time until one is fully capable of using ones arms and legs again.

"You old raccoon, what blunder did you commit?" Long Davy asked his corpulent friend. "Only a frog like you can jump right into the stork's bill!"

"Just close yours or I'll jump into it, and that right away!" Jemmy replied angrily, while he rubbed his sore wrists. "Master Shatterhand will prove, that you can't talk of any folly of ours. We surrendered without resistance since this was the only way to save our lives. Had we defended ourselves, we would have been wiped out. You'd have done the same in my place, especially since we were sure that Old Shatterhand wouldn't let us drown in this ink pot."

"Well, oldster, calm down! It wasn't meant to hurt, and you know very well how very glad I am to see you free again."

"Fine! But it's unlikely that I owe you my freedom." Turning to Old Shatterhand, he continued:

"Surely, it is only to you, sir, that I am so extraordinarily obliged. Tell me how I can thank you for it! Although my life has little value, for it's only that of Fat Jemmy's, I am ready to put it at your disposal at a moment's notice."

"You don't owe me any thanks," Old Shatterhand warded off. "Your comrades helped bravely, as well. But, most of all, you must turn to my brother Winnetou, without whose help it would have been impossible to arrive so quickly and positively at this place."

The Fat One looked admiringly at the slender, yet powerful figure of the Apache. He offered his hand and said:

"I knew that Winnetou had to be near, when Old Shatterhand shows up. Since I am to be a frog, then this stork here, who's called Long Davy, may swallow me on the spot, if you aren't the bravest Indian I've ever offered my hand to. Let me press yours heartily. A thousand thanks to you, and permit me to follow in your tracks as it pleases you."

With a shout of joy, Bob, had stepped close to Hobble-Frank and said: "Finally, finally *Massa* Bob again see his good *Massa* Frank! *Massa* Bob want strike dead all Shoshone Indians, but *Massa* Shatterhand with *Massa* Winnetou want make free you all by themselves. This why Shoshone once more stay alive."

He took Frank's hands and stroked the sore spots with touching tenderness.

Of course, right away, Jemmy and Frank wanted to learn how their liberation had been so speedily and bloodlessly effected. They were told in a few words. There was no time for an extensive story since the Shoshone had already gathered around the fire for the council.

Karl May – translated by Herbert Windolf

3. Oiht-e-keh-fa-wakon

Like a long, thin snake, the train of the Shoshone wound its way through the bluegrass prairie, which stretches from Devil's Head between the Bighorn and Rattlesnake Mountains, to the area where Greyball Creek's clear waters flow into the Bighorn River.

Bluegrass is not frequently found in the West. It grows tall and can reach man-height in soil with the right moisture. It can reach to the head of a horseman, possibly even above it. This poses great difficulties to the frontiersman, and he is well advised to follow the trails buffalo have trampled in this dense sea of grass. The wave of grass blades closing in above his head robs him of the ability to see into the distance. This is why, in cloudy weather, even experienced hunters, lacking a compass and unable to determine the sun's location, often arrived in the evening, after a troublesome ride, at the same place from where they departed in the morning. Many a hunter, having ridden in a circle, hit upon his own tracks thinking them to be someone else's, even that of an enemy. Following them anew, he then circled several times until he eventually realized to his great chagrin this potentially dangerous error.

Even to follow the aforementioned buffalo tracks isn't entirely without danger. One can suddenly come face to face with a human or animal foe. To suddenly be confronted by an old buffalo who, as a cantankerous recluse separated from a herd, is just as serious a threat as when one meets, without presentiment, a hostile Indian whose rifle is aimed at you just three paces distant. This calls for lightning fast action. He who fires first is the one to survive.

The Shoshone rode in single file, so that every horse stepped into the tracks of the one ahead. Indians maintain this order whenever they are not sure of their security. In addition, care is taken to send scouts ahead. These are the shrewdest and smartest men in the group, whose eyes will not miss the bending of a blade of grass against the wind or the softest breaking of a twig.

Sunk into himself and bent far forward, such a scout hangs on his horse as if the art of horsemanship was foreign to him. His eyes seem to be closed. He doesn't move a limb. His steed, too, moves like an automaton, walking habitually. Whoever observes them from an ambush could believe that the rider had fallen asleep in the saddle. Yet, it is just the opposite. The attention of the scout is more intense the less he lets on to it. As low as his eyelids may be, his sharp look, nevertheless, penetrates from below, ahead, to the right and the left.

A soft, very soft sound is heard, only audible to the ears of such a scout. Behind close bushes lurks an enemy, his rifle raised, aimed at the scout. In doing so the foe brushes the horn button of his jacket. The barely noticeable noise caused by this movement has, nevertheless, reached the ear of the scout. A quick, sharp look to the bush, a pull at the reins, and the horseman drops out of the saddle. And yet, he remains hanging with one foot on the saddle and with one arm by the neck straps of the horse, so that his body has totally disappeared behind that of his animal and cannot be hit by the enemy's bullet. The horse, suddenly roused from its seeming lethargy, makes two or three leaps sideways and disappears with its rider into the thicket or behind a protective tree. This all happens in less than two seconds, before the enemy can take proper aim at the scout. The spy now has every reason to take care of his own safety.

Such scouts rode a good distance ahead of the Shoshone. In the lead of the main group rode Old Shatterhand, Winnetou and Black Stag, followed by Wohkadeh and Bob.

Despite the long exposure of the ride, the Negro had still not become a better horseman. The skin on his legs had not toughened. It had become sore causing him to sit even more pitifully on his horse. With continuous 'ahs' and 'ohs', 'alas' and 'woe to me', he slid from one side to the other. He groaned and moaned in all tones of the chromatic scale and assured everyone with the most terrible grimaces that he would pay the Sioux back for his suffering. Should his threats become true, they would all face a most dreadful death at the stake.

To sit more comfortably, he had made himself a cushion from cut bluegrass. But since he was unable to keep it in place on the back of his horse, from time to time it slid off with him obviously following. And thus, at regular intervals, he ended up sitting beside it on the ground.

This drew even a smile from the otherwise taciturn Shoshone. When one of them, who understood a bit of English, called him Sliding Bob, the term went from mouth to mouth and became his nickname, happily used later on.

The western horizon had so far been flat. It now began to rise in places. Mountains appeared there, not bluish with indistinct contours, but sharply drawn and clearly embodied, despite the great distance that still needed to be covered to arrive at their base.

In this area, the air is so clear that distant points many miles away appear to be so close, that one thinks they can be reached in a few minutes. At the same time, the atmosphere is so laden with electricity that when, for instance, two people touch hands or elbows, slightly visible and felt sparks fly. The Indians, belonging to the Sonoran linguistic family, call this phenomenon '*Mo-aw-k'un*', meaning Mosquito Fire. The electric tension seeks to compensate, with repeated discharges. There can be continuous sheet-lightning without there being clouds anywhere on the horizon. Often the entire range of sight can seem to be in flames, yet the well-being of man and animal is not affected in the least. In the evening, this perpetual flashing and glowing presents an indescribable view. A frontiersman, even when accustomed to this spectacle, cannot withdraw his soul or his mind from it. He, who is used to relying only on himself, feels himself to be small and impotent in the face of such mysterious forces. He thinks of God, whom he may have forgotten for some time. As a pious memory from his youth, there arises in his mind the oft-heard words of the psalmist: "Where shall I go before your spirit and where to am I to flee from your face? Fare I to heaven, see, you are already there; bed I in hell, see, you are also there; take I the wings of dawn even there your hand would lead me on and your right hold me!" The very same is thought and felt by the Indian. '*Weh-kuonpeh-ta-wakon-shetsha*', Wigwam Fire, sheet lightning is called by the Sioux. '*Manitou ahnima ahwarrenton*', translates into 'I have seen Manitou in Lightning', says the Snake River Indian when he tells his people that he traveled by this electrical illumination.

If there is war, these electrical discharges can become highly dangerous. The Indian believes that the warrior who is killed in the night, must live in eternal darkness in the Eternal Hunting Grounds. This is why he tries to avoid all nightly fights and prefers to execute an attack at the first light of dawn. However, he who dies in the Fire of the Great Spirit, does not walk on a dark path into the beyond. Instead, he finds there the hunting and warpaths well illuminated. For this reason, the Indian does not shy from attacking at the time of the flashing light, and many, unaware of this or not watching out, have paid for their ignorance or carelessness with scalp and life.

Little Hobble-Frank had never seen this inexplicable sheet lightning in a bright sky, which is why he said to Fat Jemmy riding behind him:

"Mishter Pfefferkorn, you've been a Gymnasiast in Germany and may remember a bit of your psychological lessons. Why does it flash and shine here so much?"

"It's physical, not psychological," the Fat One corrected.

"It appearsh you don't undershtand much more of it than I do. You know, I too have my merits, believe my word, particularly when it comes to orthography and punctshuation. I know precisely how such a foreign word is shpelled, and that's why I ought to be able to also pronounce it correctly. Undershtood! Whether I say psychological or physical is all the same to the German emperor. The main thing is that one pronounces the yxilump properly."

"It's 'ypsilon' ('y' in German)"

"What? Really! I'm not to know how the second to lasht letter in my fatherland's alphabet is pronounced? If you tell me that once more, something is likely to follow, which could easily put you into a dishpositional malaise. Something like that an admirer of the sciences won't readily put up with. You don't know how to answer to my question with an academic reply, which is why you now try to secretly shlink out of this trap. But if you think you'll succeed at that, you are merschtentels mistaken in me. I'm quite the man to prove to you, that miller's fellow ain't no food mopper. I asked you about the sheet lightning, but not for the yxilump and the psychological geometry. Can you give me an answer or not?"

"Any old time!" the Fat One laughed.

"Well, then out with it! Why then is there so much sheet lightning here?"

"Because there's much electricity."

"So? Ah? That's what you call an answer? Well, then one needn't have been a Gymnasiast! Although I haven't gone to an alma vater, haven't been a shtudent, have never taken part in shtudents' drinking bouts, and haven't rubbed on Alexander, I know very well, that electricity must be there for it to shine. Every effect has its cause. If someone got his ears boxed, there musht've been another to deal it out. And when there's sheet lightning, then - then - then ..."

"Then there must be someone who lit it up," Jemmy cut in.

At first Hobble-Frank remained silent to consider the Fat One's words, only to break out angrily:

"You lishten, Mishter Pfefferkorn. It's very well that we haven't agreed on brotherhood yet, because I'd now abolish it on the shpot. Wouldn't that be a disgrace and an eternal shtain on your civil blazon. Do you believe I'd have my etymological word derivation shpoiled by you? And why do you actually cut into my mosht beautiful shpeech? If you want to complete a sentence, can't you begin it yourself. Remember that! But if I'm the beginner, then I also talk to the end, because after that, the sentence is my shpiritual and philosophical property. When I, in my sagacious and modest mean, compare the electricity with boxing ears, you don't have the leasht right to seize my comparison like a captain of brigands. A horse thief is hanged; that's the law of the prairie, and if someone runs off with a sentence of mine, I'll shoot him off his horse. I had wanted to conshtruct a terrific conclusion, but as soon as I was finished with the right promises, you hung a totally false confusion to its end. That hurt my logical delicate feelings in a most horrible way. I am ..."

"Premises, you likely meant to say," Jemmy interrupted the bumptious speech. "And it isn't confusion, but conclusion."

"So! Are you really such an distinguished expert of the antiquarian language syshtem? If someone has heard sometime in his youth in school that Rome was built on seven tiles, he right off thinks afterwards that he's quite the virtuoso of all the Latin dialects. You shpeak actually common Latin; my school mashter, however, was a high Latin man; with him everything ended regularly with *um*, *cum*, and *dumb*. That's the known language of Cicero and the beautiful Melusine. But you learned Latin in the Gymnasium only in simple verses and say:

> *"Whatever one cannot declaim,*
> *one looks at neutrally the same."*

"You might have behaved quite neutrally up to the *Oberprima* (9th and final class of the Gymnasium), only to become a prairie hunter, then brag heavily with your philological knowledge of languages and don't want to let pass my promises and my confusion. In my entire life I haven't heard of conclusion, even not in Moritzburg, which is telling a lot. Therefore, do me and yourself the favor and shtick to what's real. The talk was about sheet lightning and electricity. You say there's sheet lightning because of the electricity present. Now, I keep asking, why there's precisely in this area here so much electricity. I've never seen such a bunch of it together. Can you answer that? Now you've the besht opportunity of your life to pass the exam or to miss the nicest ecumenical consilium."

Fat Jemmy broke up laughing which is why the learned Saxon asked:

"Why are you laughing like a clarinet? Are you perhaps laughing only from embarrassment, because of my totally unexshpected development of philharmonic language dexshterity? Well, I'm very curious by what means you'll try to escape, my good mishter Pfefferkorn!"

"Yes," replied Jemmy, "your question is, of course, very difficult to answer. Even a professor would try in vain."

"So! Then you don't have an answer?"

"Maybe after all."

"Then lets hear it. I'm all ear lobe."

"Maybe the metal richness of the Rocky Mountains is the cause of this amassing of electricity."

"The metal richness? Electricity has nothing to do with it."

"Oh yes? Then why is it drawn to the lightning rod?"

"But it runs out again at the bottom, conshequently it doeshn't care to know anything of it. And many a tree is hit by lightning without having the leasht bit of iron shtuck in its coat pocket. No, I can't accept that. That would mean, for inshtance, that all iron foundries would be hit by lightning."

"Or is it because we are approaching the magnetic pole here?"

"Where is that located?"

"In northern America, certainly still a good distance from here."

"Then let it lie there for good! It, too, is innoshent of this sheet lightning."

"Or, with the rapid rotation of the Earth, might the electricity be dammed by the giant height of the Rocky Mountains?"

"Such an archimedian accumulation can't be considered. Electricity ishn't as thick as syrup; it easily crosses the mountains. No, you haven't passed your exam. Your grade is at besht a D."

"Well then, if you are the man to issue a grade to me, you must be able to do better."

"Of course, I'm able to do that, because I was a foreshtry official in Moritzburg, where I pushed my native intelligence by eager questioning and reflection to the most superlative peak. I'd actually like to know to which weighty question I would be unable to give the right pneumatic information. Mind you, I'm only an autoviaduct, because I've learned merschtentels all by myself. But once the genius is in a man, then it can't even be killed by clubbing it. The explanation you aren't coming up with as a late Gymnasiast is quite simple. The Moritzburg school mashter told me once on discretion and word of honor, during an intimate hour when no one else was in abshento, that electricity is produced by friction. You'll admit to that?"

"Gladly."

"Conshequently, electricity arises where friction exists."

"For inshtance when grating potatoes!"

"Keep your Quartaner (Quarta is the 3rd class of the Gymnasium) jokes, particularly when you talk with a man who's one of the hydraulic authorities of the artificial sciences! When I'm not dishturbed, I am of a very modest and unassuming character, because there are moments when the shpirit musht be weak, but the body shtrong and powerful. But, when the right moment of reflection comes together with the proper inshtant of higher education, my noble nature bristles against the common, ordinary temperament, and the sources of my knowledge begin to bubble and to splash that it's a wonder. I sometimes am surprised myself, when I hear the kind of treasures hidden in me. With the electricity, for example, I don't make bones about. I'm far superior to that science. Merschtentels I only play with it. I don't mind a bit more or less friction, particularly here in this area. There are mighty prairies, mighty foreshts, and mighty mountains. Now, when the wind or even a shtorm rushes across them, an immense friction is created, or is it not?"

"Yes," Jemmy admitted. He was eager to hear the Saxon's explanation.

"The shtorm rubs across the ground; the infinite millions of grass blades rub againsht each other; the infinite branches, twigs and leaves of the trees also rub at each other. The buffalo roll in the wallows, which causes magnificent friction. In short, there's a friction taking place in this area like nowhere else, which is why it's evident that an enormous shtore of electricity accumulates. There you have the simplest, indishputable explanation from the mosht competent mouth. You want any more?"

"No, no," Jemmy laughed. "I've had enough!"

"Then accept my enlightenment in all seriousness and devoted respect. But I musht forbid this laughing! Whoever laughs as much without cause betrays a sanguine-choleric common existence; a hollow, phrenological brain formation, and an insignificant loyal shpinal system. And that you're also suffering from a chronic-acute reflection you've proven, because only you alone were the cause that we were captured by the Shoshone. If this capital Old Shatterhand hadn't come to our aid, we would, for sure, have had to make the dangerous salto quartale over into the Eternal Hunting Grounds."

"It's mortale, not quartale!"

"Be quiet! Something like that won't happen again in this quarter of a year, which is why I say quartale. Our scientific conversation is now on the whole finis parterra, because we are close to the mountains now, and up front there our scouts have shtopped. They musht have discovered something important."

The little pseudo-pundit had paid little attention to his surroundings during his ultra-learned exposition. In the meantime, a quite substantial distance had been covered, and the bluegrass had disappeared. In its place festucca grasses had entered, copiously mixed with fragrant cumarin blades. A bit further on, abundant brush spread about, above which, rose the tops of several fire maples. These trees like moist ground and, therefore, were a good sign that a refreshing drink could be counted on after the hot ride.

There, beside the bushes, the scouts had stopped. When the train of horsemen approached, they signaled caution with their hands and one of them called:

"*Nambau, nambau!*"

This word actually means 'foot', but also signifies 'tracks'. The scouts asked for caution, so that the tracks they had found would not be destroyed before they could be read by the leaders.

Wohkadeh did not pay attention to their signals and rode towards them.

"*Wehts toweke!*" shouted the one who had called earlier.

This means 'young man' and, thus, is a reprimand. A young man is not likely to act as wisely as an older one. The expression contained a reproof without seriously insulting Wohkadeh. Nevertheless, he replied in a firm voice:

"Did my brothers count the winters Wohkadeh has lived? He knows very well what he is doing. He knows these tracks which include the imprints of his feet. He camped at this place with the Ogallalla before they sent him out to look for the tents of the Shoshone. In any case, they rode straight west from here to reach the foot of the Bighorn and will have left signs by whose help he can follow them quickly."

The place where they halted showed tracks made several days ago by a substantial group of horsemen, although these signs were recognizable only to an exceptionally trained eye. The trampled grasses had completely risen again, but the bushes nearby were missing the tips of twigs eaten by the horses.

Following Wohkadeh's explanation, there was no reason to stay here any longer. Thus the entire train resumed its move.

The sun stood at its zenith, which meant it was the time of day with the greatest heat. The horses had need for a short rest, but they were not to have it until water had been found.

The terrain, flat until now, began to rise. Up front, on the right and left side, long mountain ridges moved closer. The horsemen followed a wide valley meandering between the heights. It was green from the aforementioned grasses. At first, the bushes were only of a rough kind, but soon softer types appeared: bush-like balsam poplars, which here did not develop into trees, and wild pears which Americans call spike-hawthorne.

Individual trees became more numerous now. There were white ash, chestnut, macrocarpa oak, linden, and others, on whose trunks purple-red creepers climbed.

When the trail turned sharply north behind a rise, the riders saw densely wooded mountains ahead. There had to be water. Two ragged heights rose rather steeply, facing each other. Between them squeezed a narrow valley on whose bottom a narrow stream murmured its soft melody. Should they turn into it or continue in the same direction?

Old Shatterhand examined the forest's edge closely. He soon nodded to himself and said:

"Our trail leads into the valley to the left."

"Why?" Long Davy asked.

"Don't you see the spruce branch sticking in the linden trunk over there?"

"Aye, sir. It's, of course, conspicuous for a needle branch to grow on a deciduous tree."

"It's a sign for Wohkadeh. The Sioux attached it to the linden so that it points to the valley. They have taken that direction, and I think that we'll come across more such signs. Onward!"

Winnetou had silently ridden ahead having given the linden only a brief look. That was his way. He was used to acting without saying much.

When the group had covered a short distance, an exceptionally well suited place was found to set up camp. There they stopped. There was water, shade, and excellent grass for the horses.

The riders dismounted and permitted the animals to graze. The Shoshone were well supplied with sun-dried meat, and the Whites still carried provisions from the Bear Hunter's dwelling. They ate. Some of the men stretched out in the grass or moss for a brief nap, the others sat together talking.

The most restless was Bob. Since he had become sore from the ride, he hurt in several places.

"*Massa* Bob be sick, very sick," he said. "*Massa* Bob no more have skin on his legs. All skin is gone, *kaputt*, and now pants cling to legs and hurt *Massa* Bob. Who be guilty of that? The Sioux. When *Massa* Bob find them, he club them dead, until they no longer be alive! *Massa* Bob cannot ride, not sit, not stand, not lie down. It be as if *Massa* Bob have fire in legs."

"There's a remedy," said Martin Baumann, who sat next to him. "Look for coltsfoot and put the leaves on the wounds."

"But where grow coltsfoot?"

"Usually at forest edges. Maybe you'll find some right here."

"Come! I'll help you look for it."

The two started to leave. Old Shatterhand had heard their conversation and warned:

"Take your rifles along. We are here not at an East Coast market place. One never knows what the next moment will bring."

Silently, Martin picked up his rifle. The Negro also put his across his shoulder.

"Yes!" he said. "*Massa* Bob take rifle along. When come Sioux or wild animal, he shoot all to protect young massa. Come on!"

The two walked slowly along the valley's border to look for the plant, but no coltsfoot was found. Thus, they went farther and farther from the camp. It was very quiet and sunny in the valley. Butterflies fluttered above flowers, beetles hummed and buzzed from place to place. The creek's waters splashed peacefully, and the treetops were bathed in sunshine. Who would have thought of danger there?

Then Martin, who walked ahead, stopped and pointed to a track, not too far away, which wended its way through the grass from the little creek straight to the side of the valley. There it disappeared under the trees.

"What that be?" asked Bob. "A trail?"

"Yes, it is a trail. Someone must be coming regularly from the forest to fetch water."

"It be a frontiersman then?"

"Hm! A frontiersman? Here in this remote area? Unlikely"

"An animal, maybe?"

"I'd rather think that. Let's have a look at the tracks!"

They approached them for a closer inspection. From the water up to the trees, the grass had not just been trampled down across a width of several feet, but eroded so much that bare soil had appeared. Martin and Bob were facing a true pathway.

"That be no animal," the Negro opined. "Here be walking a man with boots back and forth. *Massa* Martin will agree with *Massa* Bob."

But the youngster shook his head. He probed the path closely and answered:

"This is very strange. One cannot make out any hoof or claw tracks. The ground has been so impacted that one cannot determine when this trail has last been passed. I'd bet that only a hoofed animal could trample such a trail."

"Oh, nice, very nice!" the Negro exclaimed joyfully. "Maybe it be an opossum. That be very welcome to *Massa* Bob."

The opossum, which can be up to half a yard long, has a tender, white and fat meat, but has also such a peculiar, unpleasant smell, that it is never eaten by Whites. However, Negroes don't disdain it, and there are Blacks who chase madly after this unpleasantly scented roast. Good Bob belonged to this kind of gastronome.

"What's the matter with you!" Martin laughed. "An opossum here! Do you think opossums are hoofed animals?"

"Where opossum belong is all same to *Massa* Bob. Opossum be fine, delicate meat, and *Massa* Bob now try catch opossum."

He intended to follow the trail, but Martin held him back.

"Stay, and don't make a fool of yourself! That's no opossum here, it being much too small to trample such a trail. We are dealing here with a large animal, maybe even an elk."

"Elk, oh, elk!" Bob called, smacking his lips. "Elk give much, much meat and tallow and skin. Elk be good, very good! Bob shoot elk right away."

"Stay, stay! It can't be an elk or the grass here would be eaten."

"Then *Massa* Bob look what be it. Maybe it be opossum after all. Oh! When *Massa* Bob find opossum, he make big feast."

He ran off along the tracks towards the forest-covered valley slope.

"Wait! Darn it, wait!" Martin warned. "It could be a large carnivore!"

"Opossum be carnivore, eat birds and other small critter. *Massa* Bob catch it."

He couldn't be warned and continued on. The thought of his favorite roast made him forget the required caution. Martin followed him quickly in order to be on hand in case of an unpleasant surprise. But the Negro always managed to keep ahead of the young man.

In that way, they reached the forest's border where the terrain rose rather steeply, just as it did on the other side.

The trail entered the trees in a straightway, then passed between big rocks. Here, too, it was so solid that not a single impression was recognizable.

Always ahead, the Negro climbed the height. The trees stood rather close together, and between their trunks quite a bit of brush had spread, so that one could say that the trail went right through the thicket. That's when Martin heard the jubilant voice of the Negro:

"*Massa* come, come quick! *Massa* Bob found nest of opossum."

The youngster followed the call as quickly as possible. It could not be an opossum. Thus, it was to be feared that good Bob was facing a danger the extent of which he had no idea.

"Stop! Stop!!" Martin warned loudly. "Don't do anything until I get there."

"Oh, here be hole, front door of nest of opossum. *Massa* Bob now visit opossum."

Martin now had reached the spot where the Negro was. There was a number of piled up boulders. Two of them, leaning against each other, formed a cave, in front of which hazelnut, wild mulberry, and raspberry bushes grew exuberantly. Through this brush a passage had been broken. The trail they had followed led into it, however, numerous tracks to the right and left, showed that the resident of the cave did not only pass between it and the water, but undertook other excursions.

The Negro had squatted down and had already entered the passage with his torso in order to creep into the cave.

Now, Martin realized to his horror that his concern had not been unfounded. From the now distinct tracks, he saw with what kind of animal they were dealing.

"For God's sake, back, back!" he shouted. "This is the cave of a bear!"

At the same time, he grabbed Bob's legs to pull him back. The Negro, though, did not appear to have understood him, for he replied:

"Why hold me back? *Massa* Bob courageous. He defeat whole nest of opossum."

"It's no opossum, but a bear, a bear!"

He held on to the Black with all his might. That's when a deep, angry growl arose, and, at the same time, Bob uttered a scream of terror.

"Jesus! A beast, a monster! Oh *Massa* Bob, oh *Massa* Bob!"

Lightning fast, he pushed back from the brush and leaped up. Despite the Black's dark skin, Martin saw that the blood had drained from his face.

"Is it still in the cave?" the boy asked.

Bob waved his arms in the air and moved his lips, but was unable to respond. He had dropped his rifle. His eyes rolled and his teeth grated.

That's when there was a rustling in the brush, and the head of a grizzly, a gray bear, peered out. That was enough to loosen the Negro's tongue.

"Off, off!" he screamed. "*Massa* Bob up onto tree!"

He took a mighty leap towards a thin birch tree and, with the speed of a squirrel, climbed up its trunk.

Martin had turned pale, but not from fear. He quickly grabbed the Negro's rifle and jumped behind a good-sized copper beech tree nearby. He leaned the rifle against its trunk, then reached for his own double-barreled rifle on his shoulder.

The bear had slowly emerged from the thorn bushes. His small eyes first looked for the Negro, who hung by his hands on the lower branches, then towards Martin, standing farther away. He lowered his head, opened the slavering jaws to let his tongue hang far out. He seemed to consider against which of the two enemies he should advance first. Then he rose slowly and shakily onto his hind legs. He was surely eight feet tall. His penetrating reek, more or less common to the carnivores of the wilds, spread widely.

From the moment Bob had leaped from the ground to the tree, not a minute had passed. When the Negro saw the giant animal rising so threateningly, not more than four paces from him, he clamored:

"For God's sake! Bear want eat *Massa* Bob! Up, up, quickly, quickly!"

With spasmodic moves he climbed ever farther up. Unfortunately the birch was so weak, that it bent under the load of the heavy Black. He pulled his feet up as far as possible and with both arms and legs clung tightly to the trunk. The thin top of the little tree bent further down, Bob hanging from it by all fours like a giant bat.

The bear seemed to understand that this enemy was easier to get to than the other. He turned towards the birch and by doing so offered Martin his left side. The young man, still half a boy, had reached for his chest. There, under his hunting shirt, hung the little doll, the bloody memento of his unfortunate little sister.

"Luddy, Luddy!" he whispered. "I avenge you!"

With a steady hand he aimed his rifle. The shot rang out, another one –

Terror caused Bob to let go.

"Jesus, Jesus!" he cried. "*Massa* Bob be dead, quite dead!"

With him dropping down, the birch sprung back to its natural position.

The bear twitched as if he had received a push or had been hit. He opened his terrible, toothy jaws and slowly advanced two more steps. The Negro held both arms out to him and hollered, while staying prone on the ground:

"*Massa* Bob not want to do you anything, wanted only catch possum!"

In the next moment, the daring boy stood between him and the beast. He had tossed his spent rifle away and had grabbed the Black's rifle, whose barrel he now aimed at the bear. He stood no more than two feet distant from the animal. His eyes flashed boldly, and on his tightly pressed lips lay this inexorable expression saying clearly: you or I!

But instead of firing, he lowered the rifle and jumped back. His sharp eyes had realized that this third shot was not required. The bear stood still. A rattling growl came from his throat followed by a roaring groan. A shiver went through its body, the front legs dropped, a dark stream of blood gushed over its tongue, then the animal collapsed – a convulsive jerk – the body rolled to one side, then remained motionless right next to the Negro.

"Help, help, help!" he whimpered, his arms still rigidly stretched out, as if they were without motion or joints.

"Fellow! Bob!" Martin said to him angrily. "Why are you wailing, you old coward!"

"The bear, the bear!"

"But it's dead!"

That's when the Black pulled his arms to his body, righted himself to a sitting position, looked with questioning fear back and forth from the animal to Martin and repeated:

"Dead, dead! It be true?"

"Of course."

"Really true?"

"You can see it! I bet both bullets went right through its heart."

Hearing that, Bob leaped up demonstrating that all his joints were in good order, and called joyously:

"Dead, bear be dead! Oh, oh, oh! *Massa* Bob and *Massa* Martin defeated monster! *Massa* Bob made bear hunt. Oh, now *Massa* Bob be daring and famous frontiersman! All people say what courage have daring and fearless *Massa* Bob!"

"Yes," Martin laughed, "you were so daring, that you fell from the tree like a ripe plum right in front of the bear's jaws."

The Black made a surprised face.

"Fall?" he asked. "Not fall! *Massa* Bob jumped toward bear. *Massa* Bob wanted to grab him by coat and beat dead!"

"But you stayed put on the ground!"

"*Massa* Bob stay quietly put to show he not afraid of the bear. Oh, what is bear against *Massa* Bob! Bob be hero. He take bear by ears and box his ears so many times, bear cannot count!"

He bent down and with his left hand reached for one of the small ears of the killed animal, but first quietly and cautiously, to convince himself, that it was truly dead. Then, when he was sure of it, he slapped it strongly with his right.

That's when loud voices and hurried steps could be heard.

"By the devil, a bear trail," sounded from the creek. "That can only be a big grizzly. The two didn't know it and, unsuspecting, walked towards the animal." Quick! Let's follow."

That had been Old Shatterhand's voice. Upon his first look at the trail, the experienced frontiersman had no doubt what animal had trampled the path.

"Yes, it's a grizzly," Fat Jemmy called, agreeing. "Perhaps both of them were overcome. Forward, let's enter the forest."

A confusion of other voices and hurried steps arose.

"Holla!" Martin Baumann called to the arriving folks. "Have no worry about us. All is well."

Old Shatterhand and Winnetou were the first to arrive at the place. Following them were Tokvi-tey and Long Davy, behind them Fat Jemmy and the little Saxon, after them the majority of the Indians. The others had stayed in camp, since the horses were not to be left alone.

"Truly, a grizzly!" Old Shatterhand called, seeing the killed animal. "And this one is one of the biggest. And you are alive, Martin! How very fortunate!"

He stepped to the bear to check its wound.

"Hit right into the heart, and that from a very short distance! This is great hunter's luck. Of course, I need not ask who killed the animal."

With that Bob stepped forward and said with a proud, self-assured grin:

"*Massa* Bob defeat bear. *Massa* Bob be man who is cause that bear had to give his life."

"You, Bob? Well, that doesn't sound very probable."

"Oh! It be true, very true! *Massa* Bob sit before bear's nose, so bear only see him, not *Massa* Martin, who must shoot. *Massa* Bob risk life for *Massa* Martin to have sure shot."

111

Old Shatterhand smiled. Nothing could escape his sharp, experienced eyes. His look fell onto the green birch leaves on the ground, Bob had stripped off the twigs on his climb. Some of the twigs had been broken and still hung from the branches.

"Yes, *Massa* Bob seems to have been very brave," Shatterhand told him. "When he saw the bear, he climbed the birch here in fear, without thinking that it was too weak to carry him. It bent down, and he fell off, right in front of the beast. He would surely have been lost, had the young sir not fired his shots in time. Isn't it so, mister Baumann?"

Martin had to agree, although he was actually sorry to have to correct the, otherwise, good Negro. The latter tried to justify himself:

"Yes, *Massa* Bob climb birch tree for bear to climb after and not do anything against good *Massa* Martin. *Massa* Bob tried sacrifice himself for young sir."

To his dismay he had to learn that this assurance was not believed either.

Of course, everyone wanted to learn how this dangerous adventure had happened. Martin told them. He did this in simple, plain words, without any embellishment. However, the listeners recognized the kind of cold-bloodedness and courage he had shown. He received general recognition.

"My dear, young friend," Old Shatterhand said, "I will gladly tell you that the most experienced hunter could not have acted more astutely than you. If you continue like this, there will yet be a man of whom much will be talked about."

And the usually silent Winnetou said kindly:

"My little white brother has the resoluteness of an old warrior. He is the worthy son of the famous Bear Hunter. The Chief of the Apache offers his hand."

When Martin clasped hands with Winnetou, he felt a wave of proud self-confidence sweep over him. The recognition by these two famous men was to him worth as much, even more, than if he had received a medal from some ruler.

The little Saxon poked Fat Jemmy gently in the ribs and asked:

"Isn't that a great heroic deed, he?"

"Certainly! I've the greatest respect for the little fellow."

"And do you believe now that he's dispatched already other bears?"

"Sure."

"Yes, he's *merschtentels* a very good boy. Who knows how you'd have behaved yourself in his place. I'd almosht say that you'd have had yourself rather quietly devoured by the bear."

"Well, I wouldn't have remained quite as still as that. I haven't taken this old rifle here along just to shoot sparrows."

"So! But there's the question of whether you'd be able to hit a shparrow with this crummy thing. A bear is a bit easier to aim at. Have you ever killed one?"

"Not just one."

"Listen. Don't tell me any fibs here! It's easy to claim."

"Pah! I once even slept with a bear through an entire night, and noticed only in the morning what kind of a sleeping companion I had nearby."

"That's impossible! One must become aware of something like this! Didn't the creature snore?"

"No. It panted and rattled a bit, but, no, it didn't really snore."

"Hm! You must tell me about it some time."

"Tonight, in camp. Now isn't the time."

The bear was a very welcome bag. Its meat is very tasty. The hams are even better, and the paws are thought to be delicacies. Only the heart and liver, which the Indians think to be poisonous, are thrown away. The most welcome is the bear fat, from which they make an oily liquid. This bear oil is used for applying the various colors with which they paint themselves. The Sioux use the war paints, or the ocher, to color the parting of their hair. They also rub this oil onto their skin to protect themselves against the sting of mosquitoes and other insects.

Martin responded to a questioning hand movement from the Shoshone's chief and told him:

"My brothers may take the bear's meat, but I will keep the hide."

Two minutes later the animal was separated from its coat and the meat was distributed. While the majority of the Shoshone cut the meat into thin, broad strips with their very sharp scalping knives, others occupied themselves with the preliminary preparation of the hide. All remaining bits of meat were carefully removed. Then the bear's head was split with a tomahawk to get to the brain, with which the hide's inside was rubbed.

All this went so quickly that the entire work was completed in less than a quarter of an hour so that the warriors were able to return to camp. The hide was loaded onto one of the Shoshone's horses, and the meat was put into various cooking pots and roasting ovens.

Ovens? Could the Shoshone possibly be carrying ovens? Of course, although theirs weren't exactly made of marble, ceramics, or iron. As it was, everyone put his piece of meat underneath the saddle. Riding then made it so soft and tender, that, by evening, it could be eaten with the greatest delight. A European gourmet would, of course, not find such preparation very appetizing.

The noon rest had been interrupted by the hunting adventure and was not resumed. Instead, they continued their ride.

The path led deeper into the valley, wended its way between several mountains, and finally, entered a broad valley through which the Sioux troop had traveled. It became apparent that, by following the Sioux' signs, the party had avoided a long detour. The Sioux must have been very familiar with the path they had taken. From time to time, when a directional change was necessary, they had left similar signs like the initial one. In any case, they must still have been of the opinion that Wohkadeh would return to them.

In the course of the afternoon, the riders entered an oval valley, several miles long, which was surrounded by steep cliffs. In the valley's midst rose a single, cone-shaped mountain, whose bare flanks shone white in the sunlight. On its top, a low, broad stone structure was visible, a fairly accurate likeness of a turtle.

To a geologist, there was no doubt that a lake had once been here, the shores of which had been formed by the surrounding heights. The tip of the hill, now in the valley's center, had then risen like an island from the waters.

Systematic observations have proven, that a large number of freshwater lakes once covered North America. This was during the Tertiary period. These great water collections have dispersed or evaporated, and the former lakes are now valleys, which have become the gravesites of previously living creatures. The naturalist, particularly the paleontologist, can enrich himself by the undreamt of treasures buried here. One finds there the teeth and jaws of hippopotamus, similar to today's living species, and the remains of hornless rhinoceros and turtles by the thousands. There are the skeletons of ruminant pigs, the hyanodon, and even a mighty type of tiger, armed with saber-like teeth. Today, it is generally said that the horse was introduced to America. However, excavations have shown that many genera of horses, as well as camels, lived in North America in the Tertiary. One of these types of horses was only the size of a Newfoundland dog. At present, there are only about ten species of horses on the entire planet, while in North America alone close to thirty horse genera have been shown to have lived. During these ancient times, elephants grazed by the shores of the North American lakes, and pigs wallowed in the mud, some only of cat-size, others the size of hippopotamus. On today's treeless plains of Wyoming, palm trees provided shade with leaves twelve feet in length. Elephant-size creatures lived below these palms. One kind had horns on both sides of its nose; others, to the side of their eyes, and a third, just a single horn above its nose.

When, by chance, an Indian stumbles on such primeval remains, he turns away silently and respectfully. He cannot explain their existence, and since everything mysterious is 'great medicine' to him, these remains are sacred. Only here and there will he try by means of a myth to make their presence comprehensible.

The horsemen had halted at the opening of the valley. Here, too, the Sioux had left a sign telling Wohkadeh that they had crossed it. However, Old Shatterhand, who was riding in the lead, did not follow this directive but guided his horse to the left to ride along the foot of the mountains.

"Here sticks the twig," Tokvi-tey said, pointing to the tree, in whose trunk a foreign twig had been attached. "This is the Ogallalla' sign. Why is my brother not following it?"

Old Shatterhand halted his horse and replied:

"Because I know of a better way. From this point on, I know the area very well. This mountain here is called *Pejaw-eploeh*, the Mountain of the Turtle. I have passed it three times already, only not from this side."

"Does this mountain have a particular meaning?" Fat Jemmy asked.

"It plays a role in the Crow Indian's myth. It is their Mount Ararat. The members of the Indian community also remember a great flood, the Deluge. The Crow Indians tell that all people drowned, except a single pair. The Great Spirit saved them by sending a giant turtle. The two, with all their belongings, found refuge on the back of the animal and lived there until the flood receded. The mountain we see here, is taller than the ones surrounding it. That's why it rose first as an island from the flood. The turtle crawled onto this island, and the pair of humans climbed off its back. The soul of the animal returned to the Great Spirit, but its body stayed up there and petrified to serve as a reminder of the original pair who today's red men honor. I was told this by Shunka-shetsha, Great Dog, a warrior of the Crow Indians, whom I camped with several years ago at this Mountain of the Turtle."

"Then, you do not want to take the path the Ogallalla rode?"

"No. I know of a shorter one, which will take us much faster to our destination. The Ogallalla are headed for the graves of their dead warriors. Since we know their destination, we need not lose precious time following their trail. There are not many entries to the Yellowstone. The Ogallalla don't seem to know the shortest one. From the direction they have taken, one can assume that they are headed for the great canyon, and from there will cross over to the Yellowstone, arriving at the Firehole Mountains via the Bridge River."

"Then they must cross the Rocky Mountains!"

"Of course. The grave, at which mister Baumann and his companions are to be sacrificed, is not next to the Yellowstone River but, the Firehole River. To reach it, the Ogallalla must ride a very wide arc with at least a forty-mile radius. The terrain they cross will give them so many difficulties that they won't be able to cover any decent day's distance. However, the path I'm taking runs straight towards the Pelican River. When we have forded it, we will ride between it and the Sulfur Hills to the place where the Yellowstone River flows out from the like-named lake. From there, we'll head for the Bridge River near which we will likely find the tracks of the Sioux. Then, we will ride to the upper Geyser Basin alongside the Firehole River. Although this path is also difficult, it doesn't present us with the numerous difficulties our enemies will face. This might make it possible for us to arrive at our destination before them. This would be extremely advantageous."

"If that is so, it would be irresponsible to follow the Ogallalla. Besides, it would be a lark if we arrived before them. It already gives me joy to imagine the shock on their faces. Onward then, sir! From now on, you will be our leader!"

115

The two had spoken in English. When Old Shatterhand now explained the content of the conversation to the Shoshone in their own language, the others also agreed with his intention and followed him gladly in the direction about which their chief had earlier shown such surprise.

A creek, which had dried up long ago, had once entered the old lake basin from the west and cut deeply into the ground. Its bed was very narrow and masked by such dense vegetation that it took a sharp eye to discover it. Old Shatterhand directed his horse to enter the brush. Once it had been penetrated, plant growth no longer caused major difficulties. One could follow the old watercourse without much difficulty until the narrow passage ended at undulating terrain. This consisted of small prairies, separated by wooded hills. Since these hills had a mostly east-west direction, the group of riders was pleased.

Towards evening, they arrived at a creek, which seemed to be part of the Bighorn River. Riding along it, they reached a place, which would make an excellent campsite. The men decided to halt here although darkness had not yet fallen.

Here, the creek broadened to a small, but not very deep pond. Along its banks grew very good grass, and in its clear waters, one could spot numerous trout, giving hope for a delicate evening meal. On one side, the bank rose steeply; on the other, it was level and framed by a very dense tree cover. The many branches littering the ground indicated that the past winter had caused rather heavy snow damage. The maze of broken branches formed a kind of abatis around the campsite, improving its security. And, since the wood was totally dry, there was no concern about having sufficient firewood.

"Trout grabbing!" Fat Jemmy called, while he jumped delightedly off his horse. "There will be a real wedding feast today!"

He would have loved to jump right away into the water, but Old Shatterhand objected.

"Not so fast!" he said. "Everything must be done at the right time and in the right way. Most of all, we must take care that the fish can't escape. Fetch some branches! We must first pound in two gratings."

Once the horses had been taken care of, thin branches were sharpened and pounded closely into the soft bottom of the creek at its exit from the pond, so that no fish could slip through. Then, a similar grating was inserted about twenty paces above the creek's entry to the pond. Now no fish were able to escape the enclosure.

Fat Jemmy began to take off his boots. He had already taken off his belt and put it beside his rifle next to the bank.

"Hey, little one," Long Davy said to him," I believe you plan to enter the water!"

"Of course! It will be great fun."

"Better leave that to people taller than you. Someone who can barely peek over a chair, could easily slip below the surface."

"Wouldn't be a problem. I can swim. Plus, this pond isn't very deep."

He stepped close to the water to check its depth.

"At most four feet deep," he said.

"It's deceptive. If one can look to the bottom, then it appears to be closer than it really is."

"Pah! Come here and look down! One can see every little pebble down there and – by the devil, brrr, puh, puh!"

He had bent over too far, lost his balance, and went headfirst into the pond right at its deepest part. The little, corpulent hunter went under, but surfaced immediately. He was an excellent swimmer and need not have been concerned about his bath. Unfortunately, he was wearing his fur coat, which, of course, had sunk together with him. His broad-brimmed hat floated like the leaf of a *Victoria regia* on the cool waters.

"What fun!" Long Davy laughed. Gentlemen, look at the trout one can catch there! When we catch it, this fat fish will provide many portions."

The little Saxon had stood nearby. He enjoyed 'rubbing' with Jemmy when it came to scientific matters, yet he was also dear to him, since the Fat One was also German.

"Oh, my God!" he called, jumping fearfully closer. "What did you do, mishter Pfefferkorn? Why did you jump into the pond? Might you even have gotten wet?"

"Through and through," Jemmy responded with a laugh.

He was in no danger, the water reaching only to just below his arms.

"Through and through! That can cause the mosht beautiful cold. And even in your fur! Get out right away. I'll take care of the hat. I will fish it out with a branch."

He took a long branch to grope for the head cover.

The branch was a bit too short, which is why the learned forestry official had to reach further.

"Be careful!" Jemmy cautioned, when he came out of the water. "I can get it myself; I'm already wet."

"Don't talk like that!" Frank responded. "If you think, that I'm as silly as you are, I'm shure sorry for you. A reshpectable man like myself knows to watch out. I won't fall into the water. And if the darn hat is floating farther away, I'll reach a little bit farther out and – oh, hells bells, now I'm in a pickle after all! No, this can't be happening!"

He had fallen in too. It looked so funny that all the Whites laughed. The Indians, however, maintained serious faces, although they too were surely amused by the funny event.

117

"Now, who isn't just as stupid as I?" Jemmy asked, tears of laughter streaming down his face.

Frank, standing in the water, made a very angry face.

"What's there to laugh about!" he shouted. "I'm shtanding here, a victim of my own kindness and Samaritan charity, and am even laughed about for my mercy. I'll remember that negstht time. You undershtand?"

"I'm not laughing at all; I'm crying! Don't you see that? If a respectable man like you loses his balance, then ..."

"Be quiet! I won't be teased! That I'm even wearing my tailcoat at it, is really just too much for me. And, over there, my Amazon hat is shwimming very brotherly next to yours. Castor and Phylax, it is called in mythology and also ashtronomy. It's right ..."

"It's called Castor and Pollux!" Jemmy corrected.

"Oh, be quiet! Pollux! As a foreshtry official, I've had so much to do with hunting dogs, that I know exactly, whether it's Pollux or Phylax. I won't suffer such corrections. They don't resht well with me. Nevertheless, I'll fish for the noble pair of brothers. Actually, I should leave yours floating. You don't deserve that I get myself even wetter for your hat."

He went for the two hats and brought them out.

"So," he said, "saved they are without me claiming a medal. Let's wring out your fur and, afterwards, my tailcoat. The two will cry bitter tears; they are dripping already!"

The two accident victims were now so busy with their coats that, to their regret, they could not participate in the beginning of the fish catch.

This went very rapidly. A sufficient number of Shoshone stepped into the lower end of the pond and formed a tight group across it. Slowly advancing, they drove the fish upwards into the accessible part of the creek. Other redskins had placed themselves on each side, ready to grab the advancing fish, which were caught between the upstream grating and the advancing Shoshone. The Indians literally scooped up the crowded fish, throwing them back over their heads onto dry land. In a few minutes, the fishing was finished and had produced such a yield that everyone would get his fill.

Now shallow pits were dug and laid out with rocks. The gutted fish were placed onto these rocks and were then covered with another rock layer on which a fire was lit. After some time the ashes were removed. The trout had been steamed in their own juices between the hot rocks, so the flesh literally fell off their bones.

However, these fish were not as delicious as if they'd been served in one of our restaurants or from the table of one of our gourmets. Butter was missing, also, salt. Indians almost never, or very rarely, enjoy salt. Unfortunately, the frontiersman must also do without. It is impossible for him to provision himself with a sufficient supply for his months-long wanderings, and the little he does take along is soon spoiled by the moisture it attracts.

After the meal, the horses were gathered even closer, and guards were posted. The Shoshone thought these measures unnecessary, it being so remote that the presence of a hostile human was unlikely. But Winnetou and Old Shatterhand were of the hard-won experience that one never, at no time or any place, ought to dispense with the necessary caution. Thus, four Shoshone were posted to the four sides of the camp for subsequent relief and replacement.

Of course, the guards were not to remain near the fire, and thereby visible to a potentially encroaching enemy.

The men chose to group themselves around several fires. Of course, the Whites gathered around one. Old Shatterhand, Fat Jemmy and little Frank were German. Long Davy had learned enough German from his corpulent buddy so that he could understand it, although he was unable to speak it. And, since Martin Baumann's father was of German descent, his young son was fluent enough in the language, so that they could all use it by the camp fire. Whether in the forest wilds or on the prairie, such conversations have their own peculiar charms. The experiences of those present are recounted, and the deeds of famous hunters are discussed. As great as the hardships and troubles of the West are, one does not believe how quickly the news of a daring deed, the action of a famous person, or an outstanding event travels from camp fire to camp fire. If the Blackfoot, up at the Marias River have taken up the war tomahawk, then, two weeks later, the Comanche will talk about it at the Rio Grande. And, if among the Wallawalla Indians in the Washington territory a great medicine man appears, then the Dakota of the Coteau du Missouri will speak of him in short order.

As might be expected, the men's talk first began with the day's heroic action by Martin Baumann. This reminded the little Saxon of Jemmy's promise.

"Now, what was it actually about your shleeping with a bear some time ago?" he asked. "How did it happen and where?"

"Do you think I slept in a hotel bed with it?" the Fat One laughed.

"Are you shtarting it again? I've told you already that I'm not the man who'll be teased unpunished. If you think me to be a fool for having rescued your hat by soaking my only tailcoat, I'll send you my Sekundaner (second Gymnasium class)!"

"Do you mean to say 'Sekundant' (witness & assistant in a duel)?"

"Wouldn't think of it! I shpeak my fine colloquial language following the correct shtrategic syshtem, and you can shpeak your gibberish, as you like. The essential point is you dispose of it to someone, who put up with it with superhuman patience. As it is, there may not be too much about your so-called bear shtory. Maybe, it didn't happen in true reality."

"Oh, yes! I can swear by it."

"Well then. Where?"

"At a source creek of the Platte River."

"What? By chance in the middle of the river?"

"Yes."

"There you shlept an entire night with a bear?"

"Sure!"

"Well, if that had truly happened, then both of you, that is, you and the bear, would be the greatest hoax you are trying to put on us, for you'd have drifted next morning as drowned corpses to one of the banks."

120

"Oh, you mean I slept in the water?"

"Of course!"

"No. I'm not that incautious. I had my night's camp set up on a small island."

"Ah, so! On an island. That I can accept a bit better. It gives the shtory a somewhat greater probability. By the way, there is usually little water to be found in the Platte."

"Except in the spring when the snow melts in the mountains after a warm rain. Then, the river, whose waters reach barely to one's knees, will fill its high banks within an hour. It is highly dangerous to trust oneself to this raging, dirty-yellow flood. The river then resembles a wild animal, suddenly awakened, calling for victims."

"That's undershtandable. One thinks immediately of the beautiful poet's words:

"It's dangerous to wake the glue;
and fatal is the tiger's tooth.
And getting shtuck in mud too deep,
there'll be no help from gondola nor ship."

"That musht also have been the case then with you and the bear."

"Yes, only that it isn't 'glue' but 'Leu' (Latin for 'lion'), my good Frank."

"Don't you come at me again with such a groundless explanation. You find yourself there in the greatesht contradiction with the coriphers of poetry and musical general base. Don't enter into the higher elevations where you are unfamiliar, and rather tell us in simple and modesht terms the promised shtory."

The others all laughed, which is why the little scholar, turning to Old Shatterhand, continued:

"That's right! Really laugh at this fellow! Once he realizes that he made a fool of himself, he will finally quit playing the Dongki-Scot."

"It's Don Quixote," Jemmy threw in.

Now Frank really became angry. He got up and said:

"Again! That's getting just too much for me. Someone, who in Moritzburg, frequented the library as much as myself, paying three pfennigs for a volume, has also read the Dongki-Scot. And, if I musht have my literary education again and again trampled on, I'll just get up and sit with the Indians. They'll appreciate it more if a man of my qualifications will sit with them. If my efforts to educate Fat Jemmy are for nothing, I'll claim innocence and take the weight entrushted to me someplace else. The noble shwan need not shwim with geese and ducks. His feelings of propriety object to such a social-democratic social level. Good bye, gentlemen!"

121

He intended to leave but, at Old Shatterhand's urgent request, let himself be moved to sit down again.

"Well then," he said. For your sake, I'll manage my justified anger silently and anonymously. As a fellow-countryman, you have a social right towards my person, and I don't want to shtunt it. Otherwise, you might even think that I've enjoyed a poor parental childhood education. But, I'm really curious about your bear shtory; and once Fatty has told it, I'll also, in the form of Friedrich Gerschtaeker, tell about in what way I met a bear firsht time."

"What? Jemmy asked delighted, "you, too, have had a bear adventure?"

"Me, too? Are you surprised, by chance? I tell you, that I've likely exsperienced and gone through more than your mind can comprehend. But now, shtart finally! So, it was at the Platte River?"

"No, actually at the Medicine Bow River, which empties into the Platte. It was in April, with me coming from North Park, where I'd had a bad hunt. In March, I had come up from Fort Larania and was now coming down the other side to look for beaver at the source of the Platte River. It wasn't very cold, and what little water there was not frozen. Despite several days search, I found no trace of 'fat tails'. My horse had to carry me and the heavy traps for nothing, and that on short rations. On that same day, a light breeze had risen, a condition I, old blockhead that I am, should actually have noticed. Towards evening I noticed a small island in the riverbed which, of course, was now no island, but more or less a dry rise higher than the river's banks. It consisted of a rock at whose downstream face a long, pointed sandbank had accumulated. While I looked at the island, I noticed a hut on it built of stones and sod, likely to have been erected by trappers who had camped there for some time. It looked like a good place for the night. I rode through only two feet of water to reach the island. There, I saw the tracks of a bear in the sand of the bank, which I planned to follow the next morning. From the side I came from, the island was easily accessible. I rode up, dismounted, freed the horse from the traps and the saddle and left it to look for fodder. I knew the animal very well and knew that it wouldn't run off."

"And in the hut? Was someone in there?" Frank asked.

"Yes," Jemmy nodded, smiling suspiciously.

"Who, who?"

When I entered, there sat – imagine my surprise – the Chinese emperor, eating pumpkin porridge with marinated herring!"

Everyone laughed, but Hobble Frank called angrily:

"Are you again after me?"

"No," Jemmy replied earnestly.

"Then leave your emperor in Poking, where he belongs!"

"Peking, you meant to say. To be honest, I must admit, that the hut was empty; that is empty of utensils and people. Upon closer inspection, I noticed signs from which I concluded the presence of snakes. There were all kinds of holes in the floor and the sod. Although I'm not much afraid of rattlesnakes, since they are by far not as dangerous as is thought and written about, for they flee man. Also it was still the season for hibernation. However, it wasn't at all cold that day, and the warmth of the fire could easily draw one, or several, of these animals from their holes. Since such company is by no means a pleasant one, I decided to remain outside the hut. There was plenty of driftwood for a good fire, and after I had put on a sufficient quantity, I wrapped myself in my blanket and said 'good night, Jemmy'."

"Ah, now it's coming!" said Frank, rubbing his hands expectantly.

"Yes, it will come soon, that is, the water. I didn't fall asleep right away. The wind freshened and blew oddly hollow, blowing my fire apart. I couldn't do anything about it and made no effort to maintain it. It soon died, and I finally fell asleep. I don't know how long I had slept when I was awakened by a peculiar noise. The wind had turned to a storm, whistling and groaning in various tones. And when it stopped for a second, I heard a dull rushing, roaring, and gurgling, which wasn't in the air, but around my island. I became concerned, jumped up and went to the edge of the island. It was totally surrounded by water, from which it barely rose three feet. The river's water had suddenly risen. The sky was cloudless, and by the stars' light I saw the flood passing at enormous speed. I was encircled."

"A real Crusoe!" Frank said.

"Crusoe?" Jemmy asked surprised. "Who's that?"

"You don't know that? Shame on you! Crusoe was the famous fellow, who got shtranded on a island and had to invent everything for himself. Then, a few natives joined him, and he named them Monday, Tuesday, Wednesday and Friday. Didn't you read this beautiful book?"

"Yes, of course, I read it," Jemmy replied amidst general hilarity. "Now I understand who you mean, Robinson."

"Robinson? Hm, yes, he was also with them."

"Of course he was with them, he being the main character."

"Main character? Listen, you are again mishtaken. The main character was Crusoe."

"Well, I don't want to quarrel. Strictly speaking, Crusoe is the main character in this novel, for he wrote it."

"Yes, and if he hadn't been on the island, he couldn't have written it."

"All right, but I haven't read anything of a Monday, Tuesday and Wednesday."

"That's again because of your epidemic flightiness with which you do everything. It looksh to me like you leafed over the besht pages of the book. Crusoe wouldn't have left out the first three days of the week. Such a chronological waste of time wouldn't be a credit to the good man. With such a triple weekday miss, he wouldn't have found a publisher for the book. But continue. How did you go on playing the Crusoe back then?"

By surrendering myself to the situation, since I couldn't do anything to change it, I had nothing to fear, because the island was higher than the riverbanks, I couldn't be flooded. Only at daybreak would it be possible to survey the situation. Until then I had to be patient. Of course, thinking of my horse caused me to worry. If it had been surprised by the water, it would be dead, which might also be my demise. You all know what the loss of the horse can mean to a frontiersman. Hoping that the animal's instinct had saved it, I returned to my camp. In the process, I thought I saw a shadow, which had disappeared inside the hut upon my approach. However, I did not pay any attention and lay down again."

"Finally the bear hash arrived! He musht merschtentels also have been surprised by the water. If only he'll keep quiet! It's besht if he shtays put in the hut. If he gets the idea to promenade, it could easily come to an ugly battle like the one at Leipzig."

"Fortunately, it kept quiet. Of course, I was unable to sleep now. I lay still, and when the wind paused to catch its breath, I thought I heard snorting. Did it come from the hut? Had I seen right earlier? What kind of animal was it? I thought it best to remove myself as far as possible. So I took my rifle in one hand, the blanket in the other, and crept quietly to the other end of the isle, where I bedded down so that I could keep an eye on the hut. You can imagine that the time until daybreak was like an eternity to me. Finally, light broke in the east. First I could clearly see the island, then the river's surface, then the river banks. I noticed two things, one very pleasant, namely my horse grazing across on the bank from which I had crossed to the island and something less pleasant – a bear was lying in the hut, its butt in the entry, with his head inside, so that he could not see me. It was fortunate that I was at the other end of the island when it came out of the river! Had he surprised me in my camp, I might now not be sitting here to tell our Hobble-Frank of this adventure."

"Yes," Hobble answered, "at mosht your departed ghosht would shpook over the prairie, as punishment for your failure at the Gymnasium. How did you behave now towards the bear?"

"Very kindly. I first looked at my rifle and saw that it was properly loaded. Then, I introduced myself politely. I walked silently up to the hut and shouted a 'huzza' at him. The fellow was truly asleep and must've been very tired. Who knows how much he had to fight the waters when he was taken away by them. When he heard my voice, he turned towards me. Seeing me, he rose inside the hut on his hind legs and received two bullets from me. It was no heroic deed to kill the animal. Bob could have even done it."

The Negro had been sitting with the group. He had heard enough German from his master that, even if he did not understand the individual words, he could follow their meaning.

Oh, oh," he said. "*Massa* Bob be very good frontiersman! *Massa* Bob be brave. He not afraid of bear. When *Massa* Bob see beast again, he catch right away with hands!"

"Fine!" Jemmy nodded. "Then the first animal you see, you will catch by hand."

"Yes, yes, *Massa*."

"Also if it's a bear?"

"Right then if be bear, *Massa* Bob turn his head backwards."

He stretched out his arms, spread the fingers, rolled his eyes, and showed his teeth to demonstrate how he would throw himself onto the animal. It looked as if he would devour it with skin and all.

"Maybe it will be a real opossum which he would like most," Old Shatterhand remarked. "But tell us now, master Jemmy, how you got over to the other bank?"

"By the simplest means: I walked over there. As is well known, such floods run off as quickly as they come. It was getting colder, and the water subsided by afternoon. I only had to spend one other night on the island. Then, by next morning, the water reached only up to my hips. I waded through, got my horse and loaded it with the traps as well as the paws and the hide of the bear. This was, of course, a load, which forced me to walk beside my animal. But it wasn't for long. Just short of the confluence of the Medicine Bow with the Platte River, I came across such a large beaver colony, that I had to stay for some time. There, I made a good number of furs, which I cached temporarily together with the traps. Then, I was able to continue without my load. – This was my adventure, and if Master Frank feels like it, he can tell his. I hope he escaped as luckily as I did."

"That's self-evident!" was the Saxon's reply. "And I was victorious all by myself, without anyone's help. No one was around, not even a dog like the one who once attacked the bear, who devoured our good Martin's poor Luddy. One should actually always have a dog around who will take the firsht attack if one comes close to a bear. But, unfortunately, no such bear baiters are being raised. I've seen such a fellow in Moritzburg, which the foresht ranger had obtained from Siebenbürgen, where there are many bears. The dog was almosht as big as a bear. But since there were no bears in Moritzburg, it was impossible to let him loose onto one. I've heard that these bear baiters won't attack any other game, but that they shmell bears to a mosht surprising degree. They are supposed to be infallible even with old tracks and after a rain."

"Pah! I doubt that!" Long Davy said.

125

"What? Are you calling me a liar? That can cause you to come eashily in conflict with me, getting your hair to shtand on end. I won't shtand for it!"

"Even an old, rain-washed track? Hm!"

Davy shook his head. His corpulent friend threw him a look and said:

"By quiet, Davy, you are wrong. These Siebenbürger bear baiters do have a nose whose performance is unbelievable. When I was still a student, I got to know such a dog and can give you an example, which would immediately cure your disbelief."

"Really?" Frank asked delightedly. "I'm very pleased that you include me in your protection. From it, I see that you are after all and secretly my good friend. That's why everything is to be forgiven if you do me the pleasure to tell of this exshample."

"Gladly, dear Frank. I was visiting with a friend, whose father owned a manor and a respectable hunting estate. The owner had received a Siebenbürger bear baiter as a gift, but could not put him to a test since there were no bears. The dog quickly became used to me and accompanied me on all my hikes. One beautiful day, I walked through the village with him. That's when he halted in front of a peasant's house and barked. I had no explanation for this, and since I couldn't get him away from the door, I opened it. Right away he leaped inside to another door and again barked. I also opened that one and he jumped in, me following. Who do you think, dear Frank, was in the room?"

"A bear, of course."

"There were none!"

"Then it may have been one which eshcaped a traveling bear show."

"Neither."

"Well, who was it then?"

"Only the old grandmother sitting on a sofa darning socks. Of course, she was scared silly by the dog leaping in ..."

"By the devil! He didn't bite her? Or did he also go on to darn socks?"

"Neither one. He didn't even pay attention to the woman, but jumped onto a table standing in the corner."

"Onto a table? Such a big dog! What did he want there?"

"I asked myself the same. After I had politely apologized to the woman, I stepped to the table and, guess what the dog had been looking for up there?"

"Some kind of critter, of course."

"Yes, but also no."

"What then?"

"A bear."

"What the heck! You earlier said exshactly the opposite from your current assertion."

"I'm right both ways. There was a book lying on the table, which the dog had his paw on. He was leafing with his tongue through page after page until he had found the respective one. Then, he began to growl and howl and kind of bit around, as if he had a carnivore ahead of him. It was absolutely remarkable."

"But I don't undershtand this. A bear baiter on the table with a book! That's a total terra in cognaco for me."

"Incognito, it is!"

"No, it's Cognac! That makes the besht grog (hot toddy). And should you not yet know this beverage, then you haven't lived worth a darn. On then! What kind of book was it?"

"Of course, I looked at it. It was an old children's book from about fifty, sixty years ago, with little pictures, below which were respective verses. And, amazingly, the dog had opened the page on which a beehive and a bear were pictured. Below it was the rhyme:

"So very fierce is the wild bear,
when he comes upon a honey tree."

"I was totally surprised. Out on the street, the dog had smelled the picture of an animal he had been trained on, pictured in a book that lay on the table, and had found it his duty to draw my attention to it. Of course, I told his master of the event after I returned to the manor, and he was very proud to own a dog like this. Therefore, gentlemen, you see that Hobble-Frank was quite right, when he earlier insisted that these bear baiters perform almost unbelievable feats. Of course, the story spread quickly. It was published in several hunting magazines, and a famous dog fancier purchased the respective children's book for fifty taler. Afterwards, it went from hand to hand for an ever-higher price, until it finally passed into the possession of the Parisian Academy of Arts and Sciences for thirty thousand francs. And since our Frank, due to his extreme learnedness, will surely be invited to join this Academy as a member, he'll have the best opportunity to leaf through this famous little book, to look up the 'bear' (bear = hoax in German) this dog once pulled on me. I was finally able to pass it along. Thank you, master Frank! You took it from me."

He made an ironic bow towards the little Saxon. Everyone around broke out in uproarious laughter. At first, the former forestry official made a totally perplexed face, but when he realized that Jemmy had invented the story only to tease him, he opened up:

"What! You think I now got your 'bear'? Don't you permit this shtupid thought to settle in your obshcure comprehension! Before you are able to tie a single 'bear' on me, I've put already fifty over on me. With reshpect to the active-passive telling of lies, I'm far superior to you. You are a real Muenchmeier [3], and if ..."

"Münchhausen [4] it is," Jemmy interrupted.

"Be quiet on the shpot, you fat tree frog. A 'Muench' who 'meiers' others can only be called a Muenchmeier. If this king of liars has for some time been called at times Münchhausen, thus it is due to a mishunderstanding based on a noumenal conceptual confushion between his birthplace and his home. Because, of his inoculation certificate, which is shtill on hand, he was born at the time of August the Strong in the little town of Mühlhausen, dishtrict Sondershausen, county Schaffhausen, three places ending with 'hausen', because mosht of hausen-bladder is shipped from there. With so many 'hausen' it is no surprise that this suffix has been added by mishtake to the 'Muench'. But someone like me ishn't easily deceived. My world hishtory shtudies enable me to separate such chaff from good grain, which is why I realized with my pleasantly penetrating looks, before you even shtarted with your shtory, that it was intended as a grand lie and 'Muenchmeierei'. But I let you go ahead, because I've always been a zealous admirer of parliamentary tact. I wrapped myself magnanimously into my superiority and from above observed how you lied at me from below. But now, I finally give my forbearance the finishing shtroke and demand from you in all seriousness the following: In the future give to the emperor what is the emperor's, and to Frank what belongs to him, that is the acknowledgment of his rank of dignity and the humble consideration of his personality. Only in this way is a future togetherness between the two of us possible, and I demand now of you, on the shpot, in front of these grown witnesses, the public and documented declaration whether you'll treat me with reshpect from now on or not. I owe this to my elapsed pasht and my shtill to be exshpected future. So, how is it, and how will it be? Reshpect or not?"

At first there was deep silence in the circle. The peculiar speech of the little man made the listeners want to laugh all the more since it had been presented in such total seriousness. All eyes lit up in delight; the lungs breathed in deeply and let go. Then, everyone clenched their teeth to overcome the almost insurmountable enticement to laugh. Old Shatterhand was the first to gain some control of himself.

Deeply serious, he began:

"But dear Frank, the jest has been a rather harmless one and wasn't directed against you alone. We others have also been listeners just like you and haven't

---

[3] This might be a cute jab of Karl May's on his former publisher, he had a falling out with

[4] Münchhausen was a soldier who, after his retirement from the Russian Army, lived with his wife at his manor in Bodenwerder until her death in 1790. Here, he acquired a reputation for his witty and exaggerated tales; at the same time, he was considered an honest man in business affairs.

felt insulted. Rather, take the story for what it was, an anecdote, meant to be fun. Your well known feeling for justice ought to tell you that you innocently deprived us of this pleasure."

The urgent note in which these words were spoken did not miss their effect. Frank had a soft heart, and he felt sorry at possibly having gone too far. He replied:

"If you preshent this matter in this way then, the subject takes another turn, of course. In no way was it my intention to dishturb your pleashure. But you must admit that I'm also entitled to my anthropological human rights."

"Right on. And we're happy to concede these rights to you."

"So? Then why's the Fat One ribbing me all the time?"

"You might want to ponder whether you aren't giving him cause. Don't you try to act superior to him all the time?"

"Hm! Then you admit that I'm truly *merschtentels* superior to him?"

"If I am to take your view as being correct, then I must concede it."

"Good! That's entirely enough for me. Then I'll withdraw my demand for a public apology in total judiciousness. No one is to say that I'm a dishturber of general international peace. Here's my hand, Fat One! Take it! We'll walk the paths of our lives in shweet concord. I call to you with Schiller's words: *Soyongs, Anis, Emma!*"

Unfortunately these words caused a long and uproarious laughter. The little one looked around in surprise.

"What's the matter now again?" he asked.

"A mistake you made, or rather several," Jemmy replied.

"So? Which then?"

"These words aren't from Schiller, but from the French poet Corneille and are: *Soyons amis, Cinna!* There's therefore neither talk of *Anis*, nor of *Emma*."

"Ah? You really think so? I offer you my hand for the great reconciliation feshtivities, and you thank me by correcting me again. That will bursht even the besht water pipe. If my peaceableness is rejected in such a solemn way, then we may as well shtay with our enmity and I shall ..."

"Oh, please!" Old Shatterhand entered mediatingly. "This time you truly erred, my dear Frank. I must agree with master Jemmy, and I hope you credit me with just and impartial judgment!"

"Yes, if you say so, I'll yield to superiority. You are an authentic celebrity before which I'm please to bow. Even a count and king can err, and I don't want to think me totally infallible. Then, once more, the hand, Jemmy. Et in terra pax; peace be on the whole earth! Is it correct like that?"

"Yes, totally!" the Fat One answered while shaking his hand.

"Good! That's enough for me. You acshept my worth after which everything is forgiven and forgotten."

"But only under one condition!"

"What, you're asking for a condition! What kind?"

"That you will finally tell us your bear adventure."

"I'm happy to. I promised it, and are obligated. And I won't have myself prompted for such an obligation. It damages the credit and also the reputation. If you're ready to listen, I can shtart right now. Because the affair didn't play out totally dry, almost like today, when we two, that is Jemmy and I, had to dry our clothes by the fire, he the fur and I the tailcoat, not to shpeak of the Amazon hat. My story happened as follows:"

He twirled the feather of his hat between his fingers, cleared his throat promisingly and began:

"At the time, I hadn't been yet an eternity in the United Shtates, meaning, I was shtill rather inexperienced in local affairs. With that I don't mean to say that I was uneducated, just the opposite. I had brought along a goodly portion of physical and mental advantages. Nevertheless, everything musht be learned, and what one hashn't yet seen and engaged with, one also cannot know. Every reasonable person will agree with me in that. A banker, for example, and were he ever so intelligent, cannot play the oboe on the shpot, and a learned professor of experimental ashtronomy cannot, without the necessary instructions in the required tricks, become readily a switchman. This I want to say ahead as my excuse and defense.

The shtory happened down near the Arkansas in Colorado. I had done a few things in different towns before that and had saved a small sum. With it I intended to shtart trading in the West, what's called a peddler in this country here. And why not? There's a good profit in this business, and by that time, I could make myself quite well undershtood already, since I learned English very well. It just easily flew into me."

"Yes," Jemmy nodded earnestly, "with your great talent, it is no wonder that you become quickly fluent in a foreign language."

"Isn't it so! There's no need to bother much with subshtantives and adjectives, because they shtick all by themselves in the memory. I also learned counting quickly. What's left then? A few adverbs, with which one also need not trouble, and with that one is done. I've never undershtood why the boys at school had to suffer that long with foreign languages. I believe the whole issue is shtarted the wrong way. Whether I say 'Kaese' in German, or 'fromage' in French, or 'cheese' in English, doesn't really matter at all. In foreign languages everything is 'cheese' to me anyway.

I began my travels with a nice shtore of trade goods and did such good business that, when I had arrived in the vicinity of Fort Lyon, I was rid of everything. Even my little cart I had sold at a profit. Now, I sat on horseback, rifle in hand, and my pocket full of money, and decided, just for pleashure, to ride farther into the country. Already then, I had a great desire to become a famous frontiershman."

"Which you've become!" Jemmy remarked.

"Well, not quite yet. But I think, when we now hit the Sioux, I'll not remain shtanding behind the front lines like Hannibal at Waterloo, which might make it possible to have a famous name beshtowed on me. But let's go on! At the time, Colorado had just recently become better known. Rich gold fields had been discovered, and now plenty of proshpectors and gold diggers were arriving from the East. True settlers were few. For this reason, I was somewhat surprised when, on my ride, I suddenly saw a real farm ahead of me. It consishted of a shmall log house, several fields and rather large pashtures. The settlement lay at the banks of the Purgatory, and, for this reason, there was foresht nearby. There were many maples, in particular, and I was surprised to see pipes shticking from the base of the tree trunks, from which sap dripped into the vessels placed below. It was early in the year, the besht time for preparing maple syrup. Near the log house shtood long, broad, but very shallow, wooden tubs, filled with the sap which was to evaporate. I musht remark about this detail, in particular, since it played a peculiar role in my adventure."

"The settlement surely didn't belong to a Yankee," Old Shatterhand said.

"Why do you think so?"

"Because such a fellow would have gone to the gold fields instead of quietly staying put as a squatter."

"Quite right! The man was from Norway and received me very hoshpitably. His family consishted of his wife, two sons, and a daughter, and I was invited to remain as long as possible. This I was very pleased to do, and I helped with the work to which my inherited intelligence became exceptionally useful to the good people."

"You must have helped with the butter barrel?" Jemmy joked.

"Of course! I even designed a new one, which needed no pounding, but revolved, like I'd seen it out easht, meaning, I drew it with chalk on the table; building it they could do themselves. With such favors and my intelligent superiority, I gained these peoples' trust to the exshtent that they even left me all by myself on the farm. There was a so-called house-raising frolic to take place at a neighbor's at which the entire family wanted to partishipate. This is why my presence came in very handy, me, as householder shtaying home, watching for the shtatishtical security of the farm. They rode off, and I was man alone. Out there, everybody who could be reached on horseback within half a day was called a neighbor. That's just as far as the reshpective farm was located from us. That's why the return of my hoshts could not be exshpected before a couple of days."

"That was quite a lot of trust extended you," Jemmy said.

"How so? Do you mean I could have had the thought to take off with the farm? Do I look like a dishhonest rascal?"

"There's no talk about that. If a statue were to be erected honoring honesty, you could sit as a model. That's how trust-inspiring is your appearance."

"That I would have demanded!"

"I meant it differently. This area was then, is even still today, traveled by all kinds of rabble. What could you, a single man, have done if such people would have chanced to come by to use the owner's absence for some acts of violence?"

"What would I have done? Don't take it the wrong way, but this is a very peculiar and silly question. I'd have made use of my right of residence and thrown them all out."

"You think it would have been that easy? Such people don't mind using a bullet."

"Me neither! Once you get to know me a bit closer, you'll find, that one cannot entrust just one farm to me, but even three or four. I would know how to defend them. I'm exshtremely knowledgeable in all kinds of war shtrategies and of the various arts of the higher fighting tactics. I've even once read the 'Froschmäuler War' and know, therefore, how to begin a battle and then to win it. I'm in the beginning like Moltke, in the attack like Zieten, and in the purshuit a true weasel. This is why I need not be afraid of any enemy, excshept if he attacks me in my sleep, without first duly announcing it."

"It's usually the case that one isn't told before."

"Unfortunately, that's the truth, and that the bear came also without prior notice, is how the adventure came to be, I was going to tell about. I musht mention here, that on the side of the house shtood a tall hickory tree. Up to its firsht branches it had been robbed of all its bark. The Norwegian had used it for its yellow color, he had told me. That's why the trunk was very smooth and it took quite some skill to climb it."

"No one would have asked for that," Davy remarked.

"No, no one did ask but unexshpected events may take place when even the mosht noble person is driven up such a tree. In a few minutes you will confirm this natural law. To come to shpeak about the main point: I was all by myself on the farm and was wondering with what occupation I could shweeten my long hours of solitude. Of course, I arrived at the solution, it being the mosht urgent – the treatment of the loam. In the log house, the loam floor had become defective, and the filling between the logs had become brittle and had broken out in places. This had to be taken care of, which is why the Norwegian had set up a loam pit right nexsht to the corner of the building. It was about four yards long and three yards wide. I couldn't see its depth, since it was filled to the rim. A few poles were shtuck in with which the shtuff was to be shtirred and kneaded. How delighted my hosht would be, if he'd find the walls taken care of, although not the floor! I thought of that with pleashure and decided to begin the task."

"Did you know what to do? Jemmy asked.

"I beg you, don't you come again and again across my path with such superfluous questions! It truly takes no skill to shtuff a hole or a joint with loam!

There are more difficult areas in the sciences. That's when I began shtirring with one of the poles.

The subshtance appeared too thick to me, which is why I added water, but it was too much, for now it was too thin. But I thought that by kneading it, it would take on a more plashtic compression, which is why I worked for more than an hour with all my shtrength. After a while, the loam achieved that consequence by which every adminishtrative and surveyor's desire could be satisfied. And before I could begin with my beautification work, I only had to carve myself a wooden trowel. For that reason, I wanted to enter the house since dry wood lay nexsht to the fireplace. Quite enthusiastic about my intent, I turned the corner and – faced the who or what?"

"A bear, of course." Jemmy answered.

"Yes, I shtood in front of a bear, who musht've left his asylum up in the Raton Mountains to acquaint himself with country and people like myself. This facing each other wasn't quite to my liking. The fellow made also such a sushpect face that, with a leap I'm likely never to repeat, I jumped sideways. But he just as quickly went for me. It gave my limbs a never-thought-of-flexshibility, and tearing away seemed to be pure joy. I shprang like an Indian king tiger towards the hickory, grabbed it, and shot up the trunk like a rocket. One doesn't believe what a person can accomplish in such an unsympathetic situation."

"In any case, you must have been a good climber?" asked Old Shatterhand.

"Less so, much less. One ought to assume, that I, a foreshter, had had to learn climbing, but unfortunately my natural conshtitution always revolted against this art. If I musht climb, up a ladder, for inshtance, I become totally swirly-whirly between the ears. I just can't do it. But if a bear is after me, one doeshn't ask for long whether climbing is conducive to health. One just climbs, and that with true passion, just like I did. Unfortunately, the trunk was too smooth. I didn't quite make it up to the branches, and there were also some difficulties with holding on to the trunk."

"Oh my! That could get dangerous. You had no weapon. What did the bear do then?"

"Something he could have omitted in good conshcience – he climbed after me."

"Ah, then, fortunately, it wasn't a grizzly!"

"That didn't touch me at all, because at the time a bear was a bear for me. I convulsively held on and looked down. Right on, the fellow had risen down there on the trunk, embraced it, and climbed slowly and happily after me. The task seemed to please him enormously. He was growling happily along, somewhat like a cat, only shtronger, or like the E-shtring of the viola bass, when it's pulled pizzicato with the fingers. But with me it washn't only the head that was shaking, but the entire body from the exertion of holding on. The bear came ever closer. I couldn't possibly remain at my present location. I had to get farther up. But

133

barely had I let go one hand to reach higher, when I losht my hold. Although I quickly held on again, the attraction of mother earth would not let go of its victim. I was just able to permit myself a brief, fearful sigh, then I shot vehemently down the trunk like a two hundred weight shteel hammer, and onto the bear that he too went down with me. He hit the ground, and I landed on top of him."

The little man spoke so lively and expressively that he had all ears of his listeners and, the way he described his accident, had everyone roaring with laughter.

"Yeah, you just laugh!" he grumbled. "I didn't feel at all like laughing. I had the feeling as if all parts of my body had been disassembled. It was as if I were deaf and mute so that, for a few seconds, I didn't even think of getting up."

"What about the bear?" Jemmy asked.

"I don't know what financial speculations he contemplated in his mind at that moment. I had neither the necessary time nor the proper devotion to enter into a dialog like Mentor with Telemach. Maybe, he was just as much out of it like myself, because he lay just as quietly underneath me, like I sat shpeechlessly on top of him. But then, he suddenly gathered himself up, which gave me insight towards my personal obligations. I jumped up and ran away. He followed right after me, whether it was from fear or because of his hot desire to continue the once shtarted acquaintanceship with me. I just don't know. I actually wanted to get to the door and into the house, but for that, time was too short and the bear too close. Fear gave me the shpeed of a shwallow. It was as if it had doubled, even quadrupled, the length of my legs. I shot forward like a rifle bullet, around the corner of the house and into the loam pit, right down to below my arm pits. I had forgotten everything, heaven and earth, Europe and America, all my knowledge and all the loam. I was shtuck in it like a cockroach in the baker's dough, and then there was a mighty 'shlap', as the American says, I got a push like from a train buffer and the loam exshploded over my head. My face, too, was totally covered by it, only my right eye had remained open. I turned and shquinted at the bear, who, because of his reckless temperament had forgotten to inshpect the terrain, as it was called for, and had leaped after me. Only his head was visible, but it also looked horrible. If my two facial profiles were just as loamy as his, then, of course, neither one could call for the reshpect of the other. For three seconds we looked at each other endearingly, then he turned left and I turned right, each in the praiseworthy intention to get to a more pleashant environment. Of course, he was fashter in climbing out. I was worried already that, once he eshcaped from the pit, he would shtay put to lay siege to me, but he had barely caught firm footing, when he hurtled off in the direction from where we both had come, and turned the corner without deigning to give me a single look. Farewell, big muddy beasht!"

In the eagerness of telling his story, Hobble-Frank had gotten up and had accompanied his report with respective gestures, causing his listeners to laugh like this lonely area had never heard before. If one of the listeners stopped laughing temporarily, he soon began once more. It was just too funny.

"This is truly a most funny adventure," Old Shatterhand finally remarked, "and the best of it is that it ended so harmlessly for you and, fortunately also, for the bear!"

"For him, too?" answered Frank. "Oho! I'm not yet finished. When the bear had dishappeared around the corner, I heard a noise as if a piece of furniture had been toppled. I didn't pay attention to it but was only intent on getting out of the pit. It took me quite some effort since the loam was mighty vishcous. I gained my freedom only by leaving it in possession of my boots. Then, first of all, I had to clean my face. Therefore, I went behind the house where a small creek ran past, to which I entrusted everything superfluous that could be removed from my exshternal individuality. Then, of course, I headed up front to look for the tracks and the direction in which the bear had dishappeared. That he had dishappeared, I figured, was certain. But the fellow hadn't. He sat below the hickory tree and – licked himself eagerly clean."

"The loam? Pah!" Jemmy opined while shaking his head. "As far as I know the characteristics of these animals, he would immediately go for the water."

"He didn't think of that, for he was shmarter than you, master Jemmy. Bears do love shweets, as is well known. And isn't maple syrup shweet like shugar?"

"I don't understand. Go on with your story!"

"Well, didn't I mention the wooden tubs from which the shugar sap was to evaporate. The bear had been so poorly delighted by the adventure, that his only thought had been to get away as fasht as possible. One of the tubs had been in his way, and he didn't take the time to shoot around it, but had wanted to leap over it. But since a bear can't leap like a tiger, he didn't make it across, but jumped into it and tore the tub off its base. Since the juice had been already quite vishcous, it shpread such a shtrong shugar shmell, that the careless animal had at once totally forgotten the fall from the tree, the leap into the loam pit, and myself. Inshtead of taking my 'farewell' to heart and to reshpect the implied warning, the bear had settled down under the tree to lick the shweetness with great pleashure off the loam. He was so very much engaged in this pleasant task that he didn't even notice, when I shlinked along the wall to the door and shnuck into the house. Now I was safe and took my rifle from its hook. It was loaded, of course. Since the bear sat on his behind I could aim as long as I pleased, I certainly couldn't miss. The bullet hit the animal right at that shpot where, according to the poets, the tenderest sentiments are harbored, that is, right in the heart. The bear jerked, righted itself, geshticulated a bit with his forelimbs, and sank dead to the ground. Because of his carelessness and pleashure-seeking, he shtopped to exist as a living being. Fate shtrides quickly, and every folly finds its right punishment.

135

To whomever the morning's red glow of the sky tells of his early death, he may pass in the afternoon already from maple syrup illness."

"That's a very serious and useful application," Old Shatterhand said. "It's to your honor. I actually wanted to say that you know how to present a story very interestingly. I've not heard anyone who has been able to dress up a story so wittily as you."

"Is that supposed to be a miracle? Remember the Moritzburger school mashter, who transferred his entire, exceptional knowledge to me and think of the library and the publications whose faithful subshcriber I was! In addition, I was second tenor in our glee club and lead splasher with the volunteer fire department and rescue troop. And later, too, I always listened up where there was something to be learned. Under such circumshtances, one becomes classic without noticing it oneself. Only the devotion one is treated with by others, brings one to the insight that one has elevated oneself far above the zero point of Fahrenheit and Reaumur. The human mind musht shtrive higher, because only up there, among the shtars the timely and subterranean calamities do end. Unfortunately, even an ideal nature like myself musht occupy itself with ordinary things. That's the fight for existence. That's how I do my duty and don't scare even from the biggesht bear."

"Well. Yours likely wasn't that big. A grizzly cannot climb. What was its coloration?"

"His coat was black."

"And its muzzle?"

"Was yellow."

"Ah, then it was a baribal. You needn't have been afraid of it at all."

"Oho! One could see that he had an appetite for human flesh!"

"Don't believe it. The baribal prefers fruit over meat. I'd volunteer to tackle such a silly animal. A few good fisticuffs, and it would run off."

"Yes, shure, that's you! You shatter down even a man with your fist, like your name says. But I'm much more tenderly dishposed and wouldn't try it without a weapon. By the way, at the time, I peeled the roasht from its coat and washed it, just like my outfit, which had become quite fireproof by the loam. I didn't do anything about repairing the tub walls and I didn't want to have anything to do with the content of the pit. When the Norwegian returned with his family, the bear hams had been pickled, and I was very much praised. Of course, I took care not to have all circumstances of the fatal adventure become public – hold it! What's running over there?"

As mentioned, he had gotten up while telling his story. In the course of walking he had stepped on some rocks behind him which scared off an animal from below these rocks. Out it came, and lightning-fast scrambled across the opening and into a hole in a hollow tree stump nearby. The creature's movements had been so fast, that it was impossible to identify it.

136

However, Bob, was electrified by the event. He jumped up, ran for the stump and shouted:

"A critter, a critter ran across here. It hide in hole! *Massa* Bob said he will catch with hands first animal he'll see. *Massa* Bob pull creature from tree."

"Careful! Careful!" Old Shatterhand warned. "You don't know what kind of animal it is!"

"Oh, it only be so small!"

With his index fingers, he demonstrated the animal's length.

"A small animal can be more dangerous than a big one."

"Opossum not be dangerous."

"Did you see that it was one?"

"Yes, yes. *Massa* Bob saw possum clearly. It be fat, very fat, and make roast very delicious, oh, very delicious."

He smacked his lips and licked them, as if he had the roast already.

"And I think you are mistaken. An opossum isn't as nimble as this little critter was."

"Opossum also run fast, very fast. Why *Massa* Shatterhand begrudge Negro Bob this good roast!"

"Well. If you are so convinced of not being mistaken, then do as you please. But stay away from us with this dish."

"Like very much to stay off! *Massa* Bob give no one of opossum. He eat roast all by himself, all by himself. Watch now! He pull opossum from hole!"

He pulled back his right sleeve.

"Not like that, not so!" said Old Shatterhand. "You must grab the animal with your left and take your knife into your right hand. As soon as you get hold of your catch, you pull it out and quickly kneel on it, then the animal cannot move and defend itself, and you can cut its throat."

"Good! That be good! *Massa* Bob will do like this, because *Massa* Bob be great frontiersman and famous hunter."

He now pulled up his left sleeve, took the knife in his right hand, then reached into the hole, first carefully and hesitantly. Then, when he didn't touch anything, he stuck his arm in deeper. Suddenly, he dropped the knife, yelled loudly, grimaced awfully and waved his right arm wildly in the air.

"Oh my, oh my!" he wailed. "It hurt, it hurt very much!"

"What? Did you grab the animal?"

"*Massa* Bob it have? No, it have *Massa* Bob."

"Oh my! Is it holding on to your hand?"

"Yes, has bit hard into hand!"

"Then pull, pull it out!"

"No, because hurt very much!"

"But you can't leave your hand inside. Once an animal has taken hold of you, it won't let go again. Pull therefore! And once you've got it out, quickly grab it with your other hand to hold it, while I give it the coup de grace."

He pulled his long knife from his belt and stepped next to Bob by the stump. The Black now pulled his arm out, but only very slowly while gnashing his teeth and with great lament. The animal really wouldn't let go and was pulled up to the hole's opening. Now the Negro made a quick pull. The animal came out hanging by its teeth on his left hand. With his right he grabbed it at its rear end, expecting Old Shatterhand to quickly use his knife. But instead of doing this, the frontiersman hurriedly jumped back calling:

"A skunk, a skunk! Away, men, away!"

The approximately one-and-a-half-foot-long mammal belongs to the marten-type carnivores. It has a hairy two-striped tail as long as its body with a swollen nose on its pointy-head. Its coat is black and has two snow-white stripes, one on each side, converging at its shoulder. It lives off eggs, small animals, but is even dangerous to rabbits, goes hunting only at night, and spends the rest of its time in holes in the ground and in trees.

This animal rightly deserves its Latin name, *Mephitis*. It has a gland underneath its tail from which, when attacked, it can spray an exceptionally bad smelling, pungent, yellow-oily liquid in its defense. The liquid's odor is truly horrible and adheres for several months to clothing. Since the skunk can hit its enemy from a good distance with this mephitic juice, everyone, knowing this creature keeps a good distance from it. Anyone having been hit by this juice can easily face the situation of being excluded for weeks from all human company.

So, instead of an opossum, Bob had caught a skunk. The other men had all jumped from their places and hurried off.

"Toss it away! Quickly, quickly!" Fat Jemmy called to the Negro.

"*Massa* Bob cannot throw away," the Black lamented. "It have bitten tight into his hand and – oh, ouch – ouch, oh! *Fie*, oh shameful, *fie*, by the devil! Now it spray onto *Massa* Bob. Oh, death, of hell, oh devil! How *Massa* Bob stink! No person can stand! *Massa* Bob choke to death. Away, off, off with animal, this pestilence thing!"

He wanted to shake it off his hand, but it had latched onto it so tightly, that all his efforts were in vain.

"Wait! *Massa* Bob get you off, you swine, you stinking thing!"

Reaching out with his right hand, he gave the animal a hard slap on the head. This hit stunned the skunk, but drove its teeth even deeper into the Negro's hand. Screaming from pain, he picked his knife off the ground and cut the animal's throat.

"So!" he called. "Now *Massa* Bob has won. Oh, *Massa* Bob not be afraid of any bear and of no smelly beast. All massas come here and see how *Massa* Bob has killed dangerous animal!"

But everyone took care not to come too close to him for he spread such a terrible odor that everyone, even quite distant, held his nose.

"Well, why not come?" he asked. "Why not celebrate victory with *Massa* Bob?"

"Are you crazy, fellow?" Fat Jemmy answered. "Who would come close to you? You are stinking worse than pestilence!"

"Yes, *Massa* Bob smell very bad. *Massa* Bob he notice now himself! Oh, oh, who can stand this smell?"

He made a terrible face.

"Toss the animal away!" Old Shatterhand told him.

Bob tried to follow this request, but was unable to accomplish it.

"Teeth are too deep in *Massa* Bob's hand. *Massa* Bob cannot open mouth of beast!"

He pulled on the head with lots of ahs and ohs but all in vain.

"Thunder and lightning!" he exclaimed angrily. "Skunk cannot hang on forever on hand of *Massa* Bob! Is there nobody, no good, dear man, who will help poor *Massa* Bob?"

The Saxon took pity on him. His compassionate heart made him risk separating the Negro of his dead enemy. He approached him, but only very slowly and said:

"Listen, dear Bob, I'll give it a try. Although you shmell awfully, my humanity may overcome it. But only under the condition that you don't touch me!"

"*Massa* Bob not touch *Massa* Frank!" the Negro assured him.

"Okay then! But your clothing must not touch mine either, or both of us will smell. I rather leave this honorable right to you alone."

"*Massa* Frank only come! *Massa* Bob will watch out very much!"

One could truly call this a form of heroism when the little Saxon now walked to the Black. Neither Winnetou, Old Shatterhand, Jemmy nor Davy, these otherwise so daring men, would risk it. If Frank touched, even a bit, a spot on Bob's clothing that had been hit by the liquid, he would join the fate of the expelled, unless he choose to get rid of his clothing.

The closer he came, the stronger and repulsive became the odor, almost taking his breath. But he endured it bravely.

"Now, Black, shtick your arm towards me!" he demanded. "I don't want to get too close to you."

Bob obeyed the command and, with one hand, the Saxon took hold of the upper jaw, and, with the other hand, the lower jaw of the animal, to free the Negro, succeeding only by applying all his strength. He literally had to break open the skunk's mouth. He then quickly jumped back. He felt quite dizzy, almost as if he would fall over, that's how infernally the Black smelled.

139

Bob was happy to be free again. Although his hand was bleeding, he did not pay attention to it and called:

"So, now *Massa* Bob showed how brave he is. Now believe all white and red men that black Negro not afraid?"

While speaking he approached the others. At that Old Shatterhand raised his rifle, aimed it at Bob's chest and commanded:

"Stay where you are or I'll shoot you!"

"By heavens! Why shoot dead poor, good Bob?"

"Because you are too close. Don't you touch us! Run off downstream along the creek, as far as possible, and discard all your clothing."

"Drop all clothes? Is Bob to lose his beautiful calico coat, his nice pants and vest?"

"All of it, everything! Then you come back and sit up to your neck in the pond's water. Hurry up! The longer you hesitate, the more you'll keep the smell on you."

"What misfortune! My beautiful coat! *Massa* Bob wash it, then it no longer smell!"

"No, *Massa* Bob will obey me, or I'll shoot him this very minute. One, two, thr ...!"

He approached the Negro, his rifle aimed.

"No, no!" the Black screamed. "Not shoot! *Massa* Bob run off quickly, very quickly."

He disappeared in the dark of the night. Of course, Old Shatterhand's threat had not been meant seriously, but it was the best means of getting the Negro to obey quickly. He soon returned, and now had to immerse himself in the pond and to wash himself incessantly. For this task, he received a thick mixture of bear fat and wood ash, the latter being in plentiful supply from the fires.

"Too bad for nice bear fat!" he lamented. "*Massa* Bob could rub fat into his hair to make many beautiful ringlets. *Massa* Bob be a fine ringlet man, not born nigger, having braided such fine curls, so long, so very long!"

"Just wash yourself!" said Jemmy laughingly. "Think not of your beauty but rather about our noses."

Despite having discarded his clothing and sat down in the water, the Black spread a most penetrating odor.

"But," he asked, "how long need *Massa* Bob sit here and wash himself?"

"As long as we stay here, that is, until tomorrow morning."

"*Massa* Bob cannot endure this!"

"You'll be forced to endure it. Another question is whether the remaining trout will be able to survive. I don't know whether these fish have a sense of smell, but if it's the case, they'll not be happy with the visit you're paying them."

"When *Massa* Bob can get his clothes to wash?"

"Not at all. They stay where they lie, for they have become useless."

140

"But what poor *Massa* Bob wear?"

"Yes, that's really a bad situation! There's no replacement for your outfit. You have to wrap yourself into the grizzly coat Martin got today. Maybe, farther up in the Rockies, we'll find the stores of a *marchand tailleur* where you can equip yourself with socks and a Havelock. Until then, you'll bring up the rear of our company, because for the next eight days at least, you'll not be allowed to come very close to us. Go ahead and keep washing yourself diligently! The more you rub, the sooner you'll lose the smell."

Bob kept rubbing with all his strength. Only his head rose above the surface, and it was truly funny to watch his grimaces.

In the meantime, the others had returned to the campfire. Of course, at first only the tragicomical adventure was the subject of conversation. Then, Long Davy was asked to tell of his experiences. He gladly complied and reported about his meeting with an old trapper known as a shooting virtuoso. After he had described some of the man's tricks, he added:

"But that's not everything. There are still better shots. I know two who can't be surpassed by anyone, and these two are sitting right here among us. I mean Winnetou and Old Shatterhand. Please, sir, would you be kind enough to tell us about one of your major tricks? You've experienced so much that you can just shake your sleeve, and the adventures are likely to drop out by the hundreds."

These last words had been directed at Old Shatterhand who, however, did not reply right away. He took a deep breath, as if wanting to check something wafting in the air.

"Yes, the fellow over there in the water is still very fragrant," said Jemmy.

"Oh, my inhalation wasn't for him," Old Shatterhand answered, looking sideways at his horse who had stopped grazing and was checking the air through its nostrils.

"Are you smelling something different?" Davy asked.

"No. But something may prevent me from telling one of my adventures all the way to its end."

"How so?"

Instead of answering directly, Old Shatterhand, in a low voice, turned first to Winnetou:

"*Teshi-ini!*"

This means 'watch out'! Since the others did not understand the Apache language, they remained unaware of its meaning. Winnetou nodded and reached for his rifle, pulling it very close.

Its eyes sparkling, Old Shatterhand's horse, with a snort, turned its head to the fire.

"*Is-hosh-ni!*" he called to the animal, who immediately lay down again in the grass without any further sign of disquiet.

Since Old Shatterhand also pulled his rifle closer, Jemmy, who had noticed the actions of the two men, asked:

"What have you got, sir? Your horse seems to smell something?"

"It smells the Negro's odor, nothing else," the hunter tried to calm the other.

"But both of you reached for your weapons!"

"Because I want to talk to you about the hip shot. You likely have heard about it?"

"Of course!"

Although English had been spoken, Frank commented in his Saxon dialect:

"Listen, mishter Shatterhand, there you'll have merschtentels applied a wrong term!"

"How so?"

"Because it ishn't called hip shot, but hex shot (German slang for lumbago). Whoever gets it, walks bent over and lame, because it has 'hexed' him pitiably in the back and the hipsh. Nevertheless, the exshpression hip shot is orthographical-medically totally wrong."

While Frank talked, Old Shatterhand didn't betray that he, like Winnetou sharply checked the jumbled trees and branches of the windfall at the forest's edge beyond the creek and pond. He had pulled his hat far into his face, so that his eyes were in deep shadow, and one could not see in what direction and onto which object they were focusing. He, nevertheless, answered unaffectedly:

"Please, my good Frank, I know very well what lumbago, a hex shot, is. But I had meant another kind of shot."

"Oh! Well, what kind?"

"The hip shot, as I said. With it, I mean the shot for which one doesn't aim the rifle as usual, but lifts it only up to the hip."

"But one can't aim like that!"

"It is, of course, very difficult to acquire the necessary skill. There is many a good frontiersman who will never fail his target, but will regularly miss with a hip shot."

"What was the hip shot invented for then? It's better after all to aim as it's done customarily, to be shure of hitting."

"No! There are situations in which one would be certain of death without this skill."

"That I don't undershtand."

"Let me explain it then."

Once more his eyes closely swept the area across the pond. Then, he continued:

"The hip shot is used only if one sits on the ground, so as not to let the opponent know that one intends to shoot. Just imagine that hostile Indians are nearby intent on attacking us. They send out their scouts to sneak up to find out how many we are, how our camp site lends itself for attack, and whether we are maintaining necessary caution. These scouts approach on hands and feet."

"But they musht be shpotted by our guards!" Frank objected.

"This isn't as assured as you think. I, for instance, crept up to and into Tokvi-tey's tent, although he had set up guards and despite the terrain being a flat grassy plain. But here stand trees all around, which make a surreptitious approach much easier, with our guards being, as you've heard, of the delusion that there aren't any enemies around here. Quite likely, they will not be too attentive. But let's continue! The scouts creep past our guards. They lie at the forest's edge, behind or in the windfall jumble and are observing us. If they succeed in returning to their own, we might be attacked and wiped out because we had no warning. The best remedy is to render the scouts harmless."

"That's to kill them?"

"Yes! In principle, I am against the spilling of blood, but it would be suicide in this case if one spared the enemy. He must be given a bullet so that it kills him immediately."

"*Tkih-akan* – they are close," whispered the Chief of the Apache.

143

"*Teshi-shi-thih* – I see them," answered Old Shatterhand.

"*Naki* – two!"

"*Ha-oh* – yes."

"*Shi-ntsage, ni-akaya* – you take this one, I take the other!"

Saying this, the Apache moved his hand from the left to the right.

"*Tayassi* – into the forehead," Old Shatterhand nodded.

"Tell us, sir, what secrets you are having with each other?" asked Long Davy.

"Nothing unusual! I told the Chief of the Apache that he should assist me in explaining what it is about the hip shot."

"Well. I know that already. However, as much as I tried, I never succeeded. But to get back to what you said earlier: One must have seen the spies before one can shoot."

"Of course!"

"In the darkness of the jumble over there?"

"Yes!"

"But they'll be careful not to come out of the jumble so that one can see them!"

"Hm! I'm surprised at what you are saying since I thought you to be a clever frontiersman."

"Well, I hope I'm no greenhorn!"

"Then, you must know that the spies cannot remain in the windfall. If they want to observe us they must at least lift their eyes and part of their face out of it."

"And that you claim to see?"

"Certainly!"

"Amazing! Of course, I've heard of frontiersmen who can spot the eyes of an encroaching enemy in the darkest of night. Here, our Fat Jemmy, for instance, has claimed to be able to do it, but hasn't yet had the opportunity to prove it to me."

"Well, concerning that, he could quite unexpectedly get the opportunity to experience proof of it."

"I'd be happy to see that! I've thought it impossible, but if you tell me that it's true, I believe it."

Shatterhand once more examined the forest edge, nodded satisfied and replied:

"Might you have seen the eyes of a *Tintorera*, a shark, shine during the dark in the ocean?"

"No!"

"Well then, one can see these eyes clearly. They have a phosphorescent sheen. Other eyes, even those of humans, have a similar light reflection, although not of the same magnitude. And the more the eyesight is strained in the night, the more clearly it becomes noticeable in the darkness. If there were a spy over there in the bushes observing us, I would spot his eyes and Winnetou would, too."

"That would be something!" Davy proclaimed. "What do you say to that, old Jemmy?"

"I think, I'm not blind either," Jemmy replied. "Fortunately we are safe here from such a visit. It's after all a touchy thing to get into a situation where a good hip shot becomes necessary. Isn't it so, sir?"

"Yes," Old Shatterhand nodded. "Look here, master Frank! Assuming there's a spy over there, whose eyes I've seen shining from between the leaves. I must kill him, of course, or I risk my own life. But if, as it is done customarily, I put the rifle to my cheek, he'll see that I'm planning to shoot, and he'll retreat quickly. He might even have his rifle aimed at me and will fire before I fire mine. I must avoid that by using a hip shot. Doing this, one sits quietly and seemingly unconcerned, like I do right now. One reaches for the rifle and lifts it slowly a bit higher, as if wanting to look for something or as if one intends to toy with it. One lowers the head, as if looking down keeping the eyes in the hat brim's shadow and aims sharply at the target, just like Winnetou and myself right now."

As he explained, he executed the move, as did Winnetou.

"With the right hand, one presses the stock tightly against the hip and the barrel against the knee, then reaches with the left hand across to the right and places it above the lock onto the rifle. In doing so, it is being steadied. Then, one puts the index finger of the right hand on the trigger, rights the barrel so that the bullet will hit above the eyes, that is in the forehead of the spy. It's a kind of aim that must be learned. Then one presses the trigger – there!"

His shot flashed and the Apache's sounded simultaneously. Then, lightning-fast both of them leaped up. Tossing his rifle aside and pulling his knife from his belt, Winnetou sprang like a panther up and across the creek and into the windfall.

"*Uhvai k'unun! Uhvai pa-ave! Uvai umpare*! Extinguish the fires! Don't move! Don't talk!" Old Shatterhand called in the Ute dialect of the Shoshone.

With his booted feet he simultaneously tossed the embers of the fire, he had been sitting by, into the pond. Then, he leaped after the Apache.

Upon the crack of the rifle shots, the Shoshone, as well as the Whites, had jumped up. The quick-witted red warriors followed Old Shatterhand's command the moment they heard it by tossing the embers of their fires into the water. Deep darkness now ruled, yet only four or five seconds had passed since the firing of the shots.

The demand for silence was obeyed by all, except by one, the Negro who was sitting in the water as the embers flew about his head and went out hissing.

"Jesus, Jesus!" he screamed. "Who shot there" Why throw fire onto poor *Massa* Bob? Is *Massa* Bob to burn or to drown? Is he to boil like carp? Why it be dark now? Oh, oh, *Massa* Bob not see anyone any more!"

"Silence, stupid!" Jemmy admonished him.

"Why *Massa* Bob be silent. Why not now ...?"

"Shut up, or you'll be killed! There are enemy about!"

From this very moment *Massa* Bob's voice was not to be heard any more. He sat motionless in the water, so as not to give away his presence to the enemy.

There was utter silence. Only the occasional stomping of a horse's hoof was heard. The men who had been so unexpectedly disturbed from their imagined security, had moved closer together. The Indians did not say a word; only the Whites whispered a few remarks to each other.

"What's the matter? What happened, mishter Pfefferkorn?" Hobble-Frank asked. "The two had no reason to shoot. We would have undershtood the explanation also without the shots. Or might there truly have been hoshtile people nearby?"

"For sure. What Old Shatterhand demonstrated as a mere example really happened. He did see a spy, or possibly several."

"By the devil! This could get here and there dangerous to us! It musht've been several fellows or the Apache wouldn't have shot, too. What's to do now?"

"We wait quietly for the two to return."

"Hm! They crossed the creek! Such incautious daring! What if they'll be caught over there by the shpies and be relieved of their little bit of earthly being!"

"Pah! These two men know exactly what they must do. The first thing for Old Shatterhand was to have the fires extinguished in case there were more hostiles in addition to the spies."

"Then, you think the fellows were truly shot?"

"I'd even bet, that they were hit exactly in the forehead."

"That would be really something! It would be much more than something! The eyes one needs for that! And now they musht be searching over there whether the enemy did come in greater quantity?"

Before Jemmy could reply, Old Shatterhand's loud voice rose."

"Light one fire again, but keep away from it so that you cannot be seen."

Jemmy and Davy bent down to follow the order, then retreated quickly into the darkness.

"Firsht the fire is extinguished, then it's lit again. Why that? I can't undershtand it!" Frank whispered to the Fat One.

"That's not necessary," he replied. "It hasn't been done for you to comprehend."

"But it must have a purpose!"

"That's true. Our two leaders first searched the area in darkness and must not have found anything suspicious. Now they will likely enter deeper into the forest. There they will move in a wide circle around the camp and, while creeping along the ground looking toward the fire, nothing questionable will escape their sharp eyes."

"So, that's how it's meant! Listen, my dear mishter Pfefferkorn, these two are some clever fellows! It takes more than shugar water to do all that they are capable of and what they dare. I don't think I would be able to do that. But, when it comes to a fight, I'll be the man. That you can happily believe!"

"I hope so, since you do handle your rifle very well."

"Well, and how! But have a look to the pond. Bob's shtill sitting in there. He's pulled his head down so far, that the water reaches to his mouth. He doeshn't want to be shot, nor be drowned."

"He needn't have any concern about that. Look! Here they come!"

In the fire's light they saw Winnetou and Old Shatterhand returning, each with rifle in hand and an Indian over the shoulder. The others started to crowd around them, but Old Shatterhand told them:

"There's no time for discussion. Tie the two dead onto the spare horses, then we will leave. Although only these two were spying on our camp, we don't know how many more are behind them. Quickly then."

Both corpses had a round hole in the forehead as well as in the back of the head. The bullets had penetrated, just as Old Shatterhand had said to Winnetou: "*Tayassi* – into the forehead."

While the others were also excellent shots, such unbelievably accurate shooting was a great surprise to them. The Shoshone whispered secretly with each other and threw the two famous men superstitious looks.

The departure was prepared quickly and silently. Of course, the fire had to be extinguished once more. Then Winnetou and Old Shatterhand took up the lead and the nightly ride began.

Where to, no one asked. They relied on their two leaders. Soon the valley became so narrow that they needed to ride in file. This fact, together with the called-for caution, made conversation impossible.

Of course, they had not left the Negro sitting in the water. Without clothing, he sat on his horse and had to ride at the end of the procession, since he was still wearing the skunk's smelly memento rather noticeably. Long Davy had given him his old, tattered Saltillo blanket, which had served the hunter as a saddle. Bob had wrapped it around his hips like a Pacific Islander's pareau. He had fallen out with his fate, and from his continuous soft grumbling, one could deduce that he was entertaining plenty of dreary and angry thoughts.

Thus, they proceeded for hours as quietly and as quickly as possible, first through the narrow valley, and then up a broad, bare mountainside. Again, down the other face, and across a very narrow, winding prairie. When dawn finally broke, the horsemen entered into high, darkly forested mountains. There, at the mountains' foot, the two leaders stopped and dismounted. The others followed suit.

The two corpses were taken off the horses and put down. The Shoshone formed a wide circle, knowing that an examination was to begin, the difficulties of which they were well aware. First, only the chiefs were to speak. Ordinary warriors had to wait until they were asked for advice.

The two dead were dressed the Indian way, partly in cloth, partly in leather. They were barely more than twenty years old.

"I thought so," said Old Shatterhand. "Only inexperienced warriors open their eyes completely when they spy on a hostile camp, allowing their reflection to be seen. A smart scout hides his eyes halfway below his lids. It is then difficult even for us to make out the other's look. But to which tribe do they belong?"

The question was directed at Jemmy.

"Hm!" he grumbled. "Do you believe that your question embarrasses me?"

"I believe you because, at the moment, I can't answer it myself. But they are on the warpath, that's for sure. Although the war colors are very much smudged, they are there. Black and red! The colors of the Ogallalla. But the fellows don't look like Sioux. Nothing can be deduced from their clothing. Let's search their pockets!"

Those were completely empty. Despite a thorough search, nothing was found. Last night, a rifle had been found next to each corpse. Those, too, were examined. They were loaded, but showed nothing from which one could have inferred the tribal membership of the dead.

"Maybe, they were totally harmless to us," Long Davy remarked. "They happened to come to the place where we camped and had to spy on us for their own safety. In that case, they would have left without doing us any harm, and I would regret very much for them to have lost their lives."

Old Shatterhand shook his head and answered:

"You want to be a frontiersman, master Davy? If you are truly one, one must ask you to think logically."

"Well, sir, I think I've got my five senses together."

"Really? Well, I don't want to doubt it. But the place where we were camped is such that one doesn't get there by chance. These people did follow our tracks."

"That doesn't prove anything against them!"

"No. But they very carefully removed everything from their bodies from which one could conclude the tribe they belong to. That's suspicious. They had their loaded rifles, but did not carry ammunition. That's even more suspicious, for no Indian leaves his group without powder and lead. They positively belong to a group whose scouts they were."

"Hm! Maybe they didn't even have horses."

"No? Have a look at the leather pants of this one. Aren't the legs worn on the inside? What is that from, if not from riding!"

"Maybe from some earlier time."

Old Shatterhand knelt down and put his nose to the pants. Rising again he said:

"Just smell these pants! You can't miss the horse smell. But since it is lost quickly in the wilderness, I'd bet that these two Reds were still sitting on horseback yesterday."

At that, Wohkadeh, who, until now had been standing at a respectful distance, stepped forward and said:

"The famous men may permit Wohkadeh to speak a word, although he is still young and inexperienced!"

"Speak up," Old Shatterhand nodded to him kindly.

"While Wohkadeh does not know these two red warriors, he knows the hunting shirt of one of them."

He bent down, lifted the shirt's tail, pointed to a mark on it, and explained:

"Wohkadeh cut his totem into it, since it was given to him as his shirt."

"Ah! This is a most wonderful coincidence. Now we may learn something more specific."

"Wohkadeh cannot say anything more accurate, but he thinks, that these two young warriors belong to the Upsaroca tribe. That's what the Crow Indians call themselves."

"What's the reason for my young brother's supposition?" Old Shatterhand asked.

"Wohkadeh was present when the Upsaroca were robbed by the Sioux Ogallalla. We were coming from the long mountain, the palefaces call the Foxback, to cross the northern arm of the Cheyenne River, where it passes through the Threefold and Inyancara Mountain. When we rode between the mountain and the river, we turned the corner of a forest and saw many red men bathing in the water. It was a hot day. The Ogallalla held a quick council. The bathers were Upsaroca, enemies of theirs. They decided to do them the greatest disgrace that can happen to a red warrior ..."

"By the devil!" Old Shatterhand called. "They didn't intend to steal their most precious possession, their medicine bags?"

"My white brother guessed it."

"Then, I know everything you are going to tell. But go on!"

"The Sioux-Ogallalla rode in the trees to the place where the Upsaroca' horses were grazing. There lay the clothing, weapons and medicines. A warrior will otherwise never take his medicine off his neck. The Ogallalla dismounted and sneaked up to the items. There was some brush between this place and the river, so it was easy for them to execute the theft, since they were not visible to the bathers."

"Had they not posted any guards?"

"No. They had not assumed that a troop of hostile Ogallalla would come to where the Upsaroca' horses were grazing at the time. The Sioux did not take any weapons since they had their own, but they took the ammunition and some of the clothing."

For a moment, Wohkadeh was silent.

"And then?" asked Old Shatterhand.

"Then," Wohkadeh continued, "they mounted up again, took the Upsaroca' horses and galloped off. Later, they let the bad horses go and kept only the good ones. When the booty was shared, Wohkadeh received this hunting shirt. But he did not want to be a thief, so he cut his totem into it, and secretly threw it away."

"When was that?"

"Two days before I was sent off as a scout by the Ogallalla."

"That is just recently. Six days later, you met with Jemmy and Davy. Now all is clear to me, and we are very fortunate that we noticed these two Upsaroca and killed them. Did Wohkadeh count the bathers?"

"No, but there were many more than ten."

"They must have quickly re-equipped themselves with new horses and new ammunition, and then followed the thieves. At the same time, they found the thrown-away hunting shirt, which its rightful owner picked up again."

"But it may also have happened differently," Jemmy objected. "Isn't it possible that an entirely uninvolved person found the shirt and put it on?"

"No, for in that case, he would have worn his own piece of clothing underneath. But the dead here wore only an old, tattered jacket underneath which one could see served only as a makeshift. There is no greater shame for an Indian than having his medicine stolen. He may not let himself be seen with his people until he has regained it again or replaced it with one he has taken from another he has killed. The Indian who is setting off to replace a lost medicine bag develops an almost crazy daring. It is all the same to him whether he kills a friend or an enemy, which has me convinced that we escaped an extraordinary danger last night. How then would it have been, my good Jemmy, if we had had to rely on your eyes?"

"Hm!" the Fat One replied, while his hand reached below his hat to scratch himself embarrassedly. "In that case we'd be lying somewhere peacefully but minus scalp and life. While I understand the importance of spotting the glimmer of eyes in the night, last night I was so convinced that there was no hostile being nearby that I didn't bother about it. Then, you think the Upsaroca are after us?"

"In any case, they are following us, and now even more so, since we've killed two of theirs."

"They won't know that for sure."

"They'll find the blood. Little may have flowed from the wound, but enough to notice it today in daylight."

"Then, we must be prepared for an attack tonight."

"May they come," Long Davy offered. "Wohkadeh said there were more than ten, so let's say twenty. We are twice as many."

"I don't count like this," replied Old Shatterhand. "If we let it come to a night attack, blood will flow, ours and theirs. Our win would be assured, but some of us would have to pay for this victory with their lives. We can avoid that. What does my red brother say to this?"

These words were directed at Tokvi-tey, the Shoshone's chief, who, for a while, looked contemplatively ahead, then asked:

"Will my white brothers not confer first? The red warriors will not begin anything before they have heard the opinion of the experienced."

"That we will do, but there's no time for a council like the red warriors are used to. Are the Upsaroca enemies of the Shoshone these days?"

"No. They are the enemies of the Sioux-Ogallalla, who are also our enemies. We have not taken up the war tomahawk against them, but a warrior looking for a medicine, is an enemy of all people. One must beware of him like a wild animal. My white brothers would be smart to make preparations for our safety!"

Old Shatterhand looked questioningly at Winnetou who had not said a word until now. It was truly remarkable how well these two understood each other. Without Old Shatterhand having put any plan into words, Winnetou knew his thoughts, and the Apache answered:

"My brother intends to do the right thing."

"Ride back in an arc?"

"Yes. Winnetou agrees."

"I'm glad. In that case, we'll not be the attacked but the attackers, and since it will happen during daytime, the Upsaroca will see that we are superior to them. Maybe they'll freely surrender."

"They'll be careful not to!" Jemmy suggested.

"I hope for it, nevertheless. It just depends how we approach it. If I'm not mistaken, there's a place two hours from here which is very well suited for the execution of my plan and will not require us to circle around."

"Then let's not waste time here. The longer we stay, the less time we'll have there to prepare. But what are we going to do with the bodies?"

"The scalps of these two warriors belong to Old Shatterhand and the Chief of the Apache, who killed them," Tokvi-tey answered.

"I'm a Christian. I do not scalp," the hunter said. And Winnetou answered with a rejective move of his hand:

"The chief has no need for the scalp of this boy to make his name famous. The dead are unfortunate enough to have entered the Eternal Hunting Grounds without their medicines. We ought not to kill their souls, too, by taking their scalp locks. They may be buried with their rifles beneath some rocks, for they died as warriors brave enough to approach the camp of their enemy."

The leader of the Shoshone had not expected this. With a sign of surprise he asked:

"My brothers intend to give a burial to those who were after their lives?"

"Yes," Old Shatterhand replied. "We shall put their rifles into their hands, seat them upright, their faces in the direction of the sacred quarries, and then place rocks onto them. This is how warriors are honored. Once their brothers come, while pursuing us, they will recognize that we aren't their enemies, but their friends."

"My two famous brothers act in a way I do not comprehend."

"Would you not be glad to find your own buried like this?"

"Tokvi-tey would be very glad and recognize from it that the enemies are noble warriors."

"Then demonstrate that you, too, are a noble warrior and command your men to fetch rocks to erect a mound!"

The Shoshone's comprehension was insufficient to grasp the viewpoint of the two men, and yet, they had such high regard for them that they did not refuse to follow their wish.

The two fallen men were placed into a sitting position facing northeast, one to the right, and the other to the left of the pass.

Their rifles were put into their hands, and then they were covered with rocks. Once this task was completed, the group took off again. Winnetou, however, said to Old Shatterhand:

"The Chief of the Apache will remain here to observe the arrival of the Upsaroca. The young son of the Bear Hunter may remain by his side."

This was an honor for Martin Baumann, which he knew enough to appreciate. He was happy and proud to have been extended this favor. These two then stayed back, while the others rode off under Old Shatterhand's leadership.

Now, that it was daytime, the ride proceeded much faster than during the previous night. Sometimes level, but mostly uphill, the pass cut through the long, stretched ridges. After about two hours, the pass led them through a narrow, very high canyon, its walls rising almost vertically. Only three horsemen were able to ride side by side. It was absolutely impossible to ascend the walls. That's when Old Shatterhand stopped. Pointing along the straight canyon he said:

"When the Upsaroca come, we'll let them enter here. Half of us, under the leadership of Tokvi-tey and Winnetou, will remain hidden here. As soon as I fire my revolver, they will enter the narrows behind the enemy. With me, the other half will position itself at the canyon's exit. In this way we will box in the enemy, leaving them the choice to be either shot down miserably or to surrender."

This was obvious to all. The location lent itself perfectly to this plan.

"But the Upsaroca would need to be stupid enough to enter this trap," Fat Jemmy said.

"Of course, they will not slip in right away," Old Shatterhand replied. "They will halt here and confer. The main thing will then be that they don't become aware of our warriors' presence. They must hide so well that it will be impossible to be spotted. Tokvi-tey is both a brave and smart warrior. He will issue his orders. Later, when Winnetou arrives, he will also remain here. I think I can rely on these two men to follow my orders."

This pleased the Chief of the Shoshone. It could be expected that he would take good care not to disappoint the trust placed into him. He stayed back with thirty of his men and immediately began to reconnoiter the area to take the requisite measures. Fortunately, the ground was so rocky that no tracks remained. In addition, at the canyon's mouth, the forest was so dense that it was not difficult to find good hiding.

Old Shatterhand, together with the others, rode through the canyon. It was so short that, standing at the entry, one could see its exit. At this point it, once again, became a broad pass. There, the ground was of good topsoil from which giant trees rose into the sky. Scattered throughout the trees lay numerous rocks.

If the men had expected Old Shatterhand to halt there, they were mistaken. Instead, he rode on and made his horse dance in order to leave clear and conspicuous tracks.

"But, sir," Fat Jemmy said, "I think we ought to stay here at the canyon's exit!"

"Yes, we will do that. But first, follow me for a distance and take care to leave good tracks! Actually, you needn't have to ask, master Jemmy. It's self-evident what I'm doing."

He rode on for about a quarter of an hour. Then he stopped, turned to the others and asked:

"Now, gentlemen, do you know why I rode on this far?"

"Because of the hostiles' scouts?" Jemmy answered.

"Yes. The Upsaroca will not dare enter the canyon until the scouts have convinced them that the area ahead is safe. I think they will entertain the possibility of an ambush and will be extremely cautious. We will, obviously, not make our presence known, put up no hindrances, and then wait for the rest."

"So, what are we going to do now?"

"Now we turn back to the canyon's exit, but not along our tracks, but through the forest here on this side. Follow me!"

The walls of the pass were not very steep here and could be readily climbed by the horses. Old Shatterhand rode ahead along the incline towards the canyon's exit. When he halted his horse, his group was halfway up the valley wall. From there, one could descend in seconds, even on horseback, and occupy the mouth of the canyon.

The riders dismounted and tied their steeds to the trees, then, sitting down on the soft moss, assembled in groups as they pleased. As expected, it was the Whites who found each others company. Only Wohkadeh joined them; none of the Shoshone would dare to come close.

"You think we'll need to wait long?" Jemmy asked.

"We can figure that out rather accurately," their leader answered. "By early morning, the Upsaroca will have searched for their two scouts. Once they discover what happened at our last night's camp, two hours will likely have passed. When they arrive where we erected the two grave mounds, they will open them to inspect their contents. If we assume that this will take an hour including the subsequent council they'll surely hold, we have a total of three hours. It took us five hours from last night's camp to get here. So, if they ride just as fast as we did, they ought to arrive eight hours after daybreak. This means we'll have to wait about five hours from now."

"Oh my! What are we going to do during this small eternity?"

"No need to wonder about that!" answered Hobble-Frank. "We shpeak a bit of the arts and the sciences. That's the besht one can do. It educates the head, ennobles the heart, softens the temperament, and adds to the character whose firmness is required so as not to be blown away by the shtorms of life. I won't let anything come onto the arts and sciences. These two are like my daily bread, my beginning and my end, my – *brrr*! What kind of infamous shmell is this? It shmells worse as if a dead corpse hadn't been properly buried here! Or – hm!"

He looked around and noticed the Black, leaning against the tree below which the Saxon was sitting.

"Get losht, you troublemaker!" he screamed at him. "Don't lean against my tree! Do you think I borrowed my nose from a mask lender? Get losht, fellow, and head for Africa! Our nerves have become too sensitive for your whereabouts. I fancy carnations, mignonette, and forget-me-nots, but skunk I wouldn't advise even the finesht lady to have in a shmelling bottle."

"*Massa* Bob smell good, very good!" the Negro defended himself. "*Massa* Bob not stink. *Massa* Bob wash in water, with ashes and fat of bear. *Massa* Bob be fine, noble gentleman!"

"What? You claim to be a man of high and well-scented birth! Wait, fellow, you'll not mess up my atmoshphere!"

He reached for his rifle, aimed it at Bob, and threatened:

"If you don't dishappear right away, I'll shoot both bullets five times through your body!"

"Jesus, Jesus! Not shoot, not shoot!" the Black screamed. "*Massa* Bob go away. *Massa* Bob sit far away!"

He quickly removed himself to a more distant spot, where he sat down sulking and softly grumbling.

Once more, the little Saxon proposed to talk about the arts and sciences, but Old Shatterhand told him:

"I believe we can use the time for a better purpose. We didn't sleep last night. You better lie down and take a nap. I shall keep guard."

155

"You! Why you precisely? You reshted just as little as us, in *Mosjeh*[5] Orpheus' arms."

"It's Morpheus!" Jemmy corrected.

"There you go again! Why is no one else correcting me, but always you alone! What do you want with your Morpheus! I know exshactly what it's called. Not for nothing was I a member of the glee club whose name was Orpheus. When one had sung there for awhile, particularly if there weren't too many pauses in the notes, one shlept wonderfully afterwards. Such a glee club is the besht means against shleepless nightly thoughts, which is why it is called Orpheus."

"All right. Let's leave it at that!" the Fat One laughed, stretching out on the moss. "I'd rather sleep than crack such learned nuts with you."

"For that, you are missing hair on your teeth. One who hashn't learned anything, can't do anything. So, go ahead and shleep. The world isn't going to suffer for it."

When he did not find anyone else to convince of his mental superiority, he too bedded down to try to get some sleep. The Shoshone followed the others' example, and soon all slept except for their leader. Even the horses lay down or, tiredly, hung their heads. All of this did not give the appearance that a bloody scene might well occur here in a few hours.

Old Shatterhand climbed down the incline, slowly crossed the canyon and, at its other end, looked around searchingly. He smiled, satisfied, for no tracks were noticeable that might indicate where Tokvi-tey and his men were hiding. The Shoshone had done well.

The hunter now returned to the canyon's exit and sat down on a rock. His head lowered to his chest, he sat for hours without moving. What was the famous hunter thinking? Might he be letting the memories of his so very eventful life pass before his eyes like a highly interesting panorama?

Then, hoof beats of a horse sounded. Old Shatterhand rose and listened from around the corner of a rock. When Martin Baumann approached, Old Shatterhand showed himself.

"Has Winnetou arrived too?" he asked.

"Yes. He was called by Tokvi-tey and is staying with him, as you requested. I, too, will return to them."

"That's fine by me. The Apache seems to have taken a liking of you. Value this, young friend! There is no one second to him here in the West who can be as useful to you as the Chief. I, too, have much to thank him for."

---

[5] Mosjeh - this word is a German mispronunciation of Monsieur, it is also employed by Blücher in Karl May's "Die Liebe des Ulanen". Frank is mangling Monsieur Orpheus into Mosjeh Orpheus - whilst trying to refer to Morpheus

"No second?" the youngster asked smilingly. "Aren't you the one we must be grateful to for so very much already?"

"Pah! That's peanuts! When it comes down to it, it is my fault that your father was captured. It is my hope that you will soon see him free and safe again. However, now we must talk about other things. Did you see the Upsaroca? But, my question is superfluous! It's self-evident that you saw them."

"Self-evident? What about if they hadn't come?"

"Pah! Now you want to test me," the hunter laughed highly amused. "Had they not shown up, you wouldn't be here yet, since Winnetou doesn't leave his post before he knows what's happening. And were he convinced, that the Upsaroca wouldn't come at all, he would not stay with the Shoshone, but would have already brought them here. You see, even if the examinee occasionally asks the examiner a question, it is generally redundant. So, how many Upsaroca did you count?"

"Sixteen, and two extra horses."

"Then, I figured correctly. The two extra horses are those of the killed."

"Two of them, scouts, rode quite a ways ahead. One could see that they followed our tracks all right."

"Good! They'll soon get to know the ones who left these tracks."

"We kept well hidden in the trees and let them approach rather close. Then, we followed them at a gallop and passed them under cover gaining a good lead on them. We noticed a really giant fellow in the group, apparently their leader, who was riding several horse-lengths ahead of them."

"Did you see how they were armed?"

"They all had rifles."

"That's fine. Now, you'll convey my message precisely to Winnetou. Inside the canyon there's only room for three horses side by side. Therefore, I'm asking the Apache not to use horses. As soon as the enemy has entered the canyon, he is to follow them quickly on foot."

"Aren't they then superior to us?"

"No. Just the opposite. We are superior to them."

"But they could easily ride us down!"

"Are you entertaining some tactical thoughts already? While the Upsaroca can ride only with three horses side by side, we, on foot, can post five men next to each other. We'll do this as follows: The first five will sit down on the ground, the second five will kneel behind them. Behind those, the next five will stand in a bent position, followed by the fourth set of five standing upright. This way twenty men can aim well and proper without inconveniencing each other. The remainder will stand behind them in reserve. That way the sixteen Upsaroca will get a total of forty shots, of course not all at once, if they don't surrender. Only a row at a time of our people are to fire, since only three of the enemy can be hit at a time. We must also take into account that we have to shoot the rider-less horses, if they are not to cause havoc among us. Tell this to the Apache and add that I alone will negotiate with the Upsaroca. No one else is to enter into this. When does Winnetou think they will arrive?"

"He figures an hour for their stop at the graves ..."

"Then, just like I do."

"And two hours to get here. But since the two of us took only one and one half hours, we can expect that more than an hour will pass before they arrive here."

"I think so, too. But we must get ready, nevertheless. Ride back now!"

Martin turned his horse and trotted off. Old Shatterhand climbed up to his companions, who were still asleep, and woke them. He conveyed his plan to them and assigned Davy, Jemmy, Frank, Wohkadeh, and one of the Shoshone to form the first, seated rank. Leading them down, the others were also shown their positions to prepare for the event. Much depended on proper arrangement, so that the task could be executed as quickly and precisely as possible. Old Shatterhand himself intended to stand in front of his people, between them and the enemy, to be able to negotiate with them. For this purpose, he cut several long, green branches which, all over the world, even among the wildest peoples, are used as a parley flag.

After several repeats, everything worked well. Then, when he was convinced that his men could do their duty, they all withdrew once more to their hiding place.

Now the time of waiting grew longer than before. Finally, the men heard the hoof beats of a horse.

"It seems to be a single scout sent ahead to check if the passage is safe," Jemmy said.

"That would be very advantageous to us," Old Shatterhand replied. "Were it two, then one would return with the message, while the other would likely wait down there. We would have to render him harmless, without his people noticing it."

Jemmy was correct. It was only one horseman, who exited the canyon slowly and stopped there while looking around cautiously. Neither to his left nor right did he see any signs of an enemy, but only the straight running tracks for whose distinctness Old Shatterhand had taken good care. Yet the scout, not being at ease with this, rode a goodly distance on.

"By the devil!" Jemmy said. "Is he going to ride all the way to the spot where we turned off! That would be the giveaway that we are hiding here."

"In that case, he wouldn't return to his people," Old Shatterhand retorted.

"How would you accomplish this without noise?"

"With this," pointing to his lasso.

"Then its loop would have to catch him right at his neck and close, so that he couldn't scream. That's a devilishly difficult trick. Could you do it, sir?"

"Not to worry. Stick out all ten fingers and tell me which I am to catch with the lasso! But from up here, one cannot see how far he's going to ride. I must go down. Stay quiet in the meantime, and then, when I whistle softly, come down quickly!"

He took the lasso from his shoulder and, once he had descended the decline, looped it ready for throwing. From below, he was relieved to see the Upsaroca return, and found just enough time to hide behind a large boulder. The man trotted by and disappeared back through the narrow canyon.

159

Old Shatterhand gave the agreed upon sign upon which his people came down. They brought him his two rifles, also the green branches, which he had left with them, so that he would not be hindered in case he had to throw the lasso.

He stepped to the edge to peer ahead. The Upsaroca had reached the opposite side of the canyon and briefly disappeared there. A minute later, the entire group appeared again and trotted into the narrows. Old Shatterhand watched them ride just beyond the middle of the canyon. He then drew his revolver and fired the agreed upon shot. Its sound reverberated throughout the canyon's steep, narrow walls and traveled with tenfold strength to the ears of the Apache and his group. They stormed down into the canyon, behind the Upsaroca. The latter had immediately pulled up their horses when the shot had sounded. Then, they saw Old Shatterhand and his people enter on the opposite side assuming their shooting positions.

The Indians' leader was, as Martin Baumann had reported, a truly Herculean figure, sitting like a war god on his horse. He wore wide leather pants, their seams full of tassels made from the hair of killed enemies. The rough-leather chaps, reaching from the saddle down to the stirrups, were also decorated with long strips of human hair. He wore a stag-leather hunting jacket on his broad chest, and over it, something like an armor made of stitched-on, scalelike scalp plates, each one next to the other. In his belt stuck various kinds of required items: a big hunting knife and a giant tomahawk, which could only be swung by the fist of such an athletically built person. On his head, he wore the head of a cougar, and its fur, braided into thick long ropes, hung down his back. The man's face was painted in black, red and yellow colors. In his right hand, he carried a heavy rifle from which many a deadly shot must have been fired.

This man recognized immediately that the rifles facing him were superior to his own.

"Back!" his deep voice rose, its tone literally thundering through the canyon.

With that he yanked his horse up turning it on its heels, and his men followed suit. But they now faced Winnetou's group, whose rifles stared at them like those at the canyon's other end.

"*Wakon shitsha* - bad medicine!" he called alarmed. "Turn once more! There stands a man who carries the sign of speaker in his hand. Our ears shall hear what he has to say."

He turned his horse to ride slowly towards Old Shatterhand, his people following him. The Apache did not miss taking advantage of this and followed them, taking up position so close behind the Upsaroca that they were now tightly encircled.

Old Shatterhand did not take a single step forward. The Upsaroca examined him fearlessly and asked:

160

"What does the paleface want here? Why is he blocking mine and my warriors' path?"

Old Shatterhand held his look smilingly and answered:

"What does the red man want here? Why does he pursue me and my warriors?"

"Because you killed two of our brothers."

"They came to us as enemies, and enemies must be rendered harmless."

"How do you know that we are your enemies?"

"Because you lost your medicines. I know, because the two warriors, who died from our bullets, did not carry their medicines."

"You guessed right. I am no longer the one I was. With my medicine, I also lost my name. Now my name is Oiht-e-keh-fa-wakon, the Brave who is Searching for Medicine. Let us pass or we will kill you!"

"Surrender, or it will be you, who is killed!"

"Your mouth speaks proud words. But what will be your actions?"

"You can learn them immediately. Just look ahead and behind you! A sign from me and five times ten bullets will hit your small group."

That is not brave, but cowardly. Many stinking coyotes kill even the strongest buffalo. What would be your dogs against my warriors had you not encircled us. I alone would kill half of you."

He pulled his heavy tomahawk and swung it threateningly.

"And I alone would send your entire group into the Eternal Hunting Grounds!" Old Shatterhand told him calmly.

"*Might ithanka* – is Big Mouth perhaps your name?"

"I do not fight with my name, but with my hand."

At that the Upsaroca' eyes lit up.

"Will you make this come true with me?" he asked.

"I'm not afraid of you, but laugh about your empty words!"

"Then wait until I have spoken with my warriors! Then, you shall learn that Oiht-e-keh-fa-wakon not only talks but also acts."

He turned back to his people and spoke quietly with them, softly enough that his lowered voice would only reach them. Then, he turned back to Old Shatterhand and asked:

"Do you know what *muh-mohwa* is?"

"I do know."

"Well then! We need scalps for medicine. Four men are to fight the *muh-mohwa*, you with me, and one of your red men with one of my warriors. If we win, we will kill and scalp you all; if you win, you take our scalps and live. Do you have the courage for it?"

He spoke this question in a mocking tone. Immediately, Old Shatterhand replied smiling:

"I am ready. Put your hand into mine as a sign your words are true."

He offered him his hand. This, the giant had not expected, which is why he hesitated momentarily.

Muh-mohwa is a term of the Ute language and means literally 'hand on tree'. Some tribes consider this fight as a kind of divine ordeal. Using strong straps, two men are tied with one hand to a tree and receive in the other hand the agreed upon weapon, a tomahawk or a knife. The straps are attached in such a way that they permit the fighters to move in a circle around the trunk. Since the two must face each other, one of them is tied up with the right, the other with the left hand. Thus, the one whose right hand is free to do battle usually has the advantage. As a rule, this truly terrible battle, in which the opponents tear each other to pieces, ends with the death of one. But there are also milder forms of it.

The Upsaroca was totally convinced that he had gained the greater advantage by his call. Here, in the canyon, he would be lost with his people, would he not surrender. With the muh-wohwa, he not only freed himself from his present distress, but would attain also the assured possession of all his enemies' scalps in whose hands he now found himself. He was totally convinced that he was superior to the White, and since he intended to pick the strongest and most nimble of his people as the second, it could be expected that he, too, would defeat his opponent. But to be absolutely certain in this respect he said:

"You will dare it? The Great Spirit must have confused your mind. Do you know the condition that the fight between the two victors must be carried to its end if one of each party is victorious?"

Old Shatterhand saw through him. According to the obvious body relationships, it stood to be expected that he, the 'Brave Looking for Medicine', would exit from the decisive fight as the victor, even if the other Upsaroca was defeated. Nevertheless, he quickly answered:

"I agree."

The giant looked at him half surprised, half triumphant, and quickly offered him his hand saying:

"Then give me your hand! You promise me, and I promise you in the name of my warriors, that we agree to the conditions. No one of the party, whose warriors are defeated may resist being killed."

"I promise. For you to be totally sure, we shall smoke the Pipe of Oath over it."

He pointed to the Peace Pipe, decorated with hummingbird skins, hanging from his neck.

"Yes, we shall smoke it," the giant agreed, a fierce, disdainful smile crossing his sharp features. "But this Pipe of Oath will not be a Pipe of Peace for we will fight, and after the fight, your scalps will adorn our medicine poles, and your flesh will be torn apart and devoured by vultures."

"Before that, we will find out if your fists are as strong and brave as your words," remarked Old Shatterhand.

"Oiht-e-keh-fa-wakon has never been defeated!" the Upsaroca replied proudly.

"But he has had his medicine taken. If his eyes today aren't any sharper than over there by the water where the medicine was stolen from him, my scalp will remain on my head."

This was a strong rebuke, since the loss of the medicine is the worst that can happen to an Indian. And immediately, the Red reached for his weapon again. Old Shatterhand only shrugged his shoulder and warned him:

"Keep your hand off! You will soon show anyway how brave you are. But now, let's leave this place to look for another that is suitable for *muh-mohwa*. My brothers will fetch their horses, and the Upsaroca will ride as prisoners in our midst."

He gave Winnetou a sign, and the Apache went with his people to where they had left their horses. Once returned, the other group also fetched their animals. In this way, the Crow Indians were never without supervision, and it was impossible for them to flee. Now they were taken into the middle, and the group set off.

Old Shatterhand had quietly told his people not to reveal his and the Apache's name. For the time being, the Upsaroca were not to know the name of the opponents they were to fight. As long as they were convinced they would emerge the victors from the planned fight, they were unlikely to act against the agreement.

Fat Jemmy stayed close to Old Shatterhand's side. He wasn't quite in agreement with the hunter's conduct.

"Don't take it wrong, sir, if I voice my objection," he said. "You've acted like a noble fellow towards the Reds, but such noblesse seems to be misplaced."

"How so? Do you think the Indian has no comprehension of noble sentiments? I've gotten to know many a Red, who, in this respect, would have been an example to Whites."

"That may be. There are always and everywhere exceptions. But one cannot trust these Crow Indians. They are out for new medicines, in which case consideration cannot be expected from them. We did have them nicely boxed in back there. They couldn't go forward nor backward. It would have been easy for us to wipe them out, just as one blows out some poor matches. But now you are committed to this devilish *muh-mohwa*, and who can say whether this giant isn't going to beat you down or stab you!"

"Pah! You are not usually such a bloodthirsty man. What's your reason to regret that we didn't kill these people? Having been so superior to them after we lured them into a trap where they couldn't move nor defend themselves, it would not have been an honor, but a shame to shoot them down. At that, I don't even want to speak about us being Christians and not heathen."

"Hm! You're right, of course, both as a Christian and as a human. But was there a need to kill them at all? They would have been forced to surrender, and then it would have been left to us to come to a humane agreement."

"They would not have surrendered because of their quest for new medicine. The battle would have been unavoidable. And since I can't imagine butchering people, whom God has given the same rights as myself, I preferred to accept the giant's proposal. Besides, I know the man."

"What? You know the fellow?"

"Yes. You may remember my remark when we passed the Mountain of the Turtle? I mentioned that I had camped once with the Upsaroca warrior Shunka-shatsha by this mountain. He related much about his tribe to me. In the story, he proudly mentioned his famous brother Kanteh-pehta, meaning Fire Heart in English."

"Was he referring to the great and famous medicine man of the Crow Indians?"

"That's the one. He recounted the actions of this, his brother, and also described his person. He portrayed him as being a real giant with his left ear missing. Once, in a fight with Sioux-Ogallalla, Kanteh-pehta received such a whack from a tomahawk, that it separated the ear from his head and injured his shoulder very badly. Now, look at this gigantic Upsaroca! He's missing his left ear, and from the way he holds his left arm, I gather that he was once injured there."

"Thunder and lightning! That must have been quite an encounter! But, nevertheless, I'm concerned for you, sir. You are the cleverest fellow there is, but this Kanteh-pehta has never been defeated. In pure strength, he's definitely beyond you. However, I'm convinced that he isn't on the same level with you when it comes to agility. If one is tied with one arm to a tree, it is strength, not agility, which makes the difference. This is why one can bet more on him than on you."

"Well, then," Old Shatterhand smiled, "if you are that concerned for me, there's a sure way to save me from certain demise."

"Which is?"

"You fight in my place with the Crow."

"Oh my! Wouldn't think of it! While I have strong nerves, it's not my taste to run straight into the arms of death. Remember, it's you who cooked this up, sir. You can also now enjoy it with good appetite. From the depth of my heart, I wish you a blessed meal!"

He now kept his horse back several lengths so as not to be made the same unpleasant offer once more. In his place, Winnetou directed his horse to Old Shatterhand's side.

"My white brother recognized Kanteh-pehta, the medicine man of the Upsaroca?" he inquired.

"Yes," the hunter nodded. "My brother's eyes are as sharp as mine?"

"The Crow has only one ear. Winnetou has never seen his face, but the 'Brave Looking for Medicine' cannot deceive the Chief of the Apache. I have heard what my brother spoke about with him and am ready to do battle."

"I did count on the Chief of the Apache, for I don't wish to entrust anyone else with this honor."

"Will my brother kill the big Crow?"

Winnetou had no doubt that Old Shatterhand would be the victor.

"No," the hunter replied. "The Upsaroca are enemies of the Sioux-Ogallalla. If we spare them, they will become our allies."

"The other may live too. One is not to say of Winnetou that his white brother is more merciful than he."

The party had covered perhaps a mile since leaving the canyon when the valley opened widely. The horsemen arrived on a small prairie like many around there. Mountains enclosed all of it. Some poor grass and singular bushes grew there. Only a lone tree could be spotted on the plain. It was a rather tall linden, the kind, which Indians of the Sonoran tongue call muh-mangatusahga, the white-leaf tree, because of its large, white and hairy leaves.

"*Mawa* – there!" said the Crow's leader, pointing to the tree.

"Howgh!" nodded Winnetou, directing his horse at a gallop towards the linden.

The others followed. This was where the duels would take place.

The tension, which had gripped all, was certainly not little, although none let it show. The three who knew themselves to be combatants felt the greatest inner peace: Winnetou, Old Shatterhand, and Oiht-e-keh-fa-wakon. Each one of them was convinced that he would win.

All jumped off their mounts. The horses were set free to roam, and the men sat in a circle on the ground. A stranger passing by would not have thought that enemies faced each other here, since the Upsaroca had been allowed to keep their weapons. Old Shatterhand had not demanded their surrender. In this respect, he was truly chivalrous, or, as the American says, gentleman-like.

He took as much as was required of his small tobacco supply from his saddlebag and then took the pipe from his neck and stuffed it. At last, he stood in the midst of the circle and spoke:

"The warrior doesn't speak many words, but speaks by action: My brothers are aware what is to happen here; I need not tell them. We did not kill the warriors of the Upsaroca, although their lives were in our hands. We spared them to show that we don't fear them, if we fight them man-to-man without advantage. They called us for the *muh-mohwa*, and we accepted their request. They sit among us with their weapons as free men, although they are actually our prisoners. We expect them to act without malice and cunning towards us like we towards them. They will promise this by smoking the Pipe of Oath with us. I have spoken. Now they may, too."

He sat down. The 'Brave Looking for Medicine' rose and answered:

"The white man spoke like from our heart. We need not be cunning, for we shall win. But he forgot to set the conditions for the fight."

"The fighters", he continued after a small pause, "will be tied with one hand to the tree facing one another. Each will receive his knife in the other hand and shall fight with it against his enemy. Only this one hand is permitted to be used; any other way of fighting is prohibited. But if one of the fighters can no longer hold the knife, he is allowed to continue defending himself with his fist. Who falls down is considered defeated, whether dead or alive. Whoever falls only to his knees, may rise again. Four men will fight; one against the other. First, I will fight this paleface, and then one of my people against one of the red warriors. However, the latter may also fight first. If the victors of each fight belong to different parties, they must fight each other to decide the battle. The lives and property of the defeated party then belong to the companions of the victor, and none of those who have forfeited their lives may resist being killed. The warriors of the Upsaroca are ready to smoke the Pipe of Oath on these conditions. And so that the fights are honest, and that none is protected more than the other by better clothing, all four men must fight bare-chested. I have spoken."

He took his place again. Old Shatterhand once more entered the circle and declared:

"We agree with all conditions of the Upsaroca. And so that the defeated will have no weapons with which they can resist being killed, all warriors present will take off their weapons and gather them at a place to be guarded by a Shoshone and an Upsaroca. I shall now light the Peace Pipe. Today, it will be the Pipe of Oath. By its smoke, the souls of the defeated may take wing into the Eternal Hunting Grounds to serve there the souls of the victors as slaves."

"Howgh! Howgh!" sounded from the circle.

Old Shatterhand pulled out his punk and lit the tobacco. Inhaling the smoke, he blew it towards the sky, the earth, and the four quarters, and then handed it to the leader of the Upsaroca, who took the same six draws. Then, he declared that the agreement had now been sworn to and been sealed. The others took part in the oath by each taking a draw. Finally, at a fairly distant place, the pipe was stuck by its mouthpiece into the earth, and all deposited their weapons there.

Sure of his victory, the Upsaroca now stepped to the tree, threw off his upper clothing and said:

"Now it begins. Before the sun has traveled a knife's back-width to the west, the scalp of one of the white dogs will hang from my belt."

Only now did it become apparent how tremendously powerful the man must be. He had the muscular frame of a bear. And because of what was to happen now, he was worthy of admiration. Then, Martin Baumann, the young son of the Bear Hunter, jumped up and shouted angrily:

"It is the Whites you have to thank for your life, and yet you call them dogs! You aren't worthy of having an experienced warrior fight you. Well then, here stands a young white dog who isn't afraid to show you his teeth, although you are the strongest warrior of your tribe. Before the sun has moved as far as you have said, the sin of the big-mouthed, croaking 'crow' will be torn apart by the dog."

His cheeks and eyes aglow, he threw off his hunting jacket.

"Uff, uff!" sounded admiringly from the circle.

He was the youngest of all present, which is why his courageous bearing was extraordinarily impressive.

"*Deh mehtsif* – he is a courageous one!" even escaped the giant Upsaroca.

"Very gallant," Old Shatterhand said. "That will not be forgotten, my dear young man. But you know it is I who has been challenged. Therefore, I must ask you to leave to me to prove that a white dog need not be afraid of a 'crow'."

"But he isn't worth having a man like you fight him," Martin objected. "And, if you think I'm frightened of this colossus, remember that I've killed quite a number of grizzlies already!"

"Yes, I can see that you would gladly enter into this dangerous fight, but, for the time being, be content with our admiration for your courage! I would be seen a coward, if I would agree to this substitution."

"I can, of course, not dispute this which is why I shall follow your will. However, I'm not used to having myself called a dog!"

He pulled his hunting jacket on again and stepped back. The giant gave one of his people a sign. The man stepped forward, unclothed his chest, and said:

"Here stands Makin-oh-punkreh, Hundredfold Thunder. He made his shield from the skin of his foes, and more than forty scalps has he taken. Who dares to face my knife?"

"I, Wohkadeh, shall put Hundredfold Thunder to silence. I cannot boast of a single scalp, but I've killed the white buffalo, and today shall decorate my belt with the first scalp. Who fears 'thunder'? It is the cowardly companion of lightning and only raises its voice when the danger has passed!"

Again the "Uff, uffs" arose all around when the young Indian, speaking these words, stepped up.

"Go back!" scoffed Hundredfold Thunder. I do not fight a child. A breath from my mouth would kill you. Lie down in the grass and dream of your mother who ought to feed you camas still!"

The Grave Indians, the most despised Reds, search the barren areas, where they lead their sorry existence, for an onion-like root which, in a half-rotten condition is formed by them into a disgusting cake, the so-called camas cake. Even dogs disdain eating it. Therefore, Thunder's words were meant as a great insult to the gallant Wohkadeh.

Before he could respond, Winnetou stepped forward. He gave the young Indian a signal to withdraw which he, from respect, immediately obeyed. Then Winnetou said:

"A verdict has been spoken on the two warriors of the Upsaroca. Who answered to fight them following their proud talk? Two boys, both of them convinced to become victors for they have already killed the white buffalo and the gray bear. They would strangle the two Crows with their hands. But we shall act as if the Crows are true warriors. They shall fight against men. Hundredfold Thunder has growled for the last time."

At that, Thunder asked angrily:

"Who are you to speak such words? Do you have a name? There is not a single hair of an enemy to be seen on your outfit. Have your learned only to play the *dshotunka*[6]? Then go and do so, but a knife does not belong in your hand. You would only hurt yourself."

"I shall tell my name to your soul when it leaves your body. Then, it will lament from terror and will not dare enter the Eternal Hunting Grounds. It will dwell in the clefts of the mountains, where it will howl from fear with the wind and lament with the breezes."

"Dog!" Thunder hollered. "You dare insult a brave warrior's soul! You shall receive punishment right away. We two shall fight first, before the other pair, and your scalp shall not find a place among my trophies. I shall toss it to the rats and your name, you denied to tell me, will not be heard by a single warrior!"

"Yes, we shall fight first. May it begin!" Winnetou replied.

He bared his chest, while Hundredfold Thunder signaled for his knife, which was handed to him.

A wide circle now formed around the linden. Everyone's eyes examined the figures of the two opponents. The Upsaroca, while not taller, was much broader and stronger built, than slender Winnetou. The Crow Indians noticed that with satisfaction. They were convinced that Winnetou would be defeated. However, they had no idea, that they were facing the famous Chief of the Apache. The others, knowing him, were somewhat concerned for him when they saw the strong body of the Upsaroca. But then they could stay calm, knowing the Apache's fame.

Fat Jemmy now stepped up. He had several straps, like every frontiersman carries on him, and said to Winnetou:

"You have the first round, my good sir. May it be your good omen that you are tied to the tree by the hand of a friend. But everyone may first convince himself that both straps are of equal quality."

The straps went from hand to hand and were closely examined. Now, it had to be decided who of the two was to be tied with the right hand and who by his

---

[6] A flute-like pipe.

left. Two different grass blades were used to draw lots. Winnetou drew the shorter one and was, therefore, disadvantaged, since his right hand would be tied to the tree, following which he had to fight with the less-trained, left hand. The Upsaroca greeted this favorable condition with a happy "*uh-ah* – very good, very good!"

The straps were now tied in a sling around the fighters' wrists, then slung loosely enough around the tree's trunk to permit the fighters to move around the tree. It may happen during a *muh-mohwa* that the opponents drive each other for a quarter of an hour and even longer, around the trunk before the first stab occurs. If blood then flows, they usually attack each other more heatedly so that the fight is soon decided.

Now, they stood ready, one on one side, the other on the opposite side of the tree.

Limping Frank stood next to Fat Jemmy.

"Listen, mishter Pfefferkorn," Frank said, "this is a situation where a cold shiver runs down your shpine, because not only do these two risk their lives, but also ours. This very moment, I have a feeling below my shcalp lock, as if it's already successively pulled off. I'm truly grateful for the promise to have ourselves patiently butchered, if our two champions are defeated!"

"Pah!" Jemmy replied. "Although I'm also not feeling too good about it, I think we can rely on Winnetou and Old Shatterhand."

"It shure looks like it. The Apache seems so peaceful as if he had ten matadors on hand. But, quiet! Hundredfold Thunder is shpeaking."

He had just received his knife.

"*Shihsheh* – come on!" he shouted, challenging the Apache. "Or am I to chase you around the tree until you collapse from fear without my knife having hit you!"

Winnetou did not reply. He turned to Old Shatterhand and said in Apache, which his opponent did not understand:

"*Shi din ida sesteh* – I shall neutralize his hand."

Hearing this, Old Shatterhand declared loudly, while pointing at Winnetou:

"This, our brother, has closed his heart from the thought of murder. He will defeat his enemy without taking a drop of his blood."

"Uff, uff, uff!" the Upsaroca shouted.

Hundredfold Thunder responded sneeringly to Old Shatterhand's statement:

"Your brother has turned crazy from fear. I shall shorten his suffering."

He took a step forward, so that the tree trunk no longer separated the two. Knife in fist, his eyes held Winnetou in a veritable carnivore's look. However, the Apache did not even seem to pay attention to him. Carelessly, he appeared to look into the distance, his face so quiet and unmoving, as if, what was happening, was of no concern to him. However, Old Shatterhand noticed very well that

169

every muscle and sinew of his red fighting companion was prepared for the coming attack.

The Upsaroca let himself be deceived. He suddenly jumped at Winnetou, raising his arm for the deadly stab. But instead of retreating, the Apache just as suddenly came towards him, and, with a mighty thrust rammed his fist with the knife's hilt into the enemy's arm pit. This courageous as well as powerful and well-performed action resulted in the Upsaroca being pushed back and dropping his knife. A grab by the Apache, who had also tossed his own knife away, and the Upsaroca screamed. Winnetou had twisted his hand and, in the next moment, thrust his balled fist into the man's stomach. Thunder tumbled backwards and, hanging with his hand from the tree trunk, landed on his back.

Stunned, the Upsaroca lay motionless, which the Apache found sufficient. Picking up his knife, he freed himself from the tree with a quick cut and knelt on his enemy, taking only a second.

"Are you defeated?" he asked.

The other did not reply. He breathed heavily, partly from the punch he had received, partly from anger and fear of death.

This had all happened so lightning-fast, that the Apache's individual movements had been almost impossible to differentiate. Not a sound arose from the circle of spectators. When the little Saxon wanted to shout a rejoicing "hurrah", Old Shatterhand ordered him to be silent with such a forceful arm move that he got to pronounce only the first syllable, while the second remained stuck in his mouth.

"Stab," the Upsaroca grated, giving the Apache, who was bent over him, a look of extreme hatred. Then he closed his eyes.

But Winnetou rose, cut the straps of the defeated, and said:

"Get up! I promised not to kill you, and I shall keep my word."

"I do not wish to live; I have been defeated!"

At that Oiht-e-keh-wakon stepped up to him and ordered angrily:

"Get up! Your life has been given you, since your scalp has no value for the victor. You behaved like a boy. But I still stand here to fight for us. I shall win twice, and while we will share the enemies' scalps, you will go to the wolves of the prairie to live with them. Return to your wigwam is forbidden you."

Hundredfold Thunder rose and reached for his dropped knife.

"The Great Spirit did not want me to win," he said. I will not go to the wolves. Here is my knife to end my life, which may have been given me. But first I want to see if you know better to win than myself."

He moved off a short distance to sit there in the grass. One could see that he was serious about not surviving the shame of having been defeated.

He wasn't given a single look by his people. The more hopeful, though, looked at their leader, who leaned his mighty frame against the tree trunk and challenged Old Shatterhand:

"Come here and let us draw lots!"

"I do not draw lots," he answered. "Tie me by my right hand."

"Is it, that you wish to die more quickly?"

"No, but because I think that your left hand is weaker than your right. I do not wish for an advantage over you. You have been injured."

He pointed to the Red's left shoulder, which showed a broad scar. His opponent could not comprehend this nobleness. He measured him with a look of great surprise and answered:

"Do you want to insult me! Are your people to say, when I have killed you, that it would not have happened had you not extended this favor to me? I demand we draw lots."

"Well then, let's do so."

The lot followed Old Shatterhand's suggestion, that is, it turned out in his enemy's favor. The White's right hand was tied up. Only a moment later, the two faced each other. Whoever saw the giant's muscles, which wound around his body like long-drawn cables, had to fear for Old Shatterhand.

However, the hunter displayed the same outward equanimity as Winnetou had earlier.

"You may begin," The Upsaroca invited him. "I shall permit you the first stab. Three thrusts I shall ward off. Then, you shall fall from my first stab."

At this Old Shatterhand laughed briefly. He thrust his knife into the linden's trunk and replied:

"And I dispense entirely with this weapon. Yet, you shall fall with the first attack. We don't have time for playing a long game. Pay attention then, for I begin!"

He raised his arm as if to hit and then leaped at his opponent, who let himself be deceived by this feint to stab at him. However, the White had fallen back with lightning speed, causing the thrust to fail. Another fast move by Old Shatterhand, and his fist hit the opponent's temple. The giant's body staggered for a moment and then crashed heavily to the ground.

"There he lies, his entire body on the ground! Who has won?" Old Shatterhand shouted.

Earlier, when Hundredfold Thunder had been defeated, the Upsaroca had remained quiet. They now broke out into a howl as though coming from animals' throats. The others rose to loud shouts of joy.

If anyone expected that the Crow Indians would attempt a quick flight if defeated, it did not materialize. Did they feel honor-bound by their oath, or were they too dismayed to be able to come to a quick decision? None made a move. Therefore, one could conclude that they did not want to evade death, seemingly certain now for all of them according to the earlier agreement.

Old Shatterhand pulled his knife from the trunk and cut himself loose. The white hunters stepped up to congratulate him. The friendly Indians also praised the two victors but endeavored also to quickly get their weapons making any possible opposition by the Upsaroca, including their escape, impossible.

They, however, had stopped their howling and went to where Hundredfold Thunder was sitting, taking their place next to him. Even the one who had guarded the weapons joined them, though it would have been easy for him to leap onto one of the horses and escape.

Old Shatterhand stepped toward 'Brave Looking for Medicine', who was just then coming out of his stunned condition. Opening his eyes, he saw the victor cutting the strap tying him to the tree. It took some time before he gained understanding of the situation. Then, he jumped up and gave Old Shatterhand an indescribable stare. His eyes appeared to come out of their sockets, and his voice sounded raw and stumbling when he asked:

"I – lay – on the ground! Did you defeat me?"

"Yes! Did you not speak of the condition that he, who would come to lie with his body on the ground, would be thought to be defeated?"

The Red looked at himself. Despite his size, he now presented an image of deepest fright.

"But I am not injured!" he exclaimed.

"Because I did not want to kill you. Did I not thrust my knife into the tree?"

"Then you struck me down with your bare hand?"

"Yes," Old Shatterhand smiled. "I hope you won't hold this against me. It was better for you than being knifed."

However, the Upsaroca was unable to jest. He gave his people a look of great helplessness. Then his features took on an expression of rigid resignation.

"It would have been better had you killed me!" he lamented. "The Great Spirit has forsaken us since our medicines were stolen. The warrior who is scalped can never enter the Eternal Hunting Grounds. Why did the squaws of our fathers not die before we were born!"

This man, previously so proud and sure of victory, was now faint-hearted and despondent like a child. He stumbled towards his people to sit with them, but turned once more to ask:

"Do you permit us to sing the death song before you kill us?"

"Before I give you an answer, I will pose a question to you. Come!"

Old Shatterhand led him to the Upsaroca, pointed to Hundredfold Thunder, and asked: "Are you still angry at this warrior?"

"No. He could not do otherwise. The Great Spirit wanted it like that. We have lost our medicines."

"You shall get them back, maybe even better ones."

They all looked up at him in surprise.

"Where are we to find them?" their leader asked. "Here, where we must die? Or in the Eternal Hunting Grounds which we cannot get to because we will lose our scalps?"

"You will keep your scalps and your lives. You would have killed us had we been defeated, but we agreed to your conditions only seemingly. We are Christians and do not murder our brothers. Get up! Go over there and take your weapons and your horses! You are free and can ride wherever you wish!"

But none made any effort to follow this offer.

"You say this as the beginning of the pains with which you will torture us," said Brave Looking for Medicine. We shall endure them without you hearing any sound of lament coming from our mouths."

"You are mistaken. I am serious. The war tomahawk between the Upsaroca and the warriors of the Shoshone has been lowered."

"But you knew that we were going to kill you!"

"You did not succeed, which is why we do not thirst for your blood. We need not avenge any of us. Kanteh-pehta, the famous medicine man of the Upsaroca, is our friend. He and his warriors can return unhindered to their wigwams."

"Uff! You know me?" the leader asked surprised.

"You are missing an ear, and I see the scar there by which I recognized you."

"Where from do you know the signs I bear?"

"From your brother Shunka-shetsha, the Big Hound, who told me about you."

"You also know him?"

"Yes. I once met him."

"When? Where?"

"Several summers ago. We parted at the Mountain of the Turtle."

Hearing this the medicine man, who had already sat down, jumped up again. His features assumed an entirely different expression. His eyes lost the rigid, resigned look and began to shine.

"Is your word or my ear deluding me?" he exclaimed. "If you tell the truth, then you are Non-pay-klama, the Whites call Old Shatterhand!"

"I am he, indeed."

Hearing this name the other Upsaroca rose, too. They suddenly appeared to be totally different people.

"If you are this famous hunter," their leader called," then the Great Spirit has not yet forsaken us. Yes, it must be you, for you struck me down with your fist. To have been defeated by you is no shame. I can live without squaws pointing at me."

"Also Hundredfold Thunder, who is a brave warrior, need not be ashamed to have been defeated, for the one he fought is Winnetou, the Chief of the Apache."

The Upsaroca' eyes looked referentially at Winnetou, who stepped up to offer Hundredfold Thunder his hand and said:

"My red brother did smoke the Pipe of Oath with me. Now, he will also smoke the Calumet of Peace with us, for the warriors of the Upsaroca are our friends. Howgh!"

Thunder took his hand to reply:

"The curse of the bad spirit has vanished from us. Old Shatterhand and Winnetou are friends of red men. They will not demand our scalps."

"No. You are free," Old Shatterhand repeated the previously given assurance. "We shall give you something instead of robbing you of something. We know the men who took your medicines. If you will follow us, we shall lead you to them."

"Uff! Who are the thieves?"

"A bunch of Sioux-Ogallalla, whose destination is the mountains of the Yellowstone River."

This information got the dispossessed men very much excited. Their leader exclaimed angrily:

"It was the dogs of Ogallalla! Hing-peh-te-keh, Heavy Moccasin, their chief, did wound me and took my ear without me being able to avenge myself. I did beg the Great Spirit to put me onto his tracks, however, my wish never came to pass."

Hearing this, Wohkadeh, who had stood close-by, stepped forward to say:

"You are on his tracks, because Hong-peh-te-keh is the leader of the Ogallalla, we are pursuing."

"Then the Great Spirit will at last give him into my hands. But who is this young red warrior, who wanted to fight Hundredfold Thunder, and now has such good information about the Sioux-Ogallalla?"

"It is Wohkadeh, a brave son of the Numangkake," Old Shatterhand answered. "The Ogallalla forced him to ride with them, and he was present when they took your medicines. He escaped and has rendered us already great service."

"And what do the Sioux want in the mountains of the Yellowstone River?"

"We shall tell you once we have started our camp fires. Then, you may deliberate whether you wish to ride with us."

"If you are on the tracks of the Ogallalla to fight them, we shall ride with you. They robbed us of our medicines. Wohkadeh shall tell us how it happened. Kanteh-pehta is the most famous of medicine men of the Upsaroca. That he had his great medicine stolen brought him disgrace and shame. He will not rest until he has succeeded in avenging himself. My brothers may light the fires of council. We must not lose any time, and my warriors know what great honor it is for them to ride with such famous men!"

Thus, once again, foes were changed to friends, and with the number of participants, hope grew that the, at first, so difficult appearing enterprise would succeed.

4. At P'a-wakon-tonka

The Congress of the United States has decided that the area near the source of the Yellowstone River in the Territories of Montana and Wyoming, is hereby reserved and withdrawn from settlement, occupancy, or sale under the laws of the United States, and dedicated and set apart as a public park or pleasuring-ground for the benefit and enjoyment of the people. Anyone settling there against these provisions or who is to take possession of any part thereof, is thought to have infringed upon this law and will be expelled. The park is to be put under the exclusive control of the Secretary of the Interior whose task it will be to issue, as soon as possible, all such regulations and directions he considers necessary for its care and maintenance.

Thus, a law was written and accepted by the Congress of the United States on March 1, 1872, with which a gift, whose magnitude could not be imagined at the time, was made to the citizens of the United States and the residents of other countries.

This area, which nowadays is called a National Park of the United States, generated the most curious rumors, which circulated in the eastern states. Known only to the wildest of Indians and seen only in parts by daring, lonely trappers, the area was enveloped in deepest secrecy. What one of these trappers reported was carried on and fantastically embellished. Burning prairies and mountains, boiling springs, volcanoes, spewing liquid metal, lakes and rivers filled with oil instead of water, fossilized forests with fossilized Indians and animals were to be found there.

It was only through Professor Hayden and his 1871 expedition to this wonderful region that precise information was returned, and he certainly reported the exceptional. He is to be thanked for the enactment of the above law.

The national park encompasses an area of over 6,000 square miles. Within it is the source of the Yellowstone, Madison, Gallatin, and Snake Rivers. Mighty mountain chains cross the area. A clean and invigorating air circulates the heights, and hundreds of cold and hot springs of different chemical composition offer wonderful healing powers for the recovery of the sick and the renewal of vital energy. Geysers, incomparably greater than Icelandic ones, throw their waters several hundred feet into the air. Mountains, some consisting of volcanic glass, glitter in all kinds of colors and shine in the sun's rays. Gorges, horrible like in no other area, seem to be cut into the innards of the earth, permitting a glimpse of its interior. Some of the ground forms bubbles, which rise and sink. Often it appears to be only inches thick, so that the horseman can urge his terrified horse to step forward only with difficulty. Giant holes open up, filled with boiling mud, slowly rising and sinking. It is absolutely impossible to walk for more than a quarter of an hour without coming across some kind of amazing natural wonder. All in all, there are more than two thousand geysers and hot springs. While, at one place, boiling hot water rises from the ground, quite near it a clear, cold spring bubbles up. Good and bad spirits, angels and devils, seem to fight against each other below the surface. If one looks at one place, astonished by the sublime, then, a few paces farther, one yields to the terrible. If one has admired a giant fountain at one place, rising a thousand feet above the river's level at the walls of a canyon, one can then walk across fields of carnelian, moss agate, chalcedony, opal, and other semiprecious stones, all of immense value.

And among the mountains hide beautiful lakes. The largest and most beautiful is Yellowstone Lake, which is, except for Titicaca Lake, the highest large lake on Earth. It is located almost eight thousand feet above sea level.

Its waters are high in sulfur, and its deep bays swarm with giant trout, whose flesh has a peculiar but very good taste. The surrounding forests are rich in elk, bear, and other game. On its banks numerous hot springs erupt from which the steam of the underworld whistles forth, loud and shrill, like from the valves of a locomotive.

A fearful mind will easily feel like vacating this area. The restlessly working forces of the Earth's interior are so very noticeable here, making the wanderer feel no longer safe on Earth. One may feel as if the entire mile-wide area may either sink the next moment, or lift like a gigantic, fire-spitting crater far above the peaks of the Rocky Mountains – in both cases, quite unpleasant for anyone being swallowed up or tossed upward along with everything else.

Where the Yellowstone River flows out from the lake, and where the lake's banks spread southwest towards the spot where the Bridge Creek enters, several fires were burning. They had been lit against the darkness that had fallen, and not for the preparation of dinner. For the latter, nature had pleasantly provided.

Yard-long trout, caught in the lake's cold waters, were simmering in hot water, boiling only a few feet away from the lake's bank. The little Saxon fancied himself, not a little, for having shot a wild sheep that afternoon. Boiled meat was, therefore, served with trout for dessert. The hot spring was of such small size, that it was just right to serve as a cooking pot, and because of this small volume, its run-off had such a bouillon taste, that it could be scooped up with the few available leather mugs and drunk with delight.

The company had come across the Pelican and Yellowstone Rivers, just as Old Shatterhand had advised. Tomorrow morning they intended to cross Bridge Creek to ride straight west for the Firehole River. That's where the geyser called *K'un-tui-tempa* by Indians, the Hell's Mouth, was located. In its vicinity lay the chiefs' graves, the destination of their long ride.

The ride had been completed much faster than originally thought. Although the destination was already rather close, there were still three full days to go until full moon, and Old Shatterhand was convinced that the Ogallalla could, by no means, have arrived already. In the course of the conversation, he remarked:

"They can hardly have reached the Botteler's Range, which means we are safe from them. So, keep the fires going until the moon rises later from behind the mountains. We need not expect other people here except for the Sioux. There's nothing to be concerned about."

"And how's the trail from Botteler's Range up there?" Martin Baumann asked.

"Do you want to ride it by chance, young friend?"

Martin did not notice the questioning look Old Shatterhand gave him upon this question, yet he answered with a slight, not quite controlled, embarrassment:

"I'm interested in it, because my father has to take it. I heard it is very dangerous."

"I wouldn't say that. Of course, one must avoid the vicinity of the geysers and avoid the areas where the Earth's crust is so thin that one might break through stepping onto it. One rides up from Botteler's Range in the river valley, passing several extinct volcanoes. After four to five hours, one reaches the lower canyon, which is half a mile long and may be cut a thousand feet deep into granite. After another five hours, one gets to a mountain from whose peak two parallel rock walls run almost three thousand feet down. This is called the Devil's Slide. Three hours later, one reaches the mouth of the Gardiner River, and follows it upstream, since one can no longer get upriver by the Yellowstone. Then, one rides along the Washburn Mountains and the Cascade Creek, the latter leading back to the Yellowstone. It enters the Yellowstone between its upper and lower falls. Then, one has reached the edge of the big canyon, which is probably the greatest wonder of the Yellowstone Basin."

"Do you know this wonder, sir?" Fat Jemmy asked.

Old Shatterhand secretly studied him before he replied:

"Yes. It is probably seven miles long and several thousand feet deep. Its walls drop almost vertically. Only a totally vertigo-free person can dare creep to its edge to look into the terrible depth where, down deep, the two hundred feet wide river appears like a thin thread. And yet, it was this thread that cut so deeply into the rock in the course of thousands of years. Its waves rush with terrific speed along the massive rock walls, though high above nothing can be heard of their fury. No mortal can get down there, and if he could, he would not be able to stand it for a quarter of an hour. He would run short of air. The river's water is warm, looks like oil, and has a nauseous sulfur and alumina taste, exuding an unbearable stink. If one travels up the canyon, one reaches the lower falls of the river, where it tumbles from a height of four hundred feet into the fearful depth. A quarter of an hour upriver, it again drops more than a hundred feet. From these upper falls, it would take a horseman about nine hours. This makes it, therefore, two hard days' ride from Botteler's Range to here, which is the number of days we are ahead of the Sioux-Ogallalla. Of course, this calculation can't be exact, but a few hours more or less are really of no consequence. It's enough for us to know that our enemies cannot be here yet."

"Where will they be tomorrow about this time, sir?" Martin Baumann asked.

"At the upper exit of the canyon. Do you have a reason for wanting to know it so precisely?"

"No particular one, but you can imagine that I'm accompanying my father in my mind. Who knows whether he's still alive."

"I'm convinced that he is."

"The Sioux might have killed him!"

You need not be concerned about that. The Ogallalla want to bring their captives to the chiefs' graves, which they will do, rest assured of this. The later these unfortunate men will be killed, the greater is the pain they must endure. This is why the Sioux won't think of shortening their time by an earlier death. I know these red fellows very well, and when I tell you that your father is still alive, you can believe me."

He wrapped himself into his blanket and lay down, as if he was going to sleep. But from beneath his half-closed lids he observed Martin Baumann, Fat Jemmy and Hobble-Frank, who were softly and intently talking with each other.

After a while, the Fat One rose from his place and ambled slowly and seemingly unaffectedly in the direction where the horses were grazing. Right away, Old Shatterhand got up, too, to follow him secretly. He saw that Jemmy staked his horse down, which had only been hobbled. Quickly stepping up to him, he asked:

"Master Jemmy, what did your horse do that it isn't permitted to graze freely?"

Startled the former Gymnasiast turned around.

"Ah, it's you, sir. I thought you were asleep."

"And until now, I thought you to be an honest fellow!"

"By the devil! Do you think I'm no longer one?"

"It almost appears like it!"

"How so?"

"What's the reason you were so alarmed when I came here?"

"For the simple reason that anyone would be startled who's so unexpectedly addressed at night."

"That would be a poor frontiersman. A good hunter might not even make a move if a shot is fired unexpectedly right next to his ear."

"Shure, if the bullet goes through his head, he's, of course, no longer moving!"

"Pah! You know very well that there are no hostiles here! Is it that no one was to know that you staked your horse down?"

The Fat One covered his embarrassment by an angry retort:

"Now, sir, I don't understand you. Can I no longer do with my horse as I see fit?"

"Certainly, but you needn't do it secretly!"

"There's no secrecy involved. There are some kickers among the Upsaroca' horses. My horse has already been hurt once. In order that it won't happen again, I staked it down, so he doesn't get into this restive company. If that's my sin, I hope to receive forgiveness."

He turned to go back to the camp. However, Old Shatterhand put his hand on his shoulder asking:

"Stay for a moment longer, master Jemmy. It isn't my intention to insult you, but I think I have reason to warn you. That I do this under four eyes tells you how much I value you."

Jemmy pushed his hat back, scratched his ear as his friend Davy usually did when he was embarrassed, and answered:

"Sir, if someone else would tell me that, I would let my fist wander a bit across his face, but from you, I'll accept the warning. All right, since you have loaded already, then, confound it, fire away!"

"Fine! What's the secret between you and the Bear Hunter's son?"

It took Jemmy a moment to answer:

"Secrets! I with him? Then, these secrets are so secret, that even I don't know the least about them."

"You whispered quite a bit with each other!"

"He wants to exercise his German."

"That he can also do aloud. I've noticed, that he's lately much more concerned about his father. He's afraid he will be killed by the Ogallalla, and my efforts are fruitless trying to talk him out of it. You heard earlier that he started it again. I'm afraid that he entertains thoughts, which are an honor to his love as a child, but not to his judgment. Might you know anything about this?"

"Hm! Did he tell you anything about that, sir?"

"No."

"Well then. He's having certainly more trust towards you than with me. If he's silent towards you, he'll be no more communicative with me."

"It looks to me, like you are trying to get around a direct answer?"

"Wouldn't think of it!"

"He has kept his distance from me and Winnetou since yesterday, while you are always riding with him. From it, I concluded that he's made you his confidant."

"I tell you that there, you are quite mistaken while, otherwise, you are such an exceptionally sharp-minded man."

"Then, he truly told you nothing from which one could conclude that he intends doing something I cannot approve?"

"By the devil! You're giving me quite an examination. Keep in mind, sir, that I'm no schoolboy! If someone tells me about his family affairs and problems of the heart, then I'm not permitted to answer someone else."

"All right, master Jemmy! What you just said, although rude, is nevertheless correct. I won't, therefore, press you any longer and will act as if I haven't noticed anything. However, should something happen, which would harm any one of us, I refuse to accept any responsibility for it. We are done."

He turned, though he did not walk back to camp, but in the opposite direction. He had been annoyed by Jemmy and wanted to calm his mind by taking a brief walk.

The Fat One ambled slowly back to his fire mumbling softly:

"This man has a devilishly sharp eye! Who would have thought that he noticed anything. He's right, absolutely right, and I wish I could have told him everything. But I gave my word to keep quiet, and can't break it. It would have been better if I hadn't entered into this thing. But the little Bear Hunter knew how to ask so nicely that this old, fat raccoon's heart gave up all reason. Well. I hope this thing will come to a good end!"

When Old Shatterhand had earlier left the fire, those who had stayed back had quietly talked about the same issue.

"Oh my!" Long Davy had whispered to the Son of the Bear Hunter. "There goes Old Shatterhand! Where to?"

"Who knows!"

"Maybe I do. I think he didn't sleep at all. If someone gets up like he did, then he didn't rise from slumber. He probably watched us."

"Why should he? We didn't give him any reason to mistrust us."

"Hm! I certainly did not, but you, perhaps. I've taken great care not to talk much with you, when I figured he would notice, such as earlier. But Jemmy stays with you all the time, so that anyone must think that you have some secret with him. Old Shatterhand did notice this. Now, he went after Jemmy and will see that he staked down our horses, so that we need not search long for them when we later sneak away from here. If he noticed that, then our intention has been rather given away."

"I'll do it, nevertheless!"

"I did warn you and warn you again now!"

But think about it, my dear Davy that I'm no longer capable of waiting three full days! I'm dying from anxiety for my father."

"But Old Shatterhand explained to you that the prisoners must be alive still!"

"He can easily be mistaken."

"Then, we cannot change it either."

"But then, I will be certain and can act accordingly. Do you want me to give you your word back?"

"It might be better for me."

"You say this? You, I had such great trust for," Martin said reproachingly. "Did you forget that you and Jemmy were the first to offer their help? But now I can no longer rely on you."

"By the devil! That's an accusation, I won't have resting on me. I was carried away giving you this promise because of my affection for you, and you aren't going to say that I won't keep it. I'll ride along, but under one condition!"

"Let's hear it! I'll keep it if it's possible to do so."

"We'll only spy on the Ogallalla to find out if your father is still alive."

"Yes. Agreed."

"We are not trying to free him ourselves."

"I'm of the same opinion."

"Fine! I can imagine quite well what it looks like in your heart. You see a real danger for your father. This touches my good, old soul, which is why I'll accompany you. But as soon as we've seen that he's still alive, we turn and follow the others. I only wish you had not had the idea of taking Hobble-Frank along!"

"He's earned this consideration."

"But I think he'll be more of a detriment than an advantage to us."

"Oh, you are mistaken about him. Despite his peculiarities, he's a courageous and agile fellow."

"That may be, but he's burdened with a tendency for misfortune. What he starts in the best manner, mostly fails. Such bad-luck fellows are the best of creatures, but one must avoid them."

"But I did promise him and don't want to hurt him by taking back my word. He's stayed with us in joy and pain, and it is a kind of reward for him to be taken along."

"And Wohkadeh? Is he still coming?"

"Yes. We've become such close friends that he can't stay back while I go on this ride."

"Then, it's all right, and it's only a question of getting away unnoticed. Of course, there will be quite some concern for us tomorrow morning when we are found missing, but I think the Negro will convey the instructions. Here comes Jemmy."

The Fat One approached to sit down.

"Right, Old Shatterhand doesn't trust us?" Davy asked.

"Yes. He examined me like a scoundrel," the Fat One grumbled, ill-humoredly.

"But you didn't admit to anything?"

"Of course not. But it was a bitter pill for me to swallow. I even had to resort to rudeness. He took it badly and walked off."

"And he saw that you staked our horses down?"

"At that point, I had only done it to my own. Fortunately, he had come after me right away. But let's be quiet now to put his mistrust to rest. There, the moon's rising already. Let's extinguish the fire and lie down under the trees. They'll throw some shadows, which, for a while at least, will cover our leaving.

"It's well, to have the moon's shine. It makes finding our way easier."

"It was clearly explained. Always down-river. In one way, I don't like us to be forced to deceive our comrades, but on the other hand, it won't hurt them any. Earlier, we could always put in a word, but now, Old Shatterhand and Winnetou are the commanders. Jemmy and Davy are asked only now and then for their opinion. So, it's actually time to show them that we, too, are frontiersmen who can devise a plan and execute it. But let's rest now. It won't be too much longer."

The fire was extinguished. The Indians' fires had also gone out. Talk had fallen silent. Once Old Shatterhand had returned, he lay down in the grass next to Winnetou. Now all was quiet everywhere. Only the shrill whistle of the steam escaping from the earth could be heard at regular intervals.

More than an hour passed before there was some movement below the trees where Frank, Jemmy, Davy, Martin and Wohkadeh had bedded down.

"My brothers may follow me," whispered the young Indian. "It is time. Who goes earlier, arrives earlier."

Under the trees' cover, they took their weapons and other belongings and sneaked silently towards their horses. Jemmy found his easily; the others had to search for theirs. But Wohkadeh's sharp eyes quickly succeeded in differentiating the four animals from one another.

However, they did not accomplish it without some noise. For this reason, the five escapees stayed put once they had found their horses. They listened quietly for awhile, to make sure their departure had not been noticed.

But when all remained quiet among the sleepers, they led their horses slowly off. Their hoof beats were dampened by the grass.

Of course, they did not get away totally unnoticed. Although hostiles were not expected in the vicinity, several guards had been posted who were spelled from time to time. It was a nightly requirement simply because of wild animals. They passed one of the guards. It was a Shoshone. He heard them coming and knew, of course, that they came from the nearby camp of friends. Therefore, he sounded no alarm. The moon's light, stealing through the branches, permitted him to see the horses. That there were men leaving with their horses caused him to wonder.

"What are my brothers' intentions?" he asked.

"Look at me! Do you recognize me?" Jemmy replied, stepping close to him, so that he could be seen clearly.

"Yes, you are Jemmy-petahtsheh."

"Speak quietly, so none of the sleeping are wakened. Old Shatterhand is sending us out. He knows where we are headed. Is that enough for you?"

"My white bothers are our friends. I will not prevent them from following the great hunter's commands."

They went on. When they were far enough from camp so that hoof beats could no longer be heard, they mounted up, looked for the brighter banks of the lake, and trotted along them to the Yellowstone River outflow to follow it in a northerly direction.

The Shoshone thought the incident so simple and obvious that he did not find it necessary to tell the relief guard about it later. Thus, the departure of the five daring, or rather reckless, deserters remained unknown until dawn.

Departure had been set for this early time. So, when the first bird voices sounded in the branches, everyone rose. That's when Old Shatterhand noticed first that Martin Baumann was missing. Right away, his yesterday's concern surfaced. He looked for Jemmy, and soon found that, not only he, but also Davy, Frank and Wohkadeh were missing. The hunter immediately concluded that they had left camp on horseback.

Only now the Shoshone, who had been on last night's guard duty, reported to Old Shatterhand Jemmy's explanation.

Winnetou, who was standing nearby, was unable to understand the reason for the five's secret departure, despite his usual acumen.

"They are headed for the Sioux-Ogallalla," Old Shatterhand explained.

"Then, they have lost their minds," the Apache said angrily. "They will not escape the danger they are riding towards, and will even give away our presence. But why would they want to approach the Sioux?"

"To find out whether the Bear Hunter is still alive."

"If he is dead, they cannot return him to life, and if he is still alive, they will only bring him misfortune. Winnetou can forgive the two bold boys this great mistake, but the two old, white hunters ought to be tied to a stake to be mocked by squaws and children."

That's when Bob approached. The smell of the skunk had not quite faded from him, so that no one cared to have him nearby. He was still wearing only the old horse blanket Long Davy had given him. During the night, when it got cold, he had wrapped himself in the hide of the bear Martin Baumann had killed.

"*Massa* Shatterhand look for *Massa* Martin?" he asked.

"Yes. Can you tell me about him?"

"Oh, *Massa* Bob be very smart *Massa* Bob. He know where *Massa* Martin is."

"Well then, where?"

"Be off to Sioux-Ogallalla to see captured *Massa* Baumann. *Massa* Martin have told *Massa* Bob all for *Massa* Bob to tell *Massa* Shatterhand."

"Then, it's as I thought!" Old Shatterhand said. "When did they plan to come back?"

"When have seen *Massa* Baumann, then come to Firehole River."

"Do you have some other orders?"

"No. *Massa* Bob not know more."

"Your fine *Massa* Martin has acted very stupidly here. I think he can get into real trouble with it."

"What! *Massa* Martin in trouble? Then *Massa* Bob right away mount horse to follow and save him."

He made a quick move towards the horses.

"Hold it!" commanded Old Shatterhand. "You stay! You aren't to add a second stupidity to the first, which would be even greater."

"But *Massa* Bob must save his good, dear *Massa* Martin!" the faithful Black called. "*Massa* Bob slay dead all Sioux-Ogallalla!"

"Yes, just like you slew the bear, when you climbed the birch tree from fright."

"Ogallalla be not bear. *Massa* Bob not afraid of Ogallalla!"

He stuck out his big fists and made a face as if he wanted to devour ten Ogallalla right away.

"All right, I'll try it once with you, because you love your young master so much. Get ready to ride with us in a few minutes!"

And turning to Winnetou, who stood with the chief of the Upsaroca and the chief of the Shoshone and his son, Moh-aw, he said:

"My brother shall continue the ride and expect me at *K'un-tui-tempa*, the Hell's Mouth. But the fifteen warriors of the Upsaroca, together with their chief, and Moh-aw with fifteen warriors of the Shoshone, will accompany me. We must immediately pursue these five silly people to save them should they get into trouble. I do not know when we will be able to follow the Chief of the Apache. Also, I can not determine in advance from which direction I shall come to the Hell's Mouth. My brother may dispatch men to both sides, who are to be on the lookout. It is possible that the Sioux will be at the grave of the chiefs sooner than I will be with my warriors."

Only a few minutes later, Old Shatterhand galloped off with his companions in the same direction in which the five careless people had left camp the previous night. Whether, where, and when he might catch up with them, he did not know.

Of course, they had a great lead on him. Although their nightly ride had been slow and was delayed by lack of knowledge of the terrain, by day break they had left Yellowstone Lake a good distance behind, and now they were able to let their horses run more freely.

Jemmy and Davy felt right at home. They were the ones upon which the other three had to rely, when lately so little had been asked in the way of their opinion. And if they did not know the area they were traversing, they then relied on their experience and cleverness and were totally convinced that their exploratory ride would reach a good conclusion.

186

With daylight, there was plenty to see, even more than was useful for their ride's purpose. The river's scenery was so interesting, that none of them could refrain from exclamations of admiration.

At first the river valley was rather wide and, on both sides, richly varied. When the heights lowered to the river, they soon rose again steeply into the sky. But might the formations be as they were, everywhere they showed the effects of subterranean forces.

Earlier, who knows for how many human life times, this mountain region had been a lake, which must have covered an area of many thousand square miles. Then, below its waters volcanic forces came into action. The ground rose, split, and from its cracks poured glowing lava, solidifying to basalt in the cool lake waters. Enormous craters opened, and hot rocks were exuded from them, combining with other minerals to become different conglomerates. They formed the ground onto which the numerous mineral springs could put down their deposits. Then, a mighty gathering of subterranean gases lifted the sea's bottom with immeasurable force, so that its waters ran off. They cut deep channels into the earth. Loose ground and soft stone were carried away. Cold and warmth, storms and rain, all helped to destroy and remove everything that could not offer resistance. After which, only the hard, solidified lava deposits remained.

Thus, the waters dug into the earth to a depth of a thousand feet. They ate away everything soft. They gnawed the rocks ever deeper, and in this way the grand canyons and waterfalls were formed. Nowadays, these are the wonders of the park.

That's where the volcanic banks reach high up, torn many times, then riven, and washed out by rain into forms no fantasy can imagine. At one point, one might believe to see the ruin of a knight's castle, its empty windows, the watchtower and the spot where the drawbridge spans the trench. Not far from it, slender minarets rise. One might expect the muezzin to step onto the balcony to call the faithful to prayer. Opposite it, a Roman amphitheater opens where Christian slaves fought wild animals. Next to it, a Chinese pagoda rises free and daring to the heights, and further along the river, stands an animal figure, a hundred feet tall. It appears both massive and indestructible, as if it had been erected as an idol by people from before the deluge.

But all is deceit. The volcanic eruption supplied the mass which was shaped into figures by water. And, whoever observes these products of elemental forces, feels like a microscopic worm in the dust and forgets all pride which before may have ruled him.

That's how it affected Jemmy, Davy and Martin Baumann, when they followed the river's course in the morning. They never tired of expressing their wonder. However, whatever Wohkadeh felt and thought could not be learned, since he never talked about it.

Of course, good Hobble-Frank used this opportunity to shine his scientific light in all colors, but today, he did not find a ready listener in Fat Jemmy, whose entire attention was given to seeing. He finally demanded angrily that the little Saxon be quiet.

"All right then!" the former forestry official answered. "What's it for humanity to see these wonders if it refuses to have them exshplained! That's where the great poet Gellert is right when he says: 'What's nutmeg to help the cow!' I'll, therefore, keep my nutmeg and mushtard to myself. One can have gone to the Gymnasium and shtill not undershtand anything of Yellowshtone. But I'm pleading innocence from now on. At leasht then I know where I'm at."

Where the river turns west in a wide arc, numerous hot springs opened which, in their totality, formed a substantial little river which, from between high walls, poured forth into the Yellowstone. It appeared as if, from hereon, one could no longer follow the banks of the latter, which is why the five turned left to follow the course of the little, hot river.

Neither tree nor bush grew there. All vegetation had died. The hot liquid had a dirty appearance and smelled like rotten eggs which was almost unbearable. Once they had gained the heights after an hour of hard riding, things began to change for the better. They found clear, fresh water, and soon there were bushes and, later, trees.

One could obviously not speak of a real pathway. For long distances the horses often had to work their way around boulders. It appeared as if a mountain had fallen from the sky and broken into pieces.

Often the fragments were of a wonderful configuration, frequently causing the horsemen to halt to exchange their ideas about them. Thus, time passed, and when noon arrived, they had covered only half the planned distance.

That's when they saw a rather large house ahead of them. It seemed a villa built in Italian style, surrounded by a garden with a high wall. Totally surprised they stopped.

"A home here in Yellowstone! That's entirely impossible!" Jemmy remarked.

"Why shouldn't that be possible?" Frank replied. "If there's a hoshtile on the Saint Bernhard, one may also have been built here. The poshibilities are everywhere."

"It's hospice, not hostile," Jemmy said.

"Don't you shtart with me again! If you earlier did not want to profit from my mineral knowledge, you needn't now to dig out your doubtful wishdom either! Have you ever been on the Saint Bernard?"

"No."

"Then be quiet! Only who's been up there, can talk about it. But look more closely at the house! Ishn't there a person shtanding right at the door?"

"Right. At least it seems like it. But now he's gone. It must have been just a shadow."

"So. Here you once again make a fool of yourself with your optical experiences. If there's a human shadow, there musht also be a pershon who's thrown the shadow. That's the well-known theory of Pythagoras's hypotenuse of the two catheters. And if the shadow is gone, then the sun either disappeared or the person who has thrown the shadow. But since the sun is shtill here, therefore the fellow disappeared. Whereto, we'll soon find out."

They quickly approached the building but, getting closer, realized that it had not been built by human hands, but was a work of nature. The apparent walls consisted of dazzlingly white feldspar. From afar, several openings could be easily taken for windows. A wide, tall door was also there. If one looked past it, one saw a kind of broad courtyard with natural walls split into several different-sized partitions. In the yard's center, a spring bubbled up from the ground sending its clear, cold waters out the door.

"Wonderful!" admitted Jemmy. "This place is suited perfectly for a midday rest. Shall we enter?"

"Fine with me," Frank replied. "However, we don't know yet whether the fellow living in there might be a bad one."

"Pshaw! We were mistaken. It cannot have been a person. Just to be sure, I'll do a bit of reconnoitering."

Holding his rifle ready to shoot, he rode slowly through the gateway and looked around in the yard. He then turned around and waved.

"Come on! There's not a soul in here."

"I sure hope not," Frank remarked. "I don't like to deal at all with departed souls who shtill maintain a ghostly respite here on earth."

Davy, Martin and Frank followed Jemmy's invitation. Only Wohkadeh stayed cautiously put.

"Why is my red brother not coming?" asked the Son of the Bear Hunter.

The Indian deliberately pulled some air through his nose and answered:

"Don't my brothers notice that it smells very much of horses here?"

"Of course, it must smell of them. It's ours."

"This smell came already from the door when we halted before it."

"There's neither a human nor an animal, also no tracks of either to be seen."

"Because the ground is of hard stone. My brothers ought to be cautious."

"There's no reason for any worry," Jemmy declared. "Come on, let's have a look farther inside."

Instead of letting him go ahead by himself, thus keeping their retreat open, they followed him closely next to each other to the rocky sections in the back.

Suddenly, a howling arose as if the Earth were shaking. A large number of Indians broke forth from the back and, in a minute, the four incautious men were surrounded.

189

The Reds were not on horseback but extremely well armed. A tall, lean, but sinewy fellow, marked by his headdress as a chief, called in broken English to the Whites:

"Surrender, or we will take your scalps!"

They were surrounded by at least fifty Indians. The four surprised hunters realized that opposition would be fatal.

"By the devil!" Jemmy exclaimed in German. "We rode right into their hands. These are the Sioux, for sure those we were going to spy on. But I don't think everything is lost yet. Maybe we can get away with some cunning."

Turning to the chief, he continued in English:

"We are to surrender? But we didn't do anything to you. We are friends of the red man."

"The Sioux-Ogallalla are on the war path against the Whites," the tall one replied. "Dismount and drop your weapons! We will not wait."

Fifty pairs of eyes stared scowlingly at the Whites and fifty red-brown hands lay on their knives. Old Shatterhand and Winnetou would likely not have surrendered, but Long Davy was the first to climb off his mule.

"Do as he asks," he told his companions. "We must gain some time. Our people will surely come to free us."

That's when the others also dismounted and surrendered their weapons. Hobble-Frank used the opportunity to punch Fat Jemmy into the ribs telling him, angrily:

"That's what happens, if one hashn't even learned at the Gymnasium how to shpell the word 'hostiz'! Why did you have to ride in here! You should've shtayed outside. Now the canailles have us by the throat!"

Then, he himself got a much harder punch into the ribs by one of the Indians. The Red held a knife in front of his face demanding:

"Be quiet! Or ...!"

He made a move like stabbing. Frank immediately held his hand in front of his mouth, indicating that he had no desire to make closer acquaintance with the knife.

Wohkadeh had not entered with the others. From outside, he saw his companions being encircled and, at once, drove his horse aside, so that he could not be seen through the doorway. There he jumped off, crouched on the ground, and pushed only his head far enough forward to look into the yard.

What he saw gave him cause for dismay. He knew the chief. It was Hong-peh-te-keh, Heavy Moccasin, the Sioux-Ogallalla' leader. He also knew the others. They were the fifty-six Ogallalla he had been with and from which he had escaped. The White who fell into the hands of the Indians here, so close to the chiefs' graves, was surely lost if he could not get help from outside.

What was he to do? This was brave Wohkadeh's question. To ride quickly back to the lake to fetch Old Shatterhand and his people? No. He had a better idea. It was extremely daring, but it offered at least a little hope for success. He was going to ride inside to face the Ogallalla, risking to be torn to pieces. He had to lie to them. Should the Whites comprehend his intention without him needing to explain it, and make their statements accordingly, it might be possible to achieve success.

He did not ponder much longer. It was a real hero's deed that he planned to execute. But what would Winnetou and Old Shatterhand, his two models say, once they heard about it!

The thought doubled his boldness. He mounted his horse and rode into the yard, putting on the most unaffected face possible.

Just then the four captives were to be tied up. Two, three paces of his horse, and he stopped in front of them.

"Uff!" he called loudly. "Since when do the warriors of the Sioux-Ogallala tie up the hands of their best friends? These palefaces are brothers of Wohkadeh!"

His sudden appearance caused general surprise, but was aired only by brief, low-toned exclamations. Heavy Moccasin drew his eye brows angrily together, looked the young warrior sharply up and down, and replied:

"Since when are the white dogs brothers of the Ogallalla?"

"Since they saved Wohkadeh's life."

The chief's looks literally drilled into Wohkadeh. Then he asked:

"Where has Wohkadeh been? Why did he not return at the right time, after he was sent out to spy on the warriors of the Shoshone?"

"Because he was captured by the dogs of Shoshone. But these four palefaces fought for him and saved him. They showed him a path, which led fast and easily to the Yellowstone and rode with him to smoke the peace pipe with Heavy Moccasin."

A sneer curled the chief's lips.

"Get off your horse and step over here with your white brothers!" he ordered. "You are our prisoner just like them."

The bold red boy made a surprised face and replied:

"Wohkadeh, prisoner of his own tribe? Who gives Heavy Moccasin the right to take a warrior of his own nation prisoner?"

"He himself takes the right. He is the leader of the war party and can do as he sees fit."

At that, Wohkadeh made his horse rise up and then put his heels into its flanks, forcing it to make a quick full turn on its hind legs. Since it kicked also with its front hooves while turning, the Sioux-Ogallalla who had pushed closer to him, had to back off. He gained some room. He now put the reins onto the neck of his horse and, thus, freed his left hand. Then, he gripped his rifle, so that it lay ready to shoot in his hands, and said:

"Since when are the chiefs of the Sioux-Ogallalla allowed to do as they like? What for are the gatherings of the old fathers? Who gives the chiefs their power? Who wants to force a brave warrior of the Ogallalla to obey a chief who treats the sons of his own tribe like a nigger? Wohkadeh is a young man. There are braver, wiser and more famous warriors in his tribe. But, he has killed the white buffalo and carries eagle feathers. He is no slave. He will not let himself be taken prisoner, and whoever insults him, must fight him!"

These were proud words, which were not lost on the braves. By no means do Indian chiefs carry inherited powers. They are not given the authority of European sovereigns. They cannot issue laws and regulations. They are chosen from a line of warriors, because they excelled above others either by their bravery or shrewdness or some other characteristic. No one is really forced to obey them. Even when a chief wants to go on the war path, to follow him into

192

battle is entirely voluntary. Anyone wishing to stay home can do so, but he will, of course, experience the disparagement of others. Even during a campaign, anyone can withdraw at any time. The influence and power of a chief rests only on the impression of his personality. He can be deposed at any time.

Heavy Moccasin, who owed his name to the fact that he had very big feet, and, thus, also produced large tracks, was known as a severe and willful man. Although he had gained significant merits for his tribe, his obstinacy and his pride had often been to his detriment. He was hard, cruel and bloodthirsty. The following he had in his tribe fell into two divisions, those of his adherents, and those who either openly or secretly schemed against him.

This disunion also became evident after Wohkadeh had spoken. Several Sioux sounded approving and agreeing shouts. The chief threw them an angry look and gave some of his loyal followers a signal. They quickly hurried to the entrance to occupy it so that Wohkadeh could not escape. Then, he answered the young warrior:

"Every Sioux-Ogallalla is a free man. He can do as he pleases. In that, Wohkadeh is right. But as soon as a warrior becomes a traitor to his brothers, he has lost the rights as a free man."

"Do you think me to be a traitor?"

"I do think so!"

"Prove it!"

"I shall prove it at the assembly of these warriors."

"And I shall step in front of them as a free man, my weapons in hand, to defend myself. And when I have proven that Heavy Moccasin has insulted me without reason, he will have to fight me."

"A traitor does not approach the assembly with weapons in hand. Wohkadeh will surrender his. If he is innocent, they will be returned."

"Uff! Who is going to take them?"

The young man threw a bold, challenging look around. He saw sympathy for him on several faces but most remained cold.

"No one will take them from you," the chief replied. "You yourself will put them down. And, if you will not, you will get a bullet."

"I have two bullets in my rifle."

Saying these words, he slapped his hand on the stock of his gun.

"When Wohkadeh left us, he had no rifle. Where did he get it? It was given to him by a paleface, and they make a gift only, if they gain something from it. Therefore, Wohkadeh has done them some service and they not him. Wohkadeh is a Mandan. No Sioux squaw gave birth to him. Who among these brave warriors is going to speak for him before he has answered to my accusation?"

No one moved. Heavy Moccasin gave the youngster a triumphant look and ordered him:

"Get off your horse and put down your weapons! You will defend yourself after which we will pass judgment. By your resistance, you only prove that you are not innocent."

Wohkadeh realized that he had to submit. He had resisted trying to impress those who were not well-disposed towards the chief.

"If you think so, I shall comply with it," he said. "My cause is just. I can look forward in peace to your judgment and, until then, put myself into your hands."

He dismounted and deposited his weapons at the chief's feet, who whispered something to those standing next to him. Right away they pulled out some straps to tie up Wohkadeh.

"Uff!" he cried angrily. "Did I give you permission for it?"

"I take that permission," the chief answered. "Tie him and put him alone into some corner, so that he cannot talk with the palefaces or give them a signal!"

No resistance would have helped. It would have only made things worse, which is why Wohkadeh submitted to his fate. Both his hands and feet were bound, so that he could move no longer and was put into a corner. Two Sioux were ordered to sit with him in order to prevent the possibility of his escape.

An old warrior stepped to the chief saying to him:

"Many more winters have crossed my head than yours. Thus, you ought not to be angry at me when I ask whether you truly have reason to think Wohkadeh is a traitor."

"I shall answer you, since you are the oldest warrior here. I have no real reason except that one of the captured palefaces lying back there with the horses, the youngest, looks very similar to the Bear Hunter."

"Can this be a reason?"

"Yes. I shall prove it to you."

He walked over to the captives who, without being able to help, had seen and heard what Wohkadeh had dared so uselessly for them. Unfortunately, neither Jemmy nor Davy understood enough of the Sioux language, that they could understand everything Wohkadeh had argued.

The shrewd chief put on a less hard face and said:

"After Wohkadeh left us, he committed a deed about which we have to hold council. If it is shown that the palefaces did not know him then, they will receive their freedom. What are the names of the white men?"

"Shall we tell them?" Davy asked his fat friend.

"Yes," Jemmy replied. "Maybe this will gain us some respect."

Turning to the chief he continued:

"My name is Jemmy-petahtsheh, and this tall warrior is Davy-honskeh. You will have heard these names already."

"Uff!" it sounded from the circle of the surrounding Sioux.

The chief gave them a disapproving look. He too was surprised to have these well-known hunters in his power, but didn't let on anything.

"Heavy Moccasin does not know your names," he replied. "And who are these two men?"

His question, referring to Frank and Martin, had been once again put to Jemmy. Davy whispered to him:

"For God's sake, don't tell their names."

"What is it the paleface has to tell the other?" the chief asked sternly. "Only he may answer who I asked!"

Jemmy had to decide on an untruth. He gave the first best names he could think of and declared Frank and Martin as being father and son.

The chief's looks searched from one to the other, and then, a disdainful smile crossed his face. Yet, he still said in a rather friendly voice:

"The palefaces may follow me."

He walked to the rear part of the yard.

The apparent house must once have been a giant boulder, consisting of feldspar, but interspersed by softer inclusions. The latter had been dissolved by rain, and while the feldspar had resisted the weather, a structure had arisen which resembled a long yard enclosed by high walls, whose several compartments were again subdivided.

The rearmost one was the largest. It provided enough space so that all the Ogallalla' horses had found a place there. In a corner lay six Whites tied on hands and feet. They were in a most sorry condition. Their clothing hung in tatters. Their wrists had been rubbed sore from the fetters. Their faces were covered by grime, and hair and beard hung from their heads in an indescribable condition. Their cheeks were drawn, and the eyes lay deeply in their sockets, a consequence of the hunger, thirst and pain they had suffered.

This is where the chief brought the new captives. While they were walking there Martin asked Jemmy quietly:

"Where is he going to take us? Maybe to my father?"

"Possibly. But in God's name don't let on that you know him, or all is lost."

"Here lie captured palefaces," said the chief. Heavy Moccasin does not know their language very well. I, therefore, do not know who they are. The white men may step to them to ask and then tell me."

He led the four to the corner. Jemmy, knowing, that Baumann was born German, and that the Sioux couldn't possibly understand a word of this language, approached quickly and said:

"I hope the Bear Hunter is among you. In God's name, don't let on that you know your son. He stands here behind me. We came to rescue you, but fell ourselves into the hands of the Reds. But, we are certain to soon be free again together with you. Did you give these red scoundrels your name?"

195

Baumann did not answer. The sight of his son had taken his speech away. Only after some time did he exclaim in a fatigued voice:

"Oh my God! What a delight and, at the same time, what pain! The Sioux know me, also the names of my companions."

"Fine! I hope we'll be kept here with you. Then, we'll learn more."

Although the chief did not understand a syllable, he listened carefully. He seemingly wanted to deduce the words' contents from the tone of voice. His looks swept sharply between Baumann and his son, but his observations were fruitless. Martin kept himself in close control, showing an indifferent face, although the pain he felt, seeing his father's condition, nearly caused him to cry.

Hobble-Frank almost did something incautious. His sorrow was so great, that he nearly made a move to throw himself onto Baumann. However, Long Davy grabbed his arm, held him back, giving him an angry look.

Unfortunately, the chief had noticed this. He asked Jemmy:

"Well, did they give you their names?"

"Yes. But, you knew them already."

"I thought they had lied to me. You and your companions will also stay here."

The partial friendliness he had shown so far now faded from his face. He waved the Ogallalla who had come with them closer. They emptied the captives pockets and tied them up.

"Wonderful!" Jemmy growled, seeing the content of his pockets disappear. "It's only a wonder that they don't take also our clothing. Isn't that their custom."

The new prisoners were laid next to the others. The chief left after posting some guards.

The pitiable men did not dare speak aloud, but rather whispered to each other. Martin had come to lie right next to his father, a circumstance, which was, of course, used for the exchange of some tenderness.

After a while, a Sioux came, removed the leg straps of one of the earlier captives and asked him to follow. The man was unable to walk and staggered helplessly along next to the Red.

"What may they want of him?" asked Baumann, so that Jemmy heard it.

"He's to be the traitor," Jemmy replied. "It's fortunate that I and my companions haven't said anything yet about the help we expect to come."

"But you did mention it."

"That's not a problem, yet. But let's be careful not to give him any important information, should he return. We must then first convince ourselves whether we can trust him."

Jemmy had guessed right. The man was led to the chief who received him with a scowl. The poor man was unable to remain on his feet and had to sit down.

"Do you know the fate you can expect?" the chief asked.

"Yes," said the man in a faint voice. "You told us often enough."

"Well, then tell me again!"

"We are to be killed."

"Yes, death is assured you, a most painful one. You are to be tortured at the grave site like no other paleface has yet endured, to honor the slain chiefs. What would you give if you were spared these pains?"

The White did not reply.

"If you could save your life?"

"Could it be saved?" the man asked hastily.

"Yes."

"What must I do? What do you ask of me?"

The thought of being able to save himself excited his weakened life force. His eyes began to shine and his sunken figure righted itself.

"It is very little I ask of you," the chief told him. "You are to answer just a few questions."

"Gladly, gladly!" the man exclaimed happily.

"But you must tell the truth, or you will die under tenfold pains. Did you know the Bear Hunter's home?"

"Yes."

"Have you been inside?"

"Yes. All five of us stayed several days with him before we set out on the ride to the mountains."

"Then, you also know who lived with him?"

"Of course."

"Tell me."

"He had a son and ..."

The man halted. The thought arose in him that the information asked, might be of greatest importance to the persons in question.

"Why don't you keep talking?" Heavy Moccasin asked harshly.

"Why do you ask?"

"Dog!" the chief erupted. "Do you know what you are? A worm I will squash! Speak once more such an insolent question, and I will hand you to my warriors as a target for their knives! I want to learn what I am asking for. If you don't tell me, I will learn it from another!"

Upon these angry words, the White had flinched like a dog whose master had shown him the whip. Physically half dead and mentally tortured, he no longer had the strength to resist. He dared to ask only one more question:

"And you shall give me my life and freedom if I tell you everything?"

"Yes. I did say so and shall keep my word. Are you prepared then to tell me the whole truth?"

"Yes," declared the pitiable man, deluded by the promise.

"Then speak! Does the Bear Hunter have a son?"

"Yes. His name is Martin."

"Is this the young paleface now lying with you?"

"Yes, he is."

"Uff! Heavy Moccasin's eyes are sharp. Do you also know the other white men?"

"Only the limping one. He lives with the Bear Hunter. His name is Hobble-Frank."

For a while, the chief stared pensively ahead. Then he asked:

"You are telling the truth?"

"Yes, I swear to it."

"This is it then. We are done."

The Ogallalla who had delivered the White got a signal. He took him by the arm to lift him up. At that the White asked:

"You promised me my life and my freedom. When do I get the latter?"

This question was answered by a fierce laugh of the chief's.

"You are a white dog. One need not keep one's word," he replied. "You will die like the others, because you are ..."

He stopped. A thought seemed to have suddenly come to him for his face took on a totally different, much friendlier expression. He now continued:

"You told me too little."

"I don't know more."

"That is a lie!"

"I cannot tell more than I know."

"Did the palefaces we brought earlier speak with the Bear Hunter?"

"Yes."

"What?"

"I do not know."

"If you know that they talked, you must also know what was said."

"No. Because they spoke in a language I do not understand. They also spoke very softly."

"Don't you know how they met Wohkadeh?"

"I do not even know who Wohkadeh is."

"And do you know if they are alone in this area, or if there are other palefaces around?"

"I know nothing of this either."

"Well. That is what I want to know, and you must find out. Ask them. Once you have learned it, I will let you go. You will accompany us on our return trip. When we reach the area, where there are palefaces, we bring you to them. Now, you can go. Tonight, when we have reached our camp and the palefaces are asleep, you must tell me what you learned."

The man was returned to his fellow captives, put down and once more tied by his feet.

The others remained silent, and he too kept quiet, not feeling well about the situation. He was, after all, a decent fellow. Contemplating the chief's conduct, it did not appear very likely to him that the Indian would keep his word. He realized that he had been duped and should not have said anything at all. The longer he thought about it, the more he became aware that he could not trust Heavy Moccasin. It was his duty to tell Baumann what he had talked about with the chief.

The Bear Hunter forestalled him. After a long time he asked:

"Well, master, you keep so quiet! It's evident that we'd like to hear what was wanted of you. Who did you see?"

"The chief."

"Of course. What did he want from you?"

"I'll tell you honestly. He wanted to know who Frank and Martin are, and I told him, because he promised me my freedom."

"Oh my! That was stupid. You couldn't have done worse. Then, you told him. But how about your freedom?"

"I am to receive it only after I have found out how the other masters met a certain Wohkadeh and whether there are more Whites here in the area."

"So! And you think the fellow will keep his word?"

"No. After I thought about it, I'm convinced he's out to deceive me."

"That's smart of you. And, because you are sincere, we'll forgive you your mistake. But don't think that you could have sounded us out. We figured what the chief wanted from you and would have certainly remained silent towards you."

"But what am I to tell him once he asks me again?"

"I'll tell you," Jemmy answered. "You tell him that we rescued Wohkadeh when he was a captive of the Shoshone, and then rode here with him to bring him safely to his people. There are no other Whites in the vicinity. Except for ourselves, we haven't seen another white or red man. That's all you tell him. And if he still tries to dupe you, don't fall for the trap. You can expect rescue sooner from us than from him."

"How so?"

"There you ask me far too much. Maybe I'll gain enough trust in you so I can give you some pleasant information soon."

With that the subject was closed for the time being.

The captives were obviously unable to move their limbs. Their only movement consisted in rolling from one side to the other. Jemmy used this means to get next to Baumann. He succeeded in lying to the right, and Martin to the left, of the Bear Hunter. This enabled them to convey everything, also their hope, that their captivity would only be a short one.

In the meantime, the chief had called for the most outstanding warriors to join him. Then Wohkadeh was fetched. When he stepped into this yard section where the Sioux had gathered, he found them sitting in a semicircle, in whose midst sat the chief. The prisoner had to stand facing them. Two guards took up post next to him, knives in hand.

This last fact was very serious. It was obvious that his situation had worsened. Nevertheless, he looked calmly forward to his interrogation.

After those present had observed him somberly for awhile, the chief began:

"Wohkadeh may now tell us what he experienced from the moment he left us."

Wohkadeh followed this request. He told the tale of having been discovered and captured by the Shoshone, but was then freed by the now-captured Whites. He presented it with an air of truth and yet noticed that no credence was given to his account.

When he was finished, no one said anything as to whether he was believed or not. The chief asked:

"And who are the four palefaces?"

Wohkadeh first named Jemmy and Davy, and stated that it was an honor for the Sioux that such famous hunters had come to them.

"And the two others?"

This question did not present any difficulty to him. He had already thought what he was going to answer. He gave Frank's name and pretended that Martin was his son. When the chief heard this, he did not change his expression, but asked:

"Might Wohkadeh have learned that the Bear Hunter has a son by the name of Martin?"

"No."

"And that a man lives with him whose name is Hobble-Frank?"

"No!"

He maintained his composure, although he was convinced that his game was now lost. Then the chief thundered at him:

"Wohkadeh is a dog, a traitor, a stinking wolf! Why is he still lying? Does he perhaps still think that we do not know that the Bear Hunter's son is our prisoner now? Wohkadeh brought those two and the others to free the captives. Now, he is to suffer their same fate. Tonight, by our camp fire, the council will consider the kind of death he is to die. For now, he is to be tied up so tightly that the straps will cut into his flesh!"

He was led off and tied up so hard that he could have cried out loud. Shortly thereafter, he was tied onto a horse for the group's departure.

The same happened to the other prisoners. However, Wohkadeh was kept away from them and received two warriors as a special guard.

It was sad to observe how faint and pitiful Baumann and his five companions in misfortune sat tied up on their horses. Had they not been tied together by their feet, they would have tumbled off their animals from exhaustion.

Davy whispered a few consoling words to Jemmy about the men's condition. The Fat One responded:

"Have a bit of patience, old chap! I would be very much mistaken, if Old Shatterhand isn't already nearby. What we've realized only now is what kind of stupid blockheads we are, which he surely knew this morning. In any case, he'll be after us with a bunch of Reds. I have taken care that he'll find our tracks."

"How so?"

"Look! I tore off a piece of fur and, using my teeth, tore it into little pieces. Where we lay, I left a small piece, and on our ride, I will drop one from time to time. They'll stay put since there's no wind. Once Old Shatterhand gets to this devilish 'building', he will surely find the bitty piece, and if I know him, he will understand that only Fat Jemmy with his pelt can have been there in this summer heat. He will keep on searching, find the other pieces, and thus, learn the direction we are traveling. That's more than enough for him."

The Sioux did not follow the run of the river. It would have been a detour. They rode for the heights carrying the name Elephant Back, then turned straight for the long-stretched range forming the watershed between the Atlantic and Pacific Oceans.

Fat Jemmy had not guessed entirely wrong when he thought Old Shatterhand might be already nearby. Barely three-quarters of an hour after the Sioux had disappeared behind the next heights, he came riding from the north with his Shoshone and Upsaroca, along the exact trail the horses of the five deserters had ridden.

He rode in the lead, together with the Shoshone chief's son and the medicine man of the Upsaroca, his eyes firmly on the ground. Not the least escaped him. In all truth, since this morning, he had never been in doubt about the tracks of the five.

Seeing the so-called 'building', he at first stopped short, but then answered the medicine man's question immediately:

"I remember. This is no house, but a rock formation. I have been inside already and wouldn't be surprised if those we are after, have also entered to look the place over. It is – by the devil!"

While calling out, he jumped off his horse and began to inspect the hard ground. It was precisely the spot where his direction met with the Sioux's direction of departure.

"Many people rode past here barely an hour ago," he said. "I'm afraid it may have been the Sioux! Who else could have been here in such number! I'm suspicious of the 'house'. Let's split up and surround it."

201

With Old Shatterhand in the lead, they advanced. The rock f[ ]
encircled. Then, he entered first by himself. He left word that the o[ ]
follow only when he fired a shot.

It took a rather long time until he emerged again. His expressio[ ]
serious and concerned. He said:

"I would gladly permit my red brothers to look at this inter[ ]
formation, which looks as if it had been erected by human hands. H[ ]
must not lose any time, because the white men and Wohkadeh have been
captured by the Sioux and were taken away about an hour ago."

"Is my white brother sure of that?" Fire Heart, the Upsaroca medicine man,
asked.

"Yes. I saw all their tracks and studied them closely. Fat Jemmy left a sign
for me. I hope we shall find more of them yet. He will want to draw our attention
to the direction the Sioux have taken."

He showed them the small pelt piece he had found. It held only five or six
hairs, a certain sign that the piece was from the fat one's pelt.

"What does Shatterhand intend to do?" the Red asked. "Does he want to
pursue the Ogallalla right away?"

"Yes. At once."

"Shall we not, once we return to Winnetou, find them just as well at the
river of the Fire Hole?"

"Yes, we would find them there, but I fear, that they may have killed the
captives by that time."

"They will keep them until the night of the full moon."

"Yes, the Bear Hunter and his five companions, but our friends cannot be
assured of their lives for that long. Particularly, our good Wohkadeh is in the
greatest danger for his life. They will treat him as a traitor. I suspect they have
the worst in mind for him. We must, therefore, follow them immediately. Or do
my red brothers think differently?"

"No," the giant replied. "We are pleased to have come across the tracks of
the Ogallalla so soon. Heavy Moccasin is their leader, and it is my desire to get
him into my hands. Let's ride!"

From his expression, one could clearly see, that the leader of the Sioux-
Ogallalla would die a terrible death should he fall into his hands.

Old Shatterhand once more resumed his place as leader of the group, and
they continued their ride, but now in a westerly direction instead of going east.

Since it had been difficult to follow the tracks of the five deserters, Old
Shatterhand and his companions had been riding very slowly since early
morning. The same was true now. The ground consisted of volcanic rock. One
could not speak here of real tracks. Small stones, crushed by the hooves of the
horses, formed the only uncertain clues for Old Shatterhand's sagacity. It called
for close attention, which forced him to ride very slowly.

That he was able to stay right on the Ogallalla' tracks despite these difficulties was proven by several more fur pieces which he found. Even the Upsaroca and Shoshone, extraordinarily experienced in tacking, gave each other looks expressing their admiration for the famous hunter.

After some time, the direction veered more to the left, that is to the southwest. They reached the foothills of the watershed. Whoever halts there up top, can see to the left, the channels taking their waters through the Yellowstone and Missouri to the Mississippi, that is to the Mexican Gulf. While, to the right, the waters run through the valley of the Snake River towards the Pacific Ocean.

Here, the land was no longer as bare as before. There was good soil, and the individual creeks running here were not suffused with sulfur. They carried fresh, healthy water providing nourishment to vegetation. This is why grass grew here as well as bushes and trees. From hereon, the tracks became clearer.

Unfortunately, they could not be followed much longer since the afternoon was coming to its close. So, as long as the tracks were clearly visible before dusk fell, the horses had to be driven on as far as possible.

The height of the watershed was reached, followed by a descent on the other side between boulders and brush, making for a difficult, in places even dangerous ride. However, this was of no concern to the Indians.

Then darkness fell. They had to stay with the tracks, and since these were no longer visible, they halted for the day.

Had the men been quiet until now, they did not become any more talkative in camp. They felt they were facing decisive events. In such cases, people become silent.

No fires were lit. From the tracks' freshness, Old Shatterhand had determined that the Ogallalla were barely two miles ahead. If they were camped, the pursuers could come so close, without being aware of it that the pursued would notice the pursuers' fires, and learn that they were being pursued.

After guards had been posted, everyone wrapped himself into his blanket to sleep. When morning had barely dawned and objects could be only faintly differentiated from each other, they set out again.

The Ogallalla' tracks were still visible. After maybe an hour, Old Shatterhand suggested that the Ogallalla had not camped the previous evening. Obviously, they did not want to rest until they had reached the Firehole River.

This wasn't a good sign indicating that they had something planned which was to happen quickly. Unfortunately, the pursuers could not increase their horses' speed, since plant cover had disappeared, and, in place of soft ground, hard volcanic rock appeared.

It now became impossible to see the tracks. Old Shatterhand thought rightly that, if the Sioux-Ogallalla had maintained the same direction to here, they would also follow it farther on. This is why he continued straight ahead.

He soon recognized that his assumption had not been wrong. Ahead, the Firehole Mountains rose, behind which the famous geyser basins bubble and erupt in a grand and continuous activity. Now, they found vegetation once again, even forest consisting mostly of dark spruce.

They arrived at a small creek which wound its way through the soft, grassy ground, and right where they met it, the ground was trampled by many hooves. The impressions followed the watercourse, and it was clear that the Sioux had watered their horses here. With their good luck, the tracks had been located, and from now on up the rise, they maintained such clarity that no error was possible.

No open path led upwards. They had to ride between the trees, which stood far enough apart that they did not present any hindrance. But a ride through woods is the most dangerous for the frontiersman. An enemy, of whose presence he has no inkling, may be hidden behind the next tree.

It would have been easy for the Ogallalla to think of being followed. They could not be sure what kind of admission they had coaxed from the captives through force or cunning. Had they had a presentiment of being pursued, they would have been smart to take suitable measures, of which the very best would have been to lay an ambush.

For this reason, Old Shatterhand sent several Shoshone ahead to search the terrain and to retreat should they discover anything suspicious.

Luckily this prudence proved unnecessary, due to the arrangement Fat Jemmy had made with the prisoner that the Chief of the Ogallalla had pressured to betray his fellow-captives.

Since the chief's crafty intent had been not to separate the prisoners from each other during the ride – except for Wohkadeh – they had been able to talk with each other. This had been the chief's tacit permission, who thought his assumed ally would have the opportunity to learn more about their intent and report it to him.

In the evening, Heavy Moccasin had him separated as innocuously as possible from the others to meet him for questioning. The man had given the information, which Jemmy had asked him to provide, and to give assurance that, except for Wohkadeh and the four Whites, no other people had come to Yellowstone.

The chief had believed it and, thus, had thought cautionary measures to be unnecessary.

This is why Old Shatterhand, with his Indians, acquired the height without meeting any resistance.

On top the tall forest grew dense, and prevented one from looking into the valley below, although the decline seemed to be rather steep.

Riding below the trees, they heard a peculiar, dull rushing noise, soon interrupted by a shrill whistle. This was followed by a hiss, just like when redundant steam is being released by a locomotive.

"What is that?" Moh-aw, the Shoshone chief's son, asked in surprise.

"A geyser, most likely," Old Shatterhand explained.

Since the word 'geyser' is totally unknown to Indians, he used the term *war-p'eh-pejah*, meaning warm water mountain, which the young Shoshone understood at once.

Now the terrain dropped, first slowly, then quickly, so that it wasn't easy to ride the horses. For this reason, the horsemen dismounted and walked, leading their animals behind.

The Ogallalla' tracks were still recognizable, but Old Shatterhand saw that they dated from the day before.

Having descended several hundred feet, the forest suddenly ended in a sharp line. Yet, some distance farther down, it reached all the way to the sole of the valley.

Now, the view across the valley was open, and what could be seen there was truly amazing – the wonderful natural scenic beauty.

The upper valley of the Madison, which carries here the very descriptive name Firehole River, is probably the most admirable region of the national park. Many miles long and in parts two, even three miles wide, it holds hundreds of geysers and hot springs. There are fountains, which propel their waters several hundred feet high. Sulfuric odors stream from the many cracks in the earth and the air is laden with hot steam.

Snow-white sinter, which forms the coating and the lid of subterranean boiling pots, shines glaringly in sunlight. In other places the ground is not solid but is of viscous, evil-smelling mud, whose temperature varies substantially. Here and there, the surface rises suddenly in the form of a crest – slowly, blister-like – then bursts leaving a broad, unfathomable deep hole. From within, steam shoots up so high that the eyes, when following it, make one dizzy. At random, these bubbles and holes arise and fade, soon here, soon there. Woe to him who happens to find himself on one of these spots! At this very moment, the solid ground underneath suddenly becomes hot and begins to rise. Only a death-defying leap, the fastest immediate flight, brings escape.

But while one escapes a bubble here, a second, or third, emerges next to the rider. He stands on a very thin crust, which covers the terrible depths of the Earth's interior like the easily torn, paper-like substance of a wasp's nest.

And woe also to him who, from afar, believes the aforementioned mud to be a substance that will support him! While it looks like marshy ground that one can walk across, it is held only by volcanic steam which carries it, like the gray-brown foam held and moved by water when cooking meat.

Everywhere, the ground gives under the wanderer's foot, and the impressions left fill immediately with a thick, green-yellow stinking, hellish liquid. All around it rushes, boils, bubbles, hisses, roars and groans. Giant flecks of water and mud fly about. If one throws a rock into one of these opening and closing holes, it is as if the ghosts of the underworld feel insulted. The waters and mud down there react in terrible, truly diabolical excitement. They rise, they overflow, as if wanting to draw the perpetrator into dreadful ruin.

The waters of these kettles of hexes are colored quite differently. Some are milky white, bright red, azure-blue, sulfur-yellow, yet often are also clear as glass. On top, one can see large white, silk-like filaments or a thick, lead-colored slime, which covers any object stuck into it in minutes and then, forms a solid, permanent, almost indestructible covering.

It can happen that the water in such a hole can shimmer in the most beautiful grass-green. The, suddenly small valves seem to open on its sides from which shoot streamers into the green waters, colored in all nuances of the rainbow.

One is tempted to shout every few seconds: "Magnificent! Incomparable! Heavenly!", if all this was not be so frightful, so hellish.

Old Shatterhand and his warriors arrived at this 'Fire Hole'. The Indians wanted to step out front under the trees, but he stopped them with a shout. He pointed to the opposite bank of the river. They then realized that it would be advisable to remain under cover of the forest.

Here the valley was perhaps only half a mile wide. Above the place where they had stopped, the banks narrowed so much that the river seemed to have barely room to force its dirty, maliciously shimmering waves through. Downstream was another narrows. The distance between these two narrows was not much longer than a mile.

The river, whose water was warmed by the hot springs spilling into it, killing all life, rushed closely along the valley's wall where Old Shatterhand had halted. Covered here by forest, its slope was passable, although being steep. However, the opposite wall rose vertically as if built by a mason's plumb. It consisted of black, turret-like rock, riven at its top. Receding, it formed an arc between the two narrows. However, the valley was by no means broadened by the retreat of this wall. From the dark rocks, right across from Old Shatterhand, rose a formation whose broad base reached almost to the bank of the river.

At first sight, this formation – there is hardly another, better term to describe this thing, was both incomprehensible and magnificent! One could have thought himself to be in a magic world in which fairies and elves and other unearthly beings lived their secret lives.

This terrace-like construct, was delicately articulated and fantastically ornamented, as if it consisted of freshly fallen snow and the finest ice crystals.

The lowermost, broadest terrace seemed to be cut from finest ivory. Its edge was clad in ornaments appearing like the artwork of a fantasy-rich sculptor from a distance. It formed a water-filled semicircular basin, from which rose a second terrace, glittering like it was alabaster interspersed by gold grains. This second terrace was of a smaller diameter as the lower one. And, just like the second from the first, a third terrace rose and receded from the second. As if made of delicately picked cotton, it rose slender and virginal from the second.

Its material was so airy, that one could think it unable to support the least weight. And yet, above it, towered still six more such terraces, each with its own basin, all receiving their waters from the next higher one. Then, they passed to the next lower either in slender jets, or as a finely spread mist in which the sun's rays were reflected, or in a broader discharge resembling a veil.

This natural wonder leaned, slender and radiant, shining like snow, against the dark rock wall, like the garment, woven of snow flakes, of a being from another world. Nevertheless, this garment had been fabricated by the same hands, which had piled up the black basalt and were still driving the mud volcanoes through the Earth's crust.

One needed to look only up to the tip of the wonderful pyramid to see immediately how it had been built. Just then, there rose a tall beam of water, which spread out at its top like an umbrella to then descend like rain. This caused the rushing sound Moh-aw had earlier been unable to comprehend. The water beam was followed by whistling, hissing, groaning steam, and it seemed as if the Earth might burst from the force of this eruption.

The geyser's water had built this pyramid. The fine, lightweight contents the beam expelled up top, adhered to the formation after they fell, and were thus still at work building this wonderful structure. The hot water flowed from one terrace down to the next and, in the process cooled, so that the individual basins, counting from the top, had an ever-lower temperature. A short stream of this crystal-like liquid then flowed from the lowest level into the Firehole River.

Like a devil beside an angel, a dirty, broad, almost circular, dark and dam-like structure lay next to to the magnificent pyramid. This dam consisted of a hard substance, from which rose the remains of various volcanic structures. It was as if a giant child had played with these basalt pieces, had pressed and bent them into the most strange shapes, and then attached them to the round dam.

The latter had a diameter of maybe fifty feet and constituted the perimeter of a hole, whose dark yawning maw did not promise anything good.

It was the crater of a mud volcano. It first narrowed, then widened again. When one looked down, it had the shape of two funnels, connected at their spouts.

As soon as it began to rush and roar in the magnificent fairy geyser, there rose next to it the mud inside the gloomy crater. And once the geyser's beam of water and steam had collapsed, the bubbling surface of the mud also receded into the depth. It was obvious that geyser and mud volcano stood in close relationship. The ghosts of the underworld separated the substances to be expelled, leading the crystal-clear waters to the geyser and letting the remaining excrement of the Earth run into the mud hole.

"This is *P'a-wakon-tonka*, the Devil's Water," said Old Shatterhand, pointing to the mud hole.

"Do you know it?" asked Fire Heart.

"Yes. I have been here before!"

"But you did not recall earlier how we would get here?"

"Because I had never before traveled the path we took. On my earlier travels, I came from up there and rode down-river. That's when I got to know the Water of the Devil."

Now, the Sioux-Ogallalla were camped there. They could be seen clearly. Even individual faces could be distinguished.

Their horses wandered about or lay resting. There was nothing to graze, since the ground did not produce a single blade.

Close by lay several hundredweight, or even heavier, boulders. On those the prisoners sat, each on his own 'seat'. Their hands had been tied to their backs, their feet tied with lassos to the boulder they were sitting on. They must have been sitting like this since last night, a position, which must have caused them extreme pain.

Just then, when Old Shatterhand directed his attention to the Ogallalla, they began to move. They rose from their prone positions to sit in a circle in whose center the chief took his place.

The medicine man of the Upsaroca, standing next to Old Shatterhand, shaded his eyes with his hand for a better look, glanced briefly towards the Ogallalla, and then stated angrily:

"There sits Heavy Moccasin among his dogs. He is holding council with his men."

"You know him, your enemy, and must know if it is truly him," Old Shatterhand answered.

"How could I mistake him! Look at his tall, lean figure and his face! He has robbed me of an ear. I shall take both of his. His tomahawk penetrated my shoulder. My knife will enter his heart!"

Obviously, the captives were also clearly recognizable. Old Shatterhand saw Jemmy, Davy, Martin and Hobble-Frank. He did not know Baumann and his companions. Apart from the others, Wohkadeh had been tied to a boulder in a position intended to wrench his limbs.

A Sioux walked over, untied him, and led him to the circle of men.

"The intend to interrogate him," Old Shatterhand said. "This may be his tribunal, after which they may punish him right there. Ah, I would love to hear what is being said now!"

"Why should we permit the Ogallalla to even speak with him?" the medicine man exclaimed. "Let us go down there and across. The tomahawk must eat them!"

"It doesn't work that fast," Old Shatterhand remarked. "My red brother may consider that we still have a hard climb down before reaching the river. They will see us once we step from the cover of these trees. Before we reach the river and ford it, they will have made their preparations."

"Does my white brother have a better plan?"

"Yes. We must hit them suddenly, totally unexpected. I am afraid, that they might kill their prisoners rather than have them fall into our hands. We can't go down from here for they would see us. But there the forest reaches right to the river. There we can get to the river's bank unnoticed. If we are careful, they will not even see us, since the geyser's wall will be between them and us."

"My brother is right. We will do it this way. But I have one condition:

"What is that?"

"No one is to kill the chief of the Ogallalla. I must take vengeance on him! He is mine!"

Looking down, Old Shatterhand reflected for a moment. Then he raised his head while his eyebrows narrowed:

"There are over fifty enemies over there. Much blood will flow, yet I would hope to avoid it. However, it will be totally impossible to get all into our hands without fighting them."

Bob who, during the ride, had remained at the end of the group, came forward to see the Ogallalla. Since Old Shatterhand had talked with the Indian in his language, the Black had not understood what had been spoken. He now stepped up, pointed down, and said:

"There be *Massa* Baumann and also young *Massa* Martin! Will *Massa* Shatterhand free them?"

"Yes!"

"Oh, oh! That be very good, very good! Negro Bob will help free them. Negro Bob will go right now down and cross water. *Massa* Bob not afraid of Ogallalla. *Massa* Bob be strong and bold. He kill all of them!"

He really wanted to head off, but Old Shatterhand held him back. The hunter took his telescope from his saddlebag and looked at the Sioux. Just then, Martin Baumann was untied, led into the circle to stand next to Wohkadeh. Through the lens, Old Shatterhand saw the two's faces so close that he could read the speaker's lips. It was as if the group was standing barely twenty paces from him.

The chief spoke to Martin Baumann, pointing to the mud crater. Old Shatterhand saw clearly how Martin became deathly pale. At the same time, a shrill cry rose, the kind a human throat can expel only in a moment of great terror.

One of the prisoners had shouted it. It was old Baumann. Old Shatterhand saw that the poor man tore at his fetters with all his strength. What the chief had said must have been something absolutely terrible.

And it was. It was something so devilish that only a father could scream like this for fear of his son.

The Sioux-Ogallalla had arrived at the geyser just after nightfall. They had expected that Heavy Moccasin would camp beneath the forest's trees, but had been mistaken. Despite the darkness and the difficulty of the descent, he still ordered the river crossing.

He knew the area, had been here several times, and in his mind brewed a thought more evil and terrible than the mud crater which, down there, in the dark of the night, lifted and lowered its ugly content.

Leading the climb down, while holding his horse by its reins, the chief showed his men the way. The captives, too, had to get down, which was extraordinarily difficult, since they could not be untied from their animals. But at last, all arrived safely at the river's edge.

At this location, the waters of the Firehole River were not hot, but only warm. One could cross without harm. Two Sioux each took the horse of one captive between them for the crossing. Then they camped at the mud crater.

The captives were tied to the boulders with guards posted next to them. Then, everyone lay down without being told by the chief why they were to camp here, next to the stink of the crater, where there was neither grass nor water for the horses.

Upon daybreak, the animals were taken a distance down-river where the chief knew of a clean spring, which tumbled from the rocks. Once the men returned, they pulled out some buffalo meat for their morning repast. Then, Heavy Moccasin quietly explained to his men what he had decided for Wohkadeh and young Baumann.

All thought Wohkadeh to be a traitor. Although he had not admitted anything, in their eyes he was guilty. That Martin was to suffer the same fate did not cause them the least scruple. Since all captives were destined to die, the more varied their execution, the more interesting it would be.

It was important to enjoy the pains caused the captives when they would hear pronouncement of their judgment. Then, Wohkadeh was led into the circle.

He knew, of course, that death for him was certain, but he did not believe that the sentence would be executed right away. He was convinced that Old Shatterhand and Winnetou would very soon appear which is why he faced his judges courageously.

The proceedings were spoken in a loud voice so that the other prisoners would also hear everything, provided they understood the Sioux language.

"Did Wohkadeh decide to continue denying his deeds or admit all to the warriors of the Ogallalla?" the chief asked.

"Wohkadeh did not do anything bad and has, therefore, nothing to admit," he replied.

210

"Wohkadeh is lying. Would he speak truth, his judgment would be very mild!"

"My sentence will be the same, no matter whether I am guilty or innocent. I must die!"

"Wohkadeh is young. Youth has a short memory. It often does not know the consequences of what it does. This is why we are willing to be indulgent. But, whoever has acted wrongly, must be sincere!"

"I have nothing to say!"

At that a sneering smile crossed the chief's face. He went on:

"I know Wohkadeh. He will, nevertheless, tell us everything, everything!"

"You will wait for it in vain."

"Then Wohkadeh is a coward. He is afraid. He has the courage to do evil, but lacks the courage to admit it. He is not a strong, young man but an old woman, howling from pain when stung by a fly."

The chief certainly knew the young man. His words served their purpose.

No Indian likes to be called a coward without demonstrating immediately that he is courageous. From early youth, he is used to privations, exertions, and all kinds of pain. He is not concerned with death. Following death, he is convinced he will immediately enter the Eternal Hunting Grounds. If called a coward, he is, therefore, prepared to prove the opposite, and in doing so, will even put his life on the line. So also did Wohkadeh. Barely had the chief spoken this insult, when he answered quickly:

"I have killed the white buffalo. All Sioux-Ogallalla know this!"

"But none of them were present. None saw that you truly killed it. You brought its hide. That we know, nothing more!"

"Will the buffalo relinquish his hide freely?"

"No! But once he has died, he lies on the prairie. Wohkadeh comes across it, takes its skin, carries it home, to then tell that he killed it. But the buffalo had died on its own."

"This is a lie!" Wohkadeh shouted, extremely angry about this new insult. "No buffalo which perishes keeps lying on the prairie. The vultures and coyotes eat it."

"And you are the coyote!"

"Uff!" Wohkadeh shouted, tearing on his fetters. "Were I not tied, I would show you, whether I am a cowardly prairie wolf or not!"

"You did show it already. You are a coward since you are afraid to tell the truth!"

"I did not deny it because I am afraid!"

"Why then?"

"Because of consideration for the others you hold in your hands."

"Uff! Then you admit your guilt now?"

"Yes!"

"Then tell us what you did!"

"What am I to tell! It is said in a few words. I went to the wigwam of the Bear Hunter to report that you had captured him. Then, we took off to free him."

"Who?"

"Us five. The Son of the Bear Hunter, Jemmy, Davy, Frank and Wohkadeh."

"No one else?"

"No."

"Then Wohkadeh seems to have grown very fond of the palefaces?"

"Yes! One of them is worth more than a hundred Sioux-Ogallala."

The chief's eyes swept the circle, secretly delighted with the impression the last words of the youngster must have had on the Ogallalla. Then he asked:

"Are you aware of what you dared to tell us?"

"Yes. You will kill me!"

"But with a thousand tortures!"

"I am not afraid of them."

"They will begin right now. Bring the Son of the Bear Hunter!"

Now, as Old Shatterhand had spied, Martin was led in and put next to Wohkadeh.

"Did you hear and understand what Wohkadeh said?" the chief asked.

"Yes," Martin replied calmly.

"He came to you so you would free the captives. Five mice take off to eat fifty bears! Stupidity has rent your brain; it may now eat you completely. You shall die!"

"We know that!" Martin Baumann smiled. "No man can live forever!"

The chief did not understand him right away. However, when he comprehended the words' meaning, he answered:

"I mean you will die by our hands!"

"I think this is your intention!"

"What you now only believe, you will very soon realize as truth. Do you still hope to escape? I will take it from you. You will die today, now, right away!"

He looked sharply at the two, to see what effect his words would produce. Wohkadeh acted as if he had never heard them. However, the color of Martin's face changed, although he made a great effort to hide his terror.

Heavy Moccasin sees that you are great friends," the chief continued. "He will give you the pleasure to die together."

He had thought to increase the two's dismay. But Wohkadeh said with a cheerful smile:

"You are better than I had thought! I am not afraid of death. If I can die with my white friend, it will be even sweeter."

"Sweet?" the chief laughed disdainfully. "Yes, sweet it will be. You shall thoroughly enjoy its sweetness, slowly, wholly. And since your love for each other is so rare, you shall also enter the Eternal Hunting Grounds in a very special way!"

He rose, stepped from the circle, to walk to the wall of the mud crater.

"This is your grave!" he said. "In only a few moments, it shall receive you!"

He pointed into the depth from which the stinking exhalation rose.

No one had expected this. This was more than inhuman. Martin became deathly pale. His father emitted that scream of fear Old Shatterhand and his companions had heard across the river. Martin tore forcefully at his fetters.

From the beginning of his captivity, Baumann, the father, had neither with word nor another expression, displayed how unhappy he was. He was too proud to let on. Now, however, when he heard what threatened his son, he was past all self-control.

"Not that, not that!" he called. "Throw me into the crater, me, me, but not him, not him!"

"Be quiet!" the chief threatened him. "You would scream from terror if you had to suffer your son's death!"

"No, no, you will not hear a sound, not a single one!"

"You will howl already when I describe this death to you. Do you think we will simply throw your boy and the traitor Wohkadeh into this maw? There you are very much mistaken. The mud rises and sinks as regularly as the ocean's tides, which follow the moon's cycles, as I have been told. One can know precisely when the mud comes and when it goes. It is also known how high it rises. We shall tie the traitor and your boy to lassos and toss them into the hole. But they will not drop down into it, since the lassos will hold them up. They will hang low enough for the mud to rise only up to their feet. The next time it rises, we lower them farther down, for the mud to reach their knees. In this way they will sink deeper and deeper, and their bodies will slowly fry in the hot mud from bottom to top. Do you still wish to die for your son?"

"Yes, yes!" Baumann replied. "Take me in his place. Take me!"

"No! You and the others are to die tied to the stake at the grave of the chiefs. But now, you must watch how your son will sink into this pool!"

"Martin, Martin, my son!" the father screamed in desperation.

"Father, my father!" Martin answered crying.

"Be quiet!" Wohkadeh whispered to him.

"We shall die without giving them the joy of seeing the pain on our faces."

Baumann tore at his fetters, but succeeded only in that they cut into his flesh almost to the bones.

"You hear how he cries and laments!" the chief called to him. "Be quiet. Rather be glad, for you will see everything clearer than we. Untie the prisoners from the boulders and tie them to their horses, so that they sit high and can view everything better. The two boys, though, tie up tightly and carry them to the hole!"

They immediately took care of this order. Several Sioux seized Wohkadeh and Martin, bound them with more straps, and carried them towards the crater.

The elder Baumann gnashed his teeth to prevent any sound of misery from escaping. He now sat high on his horse together with the others.

"Horrible!" snarled Davy, turning to Jemmy. "Help will come for sure, but too late for these two brave fellows. We are both guilty of their death. We should not have agreed."

"You're right, and – listen!"

The hoarse scream of a vulture could be heard. The Ogallalla paid no attention to it.

"That's Old Shatterhand's signal," Jemmy whispered. "He often mentioned it and demonstrated that scream."

"By God! Could it really be him?"

"Heaven forbid that I'm not mistaken! If I guess right, then Old Shatterhand did follow our tracks and will come down over there. Look over towards the forest! Do you see anything?"

"Yes, yes!" replied Davy. "A single tree moved. I saw its crown shake. This doesn't happen by itself. There must be someone there!"

"Now I see it, too! But, stop looking, so the Ogallalla don't become aware of it!"

And, in a loud voice, he called in German towards the crater:

"Master Martin, be confident! Help is already here. Friends just gave us a signal!"

He prudently avoided giving a name, since that would have been understood by the Ogallalla.

"Why is this dog barking!" the chief roared. "Does he also want to die in the mud?"

Fortunately, he was satisfied just giving this reprimand.

"Is it true, is it true?" Baumann whispered to the Fat One in German.

"Yes! They are in the forest over there."

"But then they will arrive too late. Before they reach the river and cross, it will be all over. And, in any case, they will be noticed by the enemy!"

"Pah! Old Shatterhand will accomplish his purpose."

The captives were secured close together on their horses, so that they could communicate in whispers. Their hands had been tied to their backs with their feet tied together underneath the horses' bellies.

"Hey, Davy," Jemmy whispered, "our animals are not held by the reins. It means we are actually half free already. Can you make your old mule obey you despite our fetters?"

"Don't worry! I'll apply my legs for the fun of it!"

"My old steed will obey, too. Hold it! Heaven help us! There it starts! Help comes too late – too late!"

At that moment, the earth below the horses' hooves began to shake, first softly then harder and a rolling roar arose from deep down.

The horses had become reasonably used to this shaking since last night, but now they carried their riders and became more restless.

The chief had earlier leaned over the wall of the mud volcano and had lowered his lasso to measure how deep the two doomed boys were to hang. Then two lassos were attached to a sturdy projection on the rim of the crater wall. The other ends had been fastened under Martin's and Wohkadeh's arms, so that the intended depth would be reached correctly.

When the roar began, all stepped back. Only two men remained standing next to the crater ready to slide the two convicted boys down once the mud rose.

It was a moment of immense tension. But for the two Baumanns, it became an unbearable eternity.

And Old Shatterhand? Why did he not come?

He had observed every move of the Ogallalla with close attention. When he saw that Wohkadeh and Martin were dragged to the crater's edge, all became clear to him.

"They want to kill them slowly in the mud," he told the Indians. "We must come to their aid right away. Quickly, hurry down over there under cover of the trees where the forest reaches down to the river. Cross over and, in a gallop, ride up the other side! Howl as loud as you can, while you advance and charge the Ogallalla with all your might!"

"Don't you want to come along?" the giant medicine man asked.

"No, I can't. I must stay here in order to make sure that no harm will come to our brothers. Off! Off! Not a moment must be lost!"

"Uff! Ahead then!"

The next moment, the Shoshone and Upsaroca had disappeared. Black Bob remained with Old Shatterhand, who ordered:

"Come get a hold of this spruce! We must shake it!"

Putting his hand to his mouth, he produced the scream Jemmy and Davy had heard. He saw that they looked up in his direction and knew that they had understood his signal.

"Why shake tree?" Bob asked.

"To give them a signal. They want to throw Wohkadeh and your young master into the crater to kill them. They are tied up and lie over there near its edge."

"What! Oh, oh! Kill *Massa* Martin! When? Right away?"

"It might be happening this very minute!"

At that, the Black dropped the rifle he had been holding.

"Murder *Massa*! That not be, that not allowed! *Massa* Bob not allow that. *Massa* Bob them kill all, all! Bob get over there right away!"

He ran off.

"Bob, Bob!" Old Shatterhand called after him. "Back, back! You are wrecking everything!"

But the Black did not listen to him. Total fury now possessed him. His young master was to be murdered! He could not allow this! Rather he wanted to die. He had not shown himself a hero before a bear, but when it was about his massa, he could become a raging creature.

He paid no attention when he dropped his rifle, but thought only of getting there as quickly as possible. Being a good swimmer, he knew that one had to enter the water at a place upstream to land at the desired spot on the opposite bank. He, therefore, did not race down the open forest decline and head straight for the water, but instead rushed upstream under the trees in great leaps. Only when he had gotten far enough he rushed out from under the cover of trees.

A smooth, black rock lay there leading directly into the water. Quickly, Bob sat down on it and slid, like on a toboggan, down this rock into the oily water, which was covered with dirty flecks of foam. He felt something hard stabbing him. It was a strong branch stuck in the river.

"Oh, oh!" he rejoiced. "*Massa* Bob has no rifle. Branch his rifle, his club!"

He tore it from the mud and began swimming with mighty strokes.

The good fellow wasn't even noticed by the Ogallalla. During his slide his black body was hard to differentiate from the dark rock. Now, in the water, his head and shoulders blended so well with the dirty surface that even better eyes than those of the Ogallalla would not have become aware of him. Anyway, all the Indians' eyes were on the mud crater. They did not pay attention to anything else.

Just then, when the subterranean roiling and roaring began, Old Shatterhand saw his allies ride for the river at the downstream narrows. He leaned his Henry Rifle against the tree behind him, and took up the two-barreled Bear Killer. He could rely on these two rifles. Most others would have shook from excitement, but this man remained very quiet, as if he intended to target-shoot with friends.

On the other side, the Sioux were stepping back from the crater. Only two remained standing there.

Then the chief raised his arm. Whether he spoke a loud command, Old Shatterhand could not hear, since the roar had become stronger. But the hunter knew exactly what this arm movement meant – Martin's and Wohkadeh's torturous death!

He put the rifle to his cheek. Twice the Bear Killer flashed, then the shooter threw this gun aside and reached for the Henry Rifle, so as to be ready should he need it. While he himself had heard the crack of his two shots, they had escaped the Sioux-Ogallalla, since it rumbled below them like rapidly following thunderclaps.

"In with them!" the chief of the Ogallalla had commanded in a loud voice while simultaneously raising his arm.

The two men who were to execute the order took a few quick steps toward the captives lying on the ground. Martin's father expelled a cry of fear, which would have been heartwrenching, could it have been heard. The next moment, his son was to disappear in the maw of the crater.

"But what was that? The two executors of the terrible sentence appeared to bend down to pick up the captives, but then collapsed right next to them where they remained lying.

The chief roared something that could not be understood. Above him, water and steam rose, whistling shrilly from the geyser's opening, and down across from it, sounds like dull canon shots, came from the mud volcano.

Heavy Moccasin jumped up, bent over to his two men, and hit them with his fist – but they did not move. He grabbed one by the shoulder and pulled him up halfway. A pair of unmoving, lifeless eyes stared at him, and he saw two holes in the man's head, one in front, the other in the back. Terrified, he dropped the corpse and reached for the other, only to notice the same.

He jumped up as if he had seen a ghost, and turned to his people. His face was distorted. He had the feeling that his skin was being torn from his head.

The Sioux could not comprehend his behavior, nor that of their two warriors. They stepped closer. Several of them bent down and looked just as terrified at what they saw as their leader.

Then, something else happened, which did not appear any less terrifying. The whistling and hissing of the geyser had almost ceased, so that one's ears could once again perceive other sounds. That's when a roar sounded from upriver, which seemed to come from the throat of a lion or a tiger.

All eyes turned towards it. They saw a black, giant figure leaping towards them, swinging a long, heavy branch in its fist. The figure dripped with the dirty, yellow-green foam of the river, and was hung with a whole mass of disheveled rushes and half-rotted reeds.

Good Bob, who had had to work his way through a whole peninsula of banks covered with plants, had not taken the time to strip off this decoration. He had the appearance of a monstrous being. In addition to his roar were his rolling eyes, and the big, shining teeth, he displayed – for a moment the Ogallalla were unable to move.

And, at that moment, he threw himself onto them, roaring and swinging his club like Hercules. They fell back from his onslaught. He penetrated the crowd and rushed at the chief.

"*Massa* Martin! Where be dear, good *Massa* Martin?" he screamed panting. "Here be good *Massa* Bob. Here, here! He destroy all Sioux! He smash all, very many Ogallalla!"

"Hurrah! That's Bob!" Jemmy called. "Victory is close! Hurrah, hurrah!"

Simultaneously, a many-voiced howl was heard coming from downstream – Indian war whoops. They are produced by the savages screaming a marrow-shattering, long drawn-out falsetto *jiiiiiiiiiiiiiiih*, while their hands rapidly clap their lips.

This well-known, danger-announcing war whoop wakened the Sioux from their frozen terror. Some jumped forward to look downstream from where the howling came. They saw the Upsaroca and Shoshone, who were approaching at a gallop. Much dismayed, they did not even take the time to count these enemies to notice that they had no need to be afraid of such a small number. The inexplicable death of their two comrades, the appearance of the satanic-looking and wildly-clubbing Bob, and now the approach of enemy Indians, all caused them to panic in fright.

"Off, off! Save yourselves!" they hollered, running for their horses.

Jemmy now took his old steed firmly between his legs.

"Free yourselves! Quickly, quickly, to our rescuers!" he called aloud.

Instantly, his horse took off, followed by Long Davy on his mule. Frank's horse immediately galloped after them without its rider having urged it on. The horses had become so excited by the shaking of the earth, by Bob's figure and his roaring attack, that no Sioux would have been able to hold them back.

Truly none? Oh, yes, there was one, chief Hong-peh-te-keh, the Heavy Moccasin. Bob had clubbed him so hard, that he had collapsed. He was fortunate, that the Black had not administered a second blow, which most likely would have killed him. Bob, seeing his young master lying on the ground, had knelt down next to him, forgetting everything else.

"My good, good *Massa*!" the faithful, but not very mindful, Black called. "Here be brave *Massa* Bob! He quickly cut straps of *Massa* Martin."

In the meantime, the chief had gotten up and pulled out his knife to stab the Negro. Then, suddenly, he heard the attackers' howl and saw his men fleeing, while his erstwhile prisoners rode off in order to get away from the Ogallalla.

He became aware that these circumstances required him also to flee, but to give up each and every advantage, was not his way. In a moment's time, he headed for his horse and swung himself into the saddle. It was fortunate that all his people had their rifles hanging from the pommel! He moved his horse close to Baumann's, whose animal shied that very moment, becoming airborne with all four feet. With a quick grab for the reins, a shrill, penetrating scream with which he urged his horse on, the chief galloped off, upstream, carrying away Baumann's horse together with its rider.

The Sioux-Ogallalla were totally convinced that no enemy would be lurking upstream. If they were able to reach the graves of the chiefs, they would be safe, since the terrain there offered excellent cover against an even stronger enemy than the one facing them now. However, they were soon to realize their great mistake, which was to become disastrous for them.

As told earlier, the previous morning, Old Shatterhand had asked Winnetou, before he departed Yellowstone Lake, to ride with the remaining warriors to the Mouth of Hell and to wait for him there. The Chief of the Apache had followed this request faithfully.

Tokvi-tey, the Shoshone's leader, who was with him, had wanted to leave right after Old Shatterhand's departure, but the Apache had vetoed it.

"My brothers may wait still," he said. "Our horses may graze some more, since there will be no fodder for them on the trail we are going to take."

"Do you know this path well?" the Shoshone asked.

"Winnetou knows all prairies and waters, all mountains and valleys, from the sea in the south up to Saskatchewan."

"But the sooner we leave, the sooner we arrive at our destination!"

"There my brother speaks truth, but there are times when it is not good to arrive at the destination before its time. We shall still arrive at the Mouth of Hell before the sun will sink into its wigwam behind the water-spewing mountains. Winnetou knows what he is doing. The brave warriors of the Shoshone can trust him. They may eat their meat in peace now. When the time has come, he will give the signal for departure.

Throwing his Silver Rifle across the shoulder, he left, disappearing under the forest trees. He did not like to give up decisions once made. Tokvi-tey had to comply.

The Indians prepared their breakfast, talking about the foolish trick the Son of the Bear Hunter had committed with his four companions.

Their meal was long finished when the Apache returned. He looked for his horse and mounted up. A wave of his hand sufficed to tell the Shoshone that their ride was to begin. They followed him, one behind the other, and made every effort to leave no visible tracks.

Even by Indian notions, Winnetou was a very taciturn man. Today, he seemed to be even less inclined than usual to be thought a talkative fellow. He kept his horse at a steady pace, keeping always a certain distance ahead of the Shoshone, who respected the famous warrior so highly that none dared approach him. Even Tokvi-tey, although a chief himself, kept behind at a respectful distance.

Thus, the group of horsemen wound their way silently and noiselessly through the forest, the dense foliage of which was not penetrated by a single direct sunbeam. In here, semidarkness ruled, which in cathedrals disposes the soul to prayer.

The mighty trunks reached up in giant columns. No low brush hindered their way. The bird songs, which had announced daybreak, had fallen silent. At times, the solitude was broken by a crack or crackle, which only emphasized the forest's silence.

Then, suddenly, a small prairie opened. The forest stopped abruptly and not long after, the ground became so rocky that only, here and there, a poor blade of grass peeked from a crack.

Winnetou slowed his horse and waited for Tokvi-tey to catch up with him. He pointed west, where blue-gray clouds seemed to rise and said:

"These are the mountains of the Firehole River, behind which the Mouth of Hell opens."

The Shoshone was glad that the Apache had broken his silence. Of course, he, too, knew that silence was one of the greatest graces of a warrior. However, in even the most sullen Indian, there arose occasionally the desire for a bit of talk, and Tokvi-tey found himself in this situation.

He had already heard earlier much about Old Shatterhand. Now that he had gotten to know him in such a wonderful way, the evidence had convinced him that the rumor about this famous man's characteristics and deeds was in no way exaggerated. Though a much older man, he revered the German as he had never before another person. To this was added a shyness, like one has for superior men, and yet, despite the barrier this shyness erected between him and Old Shatterhand, he felt deeply drawn towards the great hunter. In truth, he loved him. The mild, quiet friendliness and considerate kindness of the man, who was in the habit of striking his enemies down with his fist, had, like many other hearts, won over that of the Chief of the Shoshone.

Long since, he had wanted to learn more of Old Shatterhand from Winnetou. Wasn't the Apache the one who could give the best information about him? But, it was precisely the inseparableness of these two friends, which made it difficult to speak with one about the other.

Today, Old Shatterhand was gone, and Tokvi-tey wanted to use this opportunity to prompt the Apache to speak. This is why he was pleased when Winnetou called him to his side. Following Winnetou's pointing arm, he said:

"Tokvi-tey has never walked this area, but his ears have often heard what the old, gray-haired warriors of the Shoshone told about it. Did my brother also hear of it?"

"No."

"Deep below these mountains and canyons, a chief is buried. His soul could not enter the Eternal Hunting Grounds, although he was the most courageous warrior and had decorated many tents with the scalps of enemies he had slain. His name is K'un-p'a. My brother will have heard it?"

"No. A famous chief of this name is unknown to the Apache. K'un-p'a means 'Fire Water' in the language of the Shoshone, which the Yankees call brandy or whisky."

"Yes, Fire Water is the meaning of this chief's name, for he had sold his soul and his entire tribe to the palefaces in trade for fire water. He had raised the war tomahawk against them to eradicate them from the Earth. His warriors were more numerous than theirs, but they had rifles and – fire water. Their chief asked to confer with them. They met at a place between both war camps. While they conferred, the chief of the palefaces gave the red warrior fire water to drink. Never before had a drop crossed his lips. He drank and drank, until the evil ghost of the firewater possessed him. Then, to get more, he betrayed his warriors. All were killed; not even a single one escaped."

"And their chief?"

"He alone remained. He was the traitor, which is why the white men did not kill him. They promised him even more fire water if he would lead them to the

221

grazing grounds of his tribe. He did. The wigwams of his tribe stood where the water-spewing mountains now rise. The valley of the Firehole River was then the happiest grazing ground in the land. Grass bent its tips above a horseman, and the buffalo roamed in uncountable numbers. K'un-p'a guided the palefaces to this place. They fell upon the red men and killed them and all their wives and children. The chief sat close by and drank firewater until it burned from his mouth. He roared aloud from pain and writhed back and forth in terrible agony. His howling carried across the prairies and forests to the peaks of the mountains beyond the Yellowstone Lake. There, dwelled the Great Spirit of the red men. He came and saw what had happened and grew terribly angry. With his tomahawk, he struck a cleft into the Earth, many days travel deep, and pushed K'un-p'a into it. There the traitor lies now for many hundred suns. When he tosses from side to side in his never ending pain and raises his roaring voice, the entire area of Yellowstone Lake, as far as the Snake River, shakes. From the cracks and holes, his miserable howling rises to the surface of the Earth. The fire water streams boiling from his mouth. It fills all the clefts and crevices of the deep. It steams and rushes up. It swirls and bubbles from every abyss. It steams and stinks from every cave, and if a lonely warrior rides past and sees the Earth shake and crack under his horse's hooves, sees the boiling cauldron, from which waters rise to the clouds, and hears the roar, which sounds from a thousand maws of the depth, he gives his animal the heel and flees, for he knows that below him rages K'un-p'a, the one cursed by the Great Spirit."

Had the Shoshone expected that Winnetou would make a comment about this story, he had been mistaken. The Apache looked silently ahead. A barely noticeable smile played over his lips. Because of this Tokvi-tey asked:

"What does my brother say to this story?"

"That never before has a significant number of pale warriors ever come to the river of the Fire Hole."

"My brother is sure of this?"

"Yes."

"But this all happened many suns before. My red brother was not yet alive then."

"And Tokvi-tey, the Chief of the Shoshone, was also not yet existing. How can he, therefore, know what happened then?"

"He has heard it. The old ones told him, and they know it from the their grandfathers, who know it from their great-grandfathers."

"But when these ancient ancestors lived, there were no palefaces yet among the red men. I have heard it from someone who knows it very well, from my white brother, Old Shatterhand. When I came with him for the first time to the river of the Fire Hole, he explained to me how the holes came to be from which the cold and hot water beams erupt. He told me how the mountains and valleys, the canyons and gorges originated."

"Does he know it then?"

"Very well."

"But he was not present!"

"That is not necessary. When a warrior sees the track of a foot, he knows that a man has walked there, though the warrior was not present at the time. The Great Spirit has left such tracks, and Old Shatterhand knows how to read them."

"Uff!" the Shoshone cried in surprise.

"Listen to him yourself! Then you shall wonder even more. I did sit by his side in many a silent night and listened to his words. They were words of the great, good, Almighty Spirit. Words of love and kindness, of reconciliation and mercy. Since I have heard them, I act like Old Shatterhand – I kill no human being, for all are children of the Great Spirit, who wants to make his sons and daughters happy."

"Then, the white men are also his children?"

"Yes."

"Uff! Why then do they persecute their red brothers? Why do they rob them of their land? Why do they drive them from place to place? Why are they so full of cunning, malice and deceit towards them?"

"To answer the Chief of the Shoshone' question I would need to speak many hours. There is no time for it. I want to ask him only: Are all red men good?"

"No. There are good and bad ones among them."

"Well then, such it is also with the palefaces. Among them, too, are good and bad. Old Shatterhand belongs to that tribe of the palefaces who have never yet raised the tomahawk against the red warriors."

"What is the name of this tribe?"

"It is the tribe of the Ger-mans, which dwells far in the east beyond the Great Water."

"He is their chief?"

"No. The warriors of the Ger-mans have several chiefs, who are called kings. But their highest one is called Kai-sa. He is an old, brave warrior, who has been victorious in all battles and has never taken a scalp. His hair is white like the snow of the mountains, and his years can almost not be counted. But, his stature is tall and proud, and his horse trembles with pleasure when he climbs into the saddle. His arm is strong, and his commands are not contradicted. But, in his heart dwells love, and from his hand shines the staff of peace. His wigwam is visited by the chiefs of all peoples, and his advice is respected from the rise to the setting of the sun."

"And what is the name of this great chief?"

"Wi-he-lem[7]. You will not understand this word, for it is part of the language of the Ger-mans, and means as much as mighty protector."

"But why did Old Shatterhand not stay with his tribe?"

"Because he wished to get to know the red men. Afterwards he will return to the wigwams of his people."

"Would my red brother tell me where he saw him for the first time?"

"It was at the Rio Gila, far from here towards midday, where the Apache' horses graze. The dogs of the Comanche had crawled from their holes to bark at the brave warriors of the Apache. That is when the chiefs held a great council, and the next morning ten times ten times six Apache marched out to get the scalps of the Comanche. Winnetou was still young. He was selected to search for the Comanche' tracks, since his eyes were sharp and his ears heard the beetle's walk in the grass. He invited ten warriors to accompany him and succeeded in finding the enemy's tracks. On his return, he saw smoke rising and crept up to see what kind of men he would find at the fire. They were five palefaces. The Apache were on the warpath against the Whites, which is why Winnetou decided to attack them and to adorn himself with their scalps. The red men attacked, but to their detriment. The palefaces were surprised, but they were brave and defended themselves. One of them had leaped behind a tree and shot one red warrior after the other. Four palefaces died but also the ten Apache who were with Winnetou. Finally, only the brave paleface and Winnetou were left. The White tossed his rifle away and rushed the Red. He pulled him to the ground and took his weapons away. Winnetou was lost. He lay under the White and could not move, for his foe was as strong as the gray bear. The Apache tore open his hunting shirt to offer him his bare chest. But the other threw his knife away, stood up, and offered Winnetou his hand. His blood did flow, because Winnetou had stabbed him in the throat, yet he spared the life of the Apache. This paleface was Old Shatterhand. Since that time both men have been brothers, and shall remain brothers until death will separate them."

"And since that time you have always been together?"

"No. Old Shatterhand travels back to his country, but as soon as he returns to the prairie, he immediately visits his red brother. Both have saved each other's life so many, many times. Both have learned together and from each other, and each would gladly give his life if the other would demand it. More than ten times ten did they face many, many enemies. An entire tribe often pursued them. Superior forces have encircled them, but when they are together, they do not fear any enemy and no large number of foes. No one has yet succeeded in overcoming them. And since Winnetou did find his brother Old Shatterhand, he has realized that the Great Spirit is love and that our good Manitou is sadly covering his head when his sons tear themselves to pieces. The creator of Earth

---

[7] Referring here to Emperor William I, not the second!

did send his son Je-su, to let his red and white children know that there is to be peace in all lands. The war tomahawk must be buried, and the calumet of reconciliation must be smoked from place to place, from tribe to tribe. The Chief of the Shoshone will not comprehend this. If he wishes, he may speak himself with Old Shatterhand. Winnetou does not have the mouth for this talk, but he rides from north to south, from east to west, from tribe to tribe, to teach by his example and to demonstrate, that the red and white children of the Great Spirit can live together in love and peace, if they only want to. Once the red men have learned to live harmoniously among themselves, they will then gain the respect of the palefaces. They will then be strong enough to banish fratricide from their grazing grounds. Tokvi-tey, the Chief of the Shoshone, may contemplate my words. I shall leave him alone."

He spurred his horse on to regain the lead he had before and did not relinquish it for the rest of the ride.

His prediction that the horses would not find pasture on the way proved true. From now on the terrain stayed rocky and barren. It basically was a plain, however, numerous depressions and sharp cuts caused the horsemen time-consuming detours. The sun burned hotly. The horses had to be treated with care, since it was possible that tomorrow the group might be forced to require all their strength. This is why they rode only in step. Finally, the western ridges came closer.

This is how the morning and most of the afternoon passed. The sun had already reached the final quarter of its day's arc, when they finally arrived at the eastern foot of the Firehole Mountains.

Little by little, the rock changed to grassland, and when the ground began to rise there was, here and there, a small creek by whose banks bushes waved in a cool breeze.

Winnetou headed for a valley, which cut at right angles into the mountains. The farther they advanced, the more densely wooded its flanks became. After a short while, they arrived at a small freshwater pond where Winnetou jumped off his horse. He took off saddle and bridle, then led it into the water to refresh itself from the taxing ride. The other horsemen followed his example.

Not a word was spoken during this task. No one asked him whether he planned to camp here. He had not sat down but, leaning on his rifle, stood by the water. This was enough for the others to know that he would soon want to leave again.

Shortly thereafter, his horse left the water and came back to Winnetou on its own. He saddled it, mounted up, and rode off. He did not find it necessary to look back to see if the warriors were following him. It was simply understood.

The valley narrowed more, the steeper it rose. A watercourse whose origin lay up on the heights had formed it.

Arriving there, the horsemen found themselves in a wild forest which seemed as if it had never been entered by a human foot.

But the Apache knew his direction. He rode with great certainty under the tall trees, as if seeing a trail ahead of him. At first, he climbed hard upwards, then continued on a level and finally, beyond the ridge between widely spread giant boulders, down into the valley.

That's when, suddenly, a terrible crash sounded, as if a mighty dynamite explosion had happened, causing the horses to shy. A number of shots followed, which sounded like they came from a heavy fortress cannon. Then, there was a sputtering noise, like continuous firing, which dissolved into a rattle, crackle, rushing and hissing, as if a giant fireworks had been fired off ahead of the surprised horsemen.

"Uff!" Tokvi-tey called. "What is that?"

"This is *K'un-tui-tempa*, the Mouth of Hell," Winnetou replied. "My brother has heard the voice of the mouth. He will shortly see it also spit."

He rode forward a few paces, then stopped and turned to the red warriors:

"My brothers may come here. Down there the Hell's Mouth has opened."

He pointed into the abyss opening before him. The Indians hurried to him.

They could see now that they halted before a several hundred-foot vertical rock cliff at whose bottom lay the valley of the Firehole River. Directly in front of them, down below on the opposite bank, rose a water column of about twenty feet diameter to a height of close to fifty feet. At its pinnacle, it formed an almost ball-like knob from which numerous arm-size, and even larger water beams shot individually more than one hundred feet into the sky. The water was hot. A veil of semitransparent steam surrounded the giant fountain, which at its top separated umbrella-like.

Right behind this natural marvel, the wall stepped back from the riverbank, forming a deeply cut rock basin, on whose rear edge the sinking sun seemed to rest. Its rays fell onto the water column, through which it shone brilliantly in indescribable, magnificent color combinations. Had the observers' position been different, they would have seen tens of thousand of flickering rainbows in and around the water column.

"Uff, uff!" sounded from just about every mouth, and the Chief of the Shoshone turned to Winnetou and asked:

"Why does my brother call this place *K'un-tui-tempa*, the Mouth of Hell? Should it not better be called *T'ab-tui-tempa*, The Mouth of Heaven?"

"No. That would be wrong."

"Why? Tokvi-tey has never before seen something so magnificent."

"My brother ought not let himself be deceived. All evil appears to be beautiful at first. But a wise man judges only after he has waited for the end."

All eyes of the delighted Indians were still engrossed by the magnificent image, when, suddenly, another thunderclap sounded like before, and immediately, the scenery changed. The water column collapsed onto itself. A moment later, the hole in the ground became visible from which it had risen. One could hear a dull, roiling sound, after which the hole ejected brown-yellow steam rings in individual pulses. These pulses came faster and faster, until they came together in a shrill hiss. The individual rings combined into an ugly steam column. Then, a dark, mud-like mass was catapulted out, rising almost as high as the fountain before, but spreading a horrible stink. Individual, hard pieces flew far above the liquid substance. When this happened a dull, roaring growl sounded like one hears from a menagerie of hungry carnivores prior to being fed. These eruptions occurred in fits and starts, one after another, and in the pauses, a moaning and groaning came from the hole, as if, down there, souls of the damned resided.

"*Kats-angwa* – terrible!" called Tokvi-tey, squeezing his nose. "From this smell even the bravest warrior could die."

"Well," Winnetou asked smilingly, "is my brother now still going to call this hole the Mouth of Heaven?"

"No. Might all enemies of the Shoshone be buried in it! Shall we not rather ride on?"

"Yes. But we shall make camp right down there by the Mouth of Hell."

"Uff! Is that necessary?"

"Yes. Old Shatterhand asked us to do this, which is why we must. The Hell has spewed the last time today. It will not bother the noses of the Shoshone again."

"Then we shall follow you, but, otherwise, we would rather have stayed away from it."

The Apache now led his companions along the rock ledge to where the wall consisted of softer rocks and earth. There, the hidden forces had once reached all the way up. Hundreds of years ago, a crater had swallowed the entire wall all the way down to the river. The soft ground had slid down, forming a slope, which was now densely covered by half-rotted tree trunks and individual boulders.

The landslide was steep, and negotiating it did not look to be without danger. There were numerous sulfur-yellow-edged holes from which steam erupted, a sure sign that the terrain was undermined.

"This is where my brother wants to go down?" Tokvi-tey asked the Apache.

"Yes. There is no other way."

"Will we not break through?"

"If we are careless, it can happen easily. When Winnetou was here with Old Shatterhand, he investigated this place carefully. There are spots where the earth is no thicker than the width of a hand. But Winnetou will ride ahead. His horse is smart and will not step where there is danger. My brothers can follow me confidently."

"But did Old Shatterhand not request that we send out scouts from this side of the river to tell him about our arrival? Shall we not do this prior to fording the river?"

"We shall not do so. The Ogallalla will arrive before Old Shatterhand. It is sufficient, if we are on the lookout for them."

He directed his horse across the edge of the landslide and had it slowly climb down without him dismounting. The Indians followed him hesitatingly, but when they saw how cautiously his horse checked the ground before taking its next step, they entrusted themselves to its guidance.

"My brothers may ride far apart from each other," he advised, "so that the ground will carry only the load of a single horse. Should the horse threaten to break through, the rider must instantly pull it up by its reins and throw it backwards."

Fortunately, not a single one experienced this danger. Although several very hollow-sounding spots were passed, the group arrived safely at the river.

Hereabouts, the water was unusually warm. Its surface was blue-green iridescent and oily, while a distance upstream, its waves lapped the bank clear and transparent. There, the horses were driven into the water, which they swam effortlessly. Then, Winnetou led the group downstream right to the Mouth of Hell.

Its eruption was finished now. When the horsemen arrived and cautiously approached the hole's edge, they looked into a depth close to a hundred feet deep, now still and quiet. Nothing but the ejected mud revealed that, only minutes ago, all hell had been active here.

Now, Winnetou pointed to the rock basin behind the Mouth of Hell and said:

"There lies the Grave of the Chiefs, where Old Shatterhand defeated the three most famous warriors of the Sioux-Ogallalla. My brothers may follow me there!"

The bottom of the basin formed a nearly circular area with an approximate diameter of half a mile. Its walls were so steep that they were impossible to climb. Many holes, filled with hot mud from which steaming water escaped, made passage into it very unsafe. Neither a blade of grass, nor a meager plant was visible.

Right at the center of this valley, an artificial mound had been erected. Easily seen, it consisted of rocks, broken sulfur pieces and mud, the latter now forming a hard, brittle mass. Its height may have been about fifty feet, its width ten, and its length twenty feet. At its top several bows and lances had been implanted. They were adorned with a variety of war and death symbols, which now hung in tatters.

"Here," Winnetou said, "are buried Brave Buffalo and Evil Fire, who was the Ogallalla' strongest warrior. Nevertheless, Old Shatterhand defeated both

228

with a stroke of his fist. They sit on their horses, rifles on their knees, their shields in their left and the tomahawk in their right. The name of the third warrior was not given since he no longer possessed his medicine. And up there on the ridge, Old Shatterhand sat on his horse, before he came down for the fight to the death. He wounded one Ogallalla after another, as he did not want to kill them. Their bullets could not reach him, for the Great Spirit of the palefaces protected him."

With these words, he pointed to the rock wall from which a projection stood out at a height of about forty feet and on which several man-size boulders lay. From it, a series of similar, but much smaller projections ranged all the way to the bottom, by which one could toilsomely climb up. But how, on horseback, Old Shatterhand had been able to get up there, only a daring horseman like he could accomplish such a feat.

The Shoshone rose in exclamations of surprise. Had one other than Winnetou said this, and had it not been told of Old Shatterhand, they would have found the speaker a contemptible liar.

Tokvi-tey walked his horse slowly around the grave mound, measuring its dimensions. Then he asked Winnetou:

"When does my brother think the Sioux-Ogallalla will arrive at the Firehole River?"

"Maybe tonight."

"Then, they shall find the grave of their chiefs destroyed. Its dust shall be spread into the winds and their bones tossed into the Mouth of Hell, so that their souls must whimper with *K'un-p'a*, the great spirit of the damned, down in the depth! Take your tomahawks and tear down the mound! Tokvi-tey, the Chief of the Shoshone, will be the first."

He dismounted and took his tomahawk to begin the work of destruction.

"Stop!" Winnetou demanded. "Did you kill the three dead, you intend to dishonor?"

"No," the chief responded in surprise.

"Then keep your hand off their grave! They belong to Old Shatterhand. He left them their scalps and even helped bury them. A brave warrior does not fight the bones of the dead. Red men find pleasure in disgracing the graves of their enemies, but the Great Spirit wants the dead to rest in peace. Winnetou shall protect their grave!"

"You forbid me to throw the dogs of the Ogallalla into the Mouth of Hell?"

"I forbid you nothing, for you are my friend and brother. But if you wish to lay hands on this grave, you will need to fight me first. Should you kill me, you may do as you wish. But then, Old Shatterhand will come and call you to account. However, it will not get this far, for Winnetou, the Chief of the Apache, does not know anyone who could defeat him. My brothers have seen the Grave of the Chiefs and will now follow me to our camp site!"

He turned his horse and rode off, back to the Mouth of Hell. This time he again did not look back to see whether the others followed him.

Never had a friend spoken like this to Tokvi-tey. The Shoshone was angry, but did not dare resist the Apache. He mumbled a sullen "Ugh!" and followed him. His men joined him silently. The decisive demeanor of Winnetou's had left a deep impression on them.

Evening had fallen, when the Apache stopped not far from the Mouth of Hell and dismounted. Despite the proximity of the hellish place, a clear spring rose out of the rocks and crossed the valley to empty into the river. The place possessed nothing that made it attractive as a campsite. But his followers figured Winnetou had to know why he wanted to spend the night precisely here and nowhere else. He staked his horse, rolled his Saltillo blanket to a pillow and stretched out to rest close to the rock wall. The Shoshone followed his example.

They had gathered, talking softly with each other. The chief, who had forgotten his anger towards Winnetou, laid down next to him. It became totally dark. Several hours passed, and it appeared as if the Apache was asleep. But suddenly, he rose, took his rifle and said to Tokvi-tey:

"My brothers may keep resting. Winnetou will head out scouting."

He disappeared into the darkness. The men, staying put, did not care to sleep before knowing the result of his daring errand. However, they had to wait a long time, for it was midnight when he finally returned. He reported to all audibly and in his simple ways:

"Hong-peh-te-keh, Heavy Moccasin, is camped with his people by the Devil's Water. The Bear Hunter with his five companions; also our brothers, who left us the previous night, are his prisoners. Old Shatterhand is likely close by. My brothers may sleep. When morning breaks, Winnetou and Tokvi-tey will once more spy on the men at the Water of the Devil. Howgh!"

He lay down again. Although his information was exciting, none let on to it. The Shoshone assumed that the next morning would bring the decision. Who of them would still be alive the following evening? They did not ask this. They were brave warriors – and fell asleep easily. Of course, guards were posted.

Morning had barely dawned when Winnetou awakened the Chief of the Shoshone to walk with him to the river. Habitually, they were careful to use every conceivable cover, yet Winnetou knew that this was actually not necessary. The Sioux would not leave their camp before full daylight.

The distance from the Mouth of Hell to the Water of the Devil might be about a mile. When the two came close to the Devil's Water, greater caution was called for, since morning had brightened already, and everything could be clearly seen.

Not far from the enemy camp, the river made a turn. Standing there behind a rocky protrusion, the two chiefs could observe the Sioux. They were just in the process of gathering their horses, which had been watered downstream from the camp, and then to eat their morning meal.

Winnetou looked up to the heights above the opposite river bank from where Old Shatterhand was to come, if he wasn't there already.

"Uff!" he said softly. "Old Shatterhand is here already."

"Where?" Tokvi-tey asked.

"Up there, on the mountain."

"One cannot see him up there for the dense forest."

"Yes. But does my brother not see the crows circling above the trees? They have been roused. By whom? By Old Shatterhand surely. He will descend through the forest and will cross the river downstream from the Sioux where they cannot see him. Then, he will attack them driving them upriver. At that time, we must be standing at the Mouth of Hell, so that they cannot get through and will be driven into the valley of the chiefs' graves. My brother may come quickly for we must not lose any time."

The two returned immediately. Winnetou had guessed right, even if he could not know the details.

When the two had returned to their men, they received the necessary instructions from Winnetou and made themselves ready for battle. The enemy was to come between two firing lines.

Farther down, a terrible row erupted.

"The Water of the Devil is raising its voice," Winnetou explained. "Soon the Mouth of Hell will also erupt. Retreat a distance so that you are not hit!"

From his earlier visit, he knew that the two craters were connected. Soon the eruption of the Devil's Water had stopped, which is how he could hear the war whoops of the thirty Shoshone and Upsaroca throwing themselves onto the Sioux.

What he had predicted now occurred. The Hell's Mouth began to spew, just like last evening, when they had arrived. With thunder and hissing, the water column rose. From its top, the spreading beams were raining down in a wide circle. This produced an excellent cover for Winnetou and his men, since the oncoming Sioux could not see the Shoshone waiting for them behind the giant water fountain. Winnetou drove his horse farther to the side to be able to look downstream. He saw the enemy fleeing, one behind, or next to, the other without any order, driven by panicked terror.

"They are coming!" he called. "When I give the signal, we break from behind the spewing mouth and shall not let them get past and upstream. They must run to the left into the Valley of Graves. But do not shoot. Fright alone will drive them in!"

The foremost Sioux were close now. They truly wanted to escape upriver. But then Winnetou broke from behind the water fountain. His "jiiiiiii!" sounded piercingly through the morning air with the Shoshone joining in. The Sioux saw their way blocked and drew their horses a quarter turn around seeking escape in the rock basin.

Behind this first enemy group appeared another consisting of several horsemen. The Apache at first was unable to distinguish who they were. It consisted of a bunch of Sioux and Whites approaching in a flying gallop. Its core consisted of the Chief of the Ogallalla, Baumann, the Bear Hunter, and Hobble-Frank, the learned Saxon.

As mentioned, the prisoners, tied to their horses, had turned to their liberators. That's when a multi-voiced scream sounded. Bob had cut Martin Baumann and Wohkadeh free. He screamed when he saw the chief pulling Baumann along. Frank heard the scream and looked around. He saw the Sioux and recognized the danger his beloved master was in. Despite his fetters, only with the aid of thigh pressure, he swiftly turned his horse around and stopped before the Negro.

"Cut me loose, Bob! Quickly, quickly!" he shouted.

Bob immediately obeyed. Frank jumped off his horse, tore a tomahawk from the belt of one of the Sioux Old Shatterhand had shot, swung himself lightning-fast into the saddle again, and chased after the enemy-chief.

Bob had no horse. Martin and Wohkadeh were of no help, since their limbs were much too injured from the fetters. They could only scream. This caught Jemmy's attention. He looked back and shouted after his tall friend:

"Davy, turn around! The Sioux is abducting Baumann!"

Quickly, Bob stood before them and cut their fetters. Jemmy tore the knife from him and galloped after the Saxon with Davy following him weapon-less.

Now, the Shoshone and Upsaroca chased after friend and foe. At the same time, Old Shatterhand arrived on this side of the river, leading Bob's horse, which the Negro had left behind. No one had paid attention to the hunter, but nothing had escaped him.

"Here's your horse and rifle, good Bob," he called, tossing reins and rifle to him. "Free the other captives and then follow us, leisurely."

Loading his previously fired rifle while riding, he stormed on. He had not found the time for it before. Right after he had fired the two shots, he was certain, that the bullets had hit. Then it took all his effort to get, as quickly as possible, to the opposite bank of the river.

A warlike image presented itself now between the Hell's Mouth and Devil's Water. Sioux-Ogallalla, Upsaroca, Shoshone and Whites screamed from the top of their lungs. The fleeing paid no attention to each other. Everyone wanted to save only himself. The friends chased past the enemy without bothering them. Their only thought was to free Baumann.

Old Shatterhand stood high in his stirrups, the Henry Rifle on his back, the double-barreled Bear Killer in hand. He was way behind, but his horse's belly almost touched the earth, which is how he caught up with the Upsaroca and the fifteen Shoshone.

"Slower!" he shouted to them, while flying past them. "Just take care to drive the Sioux. Up there, Winnetou waits and will not let them pass. None is to escape. But do not kill them!"

Thus, he continued past friend and foe. His horse's hooves just swallowed the ground. It was necessary to reach the aforementioned group of horsemen before a disaster happened.

The little Saxon's horse wasn't a noble runner, but Frank hollered so loudly and persistently prodded it with the tomahawk's handle, that it tore along as if it had wings. But the animal could not maintain this for long, as could be expected.

He succeeded in catching up with the chief of the Sioux-Ogallalla and, driving his horse to the man's side, struck out with the tomahawk, shouting:

"*Shonka, ta ha na, deh peh* – Dog, come here! It's your end!"

"*Tshi-ga shi tsha lehg-tsha!*" the chief answered with scornful laughter. "Poor dwarf! Try striking!"

He turned to Frank, parrying the strike with his bare fist in such a way that his fist struck the Saxon's fist from below. The weapon flew out of Frank's hand. Then the chief grabbed his knife from his belt intending to stab the former 'forestry official' on his horse.

"Frank, watch out!" Jemmy shouted, and pushed his horse in order to catch up with the three.

"Don't worry about me!" the little one shouted back. "No Red will kill me that easily."

He had his horse slow down a pace, so that he could not be hit. Then he swung himself courageously from his saddle onto the Ogallalla' horse. He immediately embraced the Indian from behind and pressed the man's arms to his body.

The chief roared in anger. He fought to free his arms, but was unable to do so. Frank held on with all his might.

"You are doing fine!" Jemmy called. "Don't let go! I'm coming."

"Hurry up a bit! To squeeze a guy like this ishn't easy!"

Of course, this had all happened lightning-fast, much faster than one can tell. The Ogallalla held the knife in his right hand, his left holding the reins of Baumann's horse. He reared up in the saddle and turned to the right and the left, but all in vain! He was unable to free himself from Frank's embrace.

Baumann was tied up. He could not help with anything, and was unable to free himself, but he encouraged Frank to hold on tight. Although panting from exertion, he replied:

"All right! I wind myself around him like a baobab conshtrictor and won't let go until my lungs bursht."

The Ogallalla lost control of his horse, so it had slowed down. Consequently, Jemmy succeeded in catching up. Davy, too, got close. The Fat One rode his horse next to Baumann's and, using Bob's knife, cut Baumann's fetters.

"Yippee! We've won!" He called. "Tear the reins from the Red's hand!"

Baumann tried but did not have the strength. Jemmy wanted to give him the knife, but was unable to do so, since several Sioux, fleeing ahead of them, had noticed their chief's predicament. Two of them attacked Jemmy viciously, and a third attempted to throw himself onto Frank, whose arms were not free to defend himself. Seeing this, Davy gave his mount some fisticuffs between the ears, and it galloped forward, catching up with the Indian. He grabbed the man by the collar of his hunting shirt, tore him from the saddle, and tossed him to the ground.

"Hurrah! Hallelujah!" shouted Hobble-Frank. "That was rescue at the final moment! But now grab the chief by his neck. I can't do it myself any longer!"

"Right away!" the Tall One replied.

With both arms, he reached for the Red to pull him out of his saddle. But at that very moment, a terrible bang sounded, so that the two horses, being frightened, bumped into each other. Davy had difficulty keeping himself in the saddle, Jemmy, who needed all his strength to fight off the two Reds, was thrown from his horse. The same happened to Baumann, the Bear Hunter.

The confused group of horsemen had now arrived at the Mouth of Hell. The water fountain had collapsed and the mud column's eruption, which caused the horses to shy, had risen. Some of the hot, dirty substance was catapulted far and wide.

Being scared, the chief's horse had fallen to its knees, but recovered and took off to the left towards the river just when Old Shatterhand reached the group which was rolling on the ground.

The hunter, wanting to help good Frank, had to desist, since he saw that the two redskins had leaped off their horses and had thrown themselves onto Jemmy to kill him. Long Davy was much too occupied with his shying horse, and was unable to come to the aid of his corpulent friend. Thus, Old Shatterhand was forced to rescue him from this deathly danger. He halted his horse, jumped off, and stunned the two Ogallalla with two blows of the rifle butt.

Winnetou and his Shoshone still held their position between the Mouth of Hell and the river. It was his task not to let the Ogallalla pass there, but to drive them successfully into the valley of the chiefs' graves. This he had done. The fleeing redskins had turned for the valley when they had seen his group. The course of events had moved so rapidly that the Apache had not found time to engage himself. And now, he was prevented from advancing by the mud ejection. There was only one man that he was able to help out – Hobble-Frank. He saw that Frank, still sitting tightly behind the chief, clasping him with both arms, was being carried by the frightened horse towards the river. This happened so fast, that any helper was unlikely to come to the rescue before a catastrophe was to happen by the riverbank. Nevertheless, the Apache drove his horse in that direction with several Shoshone following him.

The chief of the Sioux recognized the danger into which the little Saxon's embrace had put him, which was now coming to its climax. Anger and fear doubled his strength. He pulled his arms from below Frank's – a mighty elbow thrust to both sides – and the Saxon had to let go.

"Die!" the Red shouted and struck out with his knife, from front to back, in order to stab the blade into the brave little one's body.

However, Frank quickly leaned far enough sideways so that the knife missed him. Frank no longer had a weapon. He thought of Old Shatterhand's fist blow. Grabbing the enemy by the throat with his left hand, he then reached out with his balled right hand and hit the Ogallalla' temple with such force that he, himself, felt as if his fist had cracked. But the chief sank forward.

By then, they had reached the river. In a wide arc the horse ran from the bank into the water with both riders being tossed over the animal's head.

The horse felt free now and, with a few strokes, returned slowly to the bank.

Now, Winnetou arrived. He jumped off and aimed his rifle, ready should it come to a fight in the water between the two ejected opponents. In that case, he was ready to render the Ogallalla harmless with a bullet.

At first nothing was seen of the two. Only Frank's Amazon hat drifted near the river bank. One of the Shoshone fished it out with his lance. Then, a distance downstream, but rather far from the bank, the feather-adorned bun of the Indian surfaced. Subsequently, Frank popped up a little farther downstream. He looked around, spotted the savage's head, and with some fast strokes swam towards him. The Red was not dead, but only stunned. He wanted to get away, but the little Saxon, like a rapacious pike shot towards him, jumped on his back, grabbed him with his left hand by the hair, and with his right hand began to hammer the man's temple. The Ogallalla disappeared and Frank with him. A vortex formed above them; bubbles surfaced, an arm of the Sioux appeared to vanish right away again. Then both legs of the 'forestry official' became visible for a moment together with the tails of his coat. In any case, a terrible wrestling was taking place below the surface. For Winnetou it was impossible to intervene.

Old Shatterhand, Jemmy, Davy and Baumann arrived at the river bank. Shatterhand quickly dropped all weapons, stripped off his upper clothing prepared to jump into the water. But then, Hobble-Frank surfaced, looked all around and shouted, while coughing and gasping:

"Is he shtill down?"

Of course, he was referring to the Ogallalla. Without waiting for a reply, he dove once more into the depth. When he reappeared a few moments later on the surface, he held the defeated enemy with his left hand by the hair and swam slowly to the bank.

He was received with loud jubilation, but he screamed even louder than the others:

"Jusht be quiet! My hat dishappeared without a trace. Is there perhaps one among the honored folks present who saw it shwim?"

"No," he was told.

"That is tough! Am I to lose my ostrich feather chapeau because of this Ogallalla? That ishn't worth it! Oh, I see it there merschtentels! That Shoshone there wears it on his head. In a minute, I'll go after him like a bailiff."

He hurried to the Indian to retrieve his head decoration and returned. Only afterwards was he willing to accept his comrades' congratulations.

He had defeated the enemy's leader and thought himself the greatest hero of the day.

"It shure was an effort," he said. "But for someone like me, it won't matter. Fendi, findi, fundi, said Caesar to Suleiman Pasha, and I accomplish something like that with equal ease."

"It's *veni vidi, vici*," Jemmy interrupted. "In English: I came, I saw, I conquered."

"Be quiet, humble mishter Jakob Pfefferkorn! You jump onto the Red from behind, jump with him on the horse into the water, then, down there, busht the thread of life from him. Afterwards, I don't mind, if you play your druggisht Latin language bugs. But not earlier! Your came, saw and conquered means nothing to me! For me it meant ' I jumped, I swam, I dunked him'. And that is translated into the proper Latin of Puma Nompilius, my absholutely correct: *Fendi, findi, fundi* !"

Jemmy broke up laughing. He was ready to respond, but Old Shatterhand forestalled him in a serious voice:

"Please, no such quarrels! Our good Frank has demonstrated today that he is an able, even bold, frontiersman. He defeated the chief. You will understand its meaning only later. We will have him alone to thank if we succeed in avoiding bloodshed. Here, dear Frank, shake my hand. You are a splendid fellow!"

The little Saxon shook the hand of the famous hunter and answered, while a tear of joy ran from his eye:

"This word from your mouth is a noble delight. Alexander Hauboldt said so nicely in his Kosmos: Mauve wreath posterity the hero braids, for blooming primrose only shpring awaits. When a later generation erects here a Carara marble shtone, then, together with the other combatants, also my name will be chiseled into it. Then my shpirit will descend in quiet nights and delight not to have lived for naught and jumped into the waters of the Firehole River. Peace to my ashes!"

236

It would not have been surprising for the men present, who understood German, to respond with a merry laughter. But it did not happen. Frank was just a peculiar character, but truly very kind, who communicated to the others the emotion he felt. They remained serious. Winnetou shook hands with him and said:

"*Ninte ken ni sho* – you are a good man!"

Then the Apache gave Old Shatterhand a signal with his hand that he was going to leave everything here to him, mounted up, and rode with his Shoshone past the now quiet again Mouth of Hell to the entry of the valley basin, where in its rear the fleeing Sioux had gathered.

Guarding the entrance, he met the medicine man of the Upsaroca and Moh-aw, the son of the Shoshone's chief, with their warriors. When the giant medicine man heard that his deadly enemy, Heavy Moccasin, lay defeated by the river, he hurried over there. He arrived just in time to see, that Moccasin, with Old Shatterhand's effort, had regained consciousness and was being thoroughly tied up. He jumped off his horse, tore his knife from the belt and shouted:

"This is the dog of the Ogallalla who took my ear. He must give his scalp while still alive!"

He knelt down to scalp him, but was prevented from doing so by Old Shatterhand, who told him:

"This captive is the property of our white brother Hobble-Frank. No other may lay hands on him."

There ensued an exchange of words, which Old Shatterhand with his usual energy concluded victoriously. Although angrily grumbling, the Upsaroca withdrew.

A scene now followed, which baffled all description. Baumann, the Bear Hunter, for whose liberation the expedition had been launched, had pulled Hobble-Frank to his heart. Both cried happy tears of joy.

"You, you faithful man, I surely owe my rescue to you, for the most part," the Bear Hunter was saying. "But how was it possible for you to gather such a great number of rescuers?"

Frank rejected all merit and drew his attention to the fact that there was now no time for long stories and explanations, and pointed downstream:

"There come others who deserve more gratitude than I. I did no more than my duty."

Baumann saw his five companions coming up, those who had been captured together with him by the Sioux. In front of them rode Martin, his son, Wohkadeh and Bob. He hurried towards them. When the Negro saw his master, he jumped off his horse, ran to him, sank to his knees, grabbed his hands, and called crying:

"Oh *Massa*, my dear, good *Massa* Baumann! At last, at last *Massa* Bob has his *Massa* back, who he loves from depth of heart! Right now *Massa* Bob die from joy. Now *Massa* Bob sing and jump with joy and burst and crack from delight! Oh, *Massa* Bob be glad, be happy, be blessed!"

Baumann lifted him up to pull him into his arms. But Bob resisted and declared:

"No, *Massa* not embrace *Massa* Bob. Bob have killed bad skunk, still not smell good."

"What the heck, skunk! You went to save me, and for that, I must now hug you!"

Only now did the delighted Negro permit his master's gratitude. But then father and son fell into each other's arms.

The others turned discretely away. The delight these two felt at this moment was sacred to them.

"My child, my son!" Baumann called repeatedly. "We have ourselves anew, and nothing is to part us ever again. What I did endure! And what you have endured since yesterday! Look how your arms have been cut by your fetters!"

"Yours much more, so very much more! But they will heal again, and you will soon be healthy and strong once more. But first, you must say thank you to all who risked their lives to save you. You were able to speak with my friend Wohkadeh last night, and also with Jemmy and Davy. But here is Old Shatterhand, the master of all. We have to thank him and Winnetou for the success of this undertaking. Our entire lives wouldn't suffice to compensate for what we owe them."

"I know, my son, and I'm sorry to say that I cannot do anything more than simply say: Thank you."

He offered Old Shatterhand both his hands, while tears still ran down his brown, emaciated cheeks. Old Shatterhand softly squeezed his hands, wounded from the fetters, pointed to the sky, and told him in the most cordial voice:

"Don't thank the men, dear friend, but thank the Lord up there, who gave you the strength to endure this indescribable misery. It is He, who guides and protects us, who made it possible for us to arrive at the right time. You need not thank us. We were only his tools. To him, we will send our prayers as it says in our beautiful German church hymn:

> *I called the Lord in my great need:*
> *"Oh God, do hear my cry!"*
> *That's when my helper from near death*
> *did comfort me with heaven's breath.*
> *That's why I thank you, God, I do!*
> *Oh, do thank God, thank God with me;*
> *Do honor our God!"*

He had taken off his hat and had spoken the words slowly, loud, and heartfelt like a prayer. The others, too, had bared their heads, and when he had ended, a pious, forceful 'Amen!' came from every mouth.

The chief, lying tied on the ground, had watched this process with amazement. He was unsure how to explain it to himself. In all likelihood, it was not to his advantage – or so he thought. According to his understanding, he was now irrevocably due for a painful, torturous death.

He was lifted off the ground to be carried to where everyone was headed, to the entry of the valley of chiefs' graves, where Winnetou was waiting for them with the Shoshone and Upsaroca. There, he was put down.

Old Shatterhand and the Apache, rode a short distance into the valley to observe the enemy and the arrangements they had made. Their friends saw that they exchanged a few words. Both understood each other so well that long discussions were not required. Then they returned.

Tokvi-tey walked to them and asked:

" What do my brothers intend to do?"

"We are aware that our red brothers have a voice just as good as ours, which is why we shall smoke the Pipe of Council. But prior to it, I shall speak with Hong-peh-te-keh, the Chief of the Sioux-Ogallalla," replied Old Shatterhand.

He got off his horse, Winnetou following suit. A circle was formed around the prisoner. Old Shatterhand stepped up to him and said:

"Heavy Moccasin has fallen into the hands of his enemies. His men, too, are forsaken, since they are encircled by the rocks and us. They cannot escape and will die from our bullets if the Chief of the Ogallalla does not do something to save them."

He stopped to see whether Heavy Moccasin would say anything, but since he kept his eyes closed and did not say anything, he continued:

"My red brother may tell me whether he has understood my words!"

The Red opened his eyes, gave him a hate-filled look and spit. That was his reply.

"Does the Chief of the Ogallalla think to have a mangy animal before him that he dares to spit?"

"*Wakon kana* – old woman!" the Indian grated.

This was a great insult to old Shatterhand and all those present. It may have been that it was the Ogallalla's intention to arouse his enemies' anger so that he might be killed in a rash of rage, thus avoiding slow death by torture. But Old Shatterhand responded smiling calmly:

"Heavy Moccasin has become blind. He cannot differentiate a strong warrior from an age-worn woman. I have pity for him."

"*Kot-o pun-krai shonka* – thousand dogs!" the captive hissed.

There is almost no greater insult to a brave red warrior than when someone has pity for him. These words of Old Shatterhand's angered the Indian so much that he threw an equivalent insult of 'thousand-fold doggishness' at his face.

Some of the surrounding Reds voiced an angry growl. Old Shatterhand sent them a reproving look, then bent down, and to the surprise and amazement of the captive, undid his fetters.

"The Chief of the Ogallalla is to recognize," he told him, that neither an old woman nor a dog, but a man is talking to him. He may rise!"

The Indian got up. As much as he was used to controlling his features, he could not conceal his embarrassment. Instead of his insulting words being answered with kicks and fist cuffs, he was relieved of his fetters! He could not comprehend this. He thought Old Shatterhand to be insane.

"Open the circle!" the hunter ordered the surrounding warriors.

They did, so that the Sioux was able to look into the interior of the valley. He saw his men waiting behind the chiefs' graves. From their movements, one could see that they maintained a lively discussion. His eyes lit up. He was no longer tied and carried the great fame of being an unsurpassable runner. Could he run away? At best, he could reach his people; at worst, he would be shot down. But this was better than death by torture.

Old Shatterhand had noticed the light in his eyes. He said:

"If Heavy Moccasin thinks of fleeing, he may give up such thoughts. His name tells us that he leaves a great track, but our feet are light as the wings of swallows, and our bullets never miss. He may look at me and tell me if he knows me!"

"Hong-peh-te-key does not look at a lame wolf!" the savage growled.

"Old Shatterhand a lame animal? Is this there not Winnetou, the Chief of the Apache, whose name is more famous than any of the Sioux-Ogallalla and all other Sioux tribes?"

"Uff!" escaped from the captive.

He had not expected to be facing these two men. While his look traveled from one to the other, he could not suppress the respect on his face. Old Shatterhand continued naming the others, while pointing at them with his hand:

"Even more brave warriors stand here. The Chief of the Ogallalla sees Tokvi-tey, the leader of the Shoshone, and Moh-aw, his strong son. Next to him stands Kanteh-pehta, the invincible medicine man of the Upsaroca. Over there you see Davy-honskeh and Jemmy-petahtsheh. Am I to tell you every single famous name? No. I don't feel like it. You will ..."

He stopped in mid-speech, since, at that very moment, a sudden nearby bang caused the horses to rear up. Even the otherwise so fearless warriors looked frightened. A long drawn-out moan, like the mile-wide audible sound of a foghorn sounded through the valley, and the earth began to move under the feet of the scared men. From the myriad mud holes in the valley rose steam, here gray-blue, there sulfur-yellow, from others blood-red and sooty-dark. The steam was followed by more solid material. The ejections were numerous. The air was literally darkened by the hellish exhalations and the flying mud projectiles, which spread an almost suffocating smell.

It was impossible to see farther than twenty to thirty paces. Everyone was busy trying not to be hit by the flying mud. An indescribable confusion ensued. The horses tore free and galloped off. People screamed and rushed wildly about. From the back of the valley, the Sioux-Ogallalla let out frightened howls. Their horses had also torn free and, guided by their instinct, stormed towards the valley's exit. In so doing, many stumbled into some of the bigger holes, the mud immediately closing over them. Others raced past the valley exit and through Whites and Reds. Trying to break into the open, they doubled the indescribable confusion.

Right from the outset, Old Shatterhand had maintained his cold-bloodedness. Upon the first bang, he had taken hold of the chief of the Sioux with a strong fist to prevent him from fleeing. But then he had to let go to evade one of the dangerous missiles by jumping sideways. In so doing he had collided with Fat Jemmy, who fell, tried to stay upright, but only succeeded in toppling both.

At that very moment, the Sioux's horses came stampeding by. This called for thinking first and foremost of oneself.

Because of his fright, Heavy Moccasin had not tried to fight Old Shatterhand's hold, but as soon as he was free, his intention was to escape. Shouting a shrill, triumphant scream he tore off into the valley, but he did not get very far. He had to get past Bob who, lightning fast, reached out with his inverted rifle and hit him on the head with its butt. However, due to the force of his strike, he fell himself. He tried to get up quickly but was kicked by one of the shying horses and fell back again.

"Chief running away! After him, after him!" he hollered aloud.

Only half conscious from Bob's clubbing, Heavy Moccasin momentarily stumbled hither and yon, then ran off, but not without being pursued.

Martin had heard the Negro's call. He saw the chief flee and chased after him. Was the tormentor of his father to escape? No! The limbs of the brave youngster had been hurt by the fetters, and he also was not carrying any weapon. Nevertheless, he ran after the escapee with all his might.

The chief did not even take the time to look back. He did not think he was being followed and so applied all his attention to the path he needed to follow. He was trying to get to the gravesite. But in this direction the most mud holes erupted. Thus, he turned to the right, towards the valley's wall, along which he hoped to find an easier, less dangerous route.

But he had erred. There, too, were many open steaming spots which he was forced to evade repeatedly. He had just lifted a foot to leap, when he noticed that the seemingly solid ground was actually of a viscous, unfathomable, deep consistency, which he could only escape by throwing himself quickly aside. Everywhere, cracks in the ground were opening ahead of him. He could only save himself by flying leaps, which one does only under fear of death. Yet, it was almost too late.

Though the chief had never been overcome by anyone in running and jumping, he now began to feel the effects of the rifle butt strike. His head was heavy, his eyes burned a glowing red, his lungs were giving up on him, and his legs began to tire. He wanted to rest for a moment and, for the first time, looked back. Seeing through a bloody fog, he realized that a pursuer was hard on his heels. However, he could not make out the person's features, much less that the pursuer was by all measure still a boy.

Terrified, Heavy Moccasin ran on. He had no weapon and thought the pursuer to be armed. Where was he to flee? He knew that ahead, behind, and to the left of him were open maws ready to swallow him. To his right hand side, he saw the rising rock wall. With his strength ebbing, he felt all was lost.

That's when he noticed a step-like protrusion in the rock wall and then, not far from it, a second, third, forth, rising upward. These were the rocks that saved Old Shatterhand and his horse many years ago. Here and only here, Heavy Moccasin hoped to make his escape. Using the last of his strength, he quickly climbed higher, step by step.

Just as suddenly as the mud holes had erupted earlier, so they now subsided. The air became clear again, and one could see as well as before.

That's when a fearful cry sounded through the valley. It was Bob who had shouted it.

"*Massa* Martin! My good *Massa* Martin! Chief want kill him, but *Massa* Bob save him."

Pointing to one of the rock protrusions, he hurried towards it. Martin and the chief were fighting for their lives there. With his strong arms, the Sioux had taken hold of Martin and was trying to throw him into the depths below. But he was enfeebled, his consciousness impaired. The agile, brave boy succeeded in wresting himself free again. Upon one such occasion, Martin pulled back as far as possible, gathered his strength, and with all his might charged the Indian. The Indian lost his balance, reached convulsively into the air, then lost his traction and, with a howl of fear, tumbled from the rock's nose into a yawning mud hole below, where he was swallowed by its horrible maw.

Everyone in the valley had seen it. At its entrance, loud jubilation arose; at its back, however, one could hear the howl of the Sioux-Ogallalla. They had seen how a boy had overcome their famous chief. The shame they felt as a result of this deed would never be effaced.

But above this screaming and howling, one could still hear Bob's voice. The Negro sprang from rock to rock, screaming inarticulate sounds of joy and delight. After arriving at the top, he drew the victor into his arms.

"Good boy!" said Jemmy. "My heart shook for him. Yours too, Frank?"

"Shure, mine even more!" the Saxon replied, wiping a tear of joy off his face. "I could have shweated syrup from pure fear right then and there. But now all is fine. The daring little fellow has won, and we won't make any bones about these Ogallalla now. We forsh them to put their necks under the culinary yoke."

"Culinary? What's come into your head? That's ..."

"Be so kind to shut up!" the little one interrupted sternly. "At such a moment, I'm not going to quarrel with you. Otherwise, it could easily happen to you like to the cabinetmaker with the shquare, who was eaten by the wolf together with the entire grand duchy of Poland. I see it coming that the Sioux will have to surrender. Then, a general peace treaty will be concluded here in which we, too, will participate. Shake my hand! Be disgraced, you millions! *Et in terra quax!*"[8]

He shook the Fat One's hand, who was still laughing about this renewed linguistic confusion and hurried off to congratulate Martin Baumann, who, together with Bob, was just coming down the rock wall.

The others also expressed their respect with great delight. Then, in a loud voice, Old Shatterhand turned to those present:

"Gentlemen, don't try to recover the horses now. They are safe. The Sioux's horses have also escaped. These people will realize that, even if we have not secured them here, they will be lost without their animals. They can save themselves only by surrendering to us. In addition, they will have to consider the impact of the subterranean forces, the death of their leader and – what I'd like to mention in all modesty – the presence of Winnetou and Old Shatterhand, aside from the many other famous hunters and warriors. Remain here! I shall go to them, together with Winnetou. In half an hour, it will be decided if human blood will flow or nor."

The two leaders walked towards the gravesite behind which the Sioux had gathered. It was an exceptionally bold venture that only these two men would dare, who knew that their mere names already frightened the enemy.

Jemmy and Davy talked softly with each other. They decided to do their best to support Old Shatterhand's peace efforts.

---

[8] The line in the "Ode to Joy" goes "Seid umschlungen, Millionen!" which means "be embrached, you millions!" whilst the other song goes "Et in terra pax hominibus bonae voluntatis" - of course Frank mangles it badly ... 'verschlungen' (devoured) instead of 'umschlungen' (embraced)... and ... 'Knax' instead of 'pax'. Since such verbal contortions can not be translated with any real meaning, one has to be inventive to retain Karl May's style.

Obviously, the allied Indians were not inclined to spare their enemies. The Bear Hunter and his five companions had also suffered so terribly that these six men would quite likely also call for revenge. But it could be expected that Old Shatterhand would oppose any cruelty, by force, if necessary. This could have deplorable effects, which had to be prevented.

The two friends called all those present together, and Jemmy gave a speech in which he expressed his view that leniency and reconciliation would be the best for both camps. It was to be expected that the Sioux would be annihilated if it came to a battle, but how many lives would that cost? Thereafter, it was certain that every Sioux tribe would raise its tomahawk to avenge this inhuman and useless blood bath on the initiators. Jemmy concluded his speech with the words:

"The Shoshone and Upsaroca are brave warriors. No other tribe is their equal. But the Sioux are to them like sand in the desert. Should it come to a war of revenge, many fathers, mothers, wives and children of the Snake and Crow Indians will cry for their sons and fathers. Consider that you yourselves have been in our hands! Old Shatterhand and Winnetou captured Tokvi-tey and his son Moh-aw from the midst of their camp, also defeated Oiht-e-keh-fa-wakon and Hundredfold Thunder on the tree. We could have killed all their warriors, but did not do so, for the Great Spirit loves his children and wants them to live harmoniously with each other. For once, my red brothers may see how good it feels to forgive. I have spoken!"

His speech left a deep impression. Baumann was prepared to desist from any revenge; his five companions agreed. The Indians, too, although in secret, agreed with the speaker. They would no longer be alive had Old Shatterhand wanted to destroy them. Only one was unhappy about Jemmy's words – the leader of the Upsaroca.

"Heavy Moccasin wounded me," he said. "Must the Sioux not suffer for it?"

"Moccasin is dead. The mud swallowed him together with his scalp. You have been avenged."

"But the Ogallalla stole our medicines!"

"They must return them to you. You are a strong man and could kill many of them. But the mighty bear is also proud. He disdains squashing the cowardly little rat."

These comparisons had the intended effect. The giant medicine man felt flattered. No matter if he killed or forgave his enemies, he was the victor. He remained silent.

Soon, Old Shatterhand and Winnetou returned leading the Ogallalla to the delighted surprise of everyone. The Sioux followed in single file. When they had arrived, they put their weapons onto a pile, and then silently stepped back. These actions expressed without any words that they thought it impossible to save themselves even by the bravest resistance.

Old Shatterhand's and Winnetou's eloquence had been victorious. The Sioux stood there with bent heads and aggrieved faces. This mighty blow had hit them so unexpectedly that they felt stunned.

Jemmy now stepped forward to tell Old Shatterhand of his speech and its effect. The German shook his hand gratefully. Delighted about it, he called to the Ogallalla:

"The warriors of the Ogallalla have surrendered their weapons to us since I promised them that their lives would be spared. The palefaces, Shoshone and Upsaroca want to grant them even more than life. Heavy Moccasin is dead and, together with him, the two warriors who laid hands on Wohkadeh and the Bear Hunter's son. That is enough. The warriors of the Ogallalla may take back their weapons, and we will help them to recover their horses. There shall be peace between them and us. There, at the Grave of the Chiefs, we shall all remember the dead who fell by my hand many suns ago. May the war tomahawk be buried between them and us. Then, we will all leave the River of the Firehole, and the Ogallalla will ride back to their hunting grounds. There, they can tell of good people, who disdained killing their enemies, and of the great Manitou of the Whites whose command it is that his children love even their enemies!"

The Sioux were dumbfounded about the fortunate turn of fate. They barely dared to believe it. But once they received their weapons back, they hurried to the famous hunter to express their gratitude.

The medicine man, too, felt satisfied, when he learned that all stolen medicines were still at hand. They were returned to the Upsaroca.

The horses had not run far. It was easy to capture them. Then, the two Sioux, who had been shot by Old Shatterhand, were brought forth and buried near the chiefs.

The day was spent in solemn funeral rituals. Afterwards, everyone left the unhealthy valley to seek the healthier forest, there to recover from the previous exertions.

In the evening, when the campfires burned and friend and foe, reconciled with each other, sat talking about their adventures, Frank said to Jemmy:

"The besht of our drama is its ending. Forgive and forget. In my entire life I've never, been a friend of murder and manshlaughter, because: 'What you don't want have done to you, that also not to others do', and leave the poor worm in peace, for it will feel it jusht like you! We've won. We've shown the gods, that we are heroes. Now, there's only one thing left. Do you want to?"

"Yes, but what?"

"Those who like each other, banter with each other. We've always only bumped one another, since we actually like each other very much. Shall we admit to it and claim brotherhood? Here, let's high five to it, you old rascal! Top?"

"Yes, top, top, and for the third time, top!"

"Fine! Now, I'm happy and know that the ride home will take place without upsetting our sympathetic harmony. Finally, finally, it has come to fulfillment, that beautiful verse dedicated to 'Joy', that godly spark[9]:

> *What folly had divided,*
> *Magic has retied;*
> *Frank and Jemmy now are brothers;*
> *Our enmity has died!*

---

[9] The "Ode to Joy" theme is continued here with "… der schöne Versch aus der Freude, schöner Götterfunken:" - Here we have Frank using "Freude, schöner Götterfunken", (Joy, you godly spark) a line from the Ode as its title. It should be noted too that the subsequent poetic lines are a reflection of
> Was die Mode streng geteilt;
> Alle Menschen werden Brüder,
> Wo dein sanfter Flügel weilt.

ABOUT THE AUTHOR

Karl May (1842 - 1912) is today hailed a German literary genius. His unequaled imagination gave birth to a whole collection of characters that lived through exiting and realistic adventure tales that captivated generations of German readers both young and old. Yet his writings were never available to English readers.

ABOUT THE TRANSLATOR

Herbert Windolf was born in Wiesbaden, Germany, in 1936. In 1964 he emigrated to Canada with his family to provide his German employer with technical services for North America. In 1970 he was transferred to the United States and eventually became Managing Director of the US affiliate. He has translated several literary works from German into English, among which is Karl May's, "The Oil Prince", published by Washington State University Press and "The Treasure of Silver Lake", published recently by Nemsi Books. In addition he has taught a number of science courses at a local adult education center, and has written several science essays and travelogues.

Karl May – translated by Herbert Windolf

Other Karl May Translations:

Title	Author	Publisher
The Oil Prince	by Herbert Windolf	Washington State Univ. Press
The Treasure of Silver Lake	by Herbert Windolf	Nemsi Books
The Ghost of Llano Estacado*	by Herbert Windolf	Nemsi Books
Winnetou's Heirs	by Herbert Windolf	BookSurge
Black Mustang	by Herbert Windolf and Marlies Bugmann	BookSurge
Winnetou I	by Victor Epp	Nemsi Books
Winnetou II	by Marlies Bugmann	BookSurge
Winnetou III	by Michael Michalak	Nemsi Books
Holy Night	by Marlies Bugmann	BookSurge
Oriental Odyssey I Through the Desert	by Michael Michalak	Nemsi Books
Oriental Odyssey II The Devil Worshippers	by Michael Michalak	Nemsi Books
Oriental Odyssey III Through Wild Kurdistan	by Michael Michalak	Nemsi Books
Oriental Odyssey IV The Caravan of the Dead	by Michael Michalak	Nemsi Books
Oriental Odyssey V From Baghdad to Stambul	by Michael Michalak	Nemsi Books
The Rock Castle	by Herbert V. Steiner	Nemsi Books
Thoughts of Heaven	by Herbert Windolf	Nemsi Books
Along Unfamiliar Trails	by Kince October	Nemsi Books
Old Surehand I	By Juergen Nett	Nemsi Books

* abridged